THE SAVAGE TIDE

AUDREY WILLSHER

The Savage Tide

HarperCollins*Publishers*

HarperCollins*Publishers*
77–85 Fulham Palace Road,
Hammersmith, London w6 8jb

Published by HarperCollins*Publishers* 1994
1 3 5 7 9 10 8 6 4 2

A catalogue record for this book
is available from the British Library

ISBN 0 00 224131 5

Set in Linotron Palatino by
Rowland Phototypesetting Ltd
Bury St Edmunds, Suffolk

Printed in Great Britain by
HarperCollinsManufacturing Glasgow

This book is dedicated to
BOB HARRIS,
a seventh generation Freeman
of the Company of Watermen and Lightermen.

With thanks for his invaluable advice
and for the permission to use
his father's memoirs, *Under Oars*.

Acknowledgements

For my chapters on South Africa, I acknowledge
a debt to Thomas Packenham's book, *The Boer War*.

Prologue

The man pushing the hand cart paused and peered through the drizzle at what looked like nothing more than a bundle of rags straddling the pavement and gutter. Investigating further, he nudged the bundle with his foot, dislodged a thin white arm, looped it across the toe of his boot, then let it fall back on to the wet cobblestones.

The woman with him tried to bend to make her own inspection but was hampered by her grotesque size. 'Well, does she show any sign of life?' she demanded.

Ignoring the child huddled against the still form, the man knelt and lifted an eyelid. 'Dead as mutton,' he pronounced, easing himself up again. 'Hunger and cold 'ave seen 'er off,' he went on, observing without pity the skeletal, already stiffening fingers and the emaciated features made old by want.

'Thank God for that,' said his wife and gave a sigh of relief. It had been a long night and her corns were giving her gyp.

Pleased with his find the man went on, 'Yeah, it might have stopped beatin' but she's still got a heart . . . and lungs and liver. Young too. They always pays more for a bit of young flesh at the anatomy school.'

He looked quickly around him. They were in a poorly lit, deserted courtyard, near a bone factory and tannery and the offensive smells that emitted continuously from these buildings kept most citizens away. Even so, the man knew there was no time to waste; in an hour or so the first shard of light would fracture the darkness that was so essential to the pursuit of their grisly trade.

'Come on, help get 'er on the cart afore a rozzer comes. You grab 'old of 'er legs.'

As he bent again, hauling the body to a sitting position,

1

the small girl began to scream in terror. 'Mama, mama,' she wailed and clung to her dead mother.

The woman prised the tiny fingers from the sodden garments and flung her away. 'Shurrup,' she ordered, threatening her with a raised hand. 'You want everyone to hear?'

The child cowered away from her. Curling herself up into a tight, protective ball, she thrust her thumb into her mouth and gazed with dark uncomprehending eyes as the lifeless form of the only person who'd ever cared for her was slung on to the cart and covered with sacking.

'What we doin' about the kid? Leavin' 'er 'ere?' the woman asked.

Her husband stared down a the child, assessing her value. 'By the look of 'er, she'll be worth a lot more dead than alive. We'll take her wiv us. A pillow will do the job nicely then she can join her ma at the anatomy school. We'll be doing 'er a kindness really,' he added self righteously.

'Stupid sod. Do you want a noose round yer neck?' The woman was now appraising the small girl with a more professional eye, noticing, even in the poor light, the Viking blond hair and eyes that were dark as a lascar's.

'No, she might be worth keeping. She's gonna be a real good looker. I reckon 'er maidenhead ought to be worth twenty quid of anyone's money in a few years' time.'

'Hold on, she's only about three now. I'm not support-ing 'er till she can be put on the streets,' the man protested.

'It'll be eight . . . nine years at the most I'd say. Some men, those with special tastes, like 'em as young as ten or eleven, you know that. And they pay well for a fresh young piece with no disease. Look on it as an investment. It'll be an extra pair of hands around the place as well. And as for food, well by the look of 'er she'll be glad of the scraps off our plates.'

The sound of footsteps finally convinced the man. 'Come on, get a move on,' he muttered, pushing the bewildered, tiny girl along in front of him. 'We h'ain't got all night. There's things to be attended to and it's a long way to Guy's 'orspital.'

Chapter 1

'Charity! Where the devil are you?'

Responding to the threat in the voice, a tingle of hate and fear ran down the girl's spine. 'Up 'ere, missus,' she called back, then stood up, wiping her hands on her hessian apron and hunching her shoulders in an instinctive and defensive gesture. But looking down, Charity saw that it was unlikely the narrow stairs would accommodate Mrs Grimbold's bulk and the tension in her neck eased a little.

'You finished up there?' The puffy features staring up at her wore their habitual aggrieved expression.

'Nearly, missus.'

''Ow many more you got to do then?'

Nodding her head, Charity slowly counted the steps, proud of the fact that she could count up to twelve. 'I've got five to do,' she answered precisely.

'Well finish them, then run out and fetch some fish and chips for our dinner.'

'Yes Mrs Grimbold,' Charity answered submissively. But her tongue darted out, quick as a lizard's, at the retreating back, following it with, 'Fat old sow!' when she was certain her mistress was out of earshot.

Although, so far in her twelve years of life, she'd been dealt a poor hand, Charity had inherited from an unknown forebear a subversive, rebellious streak. It helped her survive. It also made her take risks. And she'd had enough of scrubbing the bare wooden staircase with its sharp splinters that caught under her nails and made them bleed. A half hour's freedom beckoned and already she could hear the slap of sail, feel the sun on her face, see it silvering the river, and was impatient to be outside.

5

But she had to weigh this against the possible punishment if she skipped the stairs. Any insubordination always brought a belt across the backside from Grimbold if he came poking about. No, best not take the risk, she thought as she sloshed some water over the stairs, gave them a perfunctory wipe with a cloth then, heaving the bucket after her, running downstairs to the kitchen. Here she made a half-hearted attempt to tidy herself up, spitting on her apron and rubbing it across her face, then tugging her fingers through the knots in her flaxen hair. Having done what she could with this bird's-nest tangle, she hurried upstairs to the bar of The Sailor's Rest.

It was dinnertime and the pub was crowded. Gaudy young women sat sipping port and lemon and eyeing blue-jerseyed seamen of every race and colour over the rim of their glasses. Lightermen and Watermen who worked the Thames leaned on the upturned barrels that served as tables, talking in low, earnest tones; others played dominoes in silent concentration, and a haze of smoke rose to the ceiling which had been cured to a rich kipper brown over the years.

Mrs Grimbold, Charity saw, was at the end of the bar with Bill Slawson. Always it's whisper, whisper, whisper with those two, she thought and tried to step back into the shadows.

There was little chance of escaping Bill Slawson's attention though and, interrupting his conversation with Mrs Grimbold, he beckoned to her with a hooked, dirty finger. 'Come 'ere my little peach,' he wheedled.

But it gave her the creeps the way the man eyed her up and down and Charity didn't budge. Then Mrs Grimbold turned to her with a bad-tempered expression on her podgy face. 'Don't just stand there girl. Do as Mr Slawson says, he wants to have a good look at you.'

Charity had no choice but to step forward. But she steadfastly refused to meet his gaze. Instead, she studied the toes of her boots in sullen silence, fortified by the thought that Bill Slawson couldn't possibly have any idea of the depth of her loathing of him.

'Straighten yerself up,' Mrs Grimbold snapped.

Charity's obstinate response was to shuffle her feet, but Bill Slawson, who wasn't deterred by these antics, pushed his greasy bowler to the back of his head. 'My, she's ripening nicely. 'Ow old would you say she was?' he asked, his one good eye gleaming at Charity hungrily.

'Twelve or thereabouts I would say.'

'Not much longer then, eh Mrs G? Fully mature, like a piece of Stilton, that's 'ow I wants 'er.'

'The price we'll be askin', you won't be able to afford 'er, Bill. Grimbold reckons she's worth twenty quid at least and she'll go to the highest bidder.'

'I'll 'ave ter save me pennies then, won't I?' he smirked.

Although the full meaning of their conversation was lost on Charity, she felt a quiver of fear. The highest bidder? What could they mean? That she might be sent to work for Bill Slawson? The idea made her feel sick. Slimy and tooth-less, he had no wife, was reckoned to be well off and lived in one filthy room above the pawnbroker's shop he owned. But she wouldn't go. She'd run away, starve to death, rather than face that. She strained her ears to try and hear more but they were back to their whispering again and she only caught odd words like 'fence' . . . 'some nice pieces' . . . then the rest was lost in the babble of foreign tongues and the rising level of beery goodwill.

Relieved that the conversation had moved away from her, Charity yawned widely and began to fidget, which brought her to Mrs Grimbold's attention again. 'What you 'anging about for, eh?' she asked accusingly.

'You said you wanted something fetchin', missus. Fish and chips.'

'So I did,' she answered, mollified by the thought of food. 'Grimbold, what yer 'aving? Cod or 'addick?' Her stentorian tones rose easily above the noise.

'Cod, Pearlm'love,' Grimbold called back. He finished drying some glasses then, joining his wife, strained to encircle her waist and plant a kiss on her powdery cheek, which was all done with some difficulty for he was half her size.

But although Grimbold was small in stature, he had a gigantic conceit. It could be seen in the dandified air, the elaborately waxed moustache and the knife-sharp centre parting of his macassar-oiled hair.

Shaking off her husband's unwanted attentions, Mrs Grimbold took a sixpenny piece from the till. 'Right. Four ha'penny pieces of cod and a ha'porth o' chips. With plenty of salt and vinegar. And no stealing them on the way back, or you'll get what for. Mind you bring back the right change too, and no dawdling.'

With this list of do's and don'ts ringing in her ears and clutching the silver coin for dear life, Charity made her way across the sawdust floor already wet with beer and spittle. Pulling open the opaque, glass-panelled door stencilled with the words, Ales, Beers, Spirits, she stepped out into a bright October day.

Charity responded to the sunshine immediately. Resilient by nature she had already put Bill Slawson and the Grimbolds behind her. With a joyous sense of freedom she took an enormous leap from the top step, lost her balance and went sprawling across the pavement. Indifferent to her grazed palms, she lay there and watched with dismay as the coin rolled away into the gutter, coming to a stop only a fraction of an inch from the drain. Still on her hands and knees, she crawled to the curb.

'Phew, that was a close one,' she said to Queen Victoria's stern profile as she retrieved the coin. Refusing to imagine the consequences of such a loss, she wiped it free of dirt and dropped it into her pocket and continued on her way in a rather more decorous manner.

Rotherhithe, standing on a great loop in the river, was dominated by water. The Thames, its main artery, on one side, the Surrey Commercial Docks, its heartbeat, on the other. And squashed between them on the low-lying,

8

marshy ground were damp, overcrowded houses and stinking alleys where disease flourished. Rotherhithe Street, the long main thoroughfare, followed the curve of the river. A street of weatherboard houses, it was dominated by a soaring forest of ships' masts, funnels and cranes. In one place the bowsprit of a sailing ship stuck out over a back garden, and the workshops of ropemakers, chainsmiths and ships' chandlers all proclaimed the area's dependence on water for its livelihood. Charity loved the noise of it, the resinous smell of timber, the tarry smell of pitch competing with each other and she needed little excuse to stop and chat with anyone who had the time.

As she passed the local school, the dinner bell brought children charging out onto the street. Trailing behind a giggling group of girls, Charity envied them their clean aprons, neat plaits and friendships. She'd never been to school. In fact all the education she'd ever had had been picked up in the pub and she had a vocabulary rich in swear words, which she used unknowingly and with the vigour of a stevedore. She also knew how many pennies there were in a shilling, could recognize simple words like Ale and Stout, but apart from that she was completely unlettered and she yearned for the ordinariness of school life.

It was the whiff of vinegar and stale fat in her nostrils that reminded Charity of her errand. It also reminded her of the bag of crackling she might get, depending on who served her. So, induced by pangs of hunger – and hope – she hurried towards Reynolds' fish and chip shop. But it was crowded when she reached it and she had to stand in line, watching with a hungry expression as Mr Reynolds dipped pieces of fish into a greyish looking batter, then into a cauldron of hissing fat.

Unfortunately it was Mrs Reynolds who leaned over the counter. Peering down the length of her long nose with its permanent dew drop, which Charity felt must have flavoured many a bag of chips, she barked out, 'Who's next?'

9

Mrs Reynolds was a stingy old trout and, knowing she wouldn't get much out of her, Charity said quickly, 'Him,' and dragged on the sleeve of the man standing beside her. 'It's your turn, mister,' she insisted, avoiding the woman's eye.

Then to her relief Mr Reynolds saw her. 'What's it today, Charity, m'love?' he asked with a kindly smile.

'Four pieces o' cod and one o' chips . . . 'Wiv salt and vinegar,' she remembered to add.

'Right you are duckie, coming up.' He ladled the fish and chips into a newspaper and sprinkled the lot liberally with salt and vinegar. After this he twisted another piece of paper into a cone and shovelled it full to the brim with crisp brown cracklings which he then handed to the girl.

'Ta, Mr Reynolds.' Charity's face shone with gratitude.

'No wonder this place don't make a profit.' The loud resentful tones of Mrs Reynolds sent Charity scurrying from the shop.

With the warm packages clasped to her chest, Charity hurried towards the river, darting down a narrow passage that led to a flight of stairs. One of many that sliced the wall, these plying places all along the river front gave Watermen and Lightermen access to the Thames and free landing places for their barges and cargo.

The tide was out, leaving a wide expanse of black mud and beached vessels between the river and the high, slime-covered river wall. Warehouses rising straight and tall above it made it a gloomy place but the girl didn't notice this. Neither was her nose troubled by the malodorous smell of sewage. And although she heard the shriek of gulls, she hardly regarded them or the detritus littering the shoreline: driftwood, wheels, broken beds. All she could think of was food, and, parking herself down on a step, she undid the package and began to eat, stuffing the greasy food hungrily into her mouth. When she'd finished she gave a sigh of contentment, wiped her hands across her mouth then down the front of her dress and began to take stock of her surroundings.

A hundred yards or so from where she sat, some barges were moored and boys of mixed ages, their bodies pale as celery, were throwing themselves from the decks into the gangrenous looking water. Several others were mudlarking, plastered in the sludge they were scooping up in great armfuls as they searched for coal, coins or anything of the slightest value that might have been thrown from a passing ship.

None too sure of her welcome, but curious to see what treasures they might have dug up, Charity moved across the mudflats towards them, although she took the precaution of stopping a few yards away from them. 'Find anyfink interestin'?' she called.

When they heard her voice some of the boys stopped their energetic digging and looked up, and she saw that one of them was Danny Weston. A couple of years older than she was, Danny often came into The Sailor's Rest for a jug of ale for his mum, and his dad was a regular there, so she knew him quite well. Sometimes he would even smile at her and she'd decided some time ago that she liked the look of him, with his light brown hair and blue eyes.

'No, not yet,' Danny answered. His tone wasn't unfriendly and this gave her the courage to risk edging closer.

But then another member of the group, a large boy called Boscoe Hobbs whose father had recently come to blows with Grimbold over an unpaid bill, looked up and recognized Charity as the enemy. 'It's none of your bleedin' business what we've found. Go on, sling yer 'ook, pig face, we don't want the likes of you poking yer nose in round 'ere,' he shouted and aimed a great handful of sludge at her.

'Fatty!' Charity taunted in retaliation, took a nifty side-step and the mud missed her.

'Right, you're for it.'

Seeing he was coming for her, Charity turned and fled. But her boots, which were several sizes too big, impeded her progress. The soles had also parted company with the uppers and slapped noisily on the wet mud. She struggled on, but she could hear Boscoe Hobbs, panting heavily, coming closer and closer. A hand gripping her shoulder stopped her in her tracks and she was swung round with some force. 'What you got in that parcel, then?' His large moon face was red and sweating and he pushed it so close to Charity's she could see the beginnings of a downy moustache on his upper lip.

'None o' your bleedin' business,' she answered bravely.

'Oh isn't it? Well we'll soon see about that,' he snarled and, grabbing the package, the youth tried to wrest it from her arms.

'Don't you dare . . .' she screamed, holding on to the package for dear life and imagining the fate that would await her if she went back to the pub empty handed.

With the instinct of the pack, several other boys now came running up. Forming a jeering circle, they jostled her from one to the other, taunting her with words like nitbag and scabby, and aiming vicious blows at her body and legs.

Charity, who felt more defeated by their cruelty than anything inflicted by the Grimbolds, tried desperately to hold back her tears, failed and began to sob.

'Stop it you lot.' The voice was Danny Weston's and was so authoritative even Charity ceased crying. Danny as the oldest, was undisputed leader of the gang. Soon, too, he would begin his seven-year apprenticeship as a lighterman and this lent him some authority.

Several of the boys, wanting to distance themselves from the deed, backed away, but Boscoe stood his ground looking mulish. 'It was only a joke, I didn't mean nuffink'. Anyway, I don't know why you're troubling yerself, she's just a nobody, a skivvy of the Grimbolds'.'

'Shut up, Boscoe. Whatever she is, it don't give you the right to knock 'er about. Now clear off afore I give ye a dose of yer own medicine.'

With vengeful mutterings, Boscoe slunk off while Charity stood gazing at her rescuer as if he were a prince clad in raiments of gold. 'Thanks everso, Danny.'

She had the look of a kicked dog he'd once rescued, humble and grateful, and this embarrassed Danny. Already, too, he was regretting his heroic gesture and wondering if he'd ever live it down with the others, so his reply was offhand. 'It's arright, but you'd better go. And if I was you I wouldn't show my face round 'ere for a while.' He waited until she had nearly reached the stairs, thinking to himself, what a strange kid, then dismissed her from his mind.

He was already walking back to his mates when Charity reached the stairs and she stopped and watched him, admiring his jaunty swagger, her heart overflowing with gratitude, and, although she wouldn't have recognized it, something else as well. The first stirrings of love.

Chapter 2

Oblivious to the rapidly-cooling food, the newsprint staining her fingers, Charity fairly danced home. So deprived of affection was she that anyone showing her the smallest kindness earned her unquestioning devotion. And Danny, a rather ordinary boy, had been transformed, in her imagination, into a chivalrous, stout-hearted knight, ready to do battle on her behalf.

But with these barely understood feelings for Danny there also came doubts. And an awareness of her own considerable shortcomings – hair rough as sisal, clothes a tramp wouldn't have said thank you for – was closely followed by a determination to do something about it.

But as she drew nearer the Ale House her problems and Danny's virtues were temporarily superseded by the more immediate dilemma of lukewarm food. With no ready excuse for her tardiness, Charity ducked past the window of The Sailor's Rest and turned right into Canal Street. Then she turned right again, this time into a narrow alleyway running between two rows of houses and stinking of cats' pee and the decaying household rubbish piled up along its length. Avoiding the worst of it, she pushed open a high wooden gate and hurried through the back yard into the kitchen. Hardly pausing, she tipped the food out of the newspaper onto two plates, raced upstairs, and slipped through the door into the bar.

''Ere you are, missus.' Trying not to pant from her exertions, Charity banged the plates down in front of the Grimbolds then stood well back, shoulders hunched in their habitually defensive manner, waiting to ward off any blows that might come her way.

However, for once Mrs Grimbold did not find fault. Her greed was such she could consume prodigious amounts of food in one day, but she also had a palate that lacked finesse and, as she stuffed the food into her mouth with podgy fingers, apparently indifferent to coagulating fat and soggy batter, Charity relaxed.

Grimbold was more pernickety, complaining frequently of his weak digestion. Charity silently willed him to leave her a morsel of food, but Mrs Grimbold finished first, belched appreciatively, then leaned over and, to the girl's dismay, began to polish off the bits of skin lying abandoned on the side of his plate.

With an indulgent expression Grimbold pushed the plate towards his wife. 'Tuck in my pigeon, you must keep your strength up,' he said then turned to the more important matter of admiring himself in the bar mirror, smoothing his pomaded hair and bringing his moustache to stiff attention with the aid of his forefinger and thumb.

However, Charity persisted in hoping for some leftovers until both plates had been wiped clean of everything except a few sharp bones. Then, with lowered lashes veiling her hatred, she watched Mrs Grimbold daintily suck each finger clean. Her hunger boiled over into anger. It bubbled away inside her until she was unable to restrain her feelings a moment longer. 'Greedy old bitch!' The words burst out like a cork from a bottle and even against the noisy background they sounded louder than she intended.

Mrs Grimbold paused, slowly withdrew a finger from her mouth and glared at her with hard little eyes.

'What was that you said?'

'I didn't say nuffink, missus,' answered Charity, taking a precautionary step back from the raised hand.

'You'd better not. Now go and get on wiv washing up them tankards. And seeing 'ow you've got so much time on your 'ands, after that you can scrub the front steps.'

Relieved to be spared the humiliation of Mrs Grimbold's hand across her face in a crowded bar, Charity sped away down the far end of the counter. Idly sloshing glasses in water as murky as the Thames, she gazed about her. Through the haze of smoke from a score or more clay pipes, she noticed Kate sitting in the corner of the bar and waved to her. She liked Kate, for she was cheerful and pretty and, more importantly, she was generous.

'Half a mo' duckie,' she would say, if they met in the street, 'I've got somethin' for you.' Then, opening the handbag that swung from her wrist she would rummage around in a clutter of broken combs, scent bottles and powder puffs. Finally a piece of toffee with strands of hair and fluff attached to it would be offered to Charity, or a lavender-coloured cachou, along with an explanation from Kate that it would sweeten her breath.

Now when Kate saw Charity she returned her wave then beckoned her over. 'Come 'ere a minute, love, I want to talk to you.'

'She'll do nothing of the sort, she's got work to do,' interjected Grimbold. 'And so 'ave you. Off your arse girl and start looking for business, there's a ship just in.'

'I'll go when I'm good and ready,' Kate answered defiantly, then to prove it, settled back in her chair, took a sip of gin and pulled hard on a Turkish cigarette.

'You'll go now, you slut,' Grimbold roared and smashed his fist down hard on the counter.

Kate stood up. 'Who are you calling a slut?' she screamed back and the bar went very quiet as if girding itself for battle.

Then a tall, thickset man who Charity recognized as Danny's Pa detached himself from a group of lightermen. 'What's all this then?'

'That's my business, not yours,' replied Grimbold.

'In that case, she might as well come and have a drink with us.' The man beckoned to Kate. 'What'll it be pretty one?'

'She ain't having a drink. I've told 'er there's a ship just in and she hardly earns her keep as it is, that one.'

'Shut yer gob,' replied Kate, and with a toss of her head, she joined the group of men.

Charity watched Kate in astonished silence. She liked to defy the Grimbolds as often as possible but open rebellion like that, no, she could never do it, and the girl's bold effrontery filled her with admiration.

'You'll do as I say, whore.' Almost apoplectic, Grimbold's face had gone the colour of cured ham.

'Now I don't think you should go callin' her names like that. Kate's her moniker and very nice it is too, so why don't you just call her that, eh?' Jim Weston's pace across the floor was almost leisurely, his voice low. But wise men, hearing the threat in it, stepped out of his way. Because Jim was a big man, a hard man, a man with a reputation for violence, particularly after he'd had a drink or two, and only a very brave man would mess with him. Or someone like Grimbold who was just plain stupid.

'I'll call her what I li –'

Before Grimbold had time to finish the sentence a hand reached out and grabbed him by the collar, half pulling him over the counter. 'Oh no you won't. Her name's Kate. Now let me hear you say it.' Jim's fist was an inch from Grimbold's nose.

'Kate.' The name was spat out like an obscenity.

16

Mrs Grimbold, who had briefly left the bar, now returned and seeing her husband's predicament she rushed to his aid. 'Put 'im down! This minute!' she screamed.

'Right you are missus,' said the lighterman, and let go of his adversary so suddenly Grimbold had no time to regain his balance and fell heavily to the floor amid a great roar of derisive laughter.

It was like putting a match to a fuse. Cursing, Grimbold struggled to his feet. 'Someone's going to pay for this,' he roared, shaking his fists at the world in general and looking around for a victim.

But Charity had already slipped away downstairs. Out of reach of Grimbold's anger she filled a bucket and went outside to set about scrubbing the steps. It was a pointless task though with people constantly in and out, although there were diversions, like Danny coming to haul his dad home for dinner. He looked a proper masher too with a red-and-white-spotted hankie tied round his neck and a cap set at a rakish angle over one eye. When Charity saw him her chest went tight and her heart began an irregular pit-a-pat. Waiting for him to acknowledge her she leaned back on her heels, tucked a strand of hair behind her ear and smiled at him shyly. But he sped into the bar without a glance, taking the steps in two long strides.

She'd hardly had time to swallow her disappointment when Danny reappeared, his pa close behind, holding him by the scruff of the neck. He gave his son an almighty shove down the steps, at the same time bawling after him, 'You can bloody well tell yer ma I'll come for me dinner when I'm good and ready and not when she says.'

Astonished, Charity stood up, watching in alarm as Danny stumbled past her, certain he would fall. But although he staggered and his cap flew off and landed at her feet, by some miracle he kept his balance and reached the pavement still on two feet. However, his pride had taken a hammering, and when she handed him his cap, she saw that his face was red with shame. Hesitantly she reached out and touched his arm in a sympathetic gesture. But he shook her off and, after adjusting his jacket, he gave his father a look of pure hate and slunk off down the street. The swagger had gone from his step, though, and Charity had some sense of what he was feeling, of the depths of his humiliation.

Even after Danny had turned the corner, Jim Weston didn't let up on the drunken abuse of his son, calling into question his wife's fidelity and Danny's parentage.

Finally Kate came out and told him to shut up.

'Well, if a man can't be boss in his own 'ome where can he be?' he complained. But he was more pliable in Kate's hands and when she pushed him back into the pub, he went without any trouble.

'Men!' Kate exclaimed in a tone of disgust when he'd gone. Then, opening her bag, she took out a mirror. Wetting a finger with her tongue, she ran it over her eyebrows, tweaked at the curls on her forehead, unscrewed the top on a bottle and dabbed scent behind both ears. And while she was doing all this Charity gazed up at her, fascinated, inhaling the cheap perfume and thinking how pretty Kate was. She saw nothing incongruous in the heavily- and inexpertly-applied powder or the rouge that couldn't quite obliterate the bloom on her firm young cheeks. With all her soul she longed to look like Kate.

Completing her toilet, Kate snapped her handbag shut, looked about her then tripped lightly down the steps. She gave Charity a warm smile but would have passed on if the younger girl hadn't reached out and grabbed her skirt to detain her.

'I like that scent, Kate.'

Always susceptible to flattery, the girl paused and smiled. 'Do you pet? It's called Ecstasy. Want a dab?' Kate crouched down beside Charity and, unscrewing the bottle, tipped a drop on to her finger and went to rub it on the lobe of Charity's ear, but she backed away.

'No, better not.'

'Why, cos o' them?'

Charity nodded.

'Skin a bloody maggot those two wouldn't they?'

Again Charity nodded.

Moving closer, Kate said in a low voice, 'Take my advice, get away from 'ere just as soon as you can.'

'But where would I go?'

Kate waved her hand vaguely. 'Well you might get a job somewhere in a house as a maid.'

'What, lookin' like this?'

Kate studied her for several moments. 'Yeah, you've got a point there, I suppose,' she said bluntly. 'Tell you what, why don't you come along to my room one day when old Grimbold's out. I could tart you up a bit, get the knots out of your hair, maybe even wash it. How'd you like that?'

Charity touched her hair, trying to imagine it silky and smooth. 'D'you mean it?'

''Course I do.' Taking a handful of the matted locks, Kate piled it on top of Charity's head, noting with surprise the long, slender neck, the small ears and wide brow, but most of all the truly amazing eyes, dark and almond-shaped. 'You're not a bad looking kid, do you know that? And by the time I'm done with you, you'll look as pretty as a picture.'

'Will I really? As pretty as you?' asked Charity, thinking of Danny.

Kate stood up. 'I don't see why not. Anyway I must be off. Got to see a man about a dog, y'know.' She laughed and winked, then with a casual wave, sauntered off.

'When can I come?' Charity shouted after her.

'Come whenever you like, love,' Kate called over her shoulder. Although by the time she had reached the end of the street and haggled with a sailor over the price of her young body, she had already forgotten her promise to the other girl.

Chapter 3

With the unpitying eye of youth Charity stood looking down at her mistress. Pearl's mouth was open and a dribble of saliva ran down her chin. The front of her black shiny dress was stained with food: today's, yesterday's and the day before's, and without the restraining influence of corsets, her pendulous breasts hung down like ripe pears and almost touched her thighs.

'You're a disgusting old bag and I hate you, Pearl Grimbold.' Relishing her sense of power, and knowing they were alone together, Charity let the insults roll off her tongue.

Earlier that day, Grimbold had gone off on some undisclosed business. They were regular occurrences these mysterious trips, and often kept him away from home for the whole night. As usual, he'd hardly been gone five minutes before Pearl had put the closed sign up on the pub door. Then, summoning Charity into the parlour, she'd lifted her dress and presented to her despised maid-of-all-work, her mountainous backside.

'Help get me out of these,' she'd ordered and, as Charity obediently unlaced the whalebone corset, she'd found there was a horrible fascination in watching the tormented flesh expand, the waistline and hips merge then hang in great folds like the skin of an elephant. When she was finally unleashed, Mrs Grimbold groaned with pleasure, eased herself into a chair and lifted her swollen feet up on to a stool. 'That's better,' she said with a contented sigh, and began scratching her back with the toasting fork.

After this Charity found herself run off her feet trying to keep up with her demands for food and drink. All evening it was, 'Fetch this, fetch that,' pies, jellied eels, cockles, until she'd stuffed herself like a pig for market.

Hiding her contempt, Charity had done as she was told, watched the level of the rum bottle drop, and with growing excitement, made her plans. Then, although the snores coming from the parlour were enough to take the slates off the roof, Charity had still felt the need to satisfy herself that Mrs Grimbold was really out cold. Easing open the door to the parlour she had peered round it, seen the empty rum bottle on the table and felt bold enough to move further into the room.

Now, reassured that the sprawling figure would be out for the count until morning, Charity tiptoed from the room, paused one final time in the kitchen to check on the snores then let herself out into the yard. Here she had to circumnavigate empty beer barrels, crates, and a hand cart, before she reached the gate. And it always stuck after rain so she had to tug at it with both hands. Then she was sure the squeak of rusting hinges would bring Mrs Grimbold shuffling out after her. Moving with stealth and hardly daring to draw breath, she stepped into the alleyway leaving the gate open behind her.

It was dusk and at any other time the eeriness, the nebulous shapes in the narrow passage might have made her feel nervous. Tonight though, as she slid along in the shadow of the wall all she felt was a defiant tingle of excitement.

Charity couldn't see the river, but she could smell it, knew from the chill in the air that wraith-like whorls of mist would be rising from the water. The cold couldn't touch her that night though, and she wasn't aware of her inadequate cotton dress or the goose pimples rising on her arms and legs. Her own daring almost took her breath away and she kept thinking of Kate, imagining her surprise when she turned up at her door.

But first she had to get there. Passing the darkened pub did give Charity a twinge of anxiety, then she felt exposed by the lights from a cafe, and, certain it would be Grimbold, every footstep had her darting into a doorway.

Charity couldn't read the names of the streets, but she knew exactly where the house was that Kate shared with several other girls, and in spite of it being forbidden territory, she made her way straight there.

The house, three-storeyed and at the end of a terrace, was quite ordinary, and with its sooty brickwork and torn curtains there was little to distinguish it from the other houses in the street. Yet its very ordinariness menaced her and held her back and she had to force herself to turn the handle on the front door. Now, remember why you're here, she chided herself, to get yourself tarted up so that Danny will look at you in the same way his pa does Kate, in fact treat you like you was someone really special.

Keeping her fear in check, she stepped over the threshold. But in spite of her resolve, when the door swung closed behind her and she found herself in almost total darkness, Charity knew that, if she didn't keep a tight grip on herself, she'd turn tail and run. Keep calm, she muttered, then, to stop the pounding in her ears, she took several deep breaths and waited for her eyes to adjust to the gloom.

As she'd expected, she was in a narrow hall, and a faint light coming from under a door to her right guided her eyes to a staircase leading up to another floor. With no idea where Kate's room might be, she tiptoed to the door, crouched down and tried to peer through the keyhole. But the key was in the lock and somehow she couldn't find the courage to knock or call out. Then, hearing a movement in the room, she jumped back, fled in panic along the hall, caught her foot on some torn lino, tripped, mouthed a vigorous 'Soddit' and dashed upstairs to the first landing.

Here she stood very still and waited. When no one stirred, Charity relaxed a little. She saw there was another flight of stairs and was half way up when the front door opened and the silence was fractured by a chillingly familiar voice that stopped her dead in her tracks. There was also another sound. It was of a girl crying. And the heartbroken sobs moving nearer jolted Charity into taking the remaining steps in a bound. But now she was trapped on the top floor. Scared out of her wits, she sought some means of escape. She felt the hard metal of a door handle in the small of her back and fell into a room a moment before the man and the crying girl reached the landing and went into the room next to hers.

'For Christ's sake stop grizzling,' she heard Grimbold say, but the girl just sobbed more loudly. 'Do as you're told. Shut up or I'll really give you somethin' to snivel about.' Charity didn't have to imagine the threatening lift of the hand, it was all too familiar to her.

But now there was someone else coming up the stairs. Charity could hear the heavy foosteps of a man, and Grimbold went to the door. 'Ah, Lord Prendergast,' she heard him say in an obsequious tone. 'Come in.'

Curiosity had quickly put paid to any fear and Charity now pressed her ear hard against the communicating wall. The voice she heard answer was cultured, arrogant and totally unfamiliar to her. 'Well, what have you got for me, Mr Grimbold?'

'A pretty little piece, m'Lord, but I'm afraid the price has gone up.'

'Again!'

'Young girls is gettin' 'arder to come by these days. It's the changin' times y'see and that means extra expense.'

'How much, man?'

'I'll 'ave to ask for twenty quid.'

'You're getting greedy, Mr Grimbold.' The well-bred voice was cold.

'I could say the same for you, m'Lord, it's well nigh impossible to get an unbroken hymen every week, even at this age,' Grimbold retorted.

'Less of your impertinence, man, or I'll take my business elsewhere.'

'Now you wouldn't want to do that. It could mean prison, touchin' a maid under sixteen. It's against the law now, 'as been for some time.'

23

'Are you threatening me, Grimbold? Because I'm telling you, we'd both go down together.'

'But you'd 'ave far more to lose than me, I think, sir, with a noble name like yours.'

There was a pause then the unknown man's voice became more placatory. 'Here, take the money and go.'

'You want the same next week, Lord Prendergast?' Grimbold's tone was oily, subservient again.

'Of course, man, of course,' the aristocratic gentleman replied impatiently. 'Now go.' And Charity heard Grimbold clatter down the stairs and into a room at the front of the house.

While the coast was clear, Charity was tempted to make a run for it, but an instinct for self preservation made her keep very still and she heard the stranger speak to the girl again.

'Come here and sit on my lap, my dear. Don't be frightened, I shan't hurt you.' His voice sounded kinder now and the girl obviously felt reassured by his tone, for the sobbing stopped briefly. Then there was a whimper, followed by a frightened, 'No don't!' rising to a scream that made the hairs rise on the back of Charity's neck.

'Shut up,' the man barked then the screams were stifled, as if something was being pressed over her mouth.

Charity could stand it no longer, not the hopeless silence, nor the rhythmic movement of the bedsprings. Saving her own skin had become secondary to the girl's desperate plight as, like a vengeful whirlwind, she burst into the room. But she was brought up short by a scene that would haunt her through childhood into adult life. Intent on his pleasure, the man's hand was clamped over the girl's mouth and his weight pinned her to the bed. Swaying with shock and disgust, Charity clung on to the door handle. But then the mute, terrified eyes of the small girl met hers and her rage exploded. 'Stop it! Stop it!' she shrieked, and throwing herself upon the man, she began pummelling his bare back with her fists.

'Christ almighty . . .' At the abrupt termination of his

24

evening's sport, his Lordship rolled away from the girl and naked as Adam, staggered to his feet. With a murderous expression in his hard grey eyes, he reached out and grabbed Charity by the scruff of the neck and started to shake her violently. 'Who are you, damn you? Who are you?'

'Leave me alone,' Charity screamed back at him and gave him a vicious kick on the shins. Then, the other girl started to sob loudly. There was a confusion of voices as the silent house erupted, doors flew open, and men and women in various stages of undress gathered in a half-circle round the open door.

'Let go of 'er you bugger,' shouted a rough male voice and when his sentiments were echoed by several others in the circle, Lord Prendergast felt threatened enough to comply. Then another, more familiar voice broke in.

'What the devil's going on here?' demanded Grimbold, pushing his way into the room.

'You'd better ask that brat,' answered his Lordship, stepping into his trousers. He finished buttoning up his shirt, then pointed at Charity, who was trying to make herself invisible in the corner. 'If this gets out . . . I'm warning you, Grimbold . . .'

Grimbold turned to the women and their customers. 'Clear off,' he ordered. 'This is nothing to do with you. And I'm warnin' you, keep your traps shut about it too.'

He closed the door with some force, then he moved towards Charity and, holding her by the lobe of her ear, dragged her into the middle of the small room. But she just stared at the two men with a scornful expression. Indeed she stared at Lord Prendergast for so long, taking in every detail of him, the heavy frame, grey hair and full set of whiskers, that he began to move uneasily.

'Get that interfering little bitch out of my sight. And this one.' He indicated with an indifferent wave of the hand the small, forlorn victim of his lust, now modestly trying to readjust her torn clothes. 'But before you go,

Grimbold . . .' He held out his hand. 'I'll have my money back. And you can consider our business association at an end.'

Grimbold slapped a wad of notes into Lord Prendergast's palm. Then, without a word and gripping each girl by the wrist, he yanked them out of the door, down the stairs and into the street. Here, to Charity's astonishment – and Grimbold's – the child, finding a desperate sort of courage from God knows where, bent and clamped her teeth over Grimbold's hand, hanging on with the savagery of a bull terrier.

'You cow!' roared Grimbold and tried to shake her off. But the girl held on. Pain forced him to loosen his grip and in an instant she had gone.

'Run for it!' Charity shouted after her. 'And good luck,' she added provocatively as the girl was swallowed up by the night.

Grimbold, who could see his business interests being threatened at every turn, was beside himself. 'Wait till I get you 'ome, madam, I'll knock your bloody block off, wiv this.' He waved a fist under her nose.

Their noisy arrival at the pub woke Mrs Grimbold, who shot up in her chair, groaned and put a hand to her throbbing head.

'Don't be alarmed, pet,' Grimbold called, dragging Charity behind him as he groped his way through to the parlour. 'Just light the lamp, will you, there's a very serious matter to be dealt with here.'

'What you doin' home so soon anyway?' Pearl asked, in a tone of great ill humour, as she fumbled about in the dark for a lucifer. 'Oh, it's 'er, is it? I might have guessed,' she said when the lamp was lit. 'What she been up to now?'

'Poking 'er bloody nose in where she shouldn't, you know . . . down the road.' He indicated the general direction by a movement of his head. 'And we've just seen the last of a particularly valuable customer, Lord P.'

Money, particularly the loss of it, could excite Mrs Grimbold like nothing else and she moved with a surprising agility towards Charity. 'Lord Prendergast!' she shrieked, grasping the girl's face and squeezing her cheeks spitefully between her fat fingers. 'We've lost him because of this scullion?'

'Yeah, and there's the law to think about too. If they gets wind of anyfink she could be the ruination of us. So what we gonna do wiv 'er, eh?'

'She'll have to go. She's always been more trouble than she's worth; eaten us out of house and home . . . and when you think what we've done for her . . . ungrateful wench.' She shook her head in disbelief. 'Bill Slawson can't wait to get his hands on her, drools at the mouth he does. So he'll probably cough up if we make the price right.'

'It might knock some of the insolence out of 'er too,' answered her husband, relishing the prospect. 'We've always been too lenient and it never does. But he'll quieten 'er down, take the fire out of 'er.'

Charity, who had been listening to their conversation with mounting terror, managed to jerk free from Mrs Grimbold's pincer-like grip. 'I ain't going, and you'll never make me. He's disgusting. I'd throw meself in the river first.' But although her body was thrust forward in an aggressive stance and she glared at them with a fierce hatred, her heart was fluttering with the despair of a caged bird. She was trapped and knew it.

Grimbold laughed scornfully, unmoved by her threats. 'Don't talk such drivel. You've cost us a pretty penny tonight so you're just gonna have to repay it. I'll teach you to get uppity, miss.'

With nothing to lose now, Charity decided to put up a fight. Closing her eyes she began to scream, a shrill, skull-cracking scream that had Mrs Grimbold pressing her hands over her ears and grimacing in pain. 'Stop her, Grimbold, for Christ's sake, me 'ead's splitting already.'

'Shut your noise.' A violent blow was administered to

Charity's head, but this only provoked her into an even greater frenzy.

Grimbold's hand clamped over her mouth finally silenced her and as she struggled to wrench his fingers away she heard him speak. 'Open the cupboard then grab this banshee's feet, we'll soon put paid to 'er little game.'

Matted strands of hair hung down over Charity's face and her black eyes had the feral look of a cornered animal. And she fought like one too. But although her terror seemed to endow her with an almost herculean strength, it was still no match for Mrs Grimbold's weight. Even as she tried to lean against it, the door of the narrow, low-ceilinged broom cupboard was forced shut and she heard the key being turned in the lock. 'Let me out! Let me out!' she pleaded between sobs and banged with her fists against the solid oak door.

'You can cry bloody murder now, no one will hear you,' Pearl answered. Then to her husband she said, 'I'm not staying 'ere to listen to that all evening. You can take me down the pie and eel shop.'

As the lamp was extinguished and their footsteps faded away, Charity slid to the floor in a state of claustrophobic terror. It was like being buried alive and she would rather have felt ten lashes of Grimbold's belt across her back than be entombed like this, in an airless cupboard which was no larger than a coffin. Knowing she was going to suffocate, panic engulfed her and, as she battled for air, she had the sensation of being swept down into a cobwebby blackness. If she'd had any concept of God, Charity would have appealed to his mercy then. Instead her body responded in its own primitive way and when she felt a warm trickle between her legs she knew she had wet herself. But the loose curdling sensation low in her bowels was worse. Oh no, don't let me mess meself, she thought in frantic despair, squeezing the muscles in her bottom tight and inhaling deeply. But she had already lost control. By the terrible smell alone she knew nature had taken its course. Mortified, the fight gone from her, she put her thumb in her mouth and rocked back and forth in misery until she fell into a cramped, uneasy sleep.

For hours, Charity drifted in and out of sleep, hoping they would find enough pity in their hearts to release her. But it wasn't until the following morning that she heard the scraping of the key as it was turned in the lock. Confused, she lifted her head with a jerk then stood up, blinking and rubbing her eyes in the sudden light.

It was Pearl's voice she heard first. 'Christ, she's crapped all over 'erself!' the woman squawked, holding her nose. 'Stay away from me, you disgusting creature.' She shrank back as if from a leper when the bewildered girl stepped into the room.

Still dazed from her terrible ordeal, Charity didn't realize that Bill Slawson was in the room until he spoke. 'You're right, she smells like a polecat,' he agreed, then sensing a bargain added, 'twenty smackers for 'er. Not likely. Ten is the most you'll get out of me and you can take it or leave it.'

Grimbold pretended to think about it for a moment. 'Done,' he said and held out his hand, well pleased with himself.

'Now hold on. I don't carry that sort of money around with me. I ain't taking 'er 'ome ponging like that neither. I'll be back 'in the hour with the money and she better be cleaned up.'

'You won't recognize her by the time we're done, will he Pearlm'dear?

Pearl, who had her mean little eyes fixed on Charity, didn't answer.

The night in the cupboard had left Charity weak and lightheaded and too dazed to follow the conversation. It was only gradually that she began to gather her wits about her and realize she was being traded like a piece of horse-flesh. But the subversive, audacious streak that would always serve her well now found its voice and she glowered at Bill Slawson with undisguised contempt.

'You stink too . . . all the time. And I ain't coming wiv you anyway.'

'Yes you are.'

'No I'm not!' She stepped forward, an expression of implacable hatred on her face.

'And when I do get you 'ome, you're gonna get a bloody good walloping too, just for your cheek.'

'I'd rather die first.'

Hugely entertained by this dramatic statement, Bill Slawson threw back his head and roared, showing the few discoloured stumps that passed for his teeth.

'You've got spirit, I'll say that for you. Should add a bit of spice to things. I enjoy a bit of slap and tickle. Anyway, I'm sure Grimbold will see to it you don't do yerself in, not with all that money hanging in the balance.' He banged his hat more firmly on his head. 'See you in an hour then, Mrs Grimbold,' he said and with a final leer at Charity he went.

Grimbold made some excuse about draymen arriving shortly with beer and the cellar trap door having to be opened, and he, too, disappeared.

Left alone with her, Mrs Grimbold stared at Charity in her soiled rags with dislike and envy. Even in her filth, there was no ignoring the girl's beauty: the amazing eyes with their slightly oriental tilt, the honey-toned skin. It wouldn't last, though. A dose of the clap would soon put paid to those looks. Like her mother she'd be dead at eighteen.

But these musings only slightly mollified Pearl. 'I don't know why I should 'ave the job of cleaning you up, mucky bitch. You've ruined those clothes. But then you've never been grateful for what we've done; taking you in off the streets, feeding and clothing you. You wait though, once you're wi' Bill Slawson you'll be begging for us to take you back.' Anticipating Charity's fate, her eyes gleamed with malicious pleasure.

'Don't send me to 'im . . . please. I'll never breathe a word about what I saw, I promise.'

'Don't make me laugh. I wouldn't trust you an inch. Anyway it might teach you not to go snooping around and poking yer nose into things that don't concern you. Now fill a bucket, get out in the yard, strip off and get yerself washed.'

'No.' Charity stood her ground doggedly. She knew she stank to high heaven and longed for a wash. But she was shrewd enough to know that the more unappealing she looked the safer she might be from the pawnbroker's attentions. She remembered the scene in that other room, the man smothering the girl with his weight and grunting as he pushed into her and knew now that was to be her fate. The idea of it made her feel so sick she started to retch, heaving painfully and pressing her arms into her empty stomach.

But her distress awoke no pity in Mrs Grimbold. Instead, the woman grabbed a leather belt that hung over the fireplace and lashed out with it. 'Do as I say,' she screamed.

But Charity's sharp odour and Pearl's own weight put a restraint on her movements and, on a sudden impulse, Charity darted round the woman and ran out into the yard, slamming the door. Behind her she could hear Pearl screaming for her better half and she knew she hadn't a moment to spare. Fortunately the gate was as she'd left it, open, but she had the good sense to pull it hard shut before tearing off up the alleyway.

Charity's only thought was of escape and she was too filled with terror to even care where she was going. Not daring to look round, she staggered like a drunk, zigzagging her way up the alley until she found her escape blocked by a high wall. I'm done for, she thought, staring up at it. But desperation gave her strength and she hurled herself against it, found a foothold, managed to scramble over and landed with a crash in a derelict garden of overgrown bushes and empty boxes.

Charity knew from the several cats who observed her sudden arrival with inscrutable expressions and irritably flicking tails, that she was in Miss Pumfrey's back garden and so, for the moment, relatively safe. The Grimbolds would never approach Eliza Pumfrey. They were sworn enemies and had been since the day Grimbold had heaved a brick and injured one of the many strays she fed. Eliza was also elderly and her devotion to cats made her something of an oddity in the area. Often children jeered at her in the streets, called her a witch and even Charity was a little wary of her.

The boxes offered some sort of cover so when she'd got her breath back, Charity crawled into them, building them up around her like a fortress. Then she waited. She had no plan in her head but instinct told her she should lie low, at least until dusk, not that she could have summoned up the energy to move anyway.

Nevertheless, at the sound of the heavy footsteps, pausing then moving on again, Charity tensed, ready for flight. She heard the sound of boots scraping against brick and was about to break cover when a woman's angry voice stopped her.

'What are you doing trespassing on my property, Grimbold. Get down off that wall, immediately.'

Peering through a chink in her hiding place Charity watched as Miss Pumfrey came flying down the garden, brandishing a heavy walking stick above her head.

'Keep yer hair on missus. I'm only looking for that brat who works for us. She's stolen some money and run off.'

Ooh, the lying toad, thought Charity indignantly and felt a strong urge to leap up and tell him so.

But Miss Pumfrey obligingly did it for her. 'I'd never believe a word you say,' was her swift rejoinder, then she charged forward, her frizzy grey hair in disarray and looking for all the world like the witch she was rumoured to be. There was a satisfying yell of pain as ebony made contact with Grimbold's shins, then various violent ends were wished upon the lady as he overbalanced and fell back into the alleyway.

Charity's smothered giggle of delight was checked by

32

the stick being tapped against the boxes and Miss Pumfrey saying, 'You can come out now.' She tensed herself again and didn't move.

Miss Pumfrey bent down and peered through the wall of boxes at Charity, whose eyes had grown large with fear. 'You know he might come back again and I can't stand guard here all day.'

Hesitantly, Charity crawled out from her hiding place and stood up. The elderly woman managed to restrain herself from wrinkling her nose or commenting on the child's filthy appearance and instead she gave her brief instructions. 'The back door's open, keep your head down and go, now.'

Obscured from prying eyes by the thick undergrowth, Charity moved swiftly through the garden. She reached the house, Miss Pumfrey walking close behind her, and locking the door. 'You're quite safe now, he wouldn't dare come here.'

She beckoned to Charity who followed her through to the parlour behind her small haberdashery shop. As in the garden, there were cats everywhere: black ones, tabby ones, ginger ones, cats with tails missing, one-eyed cats, lame cats. Every chair was occupied as was the table, and several more were balanced like tightrope walkers along the mantelpiece.

Mrs Pumfrey studied Charity, then said, 'Right. I want you to tell me what this is all about and why you were running away. But first of all you better get out of these clothes and have a wash. I expect you're hungry too?'

Charity nodded in a dazed fashion.

'But first things first.' She lifted a kettle off the fire and indicated that Charity should follow her into the scullery. Here she filled a bowl with water, handed the girl a bar of carbolic soap and a cloth, disappeared briefly then came back with a voluminous nightgown. 'Put that on after you've cleaned yourself up and throw your own clothes outside. All they're good for is the dustcart. Meanwhile I'll get you something to eat.'

Charity waited until she had gone, then, removing her filthy rags, she washed herself thoroughly, rubbing her skin until it was raw, delighting in the luxury of hot water and soap. Then, when she'd finished and was pulling the nightgown over her head, she felt the unfamiliar pleasure of laundered cambric against her skin.

Smelling of carbolic and tripping on the hem of the outsize nightgown, she went back to the parlour, cleaner than she'd ever felt in her life before. Miss Pumfrey eyed her critically for a moment, then, scolding a beautiful tabby softly, she scooped it up from the chair and invited Charity to take its place.

She made tea and put it down in front of the girl, cut bread and spread it with rich beef dripping and watched with pity as Charity fell upon the food like a just-rescued stray. Eliza Pumfrey refilled her cup and let her demolish several more slices of bread before asking, 'Now tell me my dear, what's your name?'

Charity threw back her head, draining the cup of every last drop of tea. Then, putting it down, she rubbed her hand across her mouth and answered finally, 'Charity.'

'Charity who?'

Charity thought about this. 'Dunno.'

'So you're not related to the Grimbolds, then.'

'Gawd no.' She shook her head in vigorous denial. Even to suggest it appalled her. 'I just worked for them.'

'So what were you running away from, child?'

Charity twisted her hands and stared down at her lap in embarrassment. How could she explain it.

'Take your time,' said Miss Pumfrey when she saw the girl was becoming distressed.

'They were gonna sell me to Bill Slawson. For ten quid.' Her voice was no more than a whisper and she was dangerously close to tears.

'They're unspeakable, those two,' said Miss Pumfrey in disgust. Knowing their trade as brothel-keepers she had no doubt what the girl's fate would be. 'There's nothing they wouldn't stoop to. Certainly you can't go back there. But, in the meantime, what are we going to do about you?' Miss Pumfrey pondered, absentmindedly scratching the ears of a large ginger tom.

Charity's answer was a wide yawn. She didn't want to appear rude to someone who had shown her such kindness, but the trauma of the last twelve hours was taking its toll and she had to struggle to keep her eyes open. Then the bell rang as someone came into the shop and Miss Pumfrey was obliged to go and attend to her customer. When she returned, Charity was fast asleep in the chair, her head resting awkwardly on the arm, the thin legs dangling. Lifting the undernourished body without difficulty, Eliza laid her out on the black horsehair sofa, then, shooing several cats off a blanket, she used it to cover the sleeping girl.

Chapter 4

As Eliza stood studying Charity, noticing the bruises on her body, the matted hair, all evidence of years of cruelty and neglect, the pity she felt for the girl's plight was mixed with resentment. Compassion was all very well, but she couldn't have the child here, chipping away at her defences. She'd sworn then – how long ago it seemed – never again to allow herself to be betrayed by such emotions as love or tenderness. Caring for another human being, no, she wanted none of it. She'd experienced the terrible consequences of love, known the raw pain of rejection once, and that was enough in any life. Of course she knew she was considered a bit odd but other people's opinions meant little to her. She had her cats and they were enough; all her affection was reserved for them. They asked for little and they didn't betray. But then again the waif asleep on her sofa was an injured thing too, and not so very different from the bedraggled, ill-used strays she rescued regularly from the river. Just as she couldn't turn one of those away, Eliza knew it would need a heart with more steel in it that hers to send the girl back to the Grimbolds'. Still that didn't mean she had to be landed with her. There had to be alternatives.

Deciding an unnecessary problem was being added to her life, Eliza allowed herself to succumb to the feeling of aggrieved irritation. 'Why couldn't the wretched child have chosen someone else's garden to hide in, eh Pickles,' she said, addressing the ginger tom, who while she'd been studying the sleeping girl had leapt on to her shoulder and looped himself round her neck like a fur collar. She was still doing battle with her conscience when a damp nose nudging her cheek and a throaty, insistent purr in her ear told her it was well past Pickles' feeding time. Unaware that she was causing such heart searching, Charity slept on. But Eliza knew it wouldn't do to be taken in by the innocence of sleep. She must harden her heart, not allow her emotions to get the better of her.

Reminded once again by Pickles of her other duties she gave a vexatious sigh. Then, with a troubled shake of the head, she turned and went into the scullery to begin cutting up lights for the cats' dinner. Made frantic by the smell of food, Pickles wove himself in and out of her legs, nearly tripping her up as she went outside and rattled the knife against the plate. At the sound, cats appeared, stretching and yawning, from every corner of the garden. Watching them pick their way neatly up the path, tails raised in expectation, her irritation subsided. And, bending to share the food out between them, Eliza made her decision: this was her family and the child had no place in her life. She would not be sucked into an emotional commitment. None of it was of her doing so there was no need for guilt. The girl could go to St Olave's, the workhouse on Lower Road. It was such a simple solution she didn't know why she hadn't thought of it sooner. She would be all right there. Fed and clothed, trained for a job in service. Why, it would seem like heaven after her years of servitude with the Grimbolds.

Eliza had just about convinced herself of the rightness of her decision, when she heard a sound from the parlour. Expecting to find Charity awake she went to take a look. But the girl was still asleep and dreaming, troubled dreams, too, Eliza guessed by the restless movement of her head and the incoherent mutterings. Refusing to think what the child might have been subjected to over the years, she bent to pick up the blanket which had slipped to the floor. Tucking it more securely round her, she noticed the feverish flush on Charity's cheeks and her resolve faltered. She was so young, so vulnerable and there was so much wickedness in the world. How could she send the girl away and ever sleep easy again. Whatever her own past, she wasn't that heartless. Just as she knew she would always find room for a stray, so Eliza knew she would somehow find space for the girl in her life. 'And just let's hope I don't live to regret my moment of weakness,' she remarked to Pickles, who having eaten his fill, had now settled himself down comfortably in the crook of Charity's arm.

On that first day of her escape, Charity slept for twelve hours. She awoke to the glow of lamplight and the smell of something cooking but with no immediate understanding of why she should be lying in a strange room with a cat sitting on her chest, gazing at her with yellow, inscrutable eyes. Charity's mind was still fuzzy with sleep and, confused by the unfamiliar surroundings, she looked about her searching for clues. She was no nearer an answer when the door that divided the shop from the parlour opened and Miss Pumfrey came bustling into the room bringing back with her all the horrors of the past few hours in vivid, ghastly detail.

Not sure what to expect, Charity tensed herself, pulled the blanket up to her chin and watched with frightened eyes as Miss Pumfrey approached the bed and lifted the cat off her chest.

'So you're awake at last,' Eliza said. Then seeing

Charity's expression added, 'There's no need to look so terrified, you know, I'm not going to eat you. Anyway, now that you are awake, are you hungry?'

It was an unnecessary question because Charity couldn't remember a time in her life when she hadn't been hungry, but she nodded just the same.

'I guessed you might be.' Moving to the fire, Eliza lifted a cast iron pot on to the table and Charity watched with hungry eyes as she ladled thick soup into two deep bowls.

'Sit up then child,' Miss Pumfrey instructed her briskly.

Charity didn't need a second telling. In one swift movement she slid off the sofa and reaching out, grabbed a bowl. Throwing her head back she slurped the soup down with noisy satisfaction.

Rendered briefly speechless, Miss Pumfrey stared in astonishment then taking the bowl from Charity she said in a firm voice, 'We might as well start as we mean to go on, and that will be quite enough of that. If you are to remain here under my roof, young lady, first of all you will learn some table manners. Now would you like some more soup?'

Charity nodded her head vigorously.

'Try saying "please,"' suggested Miss Pumfrey, thinking to herself that this was all going to be just as difficult as she'd imagined.

Charity saw no reason for such niceties, but a natural intelligence combined with an instinct for survival suggested it might be in her own best interests to do as Miss Pumfrey said. She'd also heard the magic words, *If you are to remain here*, and she wasn't going to jeopardize her chances. If Miss Pumfrey wanted a please, she would get it. 'Please,' she repeated meekly and was rewarded with another plate of soup.

'Now, before we start, you'll use a spoon, like this.' Miss Pumfrey dipped a spoon into her own bowl of soup and lifted it to her mouth.

Charity watched carefully then followed suit, but grasping the handle as awkwardly as a two-year-old. Although

38

it slowed down her consumption, and much of the soup went down her nightdress, she persevered. Learning these 'table manners' Miss Pumfrey talked about was a price worth paying, she decided, if it stopped her being thrown out on her ear, or worse, sent back to the Grimbolds'. At the moment she had all she wanted, a pleasant feeling of warmth and a full belly, and, facing as she was an uncertain future, Charity decided while she had it she would enjoy it. Finishing her soup, she wiped her mouth along the sleeve of her nightie, sat back and gave a sigh of contentment. 'That was lovely,' she declared, then seeing Eliza's stern look added in a polite voice, 'And thank you very much, Miss Pumfrey.'

By the next morning Eliza found she had another problem to deal with. When she'd rashly discarded Charity's filthy rags, she'd left her without a stitch to wear. Even cut down, she knew there was no way a dress of hers would fit the girl's small frame, which left her with no choice but to make one.

Eliza had invested in the small haberdasher's she owned with money left to her when her father died. But she ran the shop without any real enthusiasm and she just about scratched a living from it. The shop did carry a variety of goods however; thread, buttons, braid, wool, and for the benefit of those more prosperous wives of local businessmen who occasionally graced her with their presence when they couldn't find the time to shop in Rye Lane, she also kept in stock a few rolls of cloth.

It was one of these she spread out on the counter for Charity to inspect. The colour was a practical but ugly brown, the material rough in texture but Charity fingered it as if it were silk.

'You like it do you child?' asked Miss Pumfrey seeing the girl's pleased expression.

'Oh yes.' Charity's eyes shone.

'Well it should see you through the winter,' said Eliza then, after a quick look at Charity to assess her size, began unrolling the material and measuring it against a brass ruler attached to the counter.

A new dress, gosh, Charity thought as she watched the scratchy material being cut, she'd never had one before. She was busy picturing herself swanking around in it when the doorbell went. Both of them looked up and both reacted differently to the customer who entered. Charity sank back against the shelves of cloth hoping to make herself invisible but Miss Pumfrey went on calmly cutting through the material. 'What can I do for you, Mr Grimbold?' she asked politely, for all the world as if he were one of her regular customers.

'Her,' Grimbold answered and, leaning over, he made a quick lunge at Charity. Then half lifting her, he pulled her against the counter, with such force it knocked the breath out of her.

Grabbing her ebony stick from under the counter, Miss Pumfrey began to lash out at him. 'Let go of her!'' she shrieked.

Grimbold had no choice. The stick cracked against his skull making his head spin and he was forced to raise his arms to ward off the blows raining down on him. 'Bugger you woman, I'll kill the pair of you,' he threatened, backing away from the virago Miss Pumfrey had become.

'No you won't. Come in here again, and I'll have the police on you. I know enough about your goings-on to have you and your wife sent down for ten years or more. Now get out of my shop.' Eliza moved round the counter, still wielding her stick and forcing Grimbold to retreat out of the door. He went, muttering more threats. Only then did Eliza allow herself to hope that would be the last they saw of him.

She found Charity crouched behind the counter, shaking violently. It was so long since she'd touched anyone in affection Eliza had to force herself to reach out to the girl. But she did, holding her trembling body awkwardly, and allowing Charity to sob onto her shoulder. 'There, there, it's all right,' she soothed, 'he's gone, and I doubt

40

if he'll come back, not if he's got any sense anyway. I've told him I'll go to the police and he knows I don't make idle threats.'

Unused to love or affection, at first Charity held herself stiffly, embarrassed by the bodily contact. But Miss Pumfrey's stout frame was warm and comforting and, knowing she'd found someone to take care of her, she relaxed. There was nothing to be frightened of any more, not Grimbold, not anyone.

In the small back parlour she was further comforted with hot sweet tea. What finally restored her spirits though, was the knowledge that all the snipping, measuring and pinning Miss Pumfrey was doing was for her benefit and would provide her with the first new dress she'd ever had in her life.

So the two of them settled down into a wary sort of relationship. Eliza often felt sorely tried by Charity's behaviour, though and even after a year she would sometimes find herself wondering why she had been so weak-willed and foolish as to take the girl in. As the daughter of a sea captain with a degree of refinement about her, she frequently lifted her hands in horror at Charity's crude language; then, as Charity was illiterate, Eliza had the task of teaching her to read and write; and the girl took up space in the cramped living quarters; and there was the expense of another mouth to feed, added to which a bed had had to be bought for her. However, weighed against this was what Charity brought to her life: a reawakening of emotions she'd thought dead. For Eliza realized she loved the girl with the same fierce protectiveness as a female cat does her kittens . . . just let anyone try and harm her . . .

Charity, too, had to make adjustments and she resented being continually corrected. Miss Pumfrey had a sharp tongue and since Charity was more than able to stand up for herself there were frequent heated exchanges. But she was also quick-witted and adaptable, besides which, she, too, was aware of the growing affection between them.

As soon as she'd learnt not to spike every other sentence with an oath, and could read and write, she was packed off to the local Board school to complete her education, armed with the surname of Brown and a birthday in September. To join in playground games, to have neat plaits, wear a clean white apron and sit behind a desk with a roomful of other children was, for Charity, a dream come true. She was so hungry for knowledge she couldn't understand why the other children were reluctant to learn, fidgeted in class and made a dash for the door as soon as the bell went. She herself hung on the teacher's every word and was always the last to leave. Soon she was forging ahead in her lessons and outstripping the other pupils. All except Mollie Payne, a girl of her own age who sat in the desk next to her. Because no matter how hard she tried, she could never catch up with the clever Mollie.

She was so in awe of her that even though they went the same way home, Charity, fearing a snub, always kept a respectful distance. But often she would try to copy Mollie's walk, head flung back, shoulders squared, her legs reaching out with long confident strides.

Too humble to imagine the other girl was even aware of her existence, Charity was so surprised when Mollie came up to her one day after school and said, 'You go the same way home as me, don't you?' she could only nod her head in confusion.

However, Mollie's next remark as she fell in step beside her, confused Charity even more. 'I'm a bluestocking, y'know.' She made this announcement with some pride.

Charity glanced down at the space between the hem of Mollie's skirt and the top of her boots and saw that her stockings were black like Charity's own. She puzzled over this briefly, decided she could hardly accuse Mollie of being a liar, so said nothing.

'D'you know what that is?' Mollie went on.

'No, I don't think so,' Charity had to admit.

'My pa says that's what women are called who are intellectual.'

'Oh, is that so.' Charity kept her tone noncommittal. She didn't want to be damned as stupid but she hadn't the slightest notion what the word 'intellectual' meant either. She promised herself though, that just as soon as she got home she would look it up in Miss Pumfrey's large, leather-bound lexicon.

'And when I'm older,' Mollie went on with hardly a pause, 'I shall be a Suffragist.'

Charity gave up pretending then. 'What's a Suf . . . Suffra . . . whatever you call it?'

Mollie stopped and stared at Charity, her broad, honest face and direct brown eyes registering appalled astonishment. 'Are you really telling me you don't know?'

Charity shook her head miserably. This was it. Shown up for the ignoramus she was. Mollie wouldn't want to be seen dead with her now.

'It's the name given to women who are fighting for the vote.'

'Why should they do that?' Charity asked in a mystified voice, somehow imagining them engaged in mortal combat.

'Don't you think women are entitled to the vote then?'

Hearing the somewhat aggressive tone in Mollie's voice and anxious to placate her, Charity replied, 'To tell you the truth, it's not something I've ever thought about. But you're so clever, Moll and you know all about these things so you'll just have to teach me.'

'With my looks I've got no choice but to be clever,' Mollie gazed at Charity's flaxen locks enviously. 'No chap's ever going to give me the eye. Not that I care, marriage is slavery by another name,' she said with a haughty toss of the head. 'Men don't like girls with brains you know, it worries them no end. To simper and flatter and hang on their every word, that's what they think we were put on this earth for. What a load of rubbish!' Mollie paused briefly before continuing her tirade. 'And what's more, opinions are for men, not us women, did you know that?'

Charity, who'd been listening in deferential silence, shook her head.

'Can you imagine me not having an opinion?'

Since she'd been having her ear bent for several minutes Charity felt that it would be hard to be anything but honest. 'Not really,' she answered with an apologetic expression, half expecting Mollie to walk off in a huff.

But instead of being offended, Mollie smiled warmly. A friendship was forged, arms were linked and then they were running along the road together, giggling foolishly.

They parted on the corner of Clarence Street where Mollie lived. 'See you tomorrow then.'

'Yeah arright,' Charity answered in a casual tone, because not for the life of her would she have shown Mollie just how desperate she was for her friendship.

'And you must come and meet my mum and dad one day. Dad will set you on the right path about politics. He knows so much about them if it was a just world he would be in Parliament.'

After this encounter there was an unspoken understanding that they would walk home together. Which they did, every day, heads together and talking umpteen to the dozen. Ideas bubbled out of Mollie and at first Charity was just a sounding-board with no opinions of her own. Pitted against her friend's high intelligence Charity felt inadequate. Deciding it was up to her to do something about it, she joined the local public library, plundering its shelves for ideas and reading voraciously. Becoming an intellectual might not be easy but she'd have a bloomin' good try.

After eighteen months of love and care, Charity's undernourished body had filled out and she'd grown both in stature and confidence. Except when she thought of the Grimbolds, for a mere glimpse of them was enough to induce in Charity a sweating, irrational fear, and an instinct to run and hide. And she would go to elaborate lengths to avoid passing The Sailor's Rest. However, one afternoon on her way home from school she found her normal route blocked by workmen repairing the road. Left with no choice but to walk past the ale house, Charity kept her panic in check with a tuneless whistle. But she couldn't resist a quick glance in the direction of the window. And sure enough, almost as if she'd been waiting for her, there stood Mrs Grimbold, arms folded and glaring at her malevolently.

The rational part of Charity's mind told her that the woman couldn't touch her now. The irrational, more powerful side made her mouth turn as dry as sand in the desert and her skin prickle with apprehension. She knew her fear was illogical but the muscles in her neck became hard, tense knots, and she felt a desperate urge to take flight.

And to give Pearl a chance to gloat, not likely. 'Just keep a grip on yerself and you'll be arright,' she muttered. So although she expected all the time to feel a heavy hand on her shoulder and spiteful fingers biting into her flesh, Charity didn't alter her pace. It took tremendous self control and she heaved a great sigh of relief when she found herself at the end of the street. Casting a final look over her shoulder she turned the corner and collided violently with someone coming in the opposite direction.

'Can't you bloody well look where you're goin',' exploded the woman, grabbing hold of the brightly-plumed hat that had been knocked askew in the collision.

'I'm ever so sorry . . .' apologized Charity, then, seeing who it was, giggled.

But it was obvious Kate didn't recognize her. Neither did she laugh. 'It ain't funny. I've just bought this titfer and you nearly ruined it,' she said in an aggrieved tone. The hat was decorated with a stuffed bird that looked as it had just alighted and pulling out a pin, Kate stabbed it into the plumage to anchor it more firmly to her head.

'I'm sorry Kate, I really am.' Charity repeated.

Hearing her name now and recognizing the voice, Kate, whose sight was poor, peered at Charity more closely.

'It's me, Charity, remember?'

'Well, I'll be blowed, so it is!' Kate exclaimed. 'Turn round and let's have a good look at you. My you've changed,' she said after Charity had done an obedient twirl. 'But then I always knew you were going to be a looker.' She looked pleased to see that her prediction had come true. 'Just thank God you got away from them two.' She jerked her head in the direction of The Sailor's Rest. 'He was fined twenty quid recently for keeping a disorderly house. Pity he wasn't sent down. But a few back 'anders always gets him off. Then there's his customers. Pillars of society most of them, but the last thing they want is his place closed.' She gave a bitter laugh.

'She saw me just now and I couldn't help it, I was scared stiff, just like the old days.'

'Don't be. When you did a bunk, Bill Slawson was beside 'imself and there was a lot of talk about how they'd brought you up, were your guardians and would see to it they got you back. But that soon died down and you'll 'ave 'eard about Bill Slawson doin' a runner an' how the police were on 'is tail over stolen jewellery. Worth a packet they say. The Grimbolds are lying low at the moment too, trying not to draw attention to theirselves, so it's my bet they're up to their ears in it as well. You're small fry these days, love, I doubt if they'll bother you. And if they do, just give me the nod. I've only got to 'ave a word in his ear and Danny's pa would go and sort 'em out good and proper. So if you do have any trouble from either of 'em, you or Miss Pumfrey, you're to let me know straight away, arright?'

Charity nodded. Her gratitude was intense. A threat had been lifted.

Chapter 5

Charity's friendship with Mollie survived their leaving school and entering the world of work, Mollie to take up a position as a clerk in a firm of tea importers in Mincing Lane, Charity to help in the shop.

Although she knew she ought to consider herself fortunate to have escaped the drudgery of domestic service or life in a factory, Mollie loathed her job and grumbled about it unendingly. However, if Charity asked her what she'd prefer to do she would shake her head: 'I dunno. What can women do? Very little really. Men have grabbed everything for themselves: money, power, legal rights, and they see to it that they exclude us from the best jobs.' Counting them off on her fingers she said, 'Do you know, we can't go into law, the church or parliament. Oh, but they've decided, a bit reluctantly mind you, that we might be capable of practising as doctors. Good of them, isn't it? Perhaps that's what I'll be, a doctor. What I've no intention of doing is staying in that fusty old place with fusty old men adding up columns of figures for the rest of my days. So, I've enrolled in an evening class.'

Charity had found work in the shop hardly any more exciting at first. But gradually Miss Pumfrey, who had little interest in the business herself, let go of the reins. Finding herself more or less in charge Charity started to think about ways of improving the business so that they wouldn't have to struggle all the time to make a living from it. But that meant nudging Eliza into parting with some money and that wasn't easy. Even Charity's well-reasoned economic argument that an initial outlay was needed if they were to reap financial rewards, fell, for a while, on deaf ears.

'You should at least have your name painted over the shop.'

'What's the point, everyone round here knows who I am.'

'It might attract a bit more business,' Charity persisted. 'And perhaps if we carried a more varied stock, women would come here instead of going to Rye Lane.'

'I can't see that happening, they've got such a choice in those big shops, I just couldn't compete.'

'You're nearer though, that's the big advantage, and we also offer a personal service.'

'I suppose we do.' Eliza's expression was thoughtful enough for Charity to feel hopeful that her ideas were taking root. Just to show who was boss, Eliza held out for a while longer, but within the month a signwriter had inscribed on the facia in green and gold paint, ELIZA PUMFREY, HABERDASHER. So pleased was she with the finished result, Eliza went and stood outside for a good quarter of an hour, pointing out her name to passers-by.

After this Charity was more or less given a free hand although there were some grumbles about waste from Eliza when the yellowing handkerchiefs, rotting socks, and fading hanks of wool that had been displayed in the window for donkey's years were thrown in the dustbin. Then, in a great spring clean Charity knocked cobwebs down, swept out dead bluebottles from corners and cleaned the window until the glass shone. She then took an inventory of the stock, and the heavy dull wools were discarded in favour of lighter materials in the beautiful jewelled colours she knew girls of her own age preferred. She draped these materials with an artistic insouciance in rainbow-like swathes across the window and business improved immediately: they moved into profit, Eliza no longer bemoaned Charity's extravagance and for the first time in her life she felt as if she'd achieved something.

Furthermore, young men who normally wouldn't be seen dead in a haberdasher's suddenly felt a compelling need to accompany their mothers on shopping trips. Or, if manly pride wouldn't allow them to enter the shop they would hang around outside, gawky and self-conscious.

'You've got another admirer,' Eliza would point out to Charity with a laugh as yet another youth peered through the window with lovesick eyes.

'Stupid idiot,' Charity would answer in a disparaging tone and freeze the young man with a glance. He'd shuffle off then, red-faced but twice as much in love. Because at seventeen Charity was as indifferent to these callow youths as she was to her own beauty. Slim, delicately-boned, she didn't simper or preen. It was left to others to admire her dark eyes, her neat head, the glorious abundance of hair which she wore in a loose knot at the nape of her neck. If she had one vanity it was her hands, and she would often stand admiring them, her slender fingers splayed.

She was perched on a stool buffing her pink, filbert-shaped nails and reading a serial in *The Girl's Own Paper* during a slack period one morning, when a man and an elderly woman, both of them dressed in sombre black, entered the shop. From his dress, Charity could see that he was a man of the cloth even before he handed her his card which read, THE REVEREND LEONARD WILLIS, ST BIDOLPH'S, ROTHERHITHE.

'Good morning, I . . . I'm your new vicar, and . . . and this is my . . . my mother, Mrs Willis.'

'Good morning sir, good morning madam,' answered Charity with a polite smile, quickly putting the magazine and chamois nail buff out of sight and standing up.

The woman, who reminded Charity of Queen Victoria and was small and almost spherical in shape, gave Charity a condescending nod but didn't return the greeting.

Her son, in complete contrast, was tall and angular with an enormous domed head and a thin neck. His lips had an unhealthy purple tinge to them, his hair was a sandy colour, and so were his eyebrows and lashes which, framing his pale eyes gave him a curiously sightless look. With his awkward body and his stammer, Charity wondered what sort of impression he made on his congregation.

'M . . . may I know your name?' asked Leonard Willis, already dazzled by Charity's halo of golden hair.

'Miss Charity Brown,' she answered reluctantly. The man's intent gaze was one she had grown familiar with since reaching womanhood but she still didn't care for it, and giving her name, she felt, was like giving away part of herself to him.

'And you . . . you are employed by Miss Pumfrey?'

What business is it of yours, Charity felt like asking. But she was also anxious to make it clear that she was no mere employee so her answer was civil enough. 'Miss Pumfrey is my guardian. I run the shop.'

'In that case Mama would li . . . like some embroidery thread and while I'm here, as part of my pastoral duties, I thought I would have a w . . . word with Miss Pumfrey.'

'I'll see if it's convenient. In the meantime,' she said in a professional manner, 'if you would care to look through these madam . . .' She placed a tray of embroidery threads on the counter then, leaving the elderly woman to choose what she wanted, went through to the parlour where Miss Pumfrey snoozed with a cat on her lap.

Charity shook her gently and she opened her eyes. 'Aunt Liza, the Reverend Leonard Willis is in the shop. He says he's the new vicar of St Bidolph's and can he have a word with you.'

'I've no time for religion tell him, so there's nothing we can usefully say to each other,' replied Eliza and closed her eyes again.'

'Please . . . Aunt Liza,' Charity pleaded, wondering how she would get rid of the man otherwise. 'If you don't come out you'll offend him, and his mother is buying some embroidery thread and we don't want to lose her custom, do we?'

Eliza gave an exasperated sigh and stood up. 'Oh all right. But he can think again if he expects me to attend his church.' Grumbling to herself and with the cat in her arms, she marched through to the shop, closely followed by Charity.

50

'Good morning, vicar, what can I do for you?' Eliza said briskly. Taking his extended hand, she gripped it like a nutcracker.

'May we . . . we expect to see you in church next Sunday, Miss Pumfrey?' the vicar asked, smiling through his pain.

'No, I'm afraid you may not.'

'Am I permitted to ask why?' The smile remained firmly fixed on the blue lips.

'Certainly. But first of all I must ask you a question. Do you believe animals have souls, vicar?'

'Indeed no, Miss Pumfrey,' said the Reverend Willis, looking suitably affronted.

'Well that's my answer then. If God can't find room in his heaven for cats, then I want to be no part of it. So it would be a waste of my time going to your church or any other.'

'Well of . . . of course you are entitled to your opinion, Miss Pumfrey but I must say I . . . I find your reasons rather strange. What about y . . . your ward, Miss Brown.'

'Charity's religious beliefs are her own affair. I don't interfere.'

Leonard Willis turned to Charity. 'Can I persuade you to come along to our little church, Miss Brown? I can assure you there is nothing Romish about it, no incense or anything like that. I presume you are Church of England.'

'To tell the truth I don't know what I am.'

'Are you tell . . . telling me . . . me you haven't be . . . been baptized?' Leonard Willis's impediment always became accentuated under stress.

'I don't think so.' Then, remembering she sometimes went to chapel with Mollie, and seeing this as a useful get-out she added, 'Although I sometimes go to chapel.'

At the mention of chapel, Mrs Willis, who so far had managed to avoid saying one word, swung round. 'Chapel?!' she repeated and with such venom, Charity gave an involuntary start of fright. Then holding up some bright hanks of silk she snapped, 'How much are these?'

Charity counted them. 'Two shillings.'

The woman threw a florin down on the counter then in an imperious voice said, 'Come Leonard,' and waddled out of the shop. Her son followed, his head thrust forward like a pigeon searching the ground for corn.

'What a strange pair,' exclaimed Miss Pumfrey when they'd gone. 'Still, we're obviously beyond redemption, thank heavens, so we might be spared their company again.'

'That's all very well but we've just lost two customers,' answered Charity who was much more businesslike.

'Count yourself lucky, m'dear. Just imagine having to endure a sermon every time they came in. And there was something about that man I just didn't care for.'

'He made my skin creep,' said Charity with a shudder.

Later that day when the shop was shut, Charity went up to her room and got out the diary Mollie had recently decided they should both keep. She pressed back the pages of the notebook, licked the end of her indelible pencil and carefully wrote: 26 JUNE 1894. Then she underlined it. Underneath, in neat handwriting, she entered just a few words: *Met the Reverend Leonard Willis today. Do not like him at all.*

Mollie wrote in her diary every day, Charity knew this because she'd told her. In their diaries, Mollie explained, they must not only write down anything unusual that happened but also commit to paper their deepest, most profound thoughts. However so far she'd found little in her life that was worth recording and except for the occasional: *Saw Danny today!!!!!!* and a few comments on the weather: *– rained – again –* the pages in Charity's rather modest notebook remained obstinately blank. Of her most intimate feelings and thoughts there was nothing.

For 30 June, however, Charity would fill her diary with over six pages of excited scribbling. Because like all riverside people, she had watched and wondered for nearly eight years, whether Tower Bridge would ever be completed. But now, after innummerable delays, this miracle of engineering with its twin Gothic towers, and central span that could be raised and lowered, was to be officially opened on Saturday 30 June, by the Prince and Princess of Wales.

And in spite of being an avowed republican who wouldn't dream of going himself, Mollie's father had very generously bought his daughter and Charity tickets to watch the ceremony from aboard the paddle steamer *Pretty Lady*.

Too excited to sleep, Charity was up extra early that morning, unhitching the zinc bath from the wall, dragging it into the scullery then waiting impatiently for the water to heat in the boiler. When she'd completed the laborious task of filling the bath with a saucepan, she got in. She soaped herself all over with the bar of rose-scented soap she'd bought specially and, when the water was a milky colour she lay back, her neck resting on the sharp edge of the bath. Forming her thumb and forefinger into an O, she blew several bubbles and rehearsed some witty and sophisticated remarks she could throw into the conversation if she bumped into Danny.

She took her time dressing, finished by pinning on a white chip hat trimmed with tulle, then, feeling rather pleased with herself, she went downstairs to show Eliza. 'Well, would I pass for a lady?' she asked only half jokingly and did a pirouette.

Eliza pretended to think about it. Standing back, chin in hand, she scrutinized her ward and cast a critical eye over the the dress she'd made for her in fine green lawn. 'I think so,' she said at last then started fussing with the dress, smoothing already immaculate seams and tugging at the hem.

Charity endured it for a couple of seconds, then gave Eliza a quick kiss. 'Must fly, Mollie's expecting me at ten.'

53

Eliza watched Charity's progress down Filbert Street and the admiring glances that followed her, with a quiet pride. Well, I haven't done a bad job, she thought, and out of pretty unpromising material, too. She remembered Charity's stubbornness and how exhausting she could be; how on more than one occasion she'd been tempted to throw it all in, to tell her to go to the devil. But perseverance had paid off and now she felt she could afford to give herself a self-congratulatory pat on the back.

There had been a bonus and that was the affection, she hardly dared call it love, that flowed between them. It was never voiced, but it was there and Eliza thanked God for it. And, what's more, this time no one could take it away from her.

Charity paused, gave Eliza a final wave and turned the corner, carefully keeping to the shady side of the street. For it wasn't yet ten and already she could feel the burning pavement through the soles of her shoes and an uncomfortable dampness under her arms. Before leaving the house, Charity had dabbed eau-de-cologne on her wrists and behind her ears but her nostrils were still overwhelmed by the smell of drains and she was glad to reach Mollie's house and to be welcomed by Mrs Payne.

Mollie and her mother shared the same expansive natures and wide, welcoming smiles and the resemblance between them was so strong that, every time she saw Mrs Payne, Charity knew she was already looking at Mollie in middle age.

'Come in, come in, my dear, I've made some lemonade. It might be a long time before you have the chance of another drink so you must both have some before you go. Let's go through to the garden, it's cooler out there.' Mrs Payne led Charity through to the small paved area outside the back door where she'd placed some kitchen chairs. 'Sit yourself down while I go and call that daughter of mine.'

Charity gave a gasp of relief and sat down, fanning her

face with a handkerchief. She saw that Mollie's dad was at the bottom of the garden staking and tying up some tall flowers she didn't know the name of. She called out, 'Good morning, Mr Payne,' and he waved back.

It was a miracle to her that he'd managed to create the garden he had out of such sour, unproductive soil and fill it with brilliant masses of colour and she'd asked him once how he'd done it. 'Horse muck, love, plain and simple,' he'd answered. 'There's more than enough of it on the streets and it's free.'

Spilling over the garden wall were pale yellow roses with blooms as big as cabbages. Charity leaned back, closed her eyes and inhaled their sweetness.

'My, you look as smart as new paint.' It was Mollie's voice and Charity heard the admiration in it even before she opened her eyes.

'So do you,' answered Charity, hiding her surprise. Because it was Mollie's opinion that fashion was the height of mindless frivolity and only a girl with feathers for a brain would concern herself with it. So Charity had never dared confess that she was not entirely indifferent to pretty clothes or even hint that she often spent hours poring over the fashion plates in journals, studying the cut of a bodice or the fullness of a sleeve.

'Mum bought it for me,' Mollie informed her, fanning out the skirt of the cool grey-and-white-striped dress for Charity's inspection.

'Yes, I'm tired of seeing my daughter in dark, serviceable colours all the time,' said Mrs Payne returning with a jug and some glasses and putting them down on an upturned orange box covered with an embroidered cloth. She poured the lemonade then called out, 'Fred, there's a drink here for you.'

Mr Payne came and sat down, wiped his sweating forehead with a red handkerchief then downed his drink in one thirsty go. He finished, smacked his lips, said, 'My, that was good, Mother,' and held out his glass for a refill.

Mollie was an only child and they were a happy family, sharing common interests and easy in each other's company. Mr Payne worked as a docker and although there was little money Mrs Payne was a good manager. Chapelgoing and politics were at the centre of their lives and they were strictly teetotal. The small terraced house was stuffed with books on every subject under the sun, learning was valued and they were intensely proud of their clever daughter. 'If only we had the money,' Mr Payne frequently said, 'there's no telling what heights our Mollie could reach.'

This remark was always followed by a deep sigh of regret but otherwise Mr Payne was a jovial man who liked to joke and tease the girls. It was on these small domestic occasions that Charity would wonder wistfully what it was like to have a real ma and pa, then immediately feel guiltily disloyal to Eliza.

They finished their drink and got up to go, Mr Payne following them to the door.

'Now see you don't go falling in the water. And watch your purses, there'll be villains of every description about today,' he warned.

'Yes Dad,' replied Mollie patiently, then turned with an apologetic shrug to Charity as they set off down the street. 'He's always fussing, that's the trouble with being an only child.'

'You should be glad, at least it shows he cares about you. You're very lucky, Mollie, in lots of ways. Take today for instance.'

'Which we're jolly well going to enjoy.' Mollie linked her arm through Charity's. 'So come on, let's put a step on it.'

At each street corner people converged and soon the girls were completely hemmed in by a relentless, swelling tide of humanity making for the river. Charity could feel excitement building up like the heat and along with it some pretty strong body odours. There was a bit of pushing and shoving, and she worried that a carelessly-held

56

cigarette might burn a hole in her dress, but by and large everyone was in a benevolent frame of mind. All many of them wanted was to get as near as possible to the Royal procession to see for themselves if the Prince had earned his nickname of Tum-tum and if the Princess Alexandra was as beautiful as her photographs showed.

Their tickets gave Charity and Mollie the privilege of a place on the launch, but that was all. When they reached the pier they found they had to wait in line like everyone else for a boat to row them out to where *Pretty Lady* was moored. But there was so much to see and exclaim over it hardly mattered.

The river was as Charity had never seen it before, flamboyant and proud in the sunshine. Larger ships were dressed over all while buildings along the waterfront were decked in flags of every nation. Anything that could float had been put into use and entrepreneurial boat owners had packed people on to their craft like sardines. Some looked as if they might sink under the weight of their human cargo. Young men, showing off a bit, stood precariously balanced in rowing boats, but the ones with the best best view of all were those who'd shinned up the masts of sailing ships.

Charity and Mollie had finally reached the head of the queue and were waiting patiently for the rowing boat to come alongside, when two louts who'd already had too much to drink, tried to push their way forward. 'Oh no you don't, it's our turn next,' said Mollie, firmly blocking their path and giving Charity a shove towards the boat. Charity just about had time to pick up her skirts in one hand and grab the boatman's hand with the other. She jumped, the boat wobbled, and she gave a scream of alarm. Then she heard an amused voice say, 'It's all right, if you fall overboard I promise I'll dive in and save you.' She looked up and saw it was Danny. She'd so longed to see him and now that she had, instead of being ready with a witty retort, she was too tongue tied to utter a word.

57

Although over the years Danny had treated her with little more than an amused contempt, Charity had loved him with a singleminded devotion. It was rumoured he was a bit of a jack-the-lad but it was easy to see why. He had looks to make any girl's heart beat that little bit faster. Tall like his father, several years of working the huge oars of a lighter had given him powerful shoulders. The summer sun had streaked his hair blond in places and his smoothly-tanned skin accentuated the intense blue of his eyes. Probably for the benefit of his female passengers, he'd rolled back his shirtsleeves to reveal muscular brown arms and although the boat carried four passengers, he rowed without any sign of effort or sweat.

'Well, what d'you think.' It was Danny speaking and Charity gave him a startled look.

'What do you mean?'

'Well I feel like a side of beef down at Smithfield, the way you've been sizing me up.' He winked and grinned. 'What I'm saying is, do you fancy me?'

'Not half as much as you fancy yourself,' Charity answered tartly and, irritated by his enormous vanity, she turned to Mollie and kept up an animated conversation with her and the two other female passengers until they reached the launch.

'Here we are; pretty ladies for the *Pretty Lady*,' Danny said gallantly when they came alongside the paddle steamer. The two other girls giggled but Mollie, who wasn't in least susceptible to male flattery just handed him threepence, the agreed fare, and climbed aboard. Charity was the last to go but when she went to pay him he pressed the coins back into her hand, closing her fingers over the money. Still clasping her hand, Danny said quietly, 'Keep it. I'd much rather have a kiss later on instead.'

With her own feelings running so deep, it angered Charity that he saw her as just an easy catch, someone to amuse himself with, and she pulled her hand away abruptly. Then, casting the money into the bottom of the boat, she said in a haughty voice, 'Thank you but I don't sell myself that cheaply, especially not to you Danny Weston.'

Danny had enough experience to know whether a girl was interested or not and this one was. Certain of himself, and intrigued by the ugly little duckling who had so quickly turned into a swan, Danny called after her, 'I'll soon change your mind for you.' But his words were drowned by the noise of a military band starting up and Charity didn't hear him.

'You took your time,' said Mollie when Charity finally flung herself down on the place Mollie had managed to secure for them both on the crowded boat.

'Did I?' replied Charity in a noncommittal voice, glad of a river breeze to cool her hot cheeks.

'Were you talking to that Danny Weston?'

'We might have exchanged a couple of words.'

'You want to watch out for him.'

'Why, for heaven's sake,' asked Charity, transferring her annoyance from Danny to Mollie.

''Seems he's quite a one for the girls, particularly good-looking ones. Likes a bit of variety too and word has it there are broken hearts scattered all over Rotherhithe.'

Charity skewered the pin more firmly into her hat and looked severe. 'I'm surprised at you, Moll, listening to gossip. And you know as well as I do, that some girls haven't got an ounce of sense where chaps are concerned. They just throw themselves at them, 'specially if they're good looking. Can you see me doing that?'

'Don't get all het up, it's just a bit of friendly advice, that's all.'

'Thanks, but I don't need it, I'm not interested.' Charity had nursed her secret for so long, she could lie without compunction, even to Mollie. And talking about it seemed to cheapen her own feelings. Because with one casual gallant act, of which he probably only had the dimmest memory, Danny had unwittingly taken possession of a young girl's heart. The trouble was, in the intervening

59

years, Charity had endowed Danny with qualities no normal young man could possibly live up to.

A military band played popular tunes and the crowd hummed and swayed in time with the music. Danny was now lost in the bustle of the crowded tideway and Charity was wondering what the chances were of bumping into him again, when Mollie nudged her excitedly. 'Hey look, here they come.' The band now struck up the National Anthem, everyone stood and an open coach with a mounted escort of Life Guards, moved on to the bridge. The sun caught their plumed helmets and cuirasses and an exultant crowd let rip with wild cheers. Although the procession crossed to the south side of the river then back again, an occasional glimpse of a royal head was about as much as the girls got. But that didn't matter. The whole atmosphere, the colour and pomp, a great swelling nationalistic pride, the sense of an invisible cord binding Prince with commoner, roused their dormant patriotism and they leapt up and down and cheered as lustily as everyone else.

There was a pause for speeches, then the Prince of Wales formally declared the bridge open and the two massive bascules slowly rose. Throats grew tight with emotion and a hush fell. Didn't this bridge, this miracle of engineering show, if proof were needed, that Britain was the greatest, most powerful nation on earth.

A thunderous salute of guns and fanfare of trumpets sent hundreds of pigeons flapping and whirling into the air in panic. The applause rose with them; ships' sirens, not to be outdone, added their bit until the more sensitive were holding their ears against the deafening, earth-shaking cacophony. Now ships were weighing anchor or slipping their moorings. Slowly, majestically, an Armada of ships, the *Pretty Lady* included, began to move under the open bridge, led by HMS *Landrail*.

It was now lunchtime and, like everyone else who'd brought them, a group sitting opposite Mollie and Charity consisting of two young women and an older and younger man, now began unpacking a hamper. Their speech and dress immediately identified them as being of a better class than most other people on the boat and the girls watched, fascinated, as starched white napkins, silver and fine china were laid out on the seat. Then, accompanied by a great deal of hilarity, a champagne cork was eased out of a bottle and the frothy liquid was poured into glasses by the young man.

The older man lifted his glass. 'A toast, to Tower Bridge and our great engineers,' he said in a commanding tone.

'The ten workmen who died building it don't count, I suppose.' Mollie addressed her remark to Charity, but she spoke loud enough for the toffs to hear and Charity was mortified when several pairs of eyes turned and stared at them coldly.

'That's right, we shouldn't forget them,' said the young man and smiled at Mollie. 'To the great British workman.'

'To the great British workman,' the other three repeated with an obvious lack of enthusiasm.

One of the girls who Charity had heard the younger man call Blanche, cut a game pie into slices and handed it around; the smell reminded Charity of how hungry she was. There would be refreshments below deck but it was too hot to struggle through a sweating crowd and a floor wet with spilt beer just to get a cup of stewed tea and a tired-looking sandwich. Chicken legs, smoked salmon and various other delicacies followed and Charity's stomach rumbled.

'Would you care for some?' asked the young man and Charity realized he was offering them both a chicken leg.

Mollie shook her head in refusal but Charity was too hungry to feel pride, and she was about to reach out for the food when Blanche spoke in a voice hard enough to cut through diamond. 'Emma, will you just look at Stephen. Altruism is all very well but he's about to give our luncheon away.'

The other members of the party looked embarrassed

and Charity blushed a deep red. But she wasn't going to let some hoity-toity miss humiliate her. 'Don't worry, I wouldn't touch your food. It would choke me to eat it.' She stood up. 'Come on Moll, let's move to where the air is fresher.'

The Royal party was making the return journey on the steam launch, *Palm*, and once they'd watched them disembark at Westminster Bridge, the *Pretty Lady*, like many other boats, turned its bow back downstream. They'd reached the end of their journey and were waiting to disembark, when Charity saw the young man called Stephen pressing his way through the crowd towards them.

She felt a sudden shame at having snubbed him. After all, Blanche's rudeness wasn't his fault. But she couldn't face him now. 'Quick, let's get going, there's that chap coming,' she said, pushing Mollie towards the gangway. But everyone else was going the same way and while they were being shoved and jostled and Charity winced with the pain of a heavy boot on her toe, Stephen caught up with them.

'I'm glad I caught you so that I could apologize for Blanche's behaviour. Unfortunately she sometimes speaks before she thinks.'

'Yes,' replied Mollie who wasn't above speaking before she thought, herself. 'I suppose you can have all the money in the world and still not be a lady.'

'I agree, it was unforgivable, but will you accept my apology?' Gazing down at Mollie, he smiled and Charity watched in astonishment as her plump cheeks turned blush pink like one of her dad's roses. Here was a side of the practical, no-nonsense Mollie she'd never seen before. Here was a girl, who in spite of her pronouncements on the opposite sex was as susceptible to a good-looking young man visibly using his charm as her weaker sisters. Still he was attractive with his hazel eyes and brown hair. Not for the likes of them of course, although if the brittle Miss Blanche what's'ername was his fiancée, she felt sorry for him. Spoilt and rich, she'd give any man a hard time. You only had to look at her to see that.

'It wasn't your fault,' Still flustered, Mollie didn't seem to know where to look.

'Shall we shake on that then?' As he took Mollie's hand, a female voice called in a peremptory tone, 'Stephen, are you coming?' Obviously at his lady friend's beck and call, he let go. But he gave them one final smile. 'It was nice to have met you both,' he said and they both watched with varying degrees of interest, as he pushed his way through the crowd, back to Blanche's side.

Angling, Charity said once they were ashore, 'He was nice, wasn't he?'

But there was to be no exchange of confidences. 'Mmm, all right, I suppose. Anyway I'm famished, let's look for something to eat.'

But everyone was of the same mind that day and when they found a stall they also found a line of people stretching back several hundred yards. So in the end, although it almost bankrupted them, they settled for a sit-down meal of fish and chips.

Their stomachs pleasantly full, they strolled over Tower Bridge, already packed with traffic and people. Charity's eyes skimmed the crowd on the look out for Danny but when she saw him he was with Boscoe, who had been so unkind to her all those years ago, and a rather over-dressed young woman called May Potter. Quickly she looked the other way. Grabbing Mollie's arm and imperilling both their lives, she pulled her friend across the road. 'Come on, I want to see what it's like up on the walkways.'

Shooting up in the lift the girls' giggles hid their nervousness, but their first tentative steps out on to the walkway had them clutching each other for support. Cautiously they edged forward and were rewarded with the sight of London spread out one hundred and forty feet below them. The impact made them gasp.

'Wow,' exclaimed Mollie. 'Isn't this amazing?'

'It certainly is.' Overawed, Charity gazed about her. This couldn't be her London, with its dirt and smells. From this height it looked like a foreign city, mysterious and exotic. And the Thames, she'd never realized before how much it curved, how like a great silver snake it looked.

'See over there, that's where we live.'

Mollie pointed downriver to Rotherhithe and its docks caught in a great watery loop, and Charity thought of Eliza, felt a stab of conscience, and decided with what money she had left, she would buy her a small gift.

When the scene downriver palled there was still another walkway and another view. Of course the tall column of The Monument and the great dome of St Paul's cathedral were familiar landmarks to Charity but she had to leave it to Mollie to put a name to the smaller churches.

With a pleasant breeze blowing through the structure, and a feeling almost of being suspended in space, the girls were kept happily entertained, sauntering back and forth. And the novelty brought other people up. Everyone wanted to be able to say they'd been on the bridge that first day, viewing their city from a new perspective, experiencing history as it happened. And, in spite of the dense crowd, Charity still nursed a hope that they might bump into Danny on his own. But although she kept her eyes peeled, she didn't see him again that afternoon.

Charity would have been quite happy to stay up there indefinitely, but after an hour or so Mollie said she ought to be thinking about getting home. 'Mum's invited relatives for supper and she'll be wanting a hand. You don't have to come if you don't want to though.'

'I can't stay here on my own, can I?'

'No I suppose not.'

'Anyway, I expect Eliza'll be pleased to see me, she's been on her own all day.' But Charity's voice carried no conviction and Mollie's conscience smote her.

64

'I'm sorry I've got to go, but we've had a marvellous time haven't we?'

'Marvellous,' Charity agreed. Then in case she sounded churlish, added, 'And thank your dad again for the ticket. Tell him it's been the best day of my life.'

But on the way home, Charity still cast envious glances backwards. There was no sign of the crowds thinning, it was too pleasant an evening for that, and down every street she could see wares being set out on stalls, and musicians, jugglers and clowns just getting into their stride. The air fizzled with excitement, the fun was about to start and Charity longed to be part of it.

Chapter 6

Charity hadn't long parted from Mollie at the corner of her street when she noticed a man who looked very like the Reverend Leonard Willis. Only ever having seen him before in clerical garb, he wasn't immediately recognizable in a light suit and boater that didn't sit well on his large head. His height and curious walk finally identified him and when she realized who it was, Charity instinctively shot back into a doorway, terrified that he would catch sight of her. She waited until he was some distance from her then crossed the road, keeping well back. Even a decent woman could be accosted in Rotherhithe, so it never did to stop, something she found difficult not to do as the vicar's pace eased off. He occasionally paused, seemed about to turn back but then walked on again, but more hurriedly, as if he were being chased. His erratic behaviour puzzled Charity until he came to a corner where one of the Grimbolds' girls, Sally-Ann by name, lounged.

''Allo love,' Charity heard her say, in a cheerful voice. 'Fancy a good time? I can give it ter you.'

She waited for the vicar to berate her loudly to give up

65

her life of sin, to forsake her chosen profession and follow God. Instead the low voices Charity could hear suggested a business transaction taking place. Satisfactorily concluded, Sally-Ann moved off, indicating with a jerk of the head that he should follow.

Leonard Willis's head swivelled round to check he wasn't being observed by any parishioners, then this cleric, who denounced fornicators and threatened them with eternal damnation from his pulpit each Sunday, sloped off after the young whore.

Charity watched him go with a taste of disgust in her mouth. Him and his phony piety she thought. Was that all men ever wanted from women, sex? What she yearned for was a pure, untainted, chivalrous love, but so far, life hadn't presented her with any evidence that it existed outside the pages of the romantic novels she read, and this depressed Charity enormously. Feeling the need to cheer herself up, with the last of her money she stopped off to buy some chocolate for Eliza and a quarter of a pound of peppermint humbugs for herself. Coming out of the shop, she was about to pop one in her mouth when she saw Danny. She paused with it half way to her mouth. 'Oh, she exclaimed, 'What are you doing here?'

'Buying fags and lookin' fer you. Do you know I hunted all over fer you today.'

Charity hadn't learnt about wiles or duplicity yet, so her smooth young face glowed with transparent pleasure. 'Did you?'

'Were you deliberately avoiding me? I couldn't find you nowhere.'

'I saw you.'

'Did you now. Why didn't you speak to me then?'

'You seemed pretty occupied. You were talking to *that* May Potter.' She hoped she conveyed by her tone her opinion of May, who played fast and loose with all the men in the neighbourhood.

A look of pained astonishment crossed Danny's face.

'You can't think I'm interested in May, for heaven's sake. She's Boscoe's bit o' skirt.'

She looked up into his blue eyes. Was he telling the truth? She so much wanted to believe him.

'Anyway, where are you off to now?'

There seemed little point in lying about it. 'Home.'

'Home? At this time of night?' His tone was incredulous. 'Nothing of the sort. I'm taking you for a drink and I'll not take no for an answer. I made a packet today as ferryman and it's burning a hole in m' pocket.' Danny took her arm in a masterful way. 'So where'll it be?'

'Anywhere, I don't mind.' Danny's fingers on her bare arms had sent an electric charge surging through her body and her emotions were in such turmoil, she couldn't think straight.

'How's about The Angel, then?'

His grip was tight, almost possessive, so that their bodies touched and Charity was very aware of the hard muscularity of his body and its faint musky odour. Charity nodded and smiled, her untried heart fluttering with joy. She'd lived moments like this in her head so many times without any real hope of fulfilment, that she'd have happily gone to Timbuktoo or the moon and back as long as it was with Danny.

'Right, off we go then.' Danny swung her round on her heels. And lapped by waves of happiness, tuned finer by the openly envious glances of other girls, Charity allowed herself to be guided towards the river.

This being a special day pubs were doing a roaring trade and some were in danger of running dry. People spilling out onto pavements jostled them, and even before they reached The Angel, Danny and Charity could hear bursts of laughter and the rise and fall of well lubricated voices. In spite of the crush of bodies, Danny insisted on taking a look inside for himself. He was back in a minute.

'They're packed together in there like salt herrings in a barrel and it's bedlam wiv the noise.'

As if to deny this, a nasal tenor started to sing, 'She

Walked Through the Fair.' Briefly the din subsided and Charity knew any customer who could lay claim to a dribble of Irish blood would have grown maudlin and moist-eyed. The last plaintive note of the ballad had hardly faded away when a woman's voice, harsh with drink and smoke, attempted a discordant rendering of, 'Down at the Old Bull and Bush.' By the sound of it, there wasn't a soul in the pub who didn't know the words of this song, and they accompanied themselves by stamping their feet on the wooden floor with boozy gusto.

'Do you want to go in and join the fun?' Danny was shouting to make himself heard.

Charity only wanted to be with Danny, not a hundred drunken strangers. She shook her head. 'No thanks. You risk being trampled to death in that place.'

'We'll have our drinks out here then. What would you like?'

'A shandy please.'

'Right, if I'm not back in twelve days send out a search party for me,' said Danny with a grin then disappeared into the scrum.

She felt awkward standing there on her own, watching scenes that had a numbing familiarity about them. A foul-mouthed husband hurling a stream of four-letter words at his wife, a woman so drunk that even when she leaned against a wall her legs wouldn't support her and she slowly slid to the ground where she stayed slumped, snoring loudly.

Having been brought up in the atmosphere of a pub, Charity was used to such things, knew they drank to blot out the sheer awfulness of their lives. But now she saw it for the first time through Mollie's eyes, realized everything her friend said was true. Drink wasn't helping these people. It ruined their health, trapped them even more firmly in poverty and was a destroyer of family life. And the habits of the parents would be copied by the children, carried on to the next generation where the whole miserable cycle would be repeated again. What a waste of human life, thought Charity. Of course this wasn't just happening in Rotherhithe, but all over London, probably the whole of England.

Having had as much as she could stomach of the revellers and wishing they hadn't come here, she moved away, and went and sat down on the stairs that led to the river. Westwards the sun was dropping towards the London skyline, and the air was cooler on Charity's skin and more pleasant. The gentle slap of water against wood soothed away the feeling of hopelessness that had suddenly gripped her. Resting her chin on her linked fingers, she watched several barges with their russet coloured sails glide slowly past. But larger ships, anchored in midstream, stretching far down the river, had to be more patient and wait for the rising of the tide. And at the exact moment the dock gates would open and thousands upon thousands of tonnage would crowd into the river then move slowly eastwards. Smoke would curl upwards, masts cross and re-cross and the river hum with commerce. Sitting there Charity remembered how not much further along the river's edge Danny had rescued her from that fat bladder of lard, Boscoe Hobbs. For five years, even though he'd ignored her for most of that time, she'd clung on to that small kindness. And now . . . it seemed unbelievable, but here she was, with Danny. But she mustn't read too much into it. It was a casual drink, nothing more and probably because he was at a loose end.

Thinking she heard his voice and impatient for his return, Charity glanced round. Strolling down the narrow alleyway that divided the pub from the property next door was Danny's father. Kate was on his arm and it struck her how alike father and son were in voice and build.

Unless she made herself known, Charity knew Kate couldn't see her because of her weak sight. And she didn't want to do that, not when Kate was with Danny's pa. The couple had a brief discussion then Kate pushed open the pub door, took a quick look inside and called back over her shoulder, 'You couldn't swing a cat in there. Let's try somewhere else.'

They wandered off hand in hand a moment before Danny emerged clutching two overflowing glasses and searching around for her.

'Over here,' she called to him.

Although he walked carefully, drink spilled on to his hands. 'One shandy. Hope it's all right,' Danny said, wiped his hands down his trouser leg then, without waiting, drank deeply from his own glass, half emptying it in one go. 'That's better,' he said, wiping the froth from his mouth and sitting down beside her on the stairs.

'I just saw your dad. You missed him by a minute.'

Danny's face darkened. 'Good job too. I suppose he was wiv that Kate woman.'

'Yeah, he was.'

'He never takes my poor old ma out, ever. Best she can hope for ternight is a black eye. Yet he treats that whore like a queen.'

'Don't call Kate a whore.'

'That's what she is, so why shouldn't I?'

'It isn't her fault. Her ma handed her over to Grimbold for a fiver when she was no more than eleven, she told me that herself. I don't like you speaking badly of her, Kate's my friend, the only one I had once, and if it wasn't for Aunt Eliza I would be doing what she is now.'

Danny took her hand. 'Don't say that, it doesn't bear thinking about.'

'Well I think about it quite a lot.'

Behind them they heard raised male drunken voices then blows being exchanged and Charity felt her shoulders tense. She finished her drink and stood up. 'I think I'd like to go home now Danny if you don't mind.'

'Not yet, the night's still young.'

'It might be for you but my aunt will wonder where I am.'

70

'You wouldn't like to try the Dover Castle?'

She shook her head emphatically. 'No, but if you want to go I'll see m'self home.'

'You don't 'ave to do that.'

'Now come on lads, break it up,' Charity heard a policeman say, trying to keep his tone light as he attempted to separate the fighting men. But they ignored him and continued to circle each other like a couple of bulls in a field, heads down and ready to ram. One man had a swollen eye and the other spat out a mouthful of blood as they passed but Charity knew by their aggressive stance, that the Bobby wouldn't stop them. As soon as he'd turned the corner, they'd be at each other's throats again.

In the narrow back streets away from the public houses it was quieter and they could hear music from some way off. Charity's heart suddenly lightened. 'Come on, let's find it,' she said, taking Danny's hand and pulling him along. Following the sound, they eventually came to a small open space where a group of people were dancing to tunes played on a hurdy-gurdy by an elderly blind woman. It was a happy, almost rural sight. No one was drunk, husbands and wives danced companionably together, while their children, aping their elders, did the same.

Danny and Charity watched for a few minutes then Danny slipped an arm around her waist. 'Shall you and me trip the light fantastic as well,' he asked, then, without waiting for her reply, drew her on to the floor and into his arms, moulding her body to his.

It was then that Charity went tense. The pleasant street scene faded and all she could see was a dingy room, a heavy-jowled man and his small victim. A pulse fluttered at the base of her throat and her fingers, linked with Danny's, trembled so much it was a relief to hear the clock chime ten so that she could move away. 'I must go home.'

'But the night has just begun.' Danny went to pull her

71

to him again, but Charity put her hands against his chest. 'My aunt will be getting anxious.'

'Oh all right.'

She allowed him to slip an arm around her waist as they walked home but when they reached the shop, Charity rather formally held out her hand. 'Thank you for taking me for a drink, Danny, it was kind of you.'

'Don't I get a kiss in return?'

'Oh no.' Charity backed away in fright. Did he think she was fast or something, like that May Potter? Next thing he'd be calling her a tart.

Danny shrugged and looked a bit sulky. 'Well, I'll probably see you around sometime. G'night.' He turned and walked away.

'Goodnight Danny.' As she watched him, her emotions see-sawed; an instinctive revulsion fought romantic longings. She was already regretting her stupidity, but she couldn't help it, that drawing away from Danny. Because as they'd danced, she'd been made aware of his maleness. And sex was something she didn't want to be reminded of. Sex was distasteful, something men took from women by force or paid girls like Kate for.

Charity waited, but Danny didn't look back and something told her he'd already erased her from his memory. But his indifference only made her angry with herself. After all, what harm would a kiss have done. He wouldn't bother with her again, not when he could have the likes of May Potter.

The back door was locked so she had to bang on it to be let in and Eliza greeted her with an anxious expression. 'My dear, where have you been?'

'Only for a drink with Danny Weston,' Charity mumbled, and brushed past her. She wasn't going to be cross-examined, was she? She felt miserable enough without that.

'That'll be Jim Weston's son, I suppose.'

'Yeah.' Charity sat down and toyed indifferently with

the cold meat and pickle Eliza had set out on a plate for her.

'Terrible temper on him, Jim Weston.'

'Yeah, I can remember him sorting old Grimbold out good and proper.'

'And I remember once years ago when he was a young man, he got into a fight. If someone hadn't parted them, it was said he would have killed the other man.'

'But Danny's not like that Aunt Eliza.' Charity answered, getting her drift.

'No, I'm sure he's not, dear,' Eliza replied and even though she had no religion she prayed that Charity was right.

'Anyway I don't know why you're bothering to tell me all this, it was only a friendly drink, I've got no particular wish even to see Danny Weston again.'

Chapter 7

Any hopes Eliza had that this might be true were shattered by the change she saw take place in Charity. She became listless and vague, mooned about the place, didn't reply when she was spoken to and took to going out for longer and longer walks on her own.

Eliza recognized the symptoms, of course she did. Remembering the great highs and lows of love, Charity's behaviour worried her no end. Charity's childhood had made her tough in many ways, but she'd come to Eliza as a small girl starved of affection. As she herself knew there were plenty of unprincipled men waiting to take advantage of a girl's vulnerability. She loved Charity dearly but Eliza often felt she failed her by not being able to express her feelings in a more physical way with spontaneous hugs and kisses. Sadly, she'd long ago lost the ability to wrap her arms round another human being, but she would still move heaven and earth to protect

73

Charity from pain, by golly she would. Eliza knew she was probably wrong in judging Danny by his father's behaviour but it was common knowledge that Jim Weston had given his poor wife a terrible time of it, right through their marriage.

Charity, unaware of Eliza's concern, went looking for Danny whenever she got the chance. On any pretext she would walk past the lighterage firm he worked for, and if she plucked up the courage she would even take a stroll down Swan Lane, the street where he lived. There was no variety to the houses – one was an exact replica of the other, all along the road. At least that was how they would appear to a stranger. But Charity knew otherwise, noticed the subtle differences that marked out a well-run home from a badly-run one: the whitened step, the clean curtains, the aspidistra standing proudly in its brass pot in the window. Danny's house was like this, the windows shone, the front was always swept.

This morning as Charity passed, Mrs Weston was where she could regularly be found, down on her knees washing and whitening the step.

'How are you this morning, Mrs Weston?' Charity asked, glad of an excuse to stop.

Mrs Weston, whom Charity had known when she used to come to the Sailor's Rest for a jug of ale, leaned back on her haunches and with both hands on her hips, eased her spine with a weary movement.

'Well let's just say I'm not one 'undred per cent, love. But there, what can't be cured must be endured.'

'I'm sorry to hear that,' Charity answered, although just by looking at her, it was evident Agnes Weston was a sick woman. She was thin, lank-haired and anaemic-looking with a fading bruise on her cheekbone that made her skin look yellow. There was no doubting who Danny had inherited his eyes from though, because hers were a vivid blue and looked incongruous against the exhausted features. In her youth, Charity supposed, she must have been pretty.

'Can I do anything to help, fetch you some medicine perhaps?'

'Bless you sweet'eart, but there ain't a medicine around that could cure my ailments. Back trouble, varicose veins, piles, me bronchials, you name it I've got it. It's nice of you to ask, though, shows a kind nature.' She stood up. 'Still, as I always says, it's not over till it's over and I must be gettin' on. I would have said pop in for a cup o' tea but my Danny's on nights at the moment and I don't want to disturb him. And the old sod'll be in soon as well wanting 'is grub and he musn't be kept waiting on any account.'

'I couldn't stop anyway, I've got to get back to the shop. But any time you need any errands done, let me know, I'd be glad to do them.'

'Thanks duckie. Do you know I'd have loved a daughter more than anything, but it wasn't to be. You see I buried two before they reached their first year, God rest their little souls. You can always talk to girls, can't you? I'm blessed with three good lads, but even the nicest of them don't understand what we women go through, do they?'

'No they don't,' Charity agreed, feeling more and more sorry for the woman with each passing minute. 'Anyway, are you sure I can't get you anything? I'd be more than glad to oblige.'

'Well you could get me some of them Holloway's Pills from the chemist. They might buck me up a bit.' She felt in her apron pocket. 'Here's a tanner, a box shouldn't cost more than that.'

'I might be a little while 'cos I've got to pop back to the shop first, but I'll be as quick as I can,' said Charity and hurried away, trying not to feel too guilty that her kindness was mixed with a degree of self interest.

Agnes Weston watched her, noting the neat, slight figure, the buoyant step of youth and thought to herself, what a nice girl, she'd do just right for my Danny. Not that he could marry yet, 'im being an apprentice, but if 'e was settled wiv one girl, it might stop 'im being led astray by some fast hussy like May Potter. Still, what

75

young lad ever took heed of what 'is ma said. Mrs Weston sighed, wrung out her cloth, wiped down the windowsill, emptied the bucket of water into the gutter, then, leaving the door on the latch, she went back indoors.

Wanting to make sure everything looked nice when the girl returned, she raked the fire, put on some coal and swept the hearth. Then, certain she could see some dust, she ran a duster along the mantelpiece and over the only present her husband had ever given her, an ornament won at a fair. It was a man in a kilt and a tam-o'-shanter and was used for keeping paper quills in. After this she took down two framed photographs. Huffing and polishing the glass vigorously she then studied them with a fond look in her eyes. The photographs were of her two eldest boys, Peter and John. Peter was in army uniform and shading his eyes against the hot sun of India. He wrote regularly. John she heard from less, but that was understandable, he was a merchant seaman and anyone knew you couldn't post letters in the middle of an ocean. He made up for it when he came home though, with gifts. Last time he'd brought her a beautiful tea set from Japan. It was decorated with dragons and made of china thin as eggshells. It looked so fragile she would never dare use it and it was locked away in a glass-fronted cabinet along with a conch shell you could hear the ocean in if you held it to your ear and a boomerang from Australia.

Danny was the only one who'd followed his father on to the river, but he complained frequently of the long hours and bad pay. She feared he, too, might have itchy feet, for he could be heard to say more and more frequently that he'd like to see something of the world. She wouldn't stop him of course but if he did follow his brothers' example, all three of her boys would be gone and then she'd have nothing.

The creak of floorboards above her head told her Danny was getting up and knowing how he liked a cup of tea first thing, Agnes filled a kettle. She was bending to put it on the fire, when an agonizing pain low in her abdomen doubled her up. She screamed out in anguish and the kettle clattered to the floor, spilling water all over the lino.

'Mum?' Danny's voice came from the top of the stairs, followed by a rapid thump of footsteps as he took them two at a time. In his anxiety he flung open the door with such force it swung back on its hinges and made a dent in the wall.

He found his mother slumped in a chair clutching her stomach. Her eyes were closed, her skin the colour of parchment and damp with sweat. 'Mum. Wha . . . what is it? Wha . . . ts wrong?' Danny's voice quavered with terror.

'A . . . a bit of indigestion that's all,' Agnes lied, her hand finding the swelling that seemed to grow a bit more each day. Anyone seeing it would think she was in the family way, except there'd been nothing of that sort between her and Jim for years.

Danny crouched down beside her and clasped her free hand. It felt cold as the marble he often transported up the river. Taking each finger in turn, he gently tried to massage some warmth back into them. 'Tell me what I can get you Mum, for heaven's sake.' Ever since he could remember he'd had this fear his mother would die and leave him. Often as a child when she was resting in the chair he would move closer to reassure himself that she was still breathing and even now as a grown man he sometimes found himself doing it.

She opened her eyes and stroked his head, biting her lip as she felt another stab of pain. 'Wipe the water up from the floor then make me a cup of tea, there's a good lad. I'll have one of me peppermints first, though, that might do the trick.' Concerned to allay her youngest son's fears she tried to smile.

'I keep telling you that you ought to see the quack. Why won't you go?' His mother's pig-headedness about her health frustrated Danny almost beyond endurance sometimes but he couldn't get her to budge on the matter.

77

'I don't want to.' Agnes answered stubbornly. If she went she would hear what she feared most. The terrible word that would be her death sentence, It was foolish of her she knew, but as long as she didn't know definitely what was wrong, she could go on feeling hope.

Danny made some tea, got out the second best cups and saucers, laid out some biscuits on a plate, then brought a stool for his mother to put her feet on. 'Now you're to stay there and rest.'

She looked up at the clock on the mantelpiece. 'I can't, the old man will be in soon. He'll need feeding.'

'He'll just have to lump it won't 'e. Take 'imself off to the pie shop, or his fancy piece can cook him something.'

Agnes Weston gave a snort of derision. 'That's likely ain't it? By the way that nice young girl who stays wiv Miss Pumfrey came by while I was doin' the step and stopped and had a chat.'

'Do you mean Charity?'

'That's right. She's getting me some pills. Isn't that nice of her?'

'Yeah,' answered Danny absentmindedly, thinking to himself, so she is interested even though she acts all coy. He was getting tired of May Potter, too, and her ever-ready availability. Charity used to be such a pathetic little waif it was hard to believe she was the same girl. She had a bit of class about her now; he liked that refined way of speaking she'd picked up from Miss Pumfrey, it really tickled him, and there wasn't another girl in Rotherhithe could equal her in looks. Trouble was he had a strong feeling there wouldn't be any messing around with her, not judging by the way she'd jumped away like a scared rabbit when he'd tried to kiss her. Still, she was a bit of a challenge and maybe if it took a bit longer to hook her it would be more fun. Some girls, like May, were too damn easy. Danny's thoughts were rambling pleasantly when he heard footsteps and saw his mother stiffen with anxiety.

'It's all right, Ma, I'll deal with him.' Danny turned to

78

face his father, who as he entered the small room, filled it with his vast bulk and brought with him the ominous smell of the ale house.

'Ma's had a bad turn, I'm gonna take her upstairs, she needs to lie down.'

'Where's me dinner then?'

'I ain't been able to manage anything today Jim. But I'll see you 'ave something real nice for your tea.' His wife's tone was conciliatory.

'Are you telling me there's nothing to eat?'

'You'll 'ave to go the pie shop, Dad. It won't hurt you for one day.'

Jim Weston swung round to face his son. His bull neck had turned dark red. It was a bad sign. 'Don't you tell me what to do, whippersnapper.'

Trying hard to curb his anger, Danny gave a nonchalant shrug. 'All right, go hungry,' he said and bent to assist his mother to her feet.

'That bitch ain't going nowhere, till I've 'ad me dinner.' exploded his father, and grabbing his son by the collar, he wrenched him away from Agnes.

But in one quick fierce movement Danny had knocked his father's arm away and his clenched fist was under his nose. 'Don't you dare call my mother a bitch.'

Jim Weston stood stock still and looking his son straight in the eye said quietly, 'Move your fist.'

Danny's eyes wavered, for he still feared his father, but his fist stayed where it was.

'Danny, do as your father says,' Agnes pleaded in an exhausted voice. 'I'm just not up to you two fighting today. I'll fry you a chop, Jim, but you'll have to wait a bit.'

She stood up. But the ceiling came down to meet her, objects spun away and when she put out her foot, she found the floor wasn't there. With a moan she collapsed back in her chair, was briefly aware of her son's anxious face hovering above her, saw his mouth move, then the world went dark.

What was left of Danny's self-control snapped. A hot blinding fury sent the blood rushing to his head and doused his fear. 'Now look what you've done, you stupid, selfish sod, made Ma pass out.'

By way of a rejoinder Jim Weston's fist shot out and hit Danny square on the chin. The sound of bone hitting bone was like a whiplash. Danny staggered, lost his balance and fell heavily, cracking his head on the edge of the table before slumping down in a senseless heap.

Charity had her hand raised to knock when Jim Weston came storming out of the door. 'Oh . . . hello Mr Weston, I've just bought these . . .' She held up a paper bag.

'Get out of my way, for Christ sake, woman,' he answered and pushed her roughly aside.

Astonished, and annoyed too at his rudeness, Charity watched him storm off down the street, thinking to herself, how awful to have a husband like that, and wondering what Kate could possibly see in him. Certainly it wasn't his manners or charm.

He'd left the door swinging but out of politeness Charity banged the knocker. She waited, then when there was no response stepped into the passageway. 'Hello Mrs Weston,' she called. 'It's me, Charity.' A total silence made her inch her way with cautious steps along the passage to the small back room. She saw Agnes Weston first, thought sympathetically, poor woman, she's so exhausted she's fallen asleep, moved into the room and almost went flying over Danny's outstretched legs. 'Oh my God,' she gasped, steadying herself against the table. Then her limbs went weak and she began to shake uncontrollably. Eliza had said Jim Weston was capable of it and she was right, they were dead . . . murdered, both of them, and it was him who had done it.

Charity's immediate and horror-struck instinct was to run from the violence that confronted her. Except that by now she was shackled by a body over which she had no control and which shook so convulsively her teeth rattled like castenets. Then somewhere in the shocked confusion of her mind it registered that there was no sign of injury or blood on either body. Had he strangled them? Certainly Jim Weston had power enough in those great hands of his. She could feel her stomach curdling and the bile syphoning up in her throat. What was she to do? In an attempt to fight off the nausea, and get a grip of herself she took several deep gulps of air. Then supporting herself against the table, Charity inched closer. She was studying Mrs Weston's features more closely, looking for telltale marks on the neck when the corpse opened its eyes and stared straight at her. Terrified almost beyond reason, she leapt back with a loud demented scream.

Although she still felt lightheaded, poor, startled Mrs Weston struggled to sit up. 'Lord love us, what an earth's the matter, my dear,' she demanded when the screams had subsided and she saw the stark fear on the girl's face.

'I . . . I . . . thought . . . I thought you were dead.'

'Good heavens no, I had a nasty turn and fainted.'

'And . . . Danny?' Dreading the answer, it took all Charity's courage to ask this question.

'A fight I should guess wiv the old man. It was heading that way when I passed out.'

'Thank God for that! And there was I thinking that Mr Weston had done you both in.' Charity let out a great sigh of relief and slumped into a chair. 'My legs have gone all funny with the shock, I must sit down.'

'Well he's certainly threatened us wi' it often enough. But probably he doesn't think we're worth swinging for.' Agnes Weston's laugh didn't quite disguise the bitterness in her voice.

There was movement from Danny then a moan and Charity saw Mrs Weston try to ease herself from her chair and fail. 'Stay where you are, I'll see to him.' Although still feeling shaky herself, Charity knelt down beside him. 'I think he's coming round,' she said and watched his eyelids flicker and slowly open. His pupils were so dilated his eyes looked black, his gaze was dazed and unfocused and there was no sign that he recognized her. But then, after several minutes he shook his head as if to clear it and gingerly felt his chin and the back of his head.

Charity scrutinized him with a tender, anxious expression. 'How are you feeling, Danny?'

'Well I've got a bloody awful headache, a great lump on my head and a painful jaw but apart from that I suppose you could say I was arright.'

'Do you know she thought we were both dead and that your pa had murdered us. Can you imagine what a shock that must have been for the poor girl,' said Mrs Weston.

'Well after that anything else can only seem an improvement, I suppose.' Danny eased himself up then, with Charity's help, got to his feet. 'But how did you come to be here anyway?' he asked in a puzzled voice.

'I was on an errand for your ma.'

'Yeah, so you were, I'd forgotten.'

'I got her some pills, they're on the dresser if she needs them. And if you're sure everything's all right I think I'd better go.'

Mrs Weston reached out and grasped her hand. 'You've been ever so kind, love. I'll never forget what you've done. And you must come to tea on Sunday, mustn't she, Danny.?'

Charity gave Danny a sideways look, not sure whether to accept or not. But his expression suggested that the idea was to his liking. 'Thank you, Mrs Weston, I'd really like to come,' she answered and the radiance of her smile lit up the small room.

'Tell you what,' said Danny, 'why don't I come and pick you up as well. About four o'clock say?'

Miss Pumfrey had never known Charity take so long to get ready to go anywhere. Dresses, blouses, skirts were tried on and discarded, advice was solicited then rejected until finally Eliza felt pressed to voice her exasperation. 'I don't know what all the fuss is about, miss, you're going to tea with the Westons, not being presented at Court.' She remarked testily. She was wasting her breath saying anything though, she knew that. And after weeks of Charity's glum looks she supposed she ought to feel glad to see her happy with life again. More than happy, actually, she was exultant, walking on air.

At three-thirty Charity finally made her decision. She knew the dark blue dress with white trimmings was the right choice when she opened the door to Danny's knock and saw the look of admiration in his eyes.

'Do you know, you're about the prettiest thing I've ever seen in my life,' he murmured in her ear as he followed her through into the parlour. Then to Eliza when they reached the small back room, 'Doesn't she look lovely Miss Pumfrey?'

'She does indeed,' Eliza replied, noticing how Charity's face glowed from Danny's compliments. She isn't up to this, she lacks the guile, just like I did, she thought, covertly studying the boy. It was easy enough to see why any young girl would be smitten by him. He was tall and hard-muscled from his job, his smile revealed even white teeth and his hair, which was thick and straight, flopped boyishly over his forehead. But was he, perhaps, just a fraction too sure of himself, she wondered, too used to an easy success with women to understand the word 'No'? She hoped not. She had her own bitter memories of how a man could persuade and charm with his silver tongue . . . but she was being over-protective of Charity and pre-judging Danny, and that would never do.

'We're off then, Aunt Liza,' said Charity, breaking into her thoughts.

'Have a nice time my dear. And give my regards to your mother, Danny and I hope she's feeling a bit better.' Eliza knew it didn't do to rake over the dead coals of a domestic dispute, but the story Charity had come home with made her feel for poor ailing Mrs Weston, who certainly didn't deserve such a pig of a husband.

'I will, Miss Pumfrey.' He smiled again. 'And I'll have Charity back here by ten, I promise.'

83

'Good.' She walked with them to the door and saw Danny bend his head to Charity's and say something. When she shyly slipped her hand through his arm, Eliza murmured to herself, 'Don't let her down Danny, don't hurt her, please.'

Tea was set in the front parlour on a starched lace table-cloth and Agnes Weston's best service. Agnes had thought long and hard before putting it out but now she was glad she had because it added a bit of class to the room and she sensed Charity was a girl who would appreciate its fragility and worth. Besides, she was out to make a good impression. She made no bones about it, she wanted to see Danny taking up with the girl, settled with her even, for that would surely put a stop to him getting ideas about seeing the world.

Feeling suddenly nervous in her role as hostess, she checked the table: shrimps, whelks, watercress, radishes, paper-thin bread and butter, seed cake and scones. Thank God the old man's working, she thought and went to the window, pulling back the lace curtain. Seeing them a few yards down the road she took off her apron, smoothed her hair and hurried to the door, flinging it open just as they reached the front step.

Constrained by the formality of the occasion when they first sat down at the table, conversation between the three of them was stilted. Charity asked Mrs Weston how she was feeling and if the pills were helping her. Assured that they were she fell silent, gazing at the crumbs on her plate and trying desperately to think of something to say. Finally in a state of nervous panic, she said, 'I do like your tea service, Mrs Weston.'

Agnes Weston's pale features lit up. 'Do you, duckie? My eldest boy, John, brought it back from Japan. He's a sailor, travels all over the world, but he never forgets 'is mum.'

'If I go I'll bring you stacks of things back too, Ma,' Danny promised.

Charity was reaching out for a slice of bread and butter when Danny spoke but his words made her hesitate, and her fingers fluttered anxiously over the plate. Danny, going away? That wasn't possible.

'Now don't you go saying things like that, my lad. I've more or less lost two sons already, it would break my heart if you went too, you know that. You're to stay and finish your apprenticeship. Another couple of years and you'll be a freeman, have your full licence. It's an honourable calling, being a lighterman, and the river's in your blood, so you should be proud of it. You're the sixth generation to go into the business. You wouldn't want to be the one to break that tradition would you?'

Danny shrugged. 'All this tradition lark, what does it matter.' He turned to Charity, showing her the palms of his hands. 'See those calluses. Well when I first started my apprenticeship as a lad, my hands would blister and bleed so badly from the oars, they looked like raw meat.' He turned back to his mother. 'But don't you worry yourself, Ma, I would never go an' leave you on your own wiv the old man. And most times I like it on the river. Well in the summer I do, anyway.'

Afer tea Mrs Weston cleared away, and while Danny went to the pub for a jug of ale, Charity helped her with the drying up in the scullery.

'How's Miss Pumfrey these days?' asked Agnes as she poured boiling water from the kettle into the brownstone sink then sloshed around with her hand to dissolve the washing soda. 'Still involved with her cats, is she?'

'Yeah. More than ever now that I run the shop. It's when she goes out looking for strays at night that I get really worried.'

'Funny how people change, ain't it? 'Cos I can remember her as a young woman. You wouldn't think it to look at her now but she was very smart in them days. And what Eliza lacked in looks she more than made up for in the proud way she carried herself. But then she had something to be proud about, her pa being a sea captain.

Fine looking man wiv his white beard, but strict I've heard. Her ma was a real refined lady as well, and there was always a bit o' money there. Lived in a very nice house they did. Mind you, there was somethin' strange about that place. It was soon after her ma died that Eliza changed. She didn't seem to care about anything after that, only her strays which she took to rescuing. But you'll know all this of course.'

Charity, who had been polishing the tines of a fork and listening intently, shook her head. 'Aunt Eliza never talks about her past.'

'Oh Lor' don't she? Perhaps I should 'ave kept me big mouth shut then.'

'Oh no. I want to know more. But I've never liked to ask her myself. She's been so kind to me I didn't want to offend her by being nosy. If she hadn't given me a home, you know, Mrs Weston, I'd have probably been sent to St Olave's.'

'It's been a two-way thing. You've been good for her, too. Cats is all very well but she needed a human being to love and you came along at just the right time to stop her becoming really odd.'

''Trouble is, Mrs Weston, it can sometime be more painful loving a human being.'

Surprised by such wisdom, Agnes Weston gave the girl a sideways glance. 'It certainly can, my dear. It certainly can.'

Danny returned then with the jug of ale, said, 'Come on you two, stop gossiping and let's get down to the real business of a game of cribbage,' got out the board and cards and effectively put an end to the conversation.

It had always puzzled Charity that Eliza never talked about her past. At first she'd put it down to a natural reserve, but her answers to any questions, even the most innocuous, were so evasive it made Charity feel as if she were prying. So, in the end she'd just stopped asking; but this afternoon she'd learned more chatting to Mrs Weston than in five years with Eliza. It was evident that somewhere, somehow, things had gone badly wrong in Eliza's life.

Since the only card game Charity ever played was 'snap' with Mollie, the rules of cribbage had first of all to be explained to her by Danny. That she had no real understanding of the game didn't appear to bother Mrs Weston at all and as she dealt the cards, she was obviously in her element. 'When the boys were all 'ome we used to play cards every Sunday night, didn't we, Danny?'

'We did indeed, Ma.'

'It feels like old times don't it, son.'

'It does, Ma,' answered Danny, trying to concentrate on his cards.

Charity smiled, a deep fondness for Mrs Weston welling up inside her, a feeling she sensed was reciprocated. She was a woman, Charity could see, with a loving, generous heart and courage, too. Like everyone else, and knowing no better, Charity had taken for granted the hardship of most waterside women's lives. But as she grew older she'd come to admire their stoicism, their refusal to accept defeat. Against enormous odds and in the face of disease, dirt, countless pregnancies, brutal husbands or even the tragic death of a child, they battled on. Mrs Weston's poor state of health had made her even more aware and, she'd found herself thinking about it more and more of late and she *burned* to help them, to do something to lighten their load. But what, she asked herself. The desire to help was all very well, but without money or skills she couldn't change their lives one jot. Of course she hadn't mentioned any of this to Mollie, because her friend considered it was sufficient to have the will to do something. Everything else would flow from that, she could hear her friend saying, and then in that robust way of hers, accusing her of being faint-hearted.

'You'll come again, won't you, dear,' said Mrs Weston when they'd finished a hand and Charity indicated she must go. 'It's been such a lovely evening and I haven't enjoyed myself so much in a long time.'

''Course I will.' Charity bent and gave her a spontaneous kiss and saw her careworn face light up.

'You've made quite an impression on my mum,' said Danny when they were walking home.

'I liked her, too.'

'And what about her son? Does he meet with your approval?' asked Danny, slipping an arm round her waist, pulling her against him.

Charity stared down at her shoes. 'I like you well enough,' she answered shyly.

'Will you come wiv me to the fair on Bank holiday Monday then?' he asked, thinking of all the quiet spots he knew in the park where he could take her when it grew dark. He was having great difficulty keeping his hands off her, but remembering how she'd shied away from him before, he didn't want to go at it like a bull in a china shop. Best to bide his time, be patient. And he was going to be the first one to uncoil that thick rope of flaxen hair, watch those dark eyes slowly rouse to passion. This was a novelty in itself, for, in Rotherhithe, virgins were about as rare as polar bears.

Charity remembered the half-promise she'd made to go to the fair with Mollie and her face fell. Briefly she was torn between loyalty to her friend and her desperate wish to spend the day with Danny. She had to wrestle with her conscience but in the end she knew she couldn't let Mollie down.

'I sort of half promised I'd go with Mollie. So unless she's going somewhere else, I'm sorry, Danny, I can't.'

'Couldn't I bring Boscoe along for Mollie?'

'You are joking, aren't you? Mollie hates Boscoe Hobbs and so do I. I don't understand what you see in him either. He's been in trouble with the law and if you're seen too often with those sort of people you tend to get tarred with the same brush.'

'I don't care. Boscoe's my mate. A bit of a rogue, I'll grant you, but good for a laugh. And you can't always take life seriously you know. Anyway, it seems to me Mollie thinks she's too good for anyone around here.'

'She probably is.'

'How's that? Her dad's no more than a docker.'

'But Mollie's clever,' answered Charity, as if this explained everything.

'It strikes me she's just toffee nosed.' Danny was beginning to get his sulky look. 'Still, if you prefer to go out wiv her instead o' me that's up to you.'

'I'd much rather spend the day with you. But if I did I'd be letting a friend down.' Charity had pulled herself away from Danny and they were now walking apart. The day, she felt, was in danger of ending badly again, which was the last thing she wanted. 'Look, I'll have a word with Mollie, see what she says.'

'OK. But if you can't come wiv me, Charity, I'll just have to ask someone else.' His meaning was implicit.

'May Potter, you mean.'

'Maybe.'

It was like a punch in the stomach. Danny was deliberately insulting her and didn't even seem to care. Well, he might treat other girls like dirt, but he wouldn't do it to her, she did have some pride. Her head came up and she stared straight at him. 'Well, if that's the sort of company you prefer to keep, don't let me stop you.' Then to Danny's surprise, holding the skirt of her dress with one hand and her hat with the other, Charity sped off down the street.

'Wait for me,' he yelled, racing to catch up with her. But she'd got too good a start on him and he reached the door just in time to have it slammed firmly in his face.

Well, who'd have credited it, thought Danny in astonishment. What had he said after all, not much. A touchy one it seemed, who needed a bit of kid glove treatment. He waited a minute or two expecting Charity to come back out, then shaded his eyes and peered in through the shop window. But there was no movement, not even a chink of light under the door. He was about to bang on the window when, reflected in the glass he saw a policeman. The Bobby was on the opposite side of the street, patting his truncheon against his thigh and regarding Danny with some suspicion.

Feeling he'd been unjustly cast in the role of villain, Danny slunk off, his irritation at Charity's unreasonable behaviour mixed with a growing sexual need. There was he expecting her to be putty in his hands, and she'd done that to him. That was women all over. You never knew where you stood wiv most of them. Still, he supposed she'd come round soon enough and in the meantime there was May. Without fail she could be found in The Angel on a Sunday night. A couple o' gins and some sweet talk usually did the trick with May and made her more than willing to oblige.

To Charity's relief Eliza was already in bed when she got in, but she still took the precaution of removing her shoes before she went upstairs. A chat was the last thing she wanted tonight.

Lighting a candle she undressed, washed her face, unpinned her hair and gave it one hundred strokes with a brush. When she'd completed her toilet, she went to her dresser, unlocked a drawer and took out her diary. Getting into bed, she drew up her legs and, resting the notebook on her knees, wrote: *Had a row with Danny.* She stared miserably at the words then added: *I think I love him.*

Committing her feelings to paper like this was just too much for Charity and a tear rolled down her cheek on to the page, smudging the word 'Love'. Pushing the notebook under her pillow, she blew out the candle, turned on her side and lay staring into the darkness, thinking to herself that love was supposed to make you happy, and yet so far all it had done was make her blinking miserable.

Monday morning was always slack in the shop, but it

was more to take her mind off Danny that Charity decided to check the stock to see what might need re-ordering. She counted out reels of cotton and boxes of buttons and was half way up a ladder, going through the rolls of material, when she heard the door open. Stupidly, she didn't know why, she turned with a smile on her face expecting it to be Danny. But the man stepping over the threshold was the Reverend Leonard Willis. Already in low spirits the sight of him sent them spiralling down to somewhere in the region of her boots.

'Goo . . . Good morning, Miss Brown.'

'Good morning vicar,' answered Charity. As she descended the ladder she had the distinct impression he was trying to peer up her skirts. Two-faced, lecherous so and so, she thought. And him all pious, yet he consorts with Kate and her kind.

She brushed dust from her skirt, tucked a wayward strand of hair behind her ear and said in a businesslike tone, 'What can I do for you this morning?'

'I ha . . . had hoped we might have had the pleasure of . . . of seeing you in our church by now. But since we haven't, I brought you this to . . . to read.' He pushed a piece of paper over the counter towards her. Charity picked it up, saw it was a religious text and more to get rid of him than out of any interest, she quickly scanned it: 'Charity suffereth long, and is kind; charity envieth not; charity vaunteth not itself, is not puffed up, doth not behave itself unseemly . . .'

The words sent a trickle of unease down Charity's spine and she couldn't read any further. When she looked up Leonard Willis's pale eyes were fixed on her and he was running his tongue over his lips. She was aware of an excitement barely held in check, which totally repelled her.

'Co . . . Corinthians,' he said at last.

'Is it?' Showing as little interest as possible, and wishing with all her heart he'd get out the shop, Charity pushed the text back to him. As she did, his hand slid across the counter to touch her fingertips. Feeling contaminated, she pulled her own hand away with a jerk and said icily, 'I'm sorry Mr Willis but I must get on. And I really don't have the slightest interest in religion. God doesn't seem to concern himself overmuch with all the suffering in the world. He doesn't even seem to be able to do much for the people in these parts and that's only a small area.'

'If w . . . we lead lives of high moral rectitude we will f . . . find our reward in Heaven.'

'Do you think *you* will then?' Charity was having trouble bottling up her anger and her tone was sharp.

Leonard Willis looked taken aback. 'M . . . mo . . . most certainly.'

Why, of all the hypocrites! Indignantly she flashed this message with her eyes, regretting she hadn't quite the courage to give voice to her opinion of him to his face.

It was obvious her contempt registered, though. His eyelids twitched in agitation and he backed towards the door. 'Well, as you say, w . . . we must all get on. There's the rest of my flock t . . . to see to. Good day to you Miss Brown.' He lifted his hat.

'Good day,' Charity replied, and shouting after him with some pleasure when she was certain he was out of earshot, 'And good riddance, too!'

Chapter 8

Danny guided the swim-headed barge into midstream, the muscles in his arms and shoulders, thick and strong as steel hawsers, allowing him to manipulate the twenty-five-foot oars with ease. It was early, five o'clock, and although he was feeling the effects of the night before, he knew couldn't afford to be less than alert or he could end up in the ditch, and a watery death was not an uncommon fate for heavy-drinking lightermen. No, in the

Pool with its constant movement of river traffic – steamers belching black smoke, colliers, brigantines at anchor – you needed your wits about you all the time. Then there were the barge-roads and buoys to negotiate.

Although he loved pitting his skill against the swirling currents and changing tides, Danny's feelings towards his work were ambivalent. When it was pitch dark with a wind of Siberian ferocity blowing up from the North sea and the ropes were icy, he hated it. He hated equally the all-enveloping, sulphurous fogs that descended without warning, blanking out the world and making navigation damn near impossible. But worse, far worse, were the dead 'uns, stirred up from the depths by his oar like a spoon in a plate of broth. Bloated, or half eaten away by rats, there was no doubt that some, like the tiny babies still trailing their umbilical cords, had died under suspicious circumstances. Many were 'jumpers,' though, poor buggers who couldn't take any more of what life threw at them.

But on a radiant July morning like this with the easeful sound of slapping water in his ears, Danny could put such disturbing incidents to the back of his mind. Today he felt nothing but love for the river and the comradeship it offered. And a sight he knew he would never tire of was watching the sun, filtered through the permanent haze that hung over the chimney pots, rise above the familiar crenellated skyline. For a brief and magical moment sooty London buildings that a moment before had been shadowy and unfocused were touched with gold. Moved and slightly ashamed, too, by his own sentimentality, Danny drew in his breath at the beauty of it.

But already the river was losing its early morning tranquility and returning to its ordinary workaday self. Boats were on the move, paddle-wheel and screw churning up the stillness. Squeaking cranes jutting from walls swung huge bales of goods from warehouses into waiting barges, and as Danny passed he took deep breaths of air made sweet with the smell of cinnamon and cloves.

Today he'd been given instructions by his lighterage firm to go up to Nine Elms and pick up a cargo of lead. This meant going up through eleven bridges and back again, and although it gave him a chance to work off his hangover, he knew it would be a hard, long slog.

And that was another thing that really narked him, the way firms exploited apprentices who'd got their 'two's, giving them the responsibilities and work of a time-served man but the wages of an apprentice. He was regularly tempted to pack it all in, get on a ship like his brother John and in the past it was only the thought of leaving his ma that had stopped him. Now, though, there was the added complication of Charity, damn her. It was her who'd driven him to May's arms last night, her and too many tankards of ale. He'd always considered it a mistake to get too fond of a girl and even worse, to let her know it. He'd seen what happened to some of his best mates. Tough blokes he'd grown up with, reduced to jelly in the clutches of some bossy female. There were no more nights out then, oh no. Instead the girl would have the idiot saving every penny he earned and before he knew what had hit 'im, wham, the poor sod was spliced.

That was the last thing he wanted. Not that he could marry, thank God, not as an apprentice. But there again he needed to watch his step, because plenty of chaps would give their eye teeth to be seen with Charity on their arm, for there wasn't a girl in the area could come within a mile of her for looks and style. Of course, he'd have liked her a bit more free and easy, but you couldn't have it all ways. And it had been daft hinting he would take May to the fair when he wouldn't be seen dead with her in public. It was Charity he was taking or no one.

He'd have to stop thinking about Charity, her flaxen hair, dark eyes and neat figure and how he was going to make it up with her tonight. He was just passing Custom House and he could smell Billingsgate on his starboard side and see white-coated porters rushing back and forth with the single mindedness of ants. Loud-mouthed, impatient, their profanities reached him across the water. Danny knew, like they did, that with the fish needing to be distributed to towns throughout England before it began to stink, time and the hot weather were against them. So jostling and cursing, they rapidly lightened Dutch schuyts of their catches of eels and oysters, fishing smacks of their cod, haddock and other North Sea fish in the race to get their loads to the market hall and the buyers offering the best prices.

In front of him, carts heavily laden with fruit and vegetables for Covent Garden rumbled over London Bridge and sleepy workmen slouched unwillingly to their jobs. But it was the tide, racing through the arches and swirling to the left and right of its buttresses, that needed all his skill and concentration now. Danny shaped up, shot through a bridge hole but as the barge gathered headway he heard from a wharf a whistle like a starling. It was Rasher Lennox, one of the crowd he went around with.

'Hows about a trip to Gattis ternight?' Rasher shouted across to him.

Danny thought for a moment. Was it to be Charity or a bit o' fun at the Music Hall. It never hurt to keep girls on their toes. Besides, Charity putting that stuck up Mollie before him, that wasn't right and what's more, she didn't like Boscoe that was for sure. So he was a bit of a scoundrel, but a bloke had to make a living, didn't he? Perhaps it wouldn't do no harm to punish her a bit longer just to show who was boss.

'Yeah, arright,' he shouted back. 'If I can make it, I'll see you there about ten.' Then for no other reason than that life seemed pretty good, Danny started to bawl tunelessly at the top of his voice:

> Sing up for Gattis,
> Cheer up for Gattis,
> Why make life a load.

Sing up for Gattis,
You know where that is,
Down in Westminster Road.

By late afternoon Charity was thoroughly fed up. Every time she thought of the creepy Leonard Willis she felt sort of unclean and any hope that Danny might come and make his peace with her faded as the day passed.

Then just before she was about to close, Mrs Green, whose husband owned a lighterage firm, came in all excited explaining that she and her daughter Alice had been invited to tea with the Reverend Willis and his mother so it was imperative that they both have new gowns.

'I want the best for my Alice,' she said by way of explanation as she demanded that Charity spread yet more rolls of material out on the counter for her inspection.

Mrs Green was usually quite careful with her money so at first Charity failed to understand why she should want to go to the expense of new dresses just to have tea in the gloomy rectory. But Mrs Green was the chatty type and while she fingered the material, comparing quality and price, her motives soon became obvious.

'You don't go to our church do you, my dear?'

'No.'

'You should. The vicar's a man of such sterling character and his sermons are wonderful.' She paused, her expression becoming pensive. 'A devoted son too, which of course is why he's still a bachelor, although his mother is looking frail these days.'

Aah, so that was what it was. With her frizzy ginger hair and spots, Alice Green was no beauty but she deserved better than to be sacrificed on the altar of her mother's vaulting social ambitions. How could anyone, a mother least of all, even contemplate such a fate for her daughter. To look across the table for the rest of your life at that weasel face, and worse, lie with him in bed. Imagine being touched by Leonard Willis, kissed by him, having a child by him. The idea was so abhorrent to her,

96

Charity gave an involuntary shudder. She was fretting about whether she should warn Mrs Green about some less savoury aspects of Leonard Willis's character, when the shop door was flung open and Mollie's cheerful countenance appeared round it.

'Want to come to a suffragist meeting tonight? Mrs Fawcett's speaking,' she called out in her exuberant way.

Charity gave Mrs Green a quick glance. 'I'll think about it.'

'Well if you do decide to come, be at my house by six.' Mollie went then, slamming the door with such energy the glass trembled in its frame.

Mrs Green winced as if in pain. 'Well I never!' she exclaimed. 'What are young women coming to! No girl with any claim to a proper upbringing would have raised her voice like that in my young day.'

'It's just Mollie's way, Mrs Green, she can never do anything quietly,' said Charity, feeling the need to apologize on her friend's behalf.

'So it would seem. And all this nonsense about votes. As the Reverend Willis preached in his sermon last Sunday, these things, politics and the like, are best left to men. They have the brain power to deal with such matters. But that's something else that's changed. We were taught to know our place, look up to our husbands and respect their judgement.'

Remembering Agnes Weston's bruised face, Charity wondered about her. Was she supposed to respect her husband and look up to him as a superior mortal? She was tempted to put this question to Mrs Green but knew if she did she risked being accused of impertinence and the shop wasn't that prosperous it could afford to lose her custom.

'But then standards are falling all the time,' Mrs Green went on. 'What can you expect, though, when young women get involved with these cigarette-smoking, suffragist types who just put silly ideas into their heads. I'll see to it that my Alice never does. You'd all do well to remember that there is great truth in the saying, "the hand that rocks the cradle rules the world," and forget about behaving like men.'

'The way a lot of men behave, no woman in her right mind would want to imitate them. And wanting the vote, that's just a question of rights, Mrs Green.' Making these points, Charity was surprised by her own vehemence, because although female suffrage was one of Mollie's favourite topics of conversation, until now she herself had found it difficult to work up any enthusiasm for the subject.

Mrs Green finally chose her material, unflattering red plaid taffeta for her daughter, brown wool for herself, and Charity wrapped it. As Mrs Green took the parcel she leaned over the counter and, clutching Charity's arm, said in a confidential tone, 'If I were you I wouldn't go to this meeting, my dear. Be a sensible girl and stay at home. You don't know what sort of unsavoury types you'll meet there. Radicals, agitators, probably even some anarchists. You'd do much better to come along to our church instead, the Reverend Willis would make you most welcome.'

I bet he would, thought Charity, as she walked with Mrs Green to the door, bid her goodnight and hung up the closed sign. Any uncertainty she'd had about attending the meeting had flown – Leonard Willis's opposition to women's rights was encouragement enough. Now she was determined to go and find out for herself exactly what the suffrage movement was all about.

It was a long way to the meeting. First they had to take the train across the river to Wapping, then an omnibus. And although Mollie insisted she knew the way, there was a lot of stopping and asking for directions before they found the hall they were looking for, somewhere off Whitechapel Road.

Footsore and hot, and already beginning to doubt the wisdom of the exercise, Charity was dismayed to see the hall full almost to overflowing with women and with apparently nowhere to sit.

But the ever-resourceful Mollie, who was standing on tiptoe and peering over the heads of the audience, had already spied some vacant seats. 'Come on, I can see two down there right in the middle of the row, let's grab them,' she said, although as they squeezed their way along a row of tired-looking women, Charity was conscious of some mild grumblings, and such comments as, 'Watch out for me corns, love.'

Breathing sighs of relief they collapsed into the chairs just in time to join in the clapping when several women, all of them smartly dressed and obviously well to do, filed on to the platform.

Mollie gave Charity a nudge in the ribs. 'The lady in the middle, that's Mrs Millicent Fawcett.'

Mrs Fawcett was a handsome looking woman with a confidence and easy grace that came from money and position. A woman to admire. 'Who are the others though?' Charity hissed.

'I dunno, but we'll find out in a minute. I just know one's a doctor and she's going to give a talk.'

Mrs Fawcett, who was obviously in charge of the proceedings was the first to stand up and speak. 'Although it is something we hope you will give your support to, tonight we have not come here to speak specifically about the vote. Tonight we want to talk about a woman's right to assert control over her own body, her fertility, and Doctor Forbes is going to speak to you about limiting families through contraception.'

Hearing these words, Charity felt herself blush scarlet. Nudging Mollie, she said primly, 'I don't think we should stay and listen to this, after all we're not married women.'

'Don't be daft, of course we're staying. You'll probably be married yourself one day. So, unless you want a dozen kids, you'd better pay attention to what she's got to say.'

Placed where they were, right in the middle of the row,

Charity saw it would be difficult to leave without drawing attention to herself. So, she was left with no choice but to do as Mollie said, although she squirmed in her chair uncomfortably when Doctor Forbes stood up to speak.

With her sensible serge skirt and hair scraped back in a bun it was immediately apparent that Doctor Forbes was a no-nonsense sort of woman. 'Now ladies,' she said in a booming voice that carried well to the back of the hall, 'I shall discuss with you the various and inexpensive methods of family limitation which will enable you to enjoy physical union with your husbands, without fear of pregnancy.'

'I don't know about enjoying anyfink,' muttered a woman sitting next to Charity, making her blush even more; but the rest of her audience sat straight backed, silent and attentive. However, when the doctor held up for inspection a piece of sponge tied with string and said, 'now this can be soaked in quinine and inserted in the vagina,' there were a few sniggers and Charity's own embarrassment was so acute she slid down in her chair, unable to look either to the left or right. She had never heard such frank language in her life before. Crude yes, but never like this, calling a spade a spade. Next something called a douche was produced, 'To be used after sexual intercourse,' the doctor explained, 'with a solution of alum, sulphate of zinc and vinegar.' She was well into her stride, advising the women how to make cheap pessaries from cocoa butter and quinine when the interruption came. A male voice from the back of the hall thundered out like an Old Testament prophet, 'This filth must stop, madam. All your advice is against the laws of God and nature.'

There was an astonished silence then a murmur of annoyance rippled round the hall as women heaved themselves round in their chairs, peering to get a better look. Who was this bloke putting his spoke in to matters that didn't concern him. And what was he doing here in the first place? A scraggy woman wearing a flat cap stood up, and with arms folded as if she meant business, shouted back, 'Why don't you just mind your own bloody business, mate. After all it's you blokes what keeps gettin' us in the family way.'

'Yeah and why don't you come down 'ere where we can get a proper look at you,' another woman goaded. 'Come on.'

The whole hall was now on its feet and, keen to join in the skirmish, Mollie leapt up on her chair. 'Or perhaps you're frightened of us?' she shouted provocatively.

And maybe he was, for they were a tough-looking bunch and it would have taken either a rash or brave man to run the gauntlet of their hostility. Although he didn't take up their invitation, the man did move into the aisle.

'Good God, I think it's that vicar chap,' Mollie exclaimed, nearly falling off her chair in astonishment.

'You mean Leonard Willis?'

'Yeah, come and take a look for yourself. You know him better than I do.' Holding out her hand, Mollie pulled Charity up beside her.

His unprepossessing features were indistinct in the poor light but Charity had no difficulty in identifying the interloper. 'It's him all right.' The two friends stared at each other. 'But how did he find out about this meeting?'

'It was well advertised, so from a poster I suppose.'

'Of all the nerve . . . Do you know, just knowing he's here gives me the creeps . . .' The words were hardly out of Charity's mouth before Leonard Willis was off on another tirade, flailing his arms and intoning, 'Sexual union in marriage is for the procreation of children not for mere gratification, the church is quite clear on the matter.'

'Ooh, what sanctimonious humbug.' Mollie was almost, but not quite, speechless.

But what struck Charity most forcibly was the change in Leonard Willis's voice. Certitude had lent it power, it had lost its hesitancy and rang out now with utter conviction.

'All this is Satan's work and I shall go directly to the police about this meeting,' he threatened. 'And you, madam,' he pointed an accusing finger at Mrs Fawcett, 'will be prosecuted.'

'Oh no she won't,' contradicted another voice. Another man! All agog now the whole audience rose to its feet. 'Neither will you call the police. There is nothing illegal about the meeting, so you are wasting your time, sir. But just to make sure, will some of you ladies guard the doors to see that he doesn't get out.'

Nothing as exciting as this had happened to the women in years. It was better entertainment than any Music Hall turn and with a bit of luck it might turn into a punch-up. But at the same time, mention of the dreaded word 'police' caused a ripple of disquiet and anxious glances towards the exit, for they knew who would come off worse in any encounter with the law.

But surely this was someone on their side, they whispered to each other. So after a slight pause for more discussion, several of the heftier members of the audience moved down the central aisle and took up their positions by the door. Looking dangerous, they stood there, arms akimbo, daring the vicar to make one false move.

'I'm sure I know that voice. Can you see who it is?' Mollie asked.

But it was pretty evident the meeting was spinning out of control now. The hall was in total uproar and with women milling around everywhere it was impossible to see much at all. Craning her neck to get a better look, Charity felt the rickety chair wobble dangerously. Fearing it might collapse under her, she was about to step down when the crowd parted and she had a perfect view of the young man. Like Mollie she felt she knew him, except that he was well bred, that was obvious from his dress and speech, and where, she asked herself, would she ever have had the chance to meet anyone like that.

By now Mollie had seen him too. She nudged Charity in the ribs and her brown eyes grew round with excitement.

'Hey, it's that chap Stephen. You remember, the one we met the day the bridge was opened.'

'So it is.' Charity was intrigued. ' But what's he doing slumming?'

Charity was shortly have her question answered, for Mrs Fawcett, obviously feeling the need to restore the meeting to some semblance of order, was banging the gavel on the table. 'Ladies! Ladies! Can we have some quiet please,' she implored, banged it again and gradually the noise subsided enough for her to speak. Now firmly in control, her gaze swept imperiously round the hall. 'Thank you. First of all I would like some questions answered. Doctor Trevelyan is here at my request, but I don't believe this other gentleman was invited to what was specifically advertised as a meeting for women only.'

'As soon as I read that on the poster I guessed the nature of your lecture, madam, and I came to put a stop to the spread of such Godless teachings,' was Leonard Willis's self-righteous rejoinder.

'You prefer infanticide, botched abortions, I suppose, sir? The tyranny of poverty. Sickly women dragged down in health by countless births,' the young man challenged in a voice thick with anger. 'I'm a doctor, I've seen women bleed to death. Is that what you would prefer rather than your God was upset?'

'No, what I'm suggesting is abstinence, self-control.'

At this there were hoots of derision, then a woman, bolder than the rest shouted, 'Oh yeah. Come round and tell that to my old man, vicar. I can just see him going wivout. If he don't 'ave 'is bit o' nooky regular, he gets fair narked 'e does.'

'Chop it off, I should, love, best form of contraception invented,' another advised and a wave of raucous laughter swept round the hall.

It was a while before calm was restored and into the brief hiatus Charity shouted provocatively, 'You want to ask him if he practises what he preaches.'

But her remark was lost in the jeers of the women, for,

103

by now they'd had enough of this mealy-mouthed cleric with his pious claptrap and a wrathful group advanced on him in a threatening manner. Leonard Willis backed away, tripping over a chair in his haste to depart, his earlier bravado replaced by an expression of terror. With good reason, too, Charity felt, because they were a fearsome bunch who looked as if they wouldn't think twice about depriving him of his manhood.

'Let him go, ladies.' It was the young doctor and he'd put himself between Leonard Willis and his adversaries. 'He's not worth your trouble.' Turning to the vicar he advised, 'If you value your safety, I should go, quickly.'

'And come back again and you'll get what for,' shouted someone else. Fists were raised and, faced with humiliation and ignominious defeat the vicar slunk off, his tail firmly between his legs.

When he'd gone, cheers of self-congratulation rang round the hall, and when Mrs Fawcett stood up to make her final speech the women listened with attentive, eager expressions.

'Now, ladies, I want you to go home and think carefully about what you've witnessed tonight. Ask yourselves, should we have control of our own bodies or do we leave it to Parliament or men of the cloth. Because as long as we are without the vote, we are powerless to change our lives.'

Perhaps the vicar's heckling helped, but Mrs Fawcett's speech earned her a standing ovation and as the women spilled out of the hall, some straight into the pub next door, others home, Charity wondered just how many had been won over to the cause of female suffrage. The women running this meeting had certainly brought about a shift in her own attitude that night, but did these well-meaning, middle class feminists with their nannies and servants, really have any grasp of what it was like to have too many mouths to feed, too little money, to feel more or less permanently exhausted. Limiting their families yes, that would interest working class women. But she'd have to ask Mollie, see if she thought acquiring the vote loomed large in their lives when there were the more practical problems of putting clothes on backs and shoes on feet to be solved. And she couldn't see them going to a male doctor either, to discuss such personal matters as family limitation. What they needed was a woman to talk it over with.

Coming out of the hall she and Mollie were separated in the crush, but scanning the crowd, Charity caught a glimpse of her friend's white boater and waved. They were weaving their way toward each other, when Charity saw with a quiver of unease that Leonard Willis was standing a short distance away, rebuking her with his pale, unblinking eyes. Like a rabbit hypnotized by a stoat, she stood stock still and, without acknowledging her, he turned away.

'Is something wrong?' It was Mollie and she was shaking her arm. 'You do look peculiar.'

Charity gave a small shudder. 'It's that Leonard Willis, he was still hanging around when I came out.'

'Did he speak to you?'

'He doesn't have to, the way he looks at me is enough.'

'I'm surprised he risked waiting.'

'I think he might have seen us inside.'

'What if he did?' asked Mollie robustly. 'It's a free country, isn't it? We're entitled to go to a meeting without asking his permission. Anyway, don't worry about him. I think he's still tied to his mother's apron strings and that's made him a bit weird.'

'He always manages to spoil my day, but he's gone now, thank heaven.'

'So has the young doctor, more's the pity. I was looking forward to talking to him. I wanted to thank him for his support.'

'Was that the only reason?'

'What d'ya mean?' Mollie gave Charity a wary look.

'I just wondered if you'd taken a bit of a shine to him, thats all.'

'Certainly not!' Mollie tossed her head indignantly, offended that Charity could even suppose a girl of her intelligence would behave like any other silly young creature over a man.

'There's no harm in liking someone, you know,' Charity said. 'No harm in even admitting it.'

'I suppose not. And he is nice, isn't he?' Mollie looked glum. 'Although of course he'd never look twice at me.'

Chapter 9

It was a wet evening with a chill in the air and the view out on to the unkempt garden with its dripping trees just about matched Charity's own low spirits. Three days and still not a word from Danny. All evening she had listened for him, lifting her head at the slightest sound. In the end, tired of Eliza's watchful gaze on her, she went upstairs to her bedroom.

Hating Danny for his neglect, bored and at a loose end, she started flicking through old copies of the *Girl's Own Paper*. In a desultory way she tried out various hairstyles, decided none of them suited her so turned instead to the cookery hints. Thrift was the keynote here. Suggestions were given on how to use up stale bread, how to make a leg of mutton last five meals and, there being no end to their versatility, new ways were given for serving sheep's head. Yuk! sheep's head. Charity wrinkled her nose in disgust, flung the magazine aside and picked up her diary. But the contents of this were even less inspiring. In fact most pages were blank. In a determined and rather bad tempered effort to rectify this she wrote across two pages in large print, BORED! BORED! BORED! giving vent to her frustration by stabbing in the exclamation marks violently with the point of her pencil.

An impatient hammering on the door made her pause, then her face lit up. She sat very still and waited. Liza would answer it and in a moment, oh joy, she'd hear Danny's voice. But there was no sound from downstairs and when the door was thumped again with even more urgency she had no choice but to run down to answer it herself.

Just to show Danny, she kept a bit of a straight face. But when she opened the door and saw Mollie standing there, rain cascading from a broken gutter on to her umbrella, her face dropped to her boots in dismay. 'Oh it's you,' she said, making no effort to hide her disappointment. 'You'd better come in.'

Bright-eyed, ruddy-cheeked and oblivious to her friend's lukewarm welcome, Mollie shook rain from her umbrella and stepped inside along with several bedraggled cats, who streaked in under her feet. Looking about ready to explode, she took an envelope from her pocket and waved it in the air. 'I've got it! I've got it!' she proclaimed, and cats scattered in all directions as she did a jubilant dance around the scullery.

'Got what?' Charity stared at her friend, wondering at her strange behaviour.

'I have to keep pinching myself but I've just heard that I've won a Senior County Scholarship and I'm going to Bedford College for three years. So maybe I'll get to be a doctor after all. As well as that they'll give me sixty pounds a year to live on. Sixty pounds! Isn't that incredible?'

It certainly was and it took Charity several minutes to digest the news. But then, in a voice that was almost accusing, she said, 'You didn't tell me you were sitting for the scholarship.'

'I didn't want to let on in case I failed. Just think, I can leave that horrible place where I'm working and I won't have to write one more letter about Assam or Darjeeling tea. Instead I shall be able to read books all day and study English, maths and physics, all the subjects I love, and get paid for the privilege.'

'You're a lucky devil, you know, getting a chance like this.' Charity just couldn't hide her envy.

107

'It's not luck, it's hard work.'

That was true enough, for no matter how tired she felt after work, Mollie took herself off to evening classes at the City of London College at least three times a week. She deserved her good fortune and only the most mean-spirited person would feel envious. Going over to her friend, Charity gave her a hug. 'I'm ever so pleased for you, Mollie, I really am. Except that I will miss you.' She didn't voice it, but a fear was already surfacing that Mollie moving on to greater things might signal the end of their friendship.

'No Miss Pumfrey then?' asked Mollie, when they'd moved through to the small parlour.

'She's probably popped out for a jug of ale and got held up by the rain.' Charity was heating milk for cocoa but a burst of rain ricochetting off the windowpane made her look up. 'At least that's where I hope she is and not out looking for strays. It'll do her chest no good at all on a night like this.'

A flash of lightning then a clap of thunder made several of the cats leap up in fright and Charity watched with some concern as the tree in the garden was whipped into a frenzy by a gale force wind.

'You'll never stop her, will you? Rescuing cats that is. It's like a crusade. Mind you there'll never be a shortage of work for her round here. The mill pond between West Lane and Gilhams Court is full of dead cats and dogs. All bloated too. Kids aim their catapults at them, they explode and it makes a stink you can smell for miles. It's digusting. No wonder all the diseases in the world seem to run rampant in these parts, they're certainly given every encouragement.'

'Well wherever she is I wish she'd hurry back. I want to tell her your news. She'll be really pleased. She's always going on about how clever you are and how it would be a crying shame if your talents were wasted.'

At nine-thirty, when Mollie got up to leave, Eliza still

hadn't returned and Charity's earlier vague concern had stiffened into a deep disquiet. 'I'm coming with you to see if I can find her. She would never stay out this long, particularly not in this weather. I'm certain something's wrong.' She stamped her feet into stout boots and buttoned herself into a weatherproof cloak.

Although the rain had eased, debris had choked the drains and gutters overflowed across the road and up on to the pavement in a swilling sea of effluvia: tin cans, cigarette butts, old newspapers, rotting vegetables and the odd dead rat.

Wrinkling their noses in disgust the girls picked their way through the mire, holding down their skirts against the wind and trying at the same time to avoid being engulfed in the great arcs of water thrown up by the passing wheels of cabs.

'I'm going to look down by the river first, she often goes there,' Charity shouted to Mollie over the howl of the wind.

'Not on your own you're not, especially at this time of night.'

Gulls struggled to fly into the storm but time and again were beaten back; riggings whistled shrilly and swollen, grape-coloured clouds scudded across the sky, making visibility poor, and it was obvious to the girls as they jumped down on to the foreshore that the river was in a turbulent mood. Sails on many barges were already in ribbons, larger ships, making for the docks and heavy with cargo were listing badly, while some smaller vessels had been torn from their moorings and, bobbing around like corks, were being blown ashore.

It was a frightening sight, watching the havoc being wreaked and Charity realized with a shiver of apprehension how merciless nature was; it would obey no command. She also saw that with the tide coming in, if Eliza was down here somewhere they hadn't a moment to lose.

'Come on, let's go,' she urged and the two of them set off along the water's edge with as much speed as the sucking mud would allow. Even with their bodies bent in obeisance to the gale it still plucked pins from their hair and sent their cloaks billowing out behind them. Every now and then they would pause to search under the swims and budgets of barges or cup their hands and call uselessly into the wind, 'Eliza, Eliza.'

They'd passed the granary warehouses and rumbling flour mills when Mollie stopped. 'It's no good, we can't go any further or we'll be in danger ourselves.'

'I've got to find her,' answered Charity, who was now beginning to experience a real fear. 'Look there's something a bit further along.' With a surge of hope, she pointed to a dark shape and hurried towards it. But it was a sodden bale of gunnies and her sense of disappointment was so strong, she kicked it with an impotent anger. Then, swinging round she said pitifully, 'What am I to do, Moll? Aunt Eliza's my family, all I've got.'

'I know.' Gently Mollie took her friend's arm. 'But we must turn back. In this weather if we get caught by the tide we won't stand a chance. And not finding her probably means she's already at home anyway.'

It was a faint hope but Charity clung to it as they stumbled back along the shore. The ships' lights stopped it from being totally dark but the soaring warehouses cast eerie shadows and Charity tried not to think that this was a place where the dregs of society lurked. Men and women from whom all human virtues had fled and who wouldn't hesitate to kill for the clothes you stood up in. She gave a shiver of apprehension and lengthened her stride, noticing that barges which earlier had been moored high on the mud, now had water eddying around them.

'Hurry,' said Mollie in a tense voice, 'We'll have to get up the next stairs we come to.'

'But supposing . . .' There was a sob in Charity's voice. 'She could be lying unconscious somewhere and if we don't find her she'll drown.'

'That's what we're going to be in a minute, drowned.

Look, the water's nearly up to our feet, and it'll reach the river wall and stairs before long. Come on.'

Mollie started to run and Charity, tearfully protesting, 'What about aunt Eliza?' followed, stumbling over pieces of flotsam in the dark and too upset to be really aware of her own danger. Until she realized she was splashing through water and the hem of her skirt was wet. She did run then, not sure if it was the wind or her blood she could hear pounding in her ears as she strained to catch up with Mollie.

'I think we're . . . safe, there's some stairs just . . . in front,' Mollie gasped over her shoulder, exclaiming a second later, 'Good God,' following it with a jubilant, 'I've found her!'

Charity, who felt her lungs would burst before she reached safety was propelled forward by these words.

'Where are you?'

'Here, by the side of the stairs. Quickly, help me lift her.'

Charity knelt down, touching Eliza's cheek. The skin felt like ice.

'Is . . . is she alive?'

'Yes, I felt her pulse. But she'll die of pneumonia if we don't get these soaking clothes off her. Heaven knows how long she's been lying here.'

Eliza was of a solid build, and it was a struggle for the girls to lift her. But somehow between them they managed to pull her to her feet. Tottering under her dead weight, they'd looped an arm each round their necks and were dragging her to the stairs when Charity noticed the sack and heard a pitiful mew.

'Wait, there's a cat back there in the sack.'

'Never mind about that, you grab her legs, I'll take her arms.' They were hampered by their own wet skirts and Eliza's weight, but eventually they dragged her to safety and lay her out on the ground.

'Phew, I'm fair done in,' gasped Mollie and collapsed flat on her back beside her.

But Charity had one final task. Pausing only to adjust Eliza's skirts sufficiently to preserve her modesty, she scrambled back down the stairs and peered into the dark waters.

'Hey, where are you going?' Mollie shot up to sitting position.

'To get the cat.'

'You idiot, come back,' Mollie screamed.

'No.' Charity's voice was firm. 'If Aunt Eliza knew I hadn't tried to save it she would never forgive me.' Reaching out she strained to grab the sack, almost losing her balance and toppling into the water as the first wave smashed against the river wall.

By the time they got Eliza home, exchanged her wet clothes for a nightdress and made her comfortable on the horsehair sofa, she was conscious, but obviously very confused, for she gave no indication that she recognized either of them. Although once she did call out in great distress, 'No, no, you mustn't take him . . .'

'What do you think she's talking about?' asked Mollie.

'I don't know,' answered Charity in a preoccupied voice, more concerned about Eliza's temperature, which she was sure was up. 'But I'm not wasting any more time, I'm going to fetch the doctor.'

'At this time of night?' queried Mollie.

'Yes. She's got a fever, it would be dangerous to neglect it.'

'Well I know Dr Campbell won't be very pleased to be called out. I've heard tell the whisky in the decanter's usually well down by this time of night. She'd probably be safer left than suffer his ministrations. And look, she's sleeping and seems comfortable enough.'

This time, though, Charity intended to trust her own judgement rather than listen to Mollie's advice. 'I can't risk leaving her till the morning. Just suppose she took a turn for the worse, I'd never forgive myself.'

'Let me call in on the doctor and you stay here. I really ought to be off or Mum and Dad will start worrying.'

'Gosh, yes, your parents, I'd forgotten all about them. Tell Dr Campbell it's urgent, that way he'll come, then you go straight off home. You've got a day's work in front of you tomorrow. And thanks for everything you've done tonight, Moll, you've been a real brick.'

'Think nothing of it. After all, isn't that what friends are for.'

'And we will stay friends, won't we? Even when you go away.'

'You goose, of course we will.'

Reassured by Mollie's words, after she'd seen her off, Charity allowed herself the luxury of a few moments of quiet contemplation. The storm had subsided and, in a break in the clouds, she could detect a few stars. The rain had washed away the fumes from the sulphur works and the air smelt fresh for a change. Charity inhaled deeply, enjoying the dank smell of wet earth and the sound of dripping foliage. This was what the country would be like all the time, she thought. In fact the country was a place that existed only in Charity's head. Her impressions, garnered from the books she read, was of Elysian fields, gambolling lambs and happy rustics and she'd promised herself that as soon as she had enough money, she would buy herself a bicycle and take herself off there.

She was about to go in and close the door when she noticed the sack she had risked her life for, struggled home with, then dumped on the step and forgotten about completely.

More for Eliza's sake than in any hope that the small creature inside might still be alive, she picked it up and took it indoors. Spreading some paper out in front of the fire, Charity carefully slit open the sacking with scissors. It lay there lifeless, a half-grown black and white kitten, its fur smeared with slime, oil and mud. During her years with Eliza, she'd seen many similarly abused cats but she'd never become immune to their suffering. And now Charity was filled with an overwhelming pity for the small, lost life. And a feeling of rage too against the brutish person capable of committing such a vile act.

She was about to re-wrap the small body and make it ready for burial, when to her astonishment the kitten opened its eyes, raised its head, then, revived by the warmth of the fire perhaps, tried to struggle to its feet. But it was too weak and it sank back on the hessian. But against all the odds it had defied death, and if it had the will to live, Charity decided, then she would do her damnedest to see that it did.

As Charity sprung to her feet, she noticed that with their normal curiosity, one or two of the other cats were observing this life-and-death drama from a respectful distance, in particular a rather elderly female tabby called Lolly. She was of variable temper, liked to queen it over the other cats, and wasn't above giving younger members of the household a cuff round the ear if they stepped out of line.

Wondering whether she ought to risk leaving the kitten on its own with her, Charity hurried into the scullery for milk and to search for the baby's bottle Eliza used for cats too young or weak to lap for themselves. When she returned to the kitchen she was brought up short by the scene in front of her. For Lolly, her maternal instincts rekindled, was gently but thoroughly washing the kitten clean, her pink, rough tongue moving rhythmically over the bedraggled fur: the ears, the neck, then, after nudging it on to its back with her nose, its tummy. Carefully, so as not to distract Lolly from her healing task, Charity tiptoed nearer and saw that the kitten was already responding. It had opened its eyes again and was making feeble noises, not quite a purr but somehow denoting pleasure. Moved beyond measure by Lolly's small gesture of love, Charity sniffed, gulped back a tear then took herself to task for being so sentimental.

The knock took her by surprise for she'd been so engrossed in the kitten, she'd quite forgotten about Dr Campbell. After giving herself a moment to compose

114

herself, she went to let him in, preparing herself for the litany of complaints she expected to be treated to for dragging him from the comfort of his home at such a late hour. Never mind that he'd charge double the price.

However, it wasn't the elderly doctor, stewed to the gills, who stood on the step, but a sober-looking young man and Charity gave a start of recognition.

'Good evening. I have come to the right house haven't I? Miss Pumfrey, eleven Filbert Street?' he enquired when Charity made no attempt to let him in.

'Oh . . . oh yes, sorry. I was expecting Dr Campbell.'

'Dr Campbell is . . . er, indisposed. I'm his new assistant, Doctor Trevelyan.'

'I'm sorry . . . you'd better come in. My Aunt's through here.' She led him into the parlour, intensely conscious of how unkempt she must look with her mudstained skirt and hair hanging in a tangle about her shoulders. And seeing the small room through his eyes, she felt ashamed of its shabbiness. Then there were all the cats. What would he think of those?

But he didn't cast either a critical eye over Charity or the room but instead went straight to the patient. 'Can you tell me exactly what happened to Miss Pumfrey,' he asked, sitting down and feeling her pulse. 'Your outspoken friend said she'd had a fall.'

This indirect reference to their exchange of views on the boat, made it clear he also remembered them. Discomposed, Charity stuttered, 'tha . . . that's right. Down by the river. She probably slipped on the stairs. I don't know how long she'd been lying there when we found her, maybe an hour, perhaps more.'

Stephen Trevelyan raised an eyebrow. 'Not the place I would have expected a woman to go walking on her own at night, particularly not in a storm.'

'She was out looking for strays and trying to rescue that little scrap.' Charity nodded in the direction of the kitten. 'Cruel, wicked people do that all the time, deliberately throw them in the river. And Aunt Liza tries to save them. She sees it as her mission in life.'

'And she's not bothered about her own safety?'

'She's not, but I am. She's never been attacked though. Everyone, even the down-and-outs, knows what she does, thinks she's strange but in their own way admire her.'

'Has she been sick at all this evening?'

'No.'

'Well she might have slight concussion, so if she remains drowsy and is sick you are to let me know immediately. For the moment, it would be best just to let her sleep. Don't worry,' he said when he saw Charity's doubtful expression, 'I shall call back first thing in the morning.'

He shut his bag, then bending, gently tickled the kitten under the chin with one finger, while Lolly watched with a proprietorial air. 'So you're the young man who's the cause of all the trouble, eh?'

Charity, who'd been filling the bottle with tepid milk knelt down beside him and put the teat to the kitten's mouth. He took it without trouble, sucking so hungrily milk dribbled out of his mouth and down his chin. 'I thought he was dead an hour ago, but look at the way he's guzzling now.'

'Yes, just like Dr Campbell with his whisky,' observed Stephen with a grin.

Charity responded with a giggle to this indiscretion, the thought passing through her mind at the same time that he really was much nicer than the older man, who even when he was sober was inclined to be grumpy.

''Tell you what, when he's fully recovered, why don't you let me have him.' Stephen suggested.

'Do you really mean it? He might not last the night.'

'Oh yes he will. He's a real fighter that little chap, I can tell. And he'll be great company for me. It can get pretty lonely at Dr Campbell's with just him and his housekeeper.'

'What will you call him?'

Stephen thought for a moment. 'Well, under the circumstances there's only one name for him, Whisky.' His wry tone made Charity laugh out loud this time, then remembering the sleeping patient, her hand flew to her mouth.

Seeing he was getting up to go and wanting to enjoy his company a bit longer, Charity said quickly, 'I was just going to make tea. Will you stay and have some, Dr Trevelyan?'

'Why not,' he answered, and putting down his bag, he made himself comfortable by the fire. 'You don't know how pleasant it is here. The fire and the cats.' And you, Stephen wanted to add, but felt two indiscretions in one evening were enough. Instead he allowed himself the pleasure of admiring her graceful movements as she went about her small domestic tasks, putting out cups and biscuits and making tea. A gentle and malleable creature he mused, although there was something faintly erotic about her windblown hair, which freed from its pins recalled loosened hair tangled with damp sheets after lovemaking. And where in heaven's name had she got those eyes? Although in a seafaring area like this with men of every nation under the sun coming and going it was hardly a question that needed asking.

There had never been a shortage of good-looking women in his life but this girl, with hair the colour of late summer corn and whose name he didn't even know, was about the loveliest creature he'd ever set eyes on. Flattered by his attentions she would be easy to woo, and certainly it would be an enjoyable diversion for him. On second thoughts, perhaps it would be unwise to allow loneliness to affect his judgement and draw him into an relationship with a girl not of his class or education. Anyway, hadn't he always despised men of his background who used working class women for their pleasure, only to cast them aside when their charms waned. He must stop it, and instead focus his thoughts on the delectable

117

Blanche, who he knew would be at his uncle's house this weekend.

Unaware of the heart-searching she was causing, Charity handed the doctor his tea and sat down in the chair opposite. 'I was at the meeting the other night where you spoke up against the Reverend Willis.'

'Oh, were you? And whose opinion are you most in sympathy with, mine or his?'

'Yours, of course.'

'I don't know why you say, "of course". His views have more support than Mrs Fawcett's and mine. The subject of family limitation is abhorrent to many people, men and women. However if they saw some of the sad cases I do as a result of unwanted pregnancies, they might change their minds. I can't see that a motherless family benefits anyone.'

'But at least you're trying to do something for the people round here, I wish I could,' Charity answered, formulating in words for the first time something that had been no more than a vague idea until now.

'Have you anything particular in mind?'

Feeling foolish, Charity shook her head. 'No, not really.'

'Have you ever considered nursing?'

'I haven't the education to train as a nurse. Anyway you need to be suited to that sort of work and I'm not sure I am.'

'You could do evening classes in sick nursing and see how you like it. And something like that is never wasted.'

'I know. Mollie my friend, she's always attended evening classes and she's just won a scholarship to Bedford College.'

'Has she now.'

Charity could see the doctor was impressed by Mollie's achievement. But she also caught a hint of surprise in his face and this annoyed her enough to challenge him.

'You don't expect girls of our class to be clever, do you?' she asked with a touch of asperity.

Taken aback by her remark and mortified that his expression had betrayed him, Stephen finished his tea and tried to think of a suitable reply. However, all he could come up with was a rather lame, 'Yes I do.'

'No you don't,' she contradicted. 'But you wait and see, Mollie will come out with the top marks in that college over the heads of all your posh girls.'

He'd offended her, Stephen could see that. And arrogant assumptions about the poor never did, he was learning that slowly. Pride, everyone had that, even the most lowly, and in his work he forgot it at his peril.

Charity stood up and took down a tea caddy from the mantelpiece. 'How much do I owe you, Dr Trevelyan?' she asked coolly, emptying coins on to the table.

Aware that he was getting his marching orders and anxious to make amends, Stephen lifted his hand. 'Don't bother, I didn't do much.' He knew as soon as he spoke that he'd committed yet another, even more glaring *faux pas*, because the atmosphere was no longer chilly but positively glacial. 'What I . . . I mean is,' he went on, stumbling over himself now to avert a monumental disaster, 'I'll settle up with you tomorrow, when I come to see Miss Pumfrey again.' He was sweating with embarrassment when he finished, marvelling at his own crassness and wondering how on earth he'd managed to misread someone's character so completely. Malleable? Not her. No, it was pretty obvious a rod of steel ran through that slender young frame.

Chapter 10

That great restorative, sleep, did its work and by the following morning Eliza insisted she felt strong as a horse and no amount of fussing could persuade her to stay in bed a minute longer.

'Do you know what happened to you last night?'

Furious at Eliza's obstinacy, Charity's eyebrows were knitted together in a scowl. 'You fell and almost died.'

'Rubbish,' Miss Pumfrey answered and swung her feet round on to the floor.

'You did. Me and Mollie found you on the foreshore, out cold with the tide coming in. You've got us to thank you're still alive. And we got the doctor, you know.'

'The doctor did you say? Why he's hopeless. And anyway I resent seeing my hard-earned money being poured straight down that man's throat.'

'It wasn't Dr Campbell. He's got a new assistant. A Dr Trevelyan. He's looking in again this morning, in a very short while too,' said Charity with a glance at the brass-faced grandfather clock. 'And his instructions were that no account was I to let you get up. So if I was you, I'd get back on that sofa, at least until he's gone.'

'Oh all right,' Eliza grumbled, for although she wasn't going to admit it to Charity, when she'd tried to stand her legs had felt extremely shaky and she had to concede she was nowhere near in as good shape as she claimed. She refused to lie down though, but sat, her bulky figure ramrod straight, watching Charity's every move as she lit the fire and set about preparing breakfast.

Charity knew she was just waiting for an opportunity to criticize. But she was determined not to give her the chance. So the bacon she served her was fried to a crisp perfection, the tea hot, sweet and strong, exactly as Eliza liked it.

As soon as she'd washed up and fed the cats, Charity went to open the shop. It was coming up to the Bank Holiday and she knew there was business to be had today. Girls would be wanting fresh trimmings for their hats, a new lace collar to brighten up a dress, or lengths of ribbon to tie in their hair in the hope of catching a young man's eye.

She'd hardly had time to roll the blind up on the door, when Mollie burst in, panting violently and trying to push an escaping blouse back into her skirt. 'Can't . . . stop, I'm on my way to work but . . . how's Miss Pumfrey?'

'On the mend, I think, but Dr Trevelyan's coming into check a bit later.'

At the mention of Stephen's name, the pink in Mollie's cheeks spread like a stain down to her neck. 'Is he? Did you get a surprise when you saw him last night? I did, I can tell you.'

'Yeah but it was a nice one. And a change from crabby old Dr Campbell and his strawberry nose.'

Mollie giggled, then gave a wistful sigh. 'He is good looking isn't he? He's got a sort of kind face too. And he didn't curse me blind because he had to make a late call.'

'You've probably got a lot in common. Pity you're going to college really,' mused Charity, running a feather duster over the shelves and counter.

Mollie looked shocked. 'You know I would never let any man stand in the way of my education.'

Charity gave her friend a sly glance. 'Not even Dr Trevelyan?' she asked and wondered what she would do if she had choices to make, not that the question was ever likely to arise.

'Not even Dr Trevelyan,' Mollie answered without a flicker of doubt.

Of course it was easy for Mollie to turn her back on love, she had brains, knew exactly where her future lay. If only I could be a bit more like that, thought Charity with a despondent sigh.

'Anyway,' Mollie went on, 'what I really came in to tell you is that I won't be seeing you over the weekend. I'm ever so sorry, but Mum and Dad are taking me to Southend as a treat for winning the scholarship.'

'Oh that's nice.' Charity tried hard to sound pleased but she was betrayed by her glum expression.

'But it means you can go to the fair with Danny instead, doesn't it? You said he'd asked you.'

'I haven't seen Danny all week. Anyway he'll probably

take May Potter. And she's welcome to him,' Charity added, hiding her desolation behind a brave toss of the head.

'Oh, I feel I've let you down now.'

'Idiot, of course you haven't. That doesn't mean I don't envy you going to the seaside, I've never been. So see you enjoy yourself, then come back and tell me all about it.'

'Not only that, I'll send you a picture postcard of Southend Pier.' Mollie consulted the fob watch pinned to her blouse. 'Oh lor' is that the time, I'll be in for it if I'm late. Still, I'm giving in my notice this morning and I'm really looking forward to that.' She departed in her usual great dash of energy, tearing off down the road, in too much of a hurry to notice the girl walking towards the shop from the opposite direction.

'Hello love, you're a stranger.'

Charity, who was in the process of tipping the day's float into the till and sorting copper from silver, looked up. 'Kate!' she exclaimed, then felt a slight twinge of guilt. She would never forget Kate's small kindnesses towards her as a child, but because of her fondess for Agnes Weston her loyalties had become divided and she'd begun to adopt the same attitude as Danny, half blaming Kate for Jim Weston's violence towards his wife. 'It's a long time since I saw you too,' she went on, turning pink at her lie. For of late she'd taken to avoiding her old friend if she could, diving down a side street if she saw her coming.

But if Kate was aware of her changed attitude, she didn't let on. 'Well never mind, eh. Let's 'ave a look at some of your 'at trimmings. Got to look me best over the holiday. Who knows I might meet m' prince charming and 'e'll take me away from all this.' Kate laughed at the sheer unlikelihood of it.

'I've got just what you want. Stuff that only came in yesterday and if you went up West you wouldn't get anything more fashionable.' Adopting a businesslike manner, Charity drew out a tray of curled ostrich feathers and aigrette plumes and laid it on the counter for Kate to inspect. Then, because Kate was inclined to gild the lily and could easily be seduced into profligacy, out came ribbons in soft summer colours of moss green, Eau-de-nil and rose. Lastly, and all tumbled together like a meadow of wild flowers, was a tray of artificial shirley poppies, cowslips, daisies and cornflowers.

'The fashion's for elaborately-adorned hats this year,' Charity advised, then seeing how short-sightedly Kate peered into each tray added, 'You really ought to have some spectacles, you know, Kate.'

'Spectacles? In my job? Give over, duckie. I'd look like a bleedin' school mistress. Mind you some of them might like that, although I don't cater for perverts, I pack 'em off somewhere else. And at least not seein' so good means you're spared knowing what ugly mugs some of those punters out there 'ave.'

Just thinking about what Kate did with men made Charity feel sick, and she was about to urge her, as she did periodically, to give it all up, when Stephen Trevelyan walked through the door. Lifting his hat, he bade them both good morning.

'Here's just the person, Kate. Ask Dr Trevelyan to have a look at your eyes.'

Kate looked cornered. 'Oh no I couldn't do that. How much are these?' She grabbed some artificial forget-me-nots and ostrich feathers and waved them under Charity's nose.

Charity did a quick calculation. 'One and six.'

Kate slapped the money down on the counter. 'Right, must be going. Ta-ra love.' She lifted her hand in a salute and was gone.

'Well what was that all about? I didn't realize I was quite so terrifying.'

'I've told Kate she needs to have her eyes looked at, but she won't.'

'I would have thought it was in most people's interests to have their eyesight corrected. What does she do for a living?'

'Uhmm . . .' Discomfited, Charity hesitated. What did she say? Kate's a whore, a prostitute? No she couldn't, it wouldn't seem proper somehow to a gentleman like the doctor. So, neatly sidestepping the question, she answered, 'She works for the Grimbolds.'

Stephen needed no further explanation. He'd only been in the district a short while, but the Grimbolds were notorious enough for him to know their line of business. And from there, guessing the girl's calling was the simplest of deductions. Done for already, he thought, and her life hardly started. It wasn't right. 'Poor creature.' His voice conveyed a genuine compassion.

'Yes, they're bad news to anyone,' Charity replied wondering what he would make of her own history, that is, if he didn't know it already.

'Anyway, I mustn't waste any more of your valuable time. Tell me, how's the patient this morning?'

'Not as well as she thinks she is but it's hard for me to keep her in bed. She thinks she ought to be up. Don't you Aunt Eliza?' asked Charity, opening the door so that the doctor could pass through into the back room.

'It's stupid to be lying here when it's obvious to anyone I'm perfectly all right.'

'Just let me take your temperature,' said Stephen and put paid to her grumbles by popping a thermometer under her tongue. 'It's up a bit. A day or two's rest over the holiday would do you no harm, Miss Pumfrey. And your niece appears capable enough of looking after you and the shop.'

'I'm not questioning Charity's capabilities, Dr Trevelyan. I just don't care to be idle.'

A hesitant knock interrupted their conversation and Charity went over to the door and opened it.

Danny, looking unusually awkward, stood there, a posy of violets in his calloused workman's hand. 'Nobody

124

seemed to hear the bell and I've bin waitin' in the shop for some while, so . . .' His voice tailed away when he saw Stephen.

Trying to gauge the relationship between them, Stephen watched the effect the young man's presence had on Charity, and saw, with a jolt of disappointment, a glow illuminate her face.

'I brought these for you.' Danny thrust the posy at Charity. It was her turn to be embarrassed now and, to hide it, she buried her nose in the modest flowers.

'I saw Mollie just now, an' she said you might have good news for me about the fair an' I was to pop round.'

'Did she?' Charity was now gazing up at Danny with such a look of transparent happiness, Stephen had to swallow his envy.

Aware that Stephen was watching them and discomfited by his interest, Charity pushed Danny back into the shop. 'Let's talk in there,' she said and as the door closed firmly behind them, Eliza sighed.

'Poor Charity, she hasn't yet learnt how to handle her emotions. And women are often fools where love is concerned, men knaves.'

'That's a cynical view of the world, Miss Pumfrey.'

'Perhaps because the world has made me that way,' she answered enigmatically. 'But wouldn't you agree that women are often misused by men?'

'Yes, I'm afraid they are.'

'So I'm right, then?'

'Not entirely, we're not all complete cads, you know and plenty of women behave badly, too.'

Miss Pumfrey scrutinized him with some interest as he packed his instruments away, then asked bluntly, 'Are you married, Dr Trevelyan?'

'No, I am not.'

'No fiancée?'

'Not as yet,' he answered, amused by her interrogation and thinking of Blanche. Did he want anything to come of their relationship or not, he wondered. He wasn't wildly in love with her, but then he'd never experienced that intoxication of the senses, that sweet fervour. In fact he'd rather cynically come to doubt its existence until he saw Charity's ecstatic, almost mystical expression as she gazed upon her beloved, saw how her whole being was focused on Danny to the exclusion of anyone else. The world could have stopped spinning and she would neither have cared nor noticed.

Stephen gave a melancholy sigh. He had to admit there was something enviable about being able to arouse such intense emotions in a woman. Blanche certainly didn't nurse similar feelings for him, nor would she ever look at him in that uncritical, adoring way. Still, she was intelligent and handsome, too intelligent and handsome to settle for the life of a Doctor's wife in a south London slum. Marriage to her would carry with it certain conditions: a fashionable practice in either Harley Street or Hanover Square treating rich, spoilt women suffering in the main from nothing but want of occupation. As a career it would offer high financial rewards, and make no emotional demands on him at all.

Realizing that while he'd been pondering on his future, his patient had been speaking to him, he gave himself a mental shake. 'I'm sorry, what were you saying, Miss Pumfrey?'

'Charity told me you've offered to take our latest refugee off our hands. I'd be most grateful if you would. Feeding them all can get to be something of an expense.'

'Oh yes, Whisky. When would you like me to collect him? I'm away for the weekend and not back until next Tuesday.'

Eliza was a shrewd judge of character and it hadn't taken her long to decide she liked the young doctor. She also wanted the best for Charity, and although subterfuge went completely against her straightforward nature, she was prepared to resort to a little scheming, if it took Charity's mind off Danny. In her opinion Stephen

Trevelyan was the best, top drawer and of sound character. Even better, he was unattached and there was no harm in aiming high.

She thought of having a relapse, then decided it would rouse his suspicions after she'd insisted she was perfectly fit, and the last thing she wanted was to frighten the young man away. But the kitten, now that was another matter. His health could give rise to concern for a week or even two, with no trouble at all. The perfect excuse, she thought, and her mouth curled in a slight smile at the cleverness of her scheme.

'Well, why don't you come and have a last look at me then, and pick Whisky up at the same time,' Eliza suggested. 'If he's fit enough, of course,' she added slyly.

Innocently unaware of the plans Miss Pumfrey was making on his behalf, Stephen agreed to this suggestion. Then, after delivering a final warning to take things easy over the weekend, he departed, letting himself out through the shop.

Charity didn't see him as he passed, didn't even acknowledge his goodbye, and although Stephen wouldn't admit to jealousy he still felt slighted. Danny was a handsome young blighter, there was no denying it, but Stephen wasn't used to being ignored by women and his vanity was grazed. Which was stupid because after all what was she? A barely-educated, waterside girl with above average looks. And probably with no ambition in life other than to marry her young man at the earliest possible opportunity. Mollie, plain but intelligent and unfortunately going off to college, obviously had far more about her.

Castigating himself for sour grapes, Stephen made his way to his next call, one he would have been making with Dr Campbell if his hangover hadn't kept him in bed.

The house was down an alleyway; rank, dark and narrow. Leprous-looking walls ran with a green slime, a few anaemic, stunted children played in the dirt, and some straggly chickens pecked at God knows what. A girl of about seven answered his knock. She was barefoot, her nose was encrusted with snot, her skinny frame covered in flea bites, and she wore an expression of deep suspicion. Behind her stood several more brothers and sisters in an equally sorry state and with the same look of mistrust on their young faces.

It was unprofessional of him he knew, but Stephen was still new enough to medicine to feel a mixture of horror, pity and although he hated admitting it, disgust, too, at the sight of these scrofulous children. I should be getting hardened to it, he told himself, gave them what he hoped was a reassuring smile and said, 'I'm Dr Trevelyan, I've come to see how your ma is.'

The girl appeared to have been struck dumb but she did open the door and she and her siblings all shuffled back against the wall and allowed him to enter. The room he stepped into was small and stuffy, the only furniture some orange boxes upturned on a bare floor. Bluebottles buzzed against an uncurtained window, and wallpaper hung from the wall like peeling skin. Resisting the urge to scratch himself, Stephen walked over to a rickety iron bedstead where an emaciated woman of probably no more than thirty lay under one filthy blanket.

'Good morning, Mrs Pike. And how are you this morning?' It was a stupid question to a woman in an advanced state of consumption, Stephen knew that, but it was his job as a doctor to maintain a cheerful countenance and keep up the awful pretence that patients would get better.

The woman's reply was to cough as if her lungs were being dragged from her. To ease her suffering, Stephen gently lifted her to a sitting position and exchanged the stained, filthy rag she was spitting blood into for a clean one.

'I really think we should try and get you into a hospital, you know, Mrs Pike.'

'Don't waste your time. I've already told Dr Campbell

128

I ain't going,' the woman wheezed when she'd got a little breath back in her ruined lungs.

'Why not? You need proper care if you are to recover.' He was lying. There was no treatment that was going to make Mrs Pike better. But Stephen felt the least he could do was see that she was eased into death in a clean bed, in relative comfort and attended by a nurse.

'Why not, you ask? Well who's going to look after me kids for a start. While I've got breath in me body they ain't going in no workhouse. I was brought up in one, I know what bleedin' awful places they are. They beat you so bad you can count yerself lucky if you come out alive from some of them.'

'What about your husband? Surely he would see to things.'

'Oh 'e buggered off didn't 'e. Couldn't take no more of it.'

Some men, thought Stephen in disgust, but continued to try to talk her into a spell in hospital, lying that if the children had to go into the workhouse it would only be as a temporary measure until she was better. He felt he was just beginning to persuade her when he heard a snuffling noise. Turning, he saw the five children lined up in a row behind him. None of them had spoken one word but all of them were crying, silently, their tears leaving a clean white trail down their filthy cheeks.

Stephen felt an unmanly constriction in his throat. Dear God, what was he thinking of, trying to separate a mother from her children. After all, what did they have but each other and there was very little time left for them as a family as it was. Defeated, he pushed two florins into the eldest child's hand, and she stood staring in disbelief at the coins lying there in her palm. 'Get your ma something tasty to eat,' he said then turned back to the mother.

'I'm leaving you some linctus to take, Mrs Pike. I shall also arrange for the District Nurse to call in, and I'll come and see you again myself on Tuesday.'

The children were gawping at him through the window

as he left and Stephen knew he'd never make a living as a doctor if he continued to dish out money to the needy and not taking a fee. Mrs Pike and her family were just one in the long list of hopeless and depressing cases he came across daily, and although he was deeply committed to his work, Stephen rarely found much to be optimistic about. But he didn't want to be defeated by the conditions like Doctor Campbell and take to the bottle.

Dr Campbell and his father had been medical students together and when at the end of his own training, he had offered Stephen a post as his assistant, Stephen had been quick to accept. It hadn't taken long to discover the extent of the other man's 'problem' and although he knew he was needed here, at the same time he often felt trapped and see-sawed between wanting to leave and staying. For if he left, who would care for these people? Certainly no doctor with ambition would linger long in Rotherhithe. There wasn't much of a living to be made here and the only rewards were hard work and grindingly long hours.

Still he'd come here full of idealistic plans, with the idea of eliminating diseases like enteric fever, typhus and diphtheria, through hygiene and education. But what the people needed, he soon realized, was a better diet and housing and there was little he could do about that. What he could do something about, though, was family limitation. He was determined to help women reduce the size of their families, although he realized that as a man, discussing the various methods of contraception with them would require a great deal of delicacy and tact.

Stephen knew he was no more deserving of his good fortune than his patients were of their many misfortunes. Nevertheless, by the end of that day, he was grateful he had the weekend to look forward to. He could see himself sinking into a morass of despair otherwise. I need to get away, put all this misery behind me for a little while, he thought, when he'd made his last call, then suffered a pang of guilt. But he couldn't deny he relished the idea of getting into a four-wheeler and driving to his uncle's

house in Harley Street. Hardly eight miles from Rotherhithe but a world away in style of life. There he would
enjoy the luxury of a leisurely bath, after which he would
change into evening clothes. From then on it would be
an evening of enjoyment and laughter, a box at the theatre
with Blanche, his cousin Emma and a few close friends,
followed by supper at Rules. On Sunday a ride in Hyde
Park would probably be suggested and if the weather
held, on Monday they might take a picnic and go boating
on the river. As Stephen started packing a valise he
idly wondered how Charity would spend her weekend.
Certainly it would be in the company of that young
man, Danny.

Chapter 11

Charity had been taken aback by the last minute change
of plan, and none too pleased. Dragging her along the
street towards Old Swan Pier, Danny had explained how
they would go to the fair afterwards but it was really
important for him to see the race for Doggett's Coat and
Badge. He never missed it and it would be starting pretty
soon so they'd better get a move on.

But Charity was hardly won over by his argument. On
today of all days, the last thing she wanted to be doing
was watch six hulking young men scull up to Chelsea.
But if Danny noticed her disappointment he didn't let
on, and Charity didn't have the courage to protest. Their
relationship was too new, too fragile for that. And more
than anything in the world she wanted to be with Danny.
She tried to remember, too, that being an apprenticed
lighterman and waterman meant Danny must have hopes
of eventually entering the race himself.

It was a bit of a crush but now that she was here on
the small steamer with Danny's arm round her waist, her
head leaning back against his shoulder, Charity decided

it didn't seem so bad. The crowd was good natured, the atmosphere lighthearted. Along with everyone else Danny had placed a bet and riverside families being close-knit and large, each participant was sure of getting plenty of support. Each area had its own champion and each boy wore his own distinctive colours. Anyone with a claim to kinship – parents, grandparents, uncles, aunts, cousins, half cousins – was waiting to follow the race in boats. Other spectators were spread out across London Bridge or standing on the wharves waiting to bellow encouragement to their favourite. Passions could run high but it was still a rather more sedate, closely controlled affair than it had been in past. Nowadays Charity knew it was unlikely if the favourite was dropping behind, that the progress up river of the other contestants would be deliberately obstructed by a boat running athwart them. There was still a slight chance of a fractured skull from an empty beer barrel being thrown, but by and large the main hazard for the competitors was other river traffic. The swell caused by tugs could sink them and there was always the danger of being dragged under the paddles of a steamer.

'Only two years to go then I'll be in one of them boats,' Danny prophesied as they watched the rowers, who had already drawn lots for their positions, take up their stations on the river.

'There's only six can race so you've got to be pretty good.' Charity reminded him.

'I've watched some of them competing in the heats and with these muscles, I tell you, there's none of 'em a patch on me. I could beat any one of them puny lot hands down,' said Danny derisively. He flexed his arm for Charity's benefit. 'Feel them.'

Obligingly Charity pressed the bulge under his jacket.

'Harder, it won't hurt me,' Danny urged because although it in no way dented his confidence, he was secretly astonished that Charity should doubt his abilities. Didn't she know he was considered one of the best apprentices on the river. He'd watched the race for

132

Doggett's Coat and Badge since he was a nipper and, realizing pretty quickly it was often the same families who won, he'd sworn to himself that one day the name Weston would appear on the roll of honour. He knew all about the history of the race, too, how some actor called Doggett way back in the previous century had started it to commemorate George I coming to the throne. The ten pound money prize wasn't to be sniffed at but what Danny wanted, like he wanted nothing else, was to win the coveted red coat and to feel the weight of the silver badge on his arm. But like the proud young men racing today, he'd only get one chance to test his strength and skill over the gruelling four-and-a-half-mile course, and that would be in the year after he became a freeman.

The six scullers were now ready. 'Keep yer fingers crossed, my money's on Pearce,' said Danny in Charity's ear. A hush fell then the Fishmongers Company bargemaster lowered the starting flag and they were off to excited screams of, 'Go to it! Go to it!' from family and friends.

Along with the flotilla of small boats, a barge full of past winners in their red coats and with the heavy silver badges proudly displayed on their arms, were also following the race. Needless to say, everyone in the barge was trying to yell advice to the contestants, much of it conflicting.

Most of it was drowned out anyway by the sound of a brass band and Charity turned to see where the noise was coming from. 'Look,' she said to Danny and they both burst out laughing. For following close behind the rowers was a tug towing a barge. Placed inside the barge's hold was a disused tram and sitting on top of it was the band. This slightly incongruous sight brought a rousing cheer from the crowd and the bandsmen responded with a vigorous but slightly off-key rendering of 'See the Conquering Hero Comes,' blowing so hard the buttons nearly flew off their jackets.

But all Danny's attention was now being given to the

race. With all the bridges and river traffic to be negotiated between here and Chelsea, this race was a real test of a young Waterman's knowledge of the sets of the tide and Danny watched their tactics closely. To begin with, he noticed, they kept to the centre of the river to take full advantage of the current. But a southerly wind prevailed today and he was pleased to see that the leading sculler was doing what he would have done, seeking protection under the warehouses on the south shore before taking the third span of Blackfriars Bridge.

All along the waterfront, wherever there was space, crowds of spectators stopped to cheer them on their way. On bridges drivers of omnibuses, in a rare display of benevolence, paused to give passengers a chance to get a better look. At St Thomas's, nurses and doctors had come out to wave to them and on the terrace of the House of Commons a fair crowd was gathered too.

'They'll be Members of Parliament,' said Danny knowledgeably.

'Is that so?' Impressed, Charity waved to them. 'Do you think the Prime Minister is there?'

'Probably,' answered Danny, thinking to himself, soon it'll be me those bigwigs are waving to and it made him feel really proud. All at once he felt an intense, undiluted happiness. For a few fleeting moments the world seemed a perfect place. But that could have been because Charity's hair, loosened by the breeze, brushed his face like golden strands of silk and he could smell it, freshly washed, in his nostrils. Her back was to him but she was moulded into the curve of his body, and he thought with amazement, I think I love this girl, then reprimanded himself severely. Stop thinking such daft things, Danny Weston, or before you know it, you'll open yer mouth, gab it all out and really make a fool of yerself.

'Not far now,' Danny said as the tug went under Vauxhall Bridge. 'And Pearce could win.' This was the last long haul before Chelsea Bridge and he could feel for the scullers now, could imagine how their lungs were near to bursting, every muscle throbbing, sweat running into their eyes, hands raw, minds dazed. And as the oars dipped in and out of the water, over and over they would be repeating to themselves, keep going, nearly there, nearly there, must finish the course.

Danny had let go of Charity and was concentrating intently now, willing Pearce to win. There was a tremendous tension in the air and the blood rushed in his ears. Pearce was out in front, the prize was in his grasp and Danny could already feel his winnings in his pocket. He put his hands to his mouth. 'Go to it, Pearce, go to it!' he bawled but by now everyone with a wager was shouting themselves hoarse too. Even Charity, caught up in the tension and thrill of the race, was yelling for Pearce to win.

Egged on by his excited followers and calling up every last ounce of energy, Pearce of Hammersmith swept first past the winning post where the Watermen's Company flag fluttered.

The cheers rose to a crescendo. 'He's won! he's won! Yippee!' Danny punched his fists in the air. 'See you brought me good luck.' Elated he grabbed Charity round the waist, lifted her up and swung her round.

'My hat, Danny, I'll lose it,' she laughed.

''ow about this instead then?' he asked and, setting her down, kissed her firmly on the lips. Charity closed her eyes to accept the kiss but when she opened them and saw over Danny's shoulder that they were being observed with amused tolerance by the crowd, her cheeks turned as scarlet as the ribbons on her boater.

His exhaustion forgotten, Pearce was waving jubilantly to his supporters. But close behind, the bodies of the defeated sagged and their heads slumped forward on their chests. This had been their one and only chance to enjoy a brief glory and they'd messed it up. Too tired to wonder why now, a postmortem on strategy would be conducted in their heads and with friends and advisers for weeks to come.

Charity had never been this far up river before and she was struck by the elegance and prosperity of Chelsea. There were no crumbling jerry-built houses crushed together in foul-smelling alleys here, at least not on the river's edge. She would like to have disembarked and promenaded up and down the embankment with its avenue of fine trees. To have taken a closer look at the large houses, to try and imagine what it would be like to have all that room, with servants at your beck and call pandering to every whim. But the small boat was already turning round and Danny all smiles took her hand. 'As soon as we get back we'll collect our winnings, then you and me are going to paint the town red.'

'Come on, take your choice, they're all of 'em thorough-breds.' Flat-capped, wiping his oil-stained hands on a rag, the showman, in competition with all the other noises of the fairground, bellowed out his invitation, treating his audience to a view of the interior of his mouth and his teeth, large and yellow and equine looking.

The sensations came at Charity from all sides. Dizzying swirling colours. The smell of hot oil, gingerbread and humbugs in her nostrils. The tinny sound of organ music, high girlish screams and the hiss of steam, all these things pumped her blood into a high state of excitement and put a blush on her cheeks. Like a greedy child she wanted to sample all the goodies, to have her fortune told, shy balls at coconuts, see the fattest woman in the world, watch a man swallow fire and take pot shots at cut-outs of politicians in the shooting gallery. For the moment, though, her sights were set on the beautifully carved and painted galloping horses suspended from their golden, barley-sugar poles.

Taking up the showman's offer, she pulled Danny towards the carousel. 'Come on, let's have a go,' she urged then without waiting for him, jumped on to the platform and pulled herself up on the back of a horse.

Paying the man, Danny followed. It was then, high

136

above the ground and with a sense of dismay, that she saw Boscoe Hobbs and May Potter, grinning and waving at them from the crowd.

'D'you see who it is,' said Danny waving back and obviously pleased to see friendly faces.

'Yeah, I see all right,' Charity retorted, gazing over their heads with a deliberately distant expression. She had nothing but loathing for Boscoe Hobbs, but it was a bit more complicated with May. She tried to tell herself she disapproved of May because she was fast, but the truth was she was jealous. Danny swore May was Boscoe's girl but Charity wasn't so sure. His denials of any involvement were a bit too emphatic.

Now, if he noticed a lack of warmth in her manner, Danny didn't let on. Instead, beckoning them, he called out, 'Hey come on, have a go, there's two gallopers here free next to us.'

This was all the encouragement the pair of them needed. Scrambling up on to the roundabout, they seated themselves on two horses immediately behind Charity and Danny.

'Arright Charity, are you?' It was May Potter's voice, sly and ingratiating.

'Yes thank you,' Charity answered coolly, hoping her rigid back conveyed to May the message that she had no wish to enter into a conversation or spend any time in her company.

'Hey, what about you an' me 'aving a go at testing our strength on the Striker after this?' Boscoe called to Danny.

'Yeah, why not,' Danny answered casually.

Seemingly unaware that he'd cast a pall over her evening's pleasure, Charity shot him furious glance. They might be friends of his but she certainly had no wish to be lumbered with such a charmless pair for a whole evening. For two pins she'd jump down and march off, making it clear he had a choice, either them or her. But she was spared knowing Danny's true preference by the noise of the music starting up.

There was a rush of wind in her ears as the carousel gathered speed. Faster and faster it went, the faces of the crowd becoming a blur, the gallopers dipping and rising, dipping and rising until, to her horror Charity felt herself slipping sideways. Clinging to the pole she hung on for dear life, certain she was about to be flung into the watching crowd. Behind her she could hear May laughing, at her, she felt certain, and humiliation was added to her terror. Closing her eyes she hung on grimly. But when Danny shouted, 'Hey, are you all right,' she opened her eyes, smiled wanly and shouted back, 'Yes fine.' But it seemed to Charity that she would be forced to go riding round and round on the carousel until domesday. When after what felt like an eternity it did slow down and come to a stop, her head was still spinning, her muscles had liquified and she was in the embarrassing situation of not being able to move. For she knew once she did, her legs would give way under her, and flat on her behind it would be impossible to maintain a superior attitude towards May Potter.

Fortunately Danny sensing her plight came to her rescue. 'You're not all right, are you?' he said, his voice full of concern and slipping an arm round her waist he helped her to the ground.

'No,' she admitted, 'I'm not. It was awful Danny, I really thought I was going to fall off,' she confessed, fighting back her tears.

'Don't worry, you're quite safe now, I'm here to take care of you,' he said, gently taking her in his arms. And, leaning weakly against him, her face pressed against his shoulder, Charity's recovery was greatly assisted by the sight of May stomping off.

'Are you coming then, Boscoe?' she called out in a huffy voice, and, watching her, Charity's eyes gleamed with triumph, as envy was evident in every step she took.

'But Danny an' me, we were gonna have a go on the Striker,' Boscoe protested. Nevertheless, to Charity's relief, he trailed off after her.

'I hope that's the last we see of those two.'

Danny released her, holding her away from him. 'Why, what've you got against 'em?'

'Do you want me to make a list? Mind you it might take a long time.'

'But Boscoe's a good mate of mine. And we're bound to bump into 'em again. The fair's not that big. So what am I supposed to say to him?' Danny spread his hands in a helpless gesture. "Sorry, I don't want to know you tonight." It would look good, wouldn't it? Anyway I reckon a foursome can have a lot of fun together.'

A suspicion was beginning to grow in Charity's mind that their meeting had not been entirely accidental. 'Did you arrange to see them here?'

'No.' He shook his head.

Charity had to believe him. If she didn't it would cast doubts on his feelings for her. Because surely, she reasoned, if you cared about someone you wanted to spend every waking moment with them. Well, she did anyway.

She still felt tempted to test his feelings, to force him into making a choice, but she wasn't sure enough of him. And with a bit of luck they wouldn't see the pair again. Besides, why give those two the pleasure of knowing they'd ruined her evening.

Danny took her arm. 'Come on, let's go and enjoy ourselves,' he said and pulled her towards the coconut shy.

'Roll up, penny a shot,' the showman bawled and Danny handed him sixpence.

'Watch this,' he said and spat on his hands. 'I'm going to win a coconut for you.'

But the promise of a coconut was of secondary importance. To Danny it was all a question of masculine pride. He wanted to impress Charity with the accuracy of his aim and the power in his shoulders, so when, after several goes, he'd still failed to knock one from its stand, he became surly. 'I've hit six of them bloody coconuts and they ain't budged an inch. I reckon they're glued in.'

'You're asking for a punch in the gob mate, making accusations like that,' said the showman moving close to Danny and glaring at him in a threatening manner.

There was nothing more terrifying than his father drunk and Danny had learnt to stand up to *him*. It had been a lesson taught by blows, but at least few people could intimidate him now. So even though the man was a bruiser with a shaven head, thick neck and tattoos down his arm, Danny refused to budge an inch. 'Prove it then, take one out, let me see you.'

'Yeah, go on,' said several other people who had gathered round.

Seeing things could be blowing up to a serious fight, Charity dragged on Danny's arm. 'Come on Danny, I don't want a coconut, I don't even like them so it's not worth arguing about. Just let's clear off out of here.'

'All right.' And to the bitter disappointment of the crowd and Charity's surprise, Danny allowed himself to be pulled away. Tonight he had no taste for a fight. A black eye or bloodied nose might arouse Charity's compassion but not her passion and he had plans for later on.

'I could have given him one, you know.' Already regretting his docility, Danny shadow boxed, fists bunched, springing around on his toes like a prize fighter.

'I'm sure you could, Danny,' answered Charity, happy to massage his pride now that she had extricated him from a dangerous situation. 'But can't we forget that and have something to eat? I'm starving, and there's a stall over there.'

When they reached the stall, Charity uhmmed and aahed for so long about whether to have shrimps, mussels, or jellied eels, the man grew impatient.

'Come on gel, make up your mind, I ain't got all night,' he complained. So, forced into a decision, Charity had the same as Danny; cockles with a hunk of bread and a glass of sarsaparilla.

She had just sprinkled her dish liberally with vinegar,

was lifting a cockle to her mouth and already anticipating its gritty, slightly rubbery texture, its hint of the sea, when she saw Boscoe and May approaching.

'You two again. What a coincidence,' said May with a smirk.

'Yes isn't it,' Charity answered in a haughty tone. She wondered why she couldn't feel more kindly disposed towards the girl and decided it must be a defect in her own character. She realised, with a touch of shame, that because May had so little to commend her, she was more a creature to pity than dislike. Scrawny, short-changed on looks, she loved to adorn herself with cheap gee-gaws and today she was decked out in dangly earrings made of green glass and a tawdry red dress with too many flounces. She was both brazen and silly and her one asset was her easy availability which men exploited ruthlessly, for she hadn't even the intelligence to charge for her favours. But then I don't know anything about her background, Charity thought, so perhaps I shouldn't make judgements. Perhaps she's just desperate for love in whatever form it came.

'If you're expectin' me to buy you somefink to eat, May, think again. You wanted to go on everyfink, well you did and now I'm skint.' Boscoe rolled the cigarette butt he was never without from one side of his mouth to the other and gave May time to think about this.

Not at all put out, May turned to Danny with a beguiling smile, although the effect was somewhat diminished by a missing tooth. 'You'll buy me a dish of jellied eels, won't you, Danny boy?'

'Buy your own,' Danny answered rudely, through a mouthful of bread.

He made no effort to hide his contempt for the girl and, seeing her face fall, Charity's antipathy immediately dissolved. Digging into her purse she handed May a sixpence. 'Here, treat yourself.'

May examined the money with an expression bordering on astonishment. 'Well that's very kind of you I'm sure.'

141

'What about me?'

Charity turned to Boscoe. 'What about you?' Her tone was frosty. She had a long memory and even if he had forgotten his spitefulness to her as a small girl, she hadn't.

'Got a few coppers to spare for me?' Making a joke of it he held out his hand with a snigger.

'Sorry, no,' she answered briefly.

'Here, Boscoe, have this, two and a kick, but see you pay me back at the end of the week.' Flush from his winnings, Danny flicked him a half crown, which Boscoe caught deftly and put in his pocket.

Watching the two of them talking together now, their voices lowered, Charity wondered, as she frequently did, why Danny wasted his time with Boscoe. As far as she was concerned he had nothing whatsoever to commend him. He was workshy, and in her opinion it was only a question of time before he felt a policeman's hand on his collar. Loyalty, that must be it, Charity thought. It was the only acceptable reason for their friendship.

Charity was finding it hard to maintain her earlier superior attitude towards May. As someone who'd been been at the receiving end of people's cruelty and scorn, she really ought to know better, she decided. Anxious now to expunge her guilt and make amends, she waited for May to finish her dish of jellied eels then said in an inviting tone, 'Shall we leave these two to find out who's the strongest and go and have our fortunes told?

May gave a squeal of excitement. 'Ooh yeah, let's,' she said and pressing her hands together she bounced up and down so energetically her earrings swung to and fro. The light caught the cheap glass and for a moment they flashed like rare emeralds.

The sign on the tent read, MADAME ARKADY, FORTUNE TELLER TO THE CROWNED HEADS OF EUROPE. TAROT CARDS OR PALMS READ. PRICE 3D.

But now that they were here, the girls didn't know what to do and they stood and giggled nervously. 'Would you like to go first, May?' offered Charity, whose nerve was now beginning to fail her.

'Not likely. It was your idea, you go.' May gave Charity a shove towards the tent just as the flap was flung back and a gipsyish sort of woman, all bangles, floating veils and fierce black eyes, stood before them.

Fixing her gaze on Charity she said, 'Now what eez it that is troubling you Marie? That eez your name, eez it not, *ma cherie?'*

Charity shook her head in dumb denial.

'I'm Marie,' May piped up, happy to lay claim to this foreign-sounding name.

Not in the least put out the woman turned to her. 'Come on in then Marie, you and your leetle friend, both at the same time, eef that is 'ow you would like it. Do not be afraid I will not, 'ow do you say, eat you.' She bared her teeth, looking for all the world as if she might, held back the flap and both girls edged uncertainly into the tent.

The interior, hung with the same gauzy material Madame Arkady was wearing, was dimly lit and smoky. 'Poo, what's that stink?' said May, wrinkling her nose and peering into the shadowy corners of the tent.

Charity's nervous giggle at May's want of tact was stopped in her throat by Madame Arkady's tigerish expression.

'Joss-sticks, *cherie*, to soothe thee soul,' she replied, then becoming practical, indicated to two gold-painted chairs. 'Sit down and before we start that'll be threepence each.' She held out her hand, settled herself comfortably and went on in a voice that was pure South London, 'Now 'oo's first.'

Charity felt a swift kick on her ankle. Suppressing a yell of pain she gave May a glare and answered, 'Me, please.'

'Cards or palm?'

'Cards please.'

'If you want the tarot cards that'll be a tanner.'

Enraged Charity stood up and pushed her chair back. 'Give us our money back. We're going.'

'Now 'old your horses love.' Madame Arkady seeing the loss of not one, but two customers, held up a placatory hand. 'Reading the cards takes a good half hour and before that I have to get myself in the right frame of mind, what's called meditate, so you can see I have to charge more. And palmistry tells you just as much. Put your hand on the table.'

Charity did as she was bid and the woman took it, stroking the palm gently. 'You have very nice hands, my dear. They show a sensitive nature and one which is easily hurt.'

Charity leaned forward. 'Do they?' In spite of her reservations she found herself growing interested.

Except for May's rather heavy nasal breathing it went very quiet as Madame Arkady studied her hand in more detail.

'Your life-line shows you had a troubled childhood. I see a mystery too, something connected with your birth, a loss perhaps.' Madame Arkady looked up for confirmation and Charity nodded her head, too astonished to speak.

'And your heart-line shows you must look out and not be too idealistic. Your ring of Solomon is very strong, which means you have a caring nature and you have marked healing lines. I also see travel ahead for you.'

'Where to?'

'It's not clear but certainly over water.'

'Across the river to Wapping is about as far as I'll ever get.'

'No, it will be over long distances.'

Finding this hard to believe, but not wishing to contradict the woman, Charity said instead, 'What about marriage, do you see that for me?'

'Most definitely. And I see something military here as well, so perhaps you will marry a soldier.'

'But I don't want to marry a soldier.' Charity protested.

'Probably you won't then. What you must realize my dear is that the hand can change. Now let me read your friend's, see if it's half as interesting as yours.'

She released Charity's hand and took May's. But whatever it was she said to the other girl, Charity didn't hear. Her mind was too full of what Madame Arkady had told her, and the word 'loss' in particular buzzed round and round in her head like a fly trapped in a bottle.

For that was what she'd felt so often as a child, an intolerable sense of loss. It would come to her just before she fell asleep, insubstantial like a dream, a yearning for something half remembered, fleeting. The sound of a soft voice, of loving arms lifting her up. Sobbing she would reach out in the darkness, longing to return to the warmth and security of that embrace.

Once she'd dared to ask Pearl Grimbold about her origins.

The woman had stared at her for a while with suspicious little eyes then said, 'Took you from the work'ouse, didn't we, out of the sheer bloody kindness of our 'earts.'

Over the years the half understood images had grown so dim they'd almost faded from her memory. Until today. Now Madame Arkady's words had drawn her back into that dream world, forced her to confront her past, left her with a compelling need to unravel the mystery of her birth.

When they finally left the tent May was chattering away umpteen to the dozen and there were two fairly impatient young men waiting for them.

'Do you know, I'm gonna 'ave two husbands, so you pair better watch out.' May gyrated her narrow hips in a provocative manner then giggled.

'Did it take 'alf an hour to tell you that?' asked Boscoe.

'Oh no, there were other things,' she added mysteriously.

'Such as?'

'None o' your business. And another thing you're all to call me Marie from now on.'

Boscoe sniggered. 'Whatever for?'

'Cos it sounds nicer than May, that's why. It's, I dunno . . . more posh.'

'You'll never be posh whatever you call yourself,' Boscoe sneered.

May didn't respond to his insults but Charity saw her hurt expression and it made her fume. How can she think so little of herself that she's willing to stand there and let that great oaf speak to her in such a way. Why doesn't she slap him round his fat chops and walk away. She was trying to think of a remark caustic enough to put Boscoe in his place, when Danny tugged on her hand.

'What did she say to you?' he asked.

'She said she's gonna marry a soldier.' May answered on her behalf, giving Danny a sly glance.

'Well, it's a load of bunkum ain't it, we all know that.'

'Why do you say that?' asked Charity hoping to provoke him.

'Well . . . eh . . . because you don't know any soldiers that's why,' Danny blustered.

'I admit I don't know any at the moment, but things change. There's your brother for instance, perhaps he'll come home from India soon.'

Danny looked thoroughly alarmed. 'You can't marry him.'

Charity laughed. 'Course I can't, I don't even know him.'

But it surprised Danny how jealous her remarks had made him feel. Peter was a handsome fella, and if he came home he could easily sweep Charity off her feet. Fortunately, he wasn't due back for another couple of years. But John often turned up out of the blue and he wasn't bad looking either. If he saw Charity he'd make a beeline for her and what girl would be able to resist a sailor who had money in his pockets and was willing to spend it. Feeling suddenly very possessive he grabbed

146

Charity's arm. 'Anyway, enough of this daft talk let's go and take a turn on something else.'

Although she made it perfectly clear by her disdainful manner that she didn't want his friendship, during the evening Boscoe made several attempts at ingratiating himself with her. But Charity refused to unbend. May was a different matter and she found herself warming to the girl, in fact, to her surprise, quite liking her. She could see she was foolish and not very bright, but she was cheerful and undemanding so when she nudged her and said out of the corner of her mouth, 'Danny'll do anyfink for you so ask him to take us on the switchback,' Charity was quite happy to oblige.

Charity decided she preferred the switchback to the carousel. She felt safer sitting in the gilded, elaborately-carved gondola. It was enclosed, intimate and she and Danny were alone together. It rose and fell like a ship at sea, tossing them about a bit, but this was fine because it meant Danny had to put his arm around her shoulder and hold her close.

By the time they got off the switchback it was growing dark. A mackerel sky was shot through with silver and every stall, booth and roundabout was illuminated with hundreds of electric lamps, their brilliance transforming the fairground's daylight shabbiness into something so magical they could only stare in silent wonder. Even Boscoe, gross and uncouth seemed affected by its beauty

'Gosh,' said May at last, 'I ain't never seen nuffink so pretty in me life.'

'Neither have I,' admitted Charity.

'I have,' Danny whispered in her ear. 'Shall we leave these two?' he asked, and without waiting for a reply took her hand and pulled her away.

'Hey where you off to?' Boscoe shouted after them. 'I thought you were goin' ter buy me a pint.'

'I'll buy you one tomorrow,' Danny called back over his shoulder.

Boscoe was so thick-skinned, Charity half expected him

to come in pursuit of them. She gave a quick look back to check but they were lost in the swirling holiday crowd out to have fun and in no mood to go home yet.

After the brilliance of the fair the darkness in the park seemed complete, although as her eyes adjusted, Charity saw that the night sky glittered with diamond bright stars. She also saw that they weren't alone, and that other couples had come seeking the anonymity of the park. There was a murmur of voices from park benches, the occasional giggle and protesting girlish squeal, then a girl's voice said sharply, 'You can just stop that!' and Charity felt glad that the darkness hid her blushes.

'Where we going Danny?' she asked after they'd covered some distance.

'To find somewhere quiet so I can put my arm round you very tight,' he replied.

His voice had changed, Charity noticed. It was thick, husky, and he was moving with some urgency, almost pulling her along behind him as if he hadn't a moment to spare. Guiding her to a large tree, he leant her against it and began to kiss her with a hungry urgency. Charity forced herself to relax, and slowly she found herself responding to the pressure of Danny's mouth. Tentatively her arms went up around his neck. 'Oh Charity, you're so lovely,' he murmured against her throat and she was aware of being pressed to the ground. But she had to fight back a protesting cry of 'No!' and because she loved him she tried not to go tense when he unbuttoned her dress, tried not to think that only loose girls like May allowed men to kiss their breasts. But then he was pulling at her skirt and his hands were sliding up her leg. Immediately that persistent image of a slack-skinned, naked man thrusting himself into one small helpless girl, rose up in front of her. Unable to suppress her revulsion a second longer, Charity squeezed her thighs tight together, making a fortress of her body. Pushing Danny's hand away, she struggled to sit up.

148

'Leave me alone, Danny . . . please.' Ashamed of her earlier abandon, she quickly buttoned her dress.

'Christ I ain't done anything yet, Charity. How can you torture me like this.' Danny's voice was reproachful.

To give herself time to think and regain her composure, Charity began tidying her hair. Filling her mouth with pins, she pulled the thick rope of hair down over her shoulder and twisted it round slightly trembling fingers. How did she say to Danny without scorching his manly pride that the thought of physical intimacy, even with him, revolted her. The coil of hair was now back firmly in place on the nape of her neck and her mouth was empty of pins and Danny was waiting for an answer. 'I don't like being touched in certain places, that's all. It . . . it makes me feel, I dunno, sort of unclean. Anyway it's wrong.'

'What's wrong about it? It's natural, for God's sake. You want to grow up, relax a bit, Charity. Life's for enjoying. If you hang on to it too long you'll be dead. But I don't like half-hearted givers, so if you don't want to, you don't want to.' His voice had taken on the sulky tone she'd become familiar with of late.

'Oh Danny, don't say that.' Fearful that she'd put their relationship in jeopardy again, she tried to pacify him. Stroking his face gently, she felt the slight roughness of stubble on his chin. 'If I let you do . . . that, I could have a baby. And would you marry me then?'

'I can't, you know that. Not until I finish me apprenticeship.'

'I see. So you don't care about my good name? It doesn't trouble you one bit that I might have a bastard child, just as long as you get what you want, is that it? And you've the nerve to feel hurt.' Outraged at his sheer selfishness, Charity sprung to her feet. She was done with humouring him. Brushing grass and twigs from her skirt, she said icily, 'Now if it's all the same to you I'd like to go home.'

Danny stood up as well. In the distance Charity could

hear laughter and music and above the fairground the night sky glowed. By comparison the park was all shadows, Danny's features a blur so she could only guess at his expression. However, the tone of his voice told her all she needed to know.

'Arright, if that's what you want.' Deliberately he turned and walked away, leaving her to follow.

Insulted beyond measure, Charity watched him in silent rage. How could he treat her like this? Her inclination was to yell after him, 'Go to the devil, Danny Weston!' but she knew she daren't let the evening end, as it so often seemed to, on a sour note. And maybe if she just told him, explained why she feared being touched, pleaded with him to be patient, perhaps it would all come right between them.

She didn't want to be seen to be giving in but the distance between them was growing. Soon he would be gone and she would be left on her own, and she was suddenly aware of eerie rustling noises. Forgetting her pride, Charity called out, 'Danny, wait,' and chased after him.

Danny didn't stop but he slowed down sufficiently to allow Charity to catch up with him. Panting, she tugged at his hand. 'Danny, why don't we talk to each other?' she pleaded, when she'd got her breath back. 'You know, discuss our feelings, try and be really close.'

'You're a typical woman, do you know that. You always want to talk about feelings.'

'What's wrong with that?'

Danny could hear the hurt in her voice and, relenting, he put his arm round her shoulder and pulled her close. 'Do you love me?'

'Yes,' she answered simply. 'I've loved you since that time you rescued me from Boscoe, do you remember?'

'As long as that?' Danny sounded impressed. 'What are you now, nearly eighteen? Then that must be six years?'

'And you?' Charity asked tentatively.

What could he say when his feelings were so confused. He didn't want to admit to love that was too final, but

Charity did affect him strongly, more strongly than any girl before. What he didn't want was to be anchored to her by marriage. Not for a long time anyway. But he liked the clean smell of her, her looks, the way she walked, her slight body, upright and proud. But most of all he wanted to have sex with her. And that was the big problem, the way she would hardly let him touch her. It was bloody frustrating and he wasn't used to it.

They were walking under lamplight now and Charity was looking up at him, her face tender, open, waiting for his answer. But he just couldn't say it, not that word 'love'. 'I do like you, Charity, better 'an any girl I know.' He meant every word of it too, but it wasn't enough and he could see he'd hurt her.

But Charity smiled a brave bright smile. 'So we're not finished then?'

''Course not, whatever made you think that?' Then, to lessen the pain, Danny bent and kissed her, murmuring against her mouth, 'Give me time, Charity, give me time.'

Chapter 12

So Charity gave Danny all the time he wanted and not a word of complaint passed her lips, even if she didn't see him for a week. And because he wouldn't allow her talk about her past, she turned more and more to her diary, finding herself filling the empty pages almost compulsively. The words poured out of her as she filled one exercise book then another, then another. Her anxieties, her pain, her memories were hurriedly scribbled down in no particular order. During any free moment in the shop she wrote. Sometimes she'd even wake in the middle of the night, light a candle and start again. Her diary became her confessional. Reams of stuff, some of it fairly incoherent, was committed to paper as she struggled to come to terms with her past.

Charity was surprised how much she remembered, because when she'd started her new life with Eliza, she had deliberately blocked out the most painful memories. Now she could recall every tiny detail, every cruelty in her childhood so vividly the tears would often roll down her cheeks and on to the page. With shaking hands, she wrote down in capital letters Bill Slawson's name and Lord Prendergast's, and wondered how many other small girls they had used for their perversions and whose lives they'd destroyed in the process.

Charity had decided that when she'd written down every single incident she could possibly remember, she would take the notebooks out into the garden and in a ritual cleansing, build a pyre and burn them. Only then would she be free of her past. But once she got into this habit of writing, it became something of an obsession and she found she couldn't stop. Other matters needed clarifying in her mind. Where she came from for instance; and she found herself recalling the fortune teller's words and got to thinking about before she was even born. After all, she'd been conceived, had a mother and father and somewhere, too, in the world there were people walking around who were cousins, uncles and aunts. And so it went on, something else would occur to her, more words would be scribbled down, and the diaries became so much part of her she couldn't bring herself to destroy them.

But in the end none of this helped to resolve her relationship with Danny and it remained as uncertain as ever, which suited Eliza just fine. Whisky was called to play his part, suffering several imaginary crises on his road to recovery, which prevented Stephen Trevelyan taking him away immediately. 'He doesn't look quite right,' she would say with a worried shake of her head, if it was suggested by Stephen he should take the kitten off her hands. After a month, though, even Eliza could no longer make a secret of the fact that the little cat, bright-eyed and mischievous, was in fine fettle and off he went to keep Stephen company at the surgery. However, she felt all was not wasted when several times she caught Stephen regarding Charity with a certain something in his eyes. Perhaps it was no more than the healthy interest of a normal young man in a pretty girl, but it was a start and with a little perseverance, Eliza felt, it could be built on.

In late September Mollie, already looking academic in a tailored tweed costume, left in a four-wheeler for Bedford College, taking with her a small trunk for her clothes and a large one for her books.

The parting between the two girls was emotional. 'Oh I will miss you Moll,' Charity sobbed.

This started Mollie off and the girls clung to each other vowing eternal friendship, and promising to write to each other every week without fail.

And indeed Charity missed Mollie and her lively mind more than she could have believed possible. And as the days passed there seemed little chance that Danny would fill the void left by her departure. Then one night he appeared out of the blue and asked if she fancied a drink.

Avoiding Liza's eyes, Charity mumbled 'yes' but she waited until they were sitting down in the pub before she said her piece.

'It's been a long time, Danny, since I last saw you.' Her reprimand was gentle enough but she could see he didn't care for it.

'I 'ave bin on nights you know,' he huffed, twisting his tankard of ale round on the table and avoiding her eye. 'Anyway I think it's better if we keep it casual like, then we're both free to do as we please. We'll still see each other, but not too regular if you see what I mean.'

'Yeah, I see what you mean.' The words were left unsaid, but Charity understood all right, she wasn't obliging enough. 'Anyway I'm going to be pretty busy myself from now on.'

'Oh, how's that?' Danny looked up showing some

interest now. She hadn't found herself another bloke, had she?

'Haven't I told you? I've joined an evening class.'

'Good for you.' There was relief in Danny's voice and a falling off of interest. Classes, they were a good idea, keep her occupied. For perish the thought that she should fall into the clutches of some other man. After all he still had first claim to her. She was his girl.

Until she'd said it, Charity had only toyed with the idea of classes. But the time had come to assert herself, she decided, so the very next day she enrolled at the local evening institute. And thereafter, once a week, she went along to learn about sick nursing. It was fairly basic stuff: how to disinfect a room, wash a patient, make a bed, take temperatures and treat bedsores. But she did learn something about the workings of her body and later amid much hilarity, the class was put to practising their bandaging skills on each other. At the end of the course they all received a certificate and Charity found she'd gained a Distinction. Proudly she carried it home to show Eliza and that night she wrote in her diary: *Perhaps, as the palmist said, I have got healing hands. Perhaps one day I'll get a chance to prove it and be able to use my skills.*

It was an idea that began to occupy Charity more and more. Sometimes she wondered what she was going to do with the rest of her life. And her restlessness and general sense of dissatisfaction was exacerbated by Mollie's letters, page after page filled with bold, large looped, handwriting, her joy in her new life leaping off the page. Vivid and hilarious, the ideas flowed effortlessly from Mollie's pen while her own letters went back, pale things in comparison. For what had she to write about when she did nothing but tend the shop all day. Mollie was gobbling up new experiences, mixing with people of high intellect and her horizons were expanding daily, while she herself seemed to be going nowhere. The perimeters of her life were Rotherhithe and an occasional night out with Danny, if she was lucky.

In November it rained incessantly and this depressed her even further. On the upper reaches of the Thames, in places like Windsor, there was serious flooding. The dreary weather showed no sign of letting up, it got light late and dark early and with the lowering clouds the interior of the shop was so gloomy Charity had to keep a lamp lit all day.

Business was poor, and there'd been no more than a trickle of custom that week. By four o'clock on the Thursday afternoon when things should have started picking up for the weekend, Charity hadn't had a single customer. She was beginning to think about closing, when to her dismay, Leonard Willis walked through the door.

He stood in the middle of the shop like a large black crow, a musty smell of old books emanating from his wet clothes, his pale eyes staring at her in that way of his, fixedly and unblinking. Charity shivered. She could feel it, a presentiment of evil; the chill of the day was as nothing compared with the icy fingers that squeezed at her heart, making it beat erratically.

What I mustn't do is encourage him, Charity thought, favour him with as much as a hint of a smile. Fighting an urge to back away, she kept her mouth pressed shut and her eyes cast down, seeing only his large, ponderous feet as he advanced towards her.

'F . . . for you,' Not the slightest bit put off by the lack of welcome, Leonard Willis pulled a book from his pocket and placed it on to the counter in front of Charity.

'I'm sorry, but I'm afraid I can't accept gifts.' Her voice was as expressionless as her eyes.

'Don't worry, my . . . my dear Miss Brown, it's nothing personal. Just a copy of the Good Book, in which all life's truths are contained. I've marked some passages for you to . . . to read.'

Charity was in a predicament. The Bible was something she would feel uneasy about rejecting no matter

155

how vague her beliefs. Realizing he was probably aware of this, her uncomplicated dislike burgeoned into a smouldering hatred.

In the same way, because he was a man of the cloth, she found it impossible to voice her true opinion of him and to her chagrin she even found herself mumbling a thanks for the unwanted gift. But she refused to pick it up and it lay there on the counter between them.

But although his breathing was a little uneven, as if under duress, Leonard Willis wasn't deterred by the hostility emanating from Charity. Rubbing the dry palms of his hands together he said in a fawning tone, 'You . . . you w . . . will read the text I've marked, won't you?'

Charity stared at him, her black, slanting eyes inscrutable and disdained to reply, but he stumbled on. 'Then p . . . perhaps you would like to come to one of . . . of our bible readings we have at the vicarage on . . . on Tuesday evenings.'

'I'm afraid I have another class that night. I'm taking a course on sick nursing.' The course had, in fact, finished but Charity had no problem lying to him.

'Well . . . well perhaps when your course i . . . is . . .' He couldn't go on. The sight of her small pink tongue had sent the blood rushing to his neck. But it was the silken texture of her skin and her mane of hair that transfixed him. Vibrant, alive, seeming to give off sparks, the lamplight had transformed it into a shining halo round her head. And that was what she was, his angel, his ideal, except that it was wicked to have carnal thoughts about celestial beings. Wicked to want to unpin the heavy knot at her neck, to see it falling like liquid gold on to her small naked breasts, to bury his face in it then to do other things to her, unmentionable things he daren't put a name to, to hurt her even. Tortured by these images, feeling his loins stir and that part of his body he couldn't control harden, Leonard Willis turned away. Wanting to scourge himself of such lustful thoughts, he cursed under his breath women's beauty and the way it made fools of men.

Wanton temptresses, she-devils, destroyers of a man's peace of mind, that's what they were, every one of them. 'Goo . . . good afternoon to you Miss Brown.' His voice was slurred and he stumbled like a drunk to the door. It was that girl's fault, not his, that he had to find relief immediately in the arms of a woman of the night. Her fault, too, that as a penance for the sin of fornication he would have to get the whore to flail him with a knotted leather whip. But as the thong cut deep into his skin, drawing blood but shuddering him to release, he knew it was Charity's face he would see, her name he would shout out, over and over again like a profanity.

Charity had watched Leonard Willis's grotesque behaviour, his spinsterish mouth working convulsively, his sweating face and staring eyes, with a kind of fascinated terror, thankful they had the counter between them. Certain he was sinking into some sort of madness, she'd managed to grab a pair of scissors and hide them in the fold of her dress, ready to protect herself if he went for her.

When he finally departed, still muttering, as if intoning a prayer, Charity's whole body sagged with relief. Swaying, she grabbed hold of the counter for support, closed her eyes and inhaled deeply. The sour, pious smell of him still lingered in the shop and she wrinkled her nose in disgust. But through the jumble of thoughts and fears one idea broke free and surfaced strongly; there was no doubt about it, Leonard Willis was unhinged and he should be locked up. And next time he came into the shop Eliza could serve him, because there was no way she was going to be put through an ordeal like that again.

It took time to compose herself and when she opened her eyes she found herself staring down at the bible, with its cheap black cardboard cover, and shuddered. Well he needn't think she was going to read it. She pulled open a large deep drawer. That was where it was going, right at the back, out of sight. She reached out to pick the book up but knowing Leonard Willis's dry hands had held it her fingers recoiled from touching it. Instead, gingerly, as if it might be contaminated, she edged the book towards the open drawer with a ruler. But she did it clumsily and it missed its target and landed face down and open on the floor. Forced to bend and pick it up, Charity saw that it lay open and was marked by a thin purple ribbon at Song of Solomon. Against her will her eyes were drawn to some verses underlined in red ink. '. . . behold, thou art fair, thou hast doves' eyes . . . thy lips are like a thread of scarlet, and thy speech is comely . . . thy two breasts are like two young roes that are twins . . . thou hast ravished my heart, my sister, my spouse . . .'

There was more, but she couldn't read on. Sickened and ready to burst into tears, the beauty and poetry of the words were lost to her. 'You disgusting old hypocrite,' she raged then in a great surge of revulsion, Charity brought her arm back and swinging it high, aimed the bible with remarkable accuracy at the second customer to walk through the door that afternoon.

'Hey what was that all about?' laughed Stephen Trevelyan, making a perfect catch like the good cricketer he was. Then, reading the gold lettering on the spine, exclaimed, 'Good heavens, the Bible. Now could this have anything to do with the Reverend Willis? I've just passed him, muttering away to himself and behaving a trifle oddly.'

Charity's reply was unequivocal. 'He's not just odd, his mind is warped. He should be locked away.' Her small face was stamped with an expression half fearful, half ferocious and quite unlike her normal demeanour.

'Why, what's he done?'

'I'd rather not talk about it.' In the blink of an eye her expression had changed and her face now wore a look of oriental impassivity.

'Now, throwing the Gospel at our vicar, well that can't be good for business,' Stephen said in an amused voice then, taking heed of the warning look in Charity's eyes, decided to shut up. It wasn't difficult to guess what the trouble had been though. Few men could be immune to Charity's beauty, even a creepy looking, desiccated specimen like Leonard Willis, although he marvelled at the man's vanity for even imagining he stood half a chance.

'I've had two customers this afternoon, one I could have done without. With the weather like it is there probably won't be any more so I'm going to close. I need a cup of tea, how about you?'

'Yes please. But I must admit I haven't come to buy anything. Before we go through, I want to ask you something. Don't look so wary,' Stephen said when he saw her guarded expression. 'I've got two tickets for the theatre and wonder if you'd like to come.'

Startled by Stephen's suggestion, Charity turned the key, shot the bolts on the door and pulled down the blind. She took so long over these tasks, Stephen thought she was going to refuse, which would have been galling. He hardly cared to admit it, but Stephen knew he was setting himself up in competition with Danny, felt jealous of the obvious hold he had over Charity and often angry at the careless manner in which he treated her. Showing a little interest would make that young man sit up. Eliza had helped plant the idea in his mind and wooing a girl of such beauty wouldn't be without its pleasures. He could offer her far more than Danny and if he pulled out all the stops, Charity wouldn't remain immune to his attentions for long.

When Charity turned back to face him her expression gave Stephen little cause for hope.

'Theatre? When?' she asked cautiously, for she'd never been to one of those in her life.

'On Friday evening to see *The Gondoliers*. It's an operetta by Gilbert and Sullivan.'

Irritated that he obviously felt the need to explain, Charity gave him a frosty look. 'Yes, I *do* know.'

There's a prickly one, Stephen thought.

'Anyway, I couldn't come, I've nothing to wear,'

Charity went on, pursuing her own line of thought.

'That must be the universal female cry. What's wrong with that pretty dress you were wearing the first time I saw you?'

Flattered in spite of herself, Charity's expression lost its aloofness. 'You rememeber that day, do you?'

'Vividly. Anyway you'd look nice in whatever you wore.'

'I still couldn't go.'

'Why not?'

'Danny wouldn't like it.'

'I see, you've arranged to go out with him.'

'Oh no, Danny goes out with his mates on Friday night. It's a regular thing.'

'In that case what is there to stop you coming out with me. Is he your keeper or something?'

'No,' she answered defensively, 'it's just that . . .'

'It's just that he can do as he pleases but you can't. Remember, what's sauce for the goose . . .'

'Is sauce for the gander . . .' Eliza finished for him, pushing open the door and marching into the shop with a look on her face that suggested she was about to sort matters out.

Charity swung round and glared at Eliza accusingly. 'Have you been eavesdropping?'

'Yes and I make no bones about it. You can't be such a little ninny that you'd turn down Stephen's offer.'

Charity looked obstinate. She knew how Eliza felt about Danny and she'd laughed at her not very subtle attempts to throw her and Stephen together. But this really was the limit. 'I need to think about it.'

'Rubbish! What can there be to think about? If it's a new dress, you'll get one, if I have to sit up all night making it. Opportunities don't come twice in this life, young lady, and you're always saying how you'd like to go to the theatre.'

Eliza was right; she was. And Danny made sure she didn't make too much claim on his time. He was forever

160

saying, just in case she forgot, 'No ties eh, Charity?'

'No ties, Danny,' she would echo obediently and it was all a bit one sided. She ought to feel flattered too, Stephen asking her out, him being a doctor and everything.

They were both watching her now, trying to gauge her thoughts. Enjoying her little bit of power, Charity waited a few moments before reaching out and touching his arm.

'Thank you, Stephen, for asking me, I'd really love to come.'

Stephen's eyes crinkled with pleasure. 'Good,' he said. 'And I can promise you a very enjoyable evening.'

'Thank goodness for a bit of sense at last from you, young miss,' commented Eliza tartly. 'Now let's go and get that cup of tea and decide what you're going to wear tomorrow. Because you're not going up West looking any old how.'

There'd been no let up in the rain. It came spilling out of the heavens, drumming on to Charity's umbrella and in the short distance from the shop to Danny's, it had soaked through her jacket and she could feel it cold and wet on her shoulderblades. She rattled the knocker for the second time and with a little less patience. Why didn't someone let her in. 'Come on, come on,' she muttered, then bending, peered through the letterbox. A pair of legs were approaching the door, and she shouted to them, 'Hurry, I'm getting drowned out here,' although the rebuke she had prepared for Danny died on her lips when she saw his strained features.

'Danny, what's the matter?' she asked, shaking the rain from her umbrella and stepping into the hall.

'It's Mum, I've had to put her to bed. She's had one of her turns again. Passed right out.'

Charity's hand reached out for the door handle. 'Do you want me to fetch the doctor?'

'She won't see no quack. Refuses point blank. You know how stubborn she is. All I can do is make sure she stays in bed and rests. But you pop up and see her while

161

I make some tea. You might even be able to talk some sense into her.'

The bedroom door was ajar, Agnes Weston's eyes were closed and her soda-roughened hands lay still on top of the white crocheted counterpane. Taking off her wet coat, Charity hung it over a chair, and tiptoed over to the bed. What immediately struck her was how yellow Agnes Weston's skin looked in contrast to the whiteness of the pillow.

When she reached the bed, Mrs Weston opened her brilliant blue eyes and smiled a weary smile. 'Hello love.'

'Hello, Mrs Weston.' Charity took her hand. 'How are you feeling?'

'I'm all right, love, just a bit washed out that's all, so I thought I'd come to bed.

'Danny said you'd fainted.'

'That boy of mine does exaggerate. It was a dizzy turn, that's all. I just need a tonic to buck me up. Me blood's a bit on the thin side that's all.'

She probably was anaemic, but Charity, who looked at people with keener eyes these days wondered if it was more than that. The yellow skin, that could be her liver. 'Why don't you let me go and get the doctor? He's ever so nice, Dr Trevelyan, not at all grumpy like Dr Campbell.'

'I don't want no doctors fussing round me.'

'Danny's really worried about you.'

'Bless him, I know 'e is, but you see, I'll be right as rain tomorrow.'

'Look, I've made some tea and toast for us all.' Danny's voice came from the landing. Pushing open the door with his foot, he proudly entered, bearing his achievement aloft on a tray.

'My, you're gonna make a good husband for some fortunate girl,' Mrs Weston said with a wink at Charity.

'Now come on, Ma, you know I can't get married,' Danny replied, pouring out the tea.

'Neither can I,' Charity announced. Practising her newly-acquired skills, she straightened the counterpane and plumped up Mrs Weston's pillows so that she could sit up. 'As soon as I'm old enough I'm going to train to be a nurse.'

The room went quiet and the only sound was the clink of Mrs Weston's spoon as she stirred her tea.

'When did you start getting these notions? Is that Doctor bloke putting ideas into your head?' asked Danny, not looking exactly overjoyed at her announcement.

She'd actually only just, that minute, made her decision but Danny didn't need to know that. However, it was an idea that had been germinating for quite a long time, nourished by the course she'd taken and the misery she saw around her. Then, today, seeing Mrs Weston so sick, it had finally taken root.

'I've been thinking about it for ages. It's what I want to do more than anything.'

'We'd better go downstairs and talk about this.'

'All right. But there's nothing really to discuss. My mind's made up.' Charity bent and gave Mrs Weston a kiss. 'If you want anything, let me know, especially if Danny's working.'

'I will, sweetheart.'

'And see you two don't go falling out,' Charity heard her calling as she descended the stairs behind Danny.

In the kitchen they stood facing each other. 'Now, if you do become a nurse, I suppose you'll be moving away.'

'Probably.'

'Well I won't have it, is that clear?'

'I'm the one who makes the decisions about my life, not you. And by the way, while we're on the subject, the reason I came round is to tell you Dr Trevelyan is taking me out tomorrow night.'

'What?' Danny exploded.

'You heard. Stephen's asked me to the theatre with him and I've accepted. It's your night out with Boscoe, so it won't make any difference to you.'

'You're not going.'

They were glaring at each other now. 'Oh yes I am. No ties, those were your words, remember Danny?'

'Well if you do go out with that doctor, don't bother to come round here again.'

'Suits me,' Charity answered defiantly and, with a toss of her head, marched out of the house, so incensed she forgot her umbrella and arrived home drenched to the skin.

Chapter 13

11 Filbert Street
Rotherhithe
24 November 1894

Dear Moll,

I hope I'm not stepping on your toes, but guess who I went out with last night? Stephen Trevelyan. And guess where he took me? To the theatre to see *The Gondoliers*. Because it was raining so hard and I had on a dark green taffeta skirt and lace blouse and Stephen was in white tie and tails, we went all the way by cab and I daren't think how much it must have cost. I was ever so keyed up at first, you know, all tongue-tied but Stephen's the sort of person who puts you at your ease and by the time we were driving along the Strand I felt like the Queen. At one stage, though, it was so chock-a-block with traffic and people and there were so many hold ups, Stephen said we might have to get out and walk. Seeing London and the buildings all lit up like that and the crowds, it took my breath away. In the theatre with all the women dressed to kill, I didn't know where to look first and I got this really weird feeling that it was all happening to someone else. But I pinched myself and I've got a bruise this morning, so it couldn't have been.

Stephen had brought opera glasses with him and I made a good study of the new hairstyles, which we can try out on each other at Christmas. And do you know what? Stephen said there were several men in the audience studying me through their opera glasses too. It seems it's all right to do this, although I must say it made me feel a bit self-conscious.

Now about the peformance itself. What can I say except that everything about it was brilliant: the music, the words, the costumes, and the cast took so many encores it looked as if we might be there until midnight.

In the interval we had a glass of champagne, another first for me. I'm not sure I liked it though, and it made me feel a bit tiddly. Stephen seems to know a lot of people and I could see they were curious about me and quite a few men came up and asked to be introduced, so I really had to watch my P's and Q's. It was a bit nerve-racking at times I can tell you. I knew I looked all right but I kept my mouth shut, just in case my accent gave me away because I didn't want to let Stephen down.

Afterwards we went to supper at a restaurant called Rules, and a bit of scandal this, apparently the Prince of Wales used to take Lillie Langtry to supper there through a special secret door. That gives you some idea how posh it was. No pie and eels or tripe and onions but great sides of beef wheeled to the table on silver platters. You could have as much as you wanted and when the waiter sliced the meat, Stephen tipped him sixpence. I wish I'd eaten more now, but what with the toffy-nosed waiters and all the cutlery and glasses and not knowing which to use, I was so nervous I could hardly swallow.

I don't know why Stephen took me really. There must be heaps of girls of his own background would give their eye teeth for an evening out with him, because as well as being a true gentleman he's really, really nice.

Danny's furious of course, but it serves him right. He hardly takes me anywhere, and he'd rather go to the Music Hall with his mates than with me.

Pen poised and looking thoughtful, Charity stopped. What else could she say. Oh yes. With a purposeful expression she bent her head and scratched on.

There's something else I want tell you, which is just as important. (It's all happening this week isn't it?) I've decided when I'm a bit older that I want to train to become a nurse. I'm too young at present, but I talked to Stephen about it last night and he thinks it a good idea and says I ought to think about becoming a district nurse. In the meantime, though, he says I should go to some more evening classes, biology perhaps and English and maths, because hospitals are only interested in training well-educated women these days.

I still haven't come down to earth after last night. I really like Stephen, (now don't go thinking I've started having romantic notions about him, he's still yours) he treated me all the time as if I was a lady and he makes me believe in myself too, encourages me, says that if I want to be a nurse badly enough, then I will be.

You'll soon be home for Christmas, Moll and you don't know how much I'm looking forward to seeing you. I bet we'll be jabbering away nonstop like we always do when you're here.

Until then, fondest love from your dear friend, Charity

Relishing her new-found confidence, Charity signed her name with a flourish like Mollie did, then read the letter through, dotting her i's and crossing her t's. Was she, she wondered with a thoughtful frown, being strictly honest when she wrote that she nursed no romantic feelings for Stephen. That might have been true until yesterday but she had to admit that when she'd opened the door to him and he was standing there in his evening clothes looking incredibly handsome, her heart had done a little somersault. And Eliza had waved them off looking like a cat that had swallowed the cream, then waited up so that she could hear every detail of the evening. Charity had been loath to admit it but Eliza had proved to be sound in her judgement of him, because it would have been impossible to spend time with Stephen and not succumb a little to his looks and humour. And as the evening progressed, it became obvious from coquettish eye movements above fans, that quite a few other women were equally taken with him.

What she knew she mustn't do though was fall into the trap of making comparisons between him and Danny, it wasn't fair. Knowing how to dress and treat a woman might seem to come naturally to Stephen but along the way he'd had ample preparation. A great deal of money had been spent in schooling him in taste and manners and it was easy to look immaculate if you could afford the best tailors in Savile Row.

Anyway, she and Danny were of the same background and straying from your class, that could only end in tears. There were warnings enough in the novels she read, the pages of which were littered with tragic tales of wronged, betrayed maidens.

She loved Danny too much ever to want anything more than friendship from Stephen, but a little light-hearted flirtation wouldn't harm anyone, especially if it helped Danny to buck up his ideas.

Charity put the letter to Mollie in an envelope, stuck on a stamp and addressed it. The ball's over, back to reality, Cinderella, she muttered to herself then ran downstairs to collect the weekend's shopping list from Eliza.

'Now watch old Thomas the butcher doesn't palm you off with a joint that's all fat, and don't go letting that Annie Mears slip you one of her stale loaves.' While she was issuing these instructions, Eliza bent and dragged the tin box in which she kept her money from under the sofa. Further orders followed as she unlocked it with a key hanging on a piece of string around her neck and counted out the money into Charity's hand. 'Be sure you check the freshness of any vegetables you buy, and don't forget to go to collect the cats' meat . . .'

But Charity had stopped listening. This was the litany she heard each Saturday. Her eyes had taken on a distant look and she was thinking to herself, about this time last night . . . when Eliza slapped her wrist and said sharply, 'Are you listening to me, my girl?'

Annoyed at being brought back to reality with such brutal suddenness, Charity lifted her shoulders in an irritable shrug. ''Course I am.'

'It's no good looking at me like that, you've got a head like a sieve when it comes to shopping.'

All right, so she'd forgotten the cats' meat once, and perhaps she didn't always check whether the bread was fresh. Charity was on the point of mentioning that these hardly counted as major offences when she remembered how Eliza had sat up half the night making her an outfit suitiable for going to the theatre in. Leaning forward she kissed her affectionately on the cheek. 'I won't forget a thing,' she promised. But this didn't stop Eliza, and her exhortations to remember this, and not forget that were still ringing in Charity's ears as she closed the back door behind her.

Thankful that just this once it wasn't raining, Charity popped Mollie's letter into the first pillar box she came to, then with that off her mind and swinging her basket, she hurried towards the shops.

It was seven o'clock in the evening and lights blazed from windows on to the wet pavements. Charity loved

Saturday nights, the noise and bustle, the smell of cooking food, the air of festivity that came from whole families out shopping together. For the man of the house would have just been paid, his pockets would be reassuringly heavy and his wife and children could count on him being in an expansive mood. No doubt his pockets would feel lighter by the end of the evening, maybe empty by Monday, but father wasn't going to worry about that now. Sunday was the day for a blow out, a fried breakfast, followed by a stroll down to the local then back home for a roast dinner. Afterwards the children would be packed off to Sunday School, ma and pa would have a lie down and perhaps one more unwanted baby would be conceived. To finish off the day, at five o'clock grandma and grandpa would come round and distended stomachs would sit down to a high tea of cold meat and pickles. At least that was how Charity liked to imagine it.

Braziers glowed red down the street and vendors bawled out in counterpoint, 'Ro . . . ast chestnuts, 'ot pertaters, pigs' trotters.' The smells were all so enticing Charity found it hard to make up her mind and she wavered between the pigs' trotters and the hot potato. In the end economy was the deciding factor, because she only had to part with a penny for a potato. It was almost too hot to hold and she had to jig it from hand to hand. But impatience and hunger got the better of her and she bit greedily into the charcoaled skin, releasing little puffs of steam and enjoying its floury texture, even though she could feel it burning the roof of her mouth. Well it might not be quite up to last night's fare, she thought, but it tasted good all the same.

While she ate, Charity looked about her. The better off shoppers, she could see, not worrying about price, were going to the barrows and shops with the best cuts of meat and freshest vegetables. The impecunious, she knew, would hang on until closing time in the hope of a bargain but in the meantime a barrow load of footwear, down at heel and foul smelling, was being meticulously picked over and boots and shoes tried on for size.

Charity finished her potato, wiped her hands and mouth with a handkerchief and walked on. But the crowds were so dense she was jostled continuously. Pushed at one moment into the gutter amongst puddles and rotting vegetables thrown from costers' barrows, then forced back onto the pavement again by a German band marching down the middle of the road, red cheeks inflated like balloons, oompaing away for all their worth on their brass instruments and rattling their collecting boxes hopefully.

'Buy a bunch o' watercresses, missis, all fresh this morning,' a ragged, barefoot girl urged, holding a bunch under Charity's nose. Although it wasn't on her list, Charity, taking pity on the waif searched for a halfpenny in her purse and gave it to the child. Then, remembering that on Saturday night when purses were full, nimble-footed young pickpockets could make a killing, she stuffed hers well into her coat pocket and walked on.

She'd just made her final purchase, some slices of pork at the cooked meat shop and was standing counting her change, when she saw Kate weaving an unsteady path towards her.

'Hey Kate, where you going?' asked Charity, reaching out and touching her arm.

Kate stared at her in a slightly befuddled way, hic-cuped, said 'Oh 'ello, duckie,' then, hoisting up her skirts, she started to perform a jig, singing at the top of her voice at the same time, 'Oh . . . we've got chickens in our back yard, we feed 'em on barley and corn, One's a bu . . .'

'Kate, stop it!' Charity scolded and pressed her hand over her friend's mouth.

Kate giggled, then several expressions flitted across her face: bewilderment, fear, misery, collapsing finally into a look of utter hopelessness. The girl struggled to contain her tears by squeezing her eyes shut but they forced them-selves out from under her closed lids and ran down her cheeks. Charity's concerned question, 'Kate, what's wrong?' was the catalyst and she burst into loud sobs. Burying her head in Charity's shoulder, she mumbled through her convulsive weeping, 'Oh lovie, lovie, I dunno what's to become of your Kate.'

Bewildered and alarmed, Charity put her arms round her, felt her protruding shoulderblades and was struck by how thin she'd become. 'Look, there's a coffee shop open across the street, let's go and sit down then you can tell me what's worrying you.' she said.

Kate's reply was to give a great shuddering sigh but she made no objection when Charity took her arm and guided her across the street. Charity found an empty booth, sat her down in it and ordered two cups of coffee. Kate's tears had abated slightly but she left her coffee untouched and sat, fingertips pressed against her forehead and with her eyes closed.

'Do you feel like talking about what's troubling you, Kate?' Charity leaned forward and touched Kate's arm in a consoling gesture.

'It's me eyes. It's me eyes, they're real bad.'

Charity sat back, relieved. 'Oh, is that all. Like I've always said, you just need some spectacles.'

'I bought some but they don't make no difference. And how am I gonna make a living, blind. I'll end up with a sign round me neck, selling Lucifers on the street, or playing the hurdy-gurdy like poor old Nancy.' She started to cry again.

'Look, why don't I come with you to see Dr Trevelyan, he'll put your mind at rest. We could go along to the surgery on Monday night.'

The idea seemed to pacify Kate. She took a gulp of the cold coffee, wiped her hand across her mouth and said in a defeated voice, 'Yeah all right. What have I got to lose.' She stood up. 'Well I think I'd better be getting along now.'

'I'll come with you,' Charity said when she noticed how unsteady Kate still was on her feet.

But even with the best of intentions she found it a struggle. Her laden shopping basket banged against her hipbone and Kate leaned on her heavily. Every few minutes Charity was forced to stop, and she'd just put down the basket and was flexing her aching arms, when Kate said suddenly, 'I feel ill,' turned, and was sick into the gutter. Then, retching and crying, vomit and tears intermingling, she sank down on her haunches and, wrapping her arms round her knees, rocked backwards and forwards like a small, unhappy child.

Charity felt at a loss. This wasn't the Kate she knew. She was always so pert and cheerful and a girl who took pride in her appearance. Now she looked a sorry sight and they were getting comments and curious glances from passers by. One couple, more openly inquisitive than the others, did stop but Charity's ferocious glare and sharp, 'Was there something?' shamed them into walking on.

Charity felt a few spatterings of rain and knowing Kate couldn't stay there crouched on the pavement indefinitely, she bent down beside her. Taking a handkerchief from her pocket she spat on it. 'Lift your face up, Kate,' she said as if to a child, and tried to rub the caked mess from her face. Then, staggering from the effort, Charity grabbed her under the armpits and pulled her to her feet. 'Come on, you'll feel better when you're back home lying down.'

Kate was now standing with both arms looped over Charity's shoulders. 'You're a good friend, d'you know that, and I loves yer very, very, very much,' she slurred, then, becoming all maudlin, she pulled Charity towards her and started to smother her face with kisses.

'And I love you too,' replied Charity. Extricating herself with difficulty from the sour smell of sick, they walked on. But Charity found she had her own fears to cope with as they drew nearer to the house. How long was it since she had been here? She couldn't even read the street sign then, Davis Street. It hadn't improved over the years

172

either. There was even less paint on doors, window frames had rotted and many had fallen out. It was an area, too, that proclaimed its trade, poorly lit with threatening shadows and Charity could feel a trickle of unease run down her spine. Everything she was trying to confront about her past, her complicated relationship with Danny, her fear of being touched intimately, was all tied up with this house and its ghastly trade in young flesh. She pushed open the door, half expecting to hear a small girl's terrified screams. Instead she came face to face with Grimbold.

'What's this, then? Pissed again are you?' Kate had fallen against him and he pushed her away.

Although Charity knew she should almost have expected it, to actually see Grimbold again was like a blow to the stomach. There's nothing he can do to you, remember that, she told herself but she could feel the sweat under her armpits and smell her own fear. Her throat muscles had constricted and she had to struggle to speak. 'She's ill, can't you see,' It took a supreme effort on her part to utter those words and Charity was surprised how normal she sounded, defiant even.

'Who are you?' The street lamp shone on to Grimbold's face but hers was in shadow. So he moved closer and although she tried not to, Charity shrank back from his scrutiny.

'Bloody 'ell – you,' Grimbold exclaimed finally. 'Come to make trouble 'ave yer?'

'Why should I do that?' she asked. Charity's natural spirit was returning and she felt more able to cope. 'If you want to know,' I've come to put Kate to bed, that's all. So if you'd just let me get past . . .' Having no wish to linger in his presence a moment longer than was necessary, she tried to push by.

'Hold on, you're not going in there snooping about.'

'Got something to hide, have you, an under age girl perhaps?'

'Get out of it . . .' His lifted hand was curled into a

tight ball. She could remember those fists, like claw hammers, and the memory of the way she saw stars when they came in contact with her skull was vivid enough for Charity to step back.

While this altercation was going on Kate had been slumped against the door with her eyes half closed and Charity assumed it was all passing over her head. But all at once, like a slumbering cat when it sees a bird, she sprang into life, claws flexed. 'Touch as much as a hair on her 'ead, and I'm warning you . . .' she spat out at Grimbold then turning to Charity, said in a quieter voice, 'Go love, like he said. I don't want him roughing you up, not on my account. You brought me home, that was good of you. I'll see meself to bed.'

To show she meant it, Kate elbowed her way past Grimbold and Charity had time to see her make an unsteady progress down the hall before the door was slammed in her face. There was a sound of raised voices, of insults and obscenities being traded, gradually growing fainter as the pair of them climbed the stairs to Kate's room.

Charity wrote her thank-you letter to Stephen on Sunday morning, taking her time over it and checking carefully her spelling and punctuation. Then, with a plan in mind, and while Eliza was having a nap after dinner, she walked round to the surgery to deliver it in person.

Dr Campbell's house and surgery, like all the other dwellings in Princes Street, was rather fine with carved doorposts and lintels and had once been the home of a sea captain. The last thing Charity wanted was for her call to be misconstrued, so her steps as she approached the house were uncertain, her ring on the bell tentative.

A thin, gimlet-eyed woman she assumed was the housekeeper answered the door. 'Yes?' the woman snapped.

'Is . . . is Dr Trevelyan in please?' she stuttered, her diffidence not helped by the woman's hostile manner.

174

'There isn't a surgery today. Doctors need some time off just like anyone else, you know.'

'I've come to see him on a personal matter, not a health one,' Charity answered, disliking her tone.

'Have you now.'

There was a wealth of meaning in those words and Charity felt herself colouring. But she was spared further humiliation by the sound of Stephen's voice along the hall.

'Who is it Miss Fry?'

Without waiting for the woman to answer, Charity leaned forward and called, 'It's me, Stephen.'

'Charity, how nice to see you, come in.' Stephen came hurrying along the hall with a welcoming smile on his face and the housekeeper was forced to stand back so that Charity could enter. As she brushed past her, Stephen said, 'That'll be all Miss Fry, thank you, but some tea and a slice or two of your delicious fruit cake might go down well.' His attempt at humouring her met with a stony silence and the front door was closed with more force than was absolutely necessary.

Stephen's rooms were on the first floor and when she entered, the first thing she saw was Whisky sitting washing himself in front of the fire and looking perfectly at ease with life. As she knelt to stroke his glossy coat, Charity looked about her. A room, she knew, could tell you a lot about a person.

The furniture was shabby, the carpet almost threadbare and the pictures on the wall were religious and in the worst possible taste. Not Stephen's own personal stuff, she decided. The books were his though. There were piles of them everywhere and from what she could gather by a squint at the titles they were on every subject under the sun.

'Better make room for Miss Fry,' he said and was removing some medical journals from a small table on to the floor when there was a knock on the door and the housekeeper entered. She put the tray down then,

175

standing with hands clasped and a disapproving expression on her face, she said, 'Will that be all, Doctor?'

Trying his best, Stephen smiled. 'Yes thank you, Miss Fry.'

'There's cold mutton and what's left of that blancmange in the larder for you and Dr Campbell's supper, I'm off at four to my sister's.'

'That's fine, I'll take care of everything.'

'The . . . er young lady will be gone by then I trust.'

Getting her drift, Stephen answered, 'Oh yes, of course.'

'That's all right then, because I'm sure Dr Campbell wouldn't want any talk.'

'Of course not.' Stephen walked to the door with her and held it open. 'I hope you have a pleasant evening at your sister's, Miss Fry.'

The housekeeper sniffed. 'I shouldn't imagine I will, not for one minute, she does nothing but complain.'

By now Charity had her hand over her mouth, desperately trying to control her giggles. But when Stephen closed the door on Miss Fry, came back and said with a very straight face, 'Little Miss Sunshine I call her,' the giggles rose like bubbles in her throat and she exploded with laughter.

'Poor woman, I do feel sorry for her. I think she's been in love with Dr Campbell for years.'

'Really?' The idea that someone could actually nurse feelings of tenderness for someone as cantankerous as Doctor Campbell seemed quite bizarre to Charity. Then she realized she shouldn't be making those sort of judgements. What made one person fall in love with another was always going to be one of life's imponderables, she should know that. So, in an attempt to make amends she went on, 'Still he was probably quite good looking when he was young.' Before he succumbed to the booze and his face turned the colour of a plum, she was careful not to add.

'Possibly. Now, how do you like your tea, strong or weak?' Stephen had the teapot poised over a cup.

'Weak please.' Eliza's tea was always like tar, and not the sort to drink if one wanted to appear ladylike, Charity decided.

She refused the proffered slice of fruit cake, not caring for its dry, burnt look and when she'd taken a sip of tea, she handed Stephen her letter. 'It's to thank you for Friday. It was the best evening of my life, and I'll never forget it.'

'Perhaps we could repeat it sometime.'

'Perhaps.' Watching him over the rim of her cup, Charity thought, is he being polite or does he mean it. And if they did have another evening out together, what would Danny do? Raise Cain probably. But then it would serve him right for neglecting her. It was quite likely Stephen would move away soon anyway. Dr Campbell's assistants never stayed long. They found it hard to cope with his irascibility and there were no prospects here for anyone with ambition. If Stephen took her out once or even a dozen times, it would only be to alleviate some of his loneliness.

However, Charity reasoned, they seemed to get on, so where was the harm in it? No hearts were going to be broken, and he would take her to places she'd never have a chance to see otherwise. Her youth could waste away hanging around for Danny. And it would do him no harm to get a taste of his own medicine, to suffer the sort of jealousy that made you think your head was going to explode with the pain of it. In fact the more thought Charity gave to the subject the more the idea appealed. It would serve Danny jolly well right.

Stephen put more coal on the fire then lit the lamp. Charity looked at the clock. It was quarter to four. She'd have to move soon or risk scandalizing Miss Fry. 'I know it's your day off but can I talk to you about Kate? You know the girl you met in the shop one day.'

'I remember, the one who works for the Grimbolds.'

'That's right. Well, I met her last night, and in a pretty

sorry state she was, too. She's always been a bit short-sighted but now she's somehow got hold of the idea that she's going blind. She won't come on her own so can I bring her to see you tomorrow evening?'

'Of course you can.'

'I just want to make sure she sees you and not Dr Campbell. He'd frighten her to death.'

'Come at six and she should be my first patient.'

The clock on the mantelpiece chimed four. Charity stood up. 'Thank you for the tea. I'd better go now.'

'It's nearly dark, I'll walk back with you.'

'There's no need.'

'Oh yes there is. There are some shady characters out there.'

Charity didn't like to tell him she had walked the streets of Rotherhithe unchaperoned for the best part of eighteen years. Downstairs the front door banged loudly, challenging her to stay a moment longer. She picked up her coat, Stephen came and helped her into it, disappeared into another room then came back wearing an ulster and carrying a large umbrella.

The rain when they got outside was pounding off the pavement and the road was practically submerged in water. The appalling weather had kept everyone at their firesides and they had the streets to themselves.

'Come on, let's run,' said Stephen and huddled together, his hand gripping her arm, their view obstructed by the large umbrella, they raced down the street, leaping over puddles and for no particular reason, laughing childishly.

'And just where the bloody hell have you bin?' They were half way down Filbert Street, and the anger in the voice stilled their laughter and brought them up short.

Stephen raised the umbrella. With a face like thunder, Danny stood blocking their path, legs apart and arms akimbo, his wet hair flattened against his skull.

'May I ask what it has got to do with you?' enquired Stephen.

Toffee-nosed geezer, Danny thought, Stephen's patrician tones making his hackles rise even more. 'It's got everything to do wiv me. Charity's my girl.'

'Of all the nerve . . .' Charity was almost rendered speechless. 'You mean I'm your girl when it suits you.'

'We've got an understandin' you know that.'

'What I understand, Danny is that you mess me about.'

'Well you'd better choose. It's 'is lordship or me.'

'Don't be so stupid, Danny, there's no choosing to do.' Charity was hot with embarrassment.

But Stephen had gripped her arm again. 'This is a ridiculous conversation, which is getting nowhere. And I see no point in standing here getting drenched. Now if you'd just let us pass . . .'

'When I'm good an' ready.' Danny flexed his powerful shoulders and slapped his fist into the palm of his hand in a threatening manner. Never had he looked more like his pa.

He couldn't . . . he wouldn't . . .

But if he'd hoped to cow Stephen he was mistaken. Moving Charity to one side, Stephen took a step forward. They were almost the same height and, facing up to Danny, Stephen said in a very controlled voice, 'Bully-boy tactics will cut no ice with me, Danny. I learnt to box at school and I'm warning you, I was pretty good.'

It had all happened so quickly that for a few seconds, Charity could hardly believe her eyes. Would they really fight, here in the street in the pouring rain. It looked like it, unless she stopped them, for male pride was at stake now and neither would give in. 'This is ridiculous. Will you two please stop it!' Her voice was a notch away from hysteria and so shrill she hardly recognized it herself.

But at least it diverted them from actions they would later regret. Glad not to have lost face by backing down, both men did as she bid. Danny's arms fell to his side and Stephen turned to her looking apologetic. 'Sorry.'

'I should think so. I don't intend to stand here watching two grown men behave like schoolboys over nothing.

179

Stephen, take me home please, and you Danny, move out of the way.' Charity's tone was so imperious, he stood aside.

'Thank you.' She gave Danny a queenly smile, then, knowing it would infuriate him, she slipped her arm through Stephen's. Danny glowered but she didn't care. Power, how sweet it tasted. In very few situations in her life had Charity ever felt she had the upper hand, but she did at this instant and it gave her confidence to fire her parting shot. 'And don't think I'm finished. I shall have more to say to you about your behaviour later on, Danny Weston.'

Chapter 14

'I'm sorry, but Kate's health is not a matter I can discuss with anyone, not even you, Charity, it would be unethical. What passes between a doctor and his patient must be absolutely confidential. You do understand that, don't you?'

'Oh . . . yes . . . of course, Stephen,' Charity had stumbled, 'I'm sorry, I didn't mean to be nosy, I just wanted to know how she was.'

Stephen knew as soon as he saw the faint flush staining her cheeks that his unnecessarily officious manner must have sounded like a snub. Quickly he hastened to make amends. 'You're not being nosy, my dear. Kate's lucky to have a friend like you and it's quite natural you should be asking after her. Why don't you go and see her, I think she badly needs someone to talk to.'

'Yes all right, I'll do that,' she'd answered.

But somehow she hadn't yet got round to it. Caught up in the excitement and rush that preceded Christmas, she quite forgot about Kate. The shop was extra busy and the till didn't stop ringing right up until they closed on Christmas Eve. Then, on Boxing day, she was invited round to Mollie's where a clan of cousins, aunts and uncles was gathered. In keeping with their strict chapel beliefs, the festive spirit was kept going with nothing stronger than lemonade and Mrs Payne provided a marvellous spread of cold meats, pickles, trifle, junket, mince pies and Christmas cake. They played charades and musical chairs then everyone was expected to do a party piece. An uncle did conjuring tricks, Mollie sang. When it came to her turn, Charity recited 'The Solitary Reaper' by William Wordsworth, which she'd had the good sense to memorize. The evening ended on a happy note with a sing-song round the piano.

It seemed that Mollie had no sooner arrived with all her news and gossip of the big wide world than she'd gone, off to stay with a college friend in Hampstead, who had, Mollie informed Charity, 'an amazingly talented brother called Caspar,' and, from her tales, rather eccentric parents, too. Stephen wasn't mentioned once during the holiday. Caspar was the name that now sprang most readily to Mollie's lips. After Mollie left, everything went flat again, like a burst balloon after a party.

However, she'd felt a slight lifting in her post Christmas gloom when Stephen came breezing into the shop a day or two later. 'Come on young lady, I need to get away from this place and its problems for an hour or two. Put on a strong pair of shoes, we're going for a walk, somewhere that'll blow the cobwebs away.'

Charity had looked at Eliza for consent. 'Yes, go on, go,' Eliza said, shooing her towards the door.

Quickly she'd hunted out her stoutest boots and they'd headed for Greenwich on the omnibus. Here, after pointing out the perfect proportions of the Queen's House, Stephen had grabbed her hand and dragged her up the hill to the Observatory.

Charity arrived at the top panting and what little breath she still had in her was snatched away by a strong wind.

But Stephen seemed unaffected by the climb. 'Isn't this marvellous,' he said and flinging his arms wide, he took in great lungfuls of air. 'Fresh air, it's better than all the champagne in the world. And take a look at that view, Charity, you can see right to the Isle of Dogs.

'They say there used to be gibbets all along that shore. Bodies would be left swinging and the tides would wash over them until there was nothing left but bleached bones.

'Barbaric lot, the human race. I know criminals have to be punished but there ought to be better ways. But let's talk about something more cheerful,' he'd said and she could still remember his exact words. 'Tell you what, when the weather improves and the days get longer, why don't you let me show you the real country? We'll take the train, go to Kent.'

'It seems quite countrified up here.'

'Ah, but you wait until you see Kent.' He swept his hand out towards the horizon and Charity knew by the look in his eyes that in spirit he was already there. 'Oast houses, woods full of bluebells, blossom as far as the eye can see. I swear there's no place on earth so beautiful in spring.'

Spring, Charity thought with a melancholy sigh, green shoots, daffodils, warm sun stirring the earth into life. But with window sills and gutters bearded with icicles and the ice having to be scraped from the inside of windows every morning, in this dark part of January, it was almost impossible to imagine. And had Stephen even meant what he'd said, she wondered, staring out through the shop window at the falling snow. Well she couldn't ask him. Because a day after their walk he'd left for Scotland to join a 'house party,' as he called it, for the New Year. Enjoying himself no doubt with glossy young women of his own class. Charity sighed again and her confusion grew, because she hardly dared admit how drawn she felt to Stephen. But it was natural enough, wasn't it, to enjoy being treated with courtesy and respect, having your opinions sought, your wishes considered. And although she'd sworn not to, Charity had started making comparisons between Stephen and Danny, noticing small things which she silently criticized: Danny's rougher way of speaking, his manners. Since the incident between him and Stephen, she had been less starry-eyed, while Danny had become far more attentive, particularly after the fierce ticking off she had given him.

'You made a right exhibition of yourself that day, Danny, and I've never felt so embarrassed in my life. I can't imagine what Stephen thought.'

'It was seein' you wiv him. It all happened in a flash. I was so jealous I just saw red.'

'But what right have you to be jealous? We've got no claim on each other, you're always telling me that.'

'S'pose so. But that's how I am, I can't 'elp meself.' Danny gave a half smile as if expecting absolution.

But just this once Charity had been determined not to let him get round her. 'Well, you'd better change, hadn't you?' she'd snapped.

Danny had linked his fingers with Charity's and pulled her towards him. Assessing her mood, he had looked deep into her eyes and said softly, 'But it's because of the way I feel about you, that's the only reason I behaved badly.' He watched as Charity's expression softened and he pressed on. 'An' I'm truly, truly sorry, so will you forgive me?'

He had looked so genuinely remorseful, Charity had to struggle to remain indignant. 'Why should I?'

'Because you're my girl, that's why,' Danny answered and lifting her chin, he kissed her.

In the comfort of his arms, his jacket rough against her cheek, Charity sighed. Why could she never hold out against Danny? Because she loved him, she supposed. Anyway, what was the point in harbouring ill-feeling, it served no purpose in the end. If they didn't make it up, she'd be the loser. And Danny being prepared to have a fight like that with Stephen showed he felt something.

With the air cleared between them, Danny seemed to turn over a new leaf, even going as far as occasionally sacrificing his Friday nights with his mates to take Charity out instead. And it was Danny who mentioned Kate was ill.

'The old man's walking around like a bear wi' a sore head. Seems his lady friend has taken to her bed.'

They were having a drink together in The Angel. It was too early for the serious drinkers and with the freezing weather outside, the fire in the grate was a comforting sight. Danny had his arm round her, her head was on his shoulder and that was exactly how Charity liked it. She and Danny, companionable and close. However, Danny's news made her sit up. 'Are you talking about Kate?'

'That's the one.'

Charity felt a rush of guilt. 'Gosh I haven't seen her since before Christmas. Perhaps I ought to pop round there.'

'What, now?'

'Yes, now.'

'Why trouble yourself, she's only a whore.'

'Danny. I've told you, don't call her that.' Charity began to feel concerned. 'Who's looking after her?'

Danny shrugged. 'How should I know. The Grimbolds maybe. I can just see them two as ministering angels.' He laughed heartily at his wit, then emptied his tankard with a satisfied smack of his lips. 'I think I'll have another.'

Charity stood up. 'Well you can if you like but I'm going to see how Kate is, she might need food.'

'I would have thought you could have waited until tomorrow.' Danny grumbled, but he did follow her out.

After the warmth of the pub, the freezing air numbed their cheeks and lips and vaporized their breath.

'God almighty,' Danny exclaimed forcibly. He'd set off a shade too confidently and his feet went from under him on the glassy surface. He slid, falling flat on his back, pulling Charity with him and she landed on top of him with a surprised shriek.

They lay there, rolling around in the snow like a couple of young animals, convulsed with laughter. Then Danny said, 'Even though it's bloody cold, I think I like this. Come here.' And pulling her head down, he kissed Charity gently.

Her lips were numb but they warmed under the pressure of Danny's mouth and so did her blood, and she could feel little spurts of fire in her head, fingertips and down between her legs. But then Danny started pulling at her bulky clothes and immediately her body tensed. 'We'll freeze to death if we stay here,' she said and scrambled to her feet.

Danny banged his fists on the frozen ground in frustration. 'Why do you always back away from me Charity?'

'Because I'm frightened, that's why,' she said in a small voice, hating her own stupid fears.

'But I'd never hurt you, you know that,' Danny said gently. She pulled him to his feet and he came to her enfolding her in an embrace.

'I know.' She leant her face against his chest. 'But you've got to give me time. Unless of course you'd prefer me to be like May and go with anyone.'

'You know I wouldn't.'

'Well don't keep on then. It always spoils everything between us.'

She waited for his jaw to set hard as it usually did when she said something like this, but instead he just gave a philosophical sigh.

'Oh, all right, I'll keep my mouth shut, I promise.' Danny kissed her on the cheek, took her hand and pulled it through his arm and they walked on. He had to be a bit careful these days, or he could end up frightening her into another man's arms, that posh doctor with his la-di-da ways, for instance. He was always sniffing around, taking her out, unsettling her, giving her ideas he didn't ought. Danny wished he'd bumped him one like he'd intended that day, just to show 'im. You could bet your boots it was him who'd put that daft notion of being a nurse into her head. Nurse! Who'd ever heard of such a thing!

'Well, we're here. This is where Kate lives.'

Charity broke into his thoughts and he looked up at the crumbling facade. 'Christ, what a dump. I hope you're not expecting me to come in. There's a pub round the corner, I'll wait for you there. And be quick, I don't want to spend all evening on me tod.'

Charity would have preferred Danny to wait, at least until she'd opened the door. It was still there, that old irrational fear. But she knew she had to learn to come to terms with it, so she didn't try to call him back. There were some things in life you needed to face on your own, if they weren't to control you.

The house presented blank eyes to the world and it was the same inside, a total darkness. But Charity could remember the layout of the house and she fumbled her way up the stairs to the first floor where she knew Kate's room was. Like a blind person she felt her way round the wall, hands outstretched, and at last found a doorknob. She turned it carefully, but it was locked and when a gin-roughened voice from the other side of the door shouted, 'Who's that? What d'ya want?' she started back in fright.

'I'm looking for Kate.' Charity wished her voice didn't sound so timorous.

'She's next door.'

'Thanks.'

She knew as soon as the door gave way to her touch that it was Kate's room. There was the cheap, stale smell of Ecstasy and overlaying it, worse smells, smells that turned her stomach and made her want to hold her nose. Apart from a faint glow from a dying fire the room was in darkness. Calling out quietly, 'Kate, are you there?' Charity moved into the room, stumbling over dozens of

186

empty bottles, which went clattering away across the bare wooden floor.

A bundle on the bed stirred and a voice said faintly, 'Who is it?'

'Me, Charity. I heard you hadn't been well so I thought I'd come and see how you were getting along. Shall we have some light?' Without waiting for an answer Charity fumbled around on the dressing table amongst pots of cream and boxes of powder, found some vestas and lit the lamp.

It was a room in chaos. Dresses and underclothes were strewn over chairs, boots and shoes scattered about the floor. Half-eaten food was rotting on plates and an over-flowing chamber pot was the source of the noxious smells. But these were minor problems compared to the state Kate was in.

She lay facing the wall, her legs drawn up to her stomach like a child. When she didn't move, Charity leaned over and touched her lightly and she rolled on to her back and stared up at her with a blank expression.

'Shall I help you sit up?'

She nodded and with the aid of cushions, Charity eased her into a comfortable position, then sat down on the bed herself. 'How are your eyes, Kate?'

'No worse an' no better than anything else about me.' Her voice was hoarse, and there was slight slurring of her speech which Charity put down to the now empty bottles. Until she saw that the glands in her neck were so enlarged she couldn't move her head without wincing with pain.

Looking at her now, unwashed, her nightdress stained, it was hard to remember how particular Kate had always been about herself.

'Has anybody been coming in while you've been ill?'

'Yeah, the other girls do what they can. And Jim brings me food but I can't eat, me throat's too sore.'

'But you must eat if you're not well, otherwise you won't get your strength back.'

'I'll never get me strength back, I'm done for.' Kate's tone was one of resignation.

'You mustn't say such things. Of course you're not done for.' Charity tried to sound reassuring but she still felt a chill of apprehension. Failing eyesight alone couldn't account for the condition Kate was in. She stood up trying to hide her fears behind a brisk efficiency. 'Anyway, is there any water round here? I'm going to give you a wash, you'll feel heaps better then.'

'You can't, the tap in the yard's frozen.'

'I could heat some snow up in a saucepan.'

'I ain't got a saucepan, love.'

'A kettle then.'

'I usually borrow Mabel's next door.'

Charity began to feel frustrated. The room needed ventilating but she daren't open the window because of the freezing night air. And without water she couldn't even begin to clean up Kate or the room.

'Have you got a clean nightdress?'

Kate waved a thin arm in the direction of the dressing table. 'You'll probably find something in one of them drawers. You couldn't pop out and get me a bottle of gin, could you love, so that I could drown me sorrows?'

'You want proper nourishment, not gin,' said Charity in a firm tone. Opening first one drawer then another she searched amongst a clutter of garters, lacy red and black satin corsets and underwear until she found a clean nightgown.

Even lifting her arms so that Charity could remove the soiled nightdress was clearly an exhausting business for Kate. Naked, there was hardly a scrap of flesh on her. Then Charity noticed the dark red patches across Kate's back and shoulders. Repelled, she stepped back and wiped her hands down her dress. If whatever Kate had was catching, she could end up in the same state. For a minute she was tempted to make some excuse and leave.

Fine nurse you'll make, she admonished herself, if you can't even deal with this. Hiding her distaste, Charity

188

reached under the bed for the chamber pot. It overflowed with urine and excrement. 'I'm just going to empty this.'

'That's no job for you, duckie.'

'Someone's got to do it.' Charity replied resolutely and lit a stump of candle. Nose screwed up, head averted and with the chamber pot held at arms length, she moved cautiously down the stairs. It was easy to find the back yard, easier still the evil smelling privy, her nose guided her to it. Quickly, and with a great sense of relief she disposed of the contents.

Back in Kate's room Charity set about restoring it to some order. Stale food was scraped into an old newspaper and put on the fire, empties collected and shoved in a cupboard, clothes folded neatly away. She held a sheet of newspaper in front of the dying fire until it glowed red again, then built it up with slack so that it would last through the night.

'That's better,' Charity surveyed the room with a quiet satisfaction. She'd made order out of chaos and Kate had even perked up a bit. 'Could you give my hair a brush, love?' she asked.

''Course I can.' Charity found a brush amongst the clutter on the dressing table, and taking care not to hurt her, pulled it through the tangle of Kate's hair. But the knots resisted the brush and when she gave a slight tug, Charity found she was pulling away a great handful of hair. She stared in a stupefied way at the bare patch on Kate's crown then the swatch of hair in her hand and not knowing what else to do, hastily shoved it in her pocket. She suddenly felt very frightened for Kate and unable to cope.

'I'd better be going, Kate. Danny's waiting for me. But I shall be back in the morning and I'll come every day until you're better.'

'That's right, love,' Kate repeated, 'until I'm better.'

It was snowing heavily when she got outside. It stuck to her lashes and hair, it almost covered her boots and the hem of her skirt dragged wet and heavy behind her.

But Charity was too preoccupied to even notice. Chin sunk into the collar of her coat, hands deep in her pockets, she puzzled over Kate's decline. It was lying there all day in that unhealthy atmosphere that was sapping the strength out of her, she decided and felt more reassured. She would soon see to that. What the place needed was a good scrub out with carbolic and she could do that tomorrow. Then with some of Eliza's nourishing soups to build her up in no time at all, she'd be fit as a fiddle.

By now the snow was so thick, road and pavement were indistinguishable but a sudden painful jolt to her spine told her she'd stepped off the kerb. Charity then had the uncomfortable sensation of melting snow running down the inside of her boots. She knew snow muffled sound but she was struck by how eerily quiet it was. There were no wheel marks in the road and hers were the only footsteps in the freshly fallen snow. And the pub where she was supposed to meet Danny, she was astonished to see, was closed. She went to the door, rattled the handle and peered through the glass panel into total darkness. Then the church clock started to chime and she stood counting until the last stroke faded away. Midnight. That meant she must have been with Kate for over two hours. And had left Danny twiddling his thumbs. She would definitely be hearing about that tomorrow.

Stephen stood outside Kate's door and sniffed. Carbolic, cleanliness, not a smell he usually associated with this misbegotten place. Attending cases such as Kate's always weighed him down with feelings of hopelessness. People put such faith in doctors, imagined they could perform miracles, but sometimes all they could do was ease people gently into death.

The holiday in Scotland had been something of a disaster as well. Blanche had flirted outrageously with a young guards officer whose father just happened to have a castle and a title. The castle was probably a crumbling heap but she'd been sufficiently impressed by him to extend her visit. And knowing Blanche and her snobberies she'd probably even forego a comfortable lifestyle for the chance of a title. Anyway, it had culminated in a tremendous row and he'd left making it clear their relationship was at an end.

He was also having increasing problems dealing with his conflicting lifestyles. And when he had to come back to a young girl whose life had been cut short by poverty and the needs of men, it only increased his sense of pessimism.

Stephen knocked, waited for Kate to call, 'Come in,' pushed open the door and was slightly taken aback to find Charity down on her hands and knees, attacking the dirty floorboards with a scrubbing brush. When she saw him, she leapt to her feet. 'I thought I'd do a bit of tidying up.' She spoke as if almost apologizing for her small act of mercy.

She had a piece of sacking tied round her waist, loosened tendrils of hair framed her face and her cheeks were rosy from her exertions. Never had she looked so beautiful, and the contrast between her and the dying girl on the bed was so unbearably poignant Stephen had to turn away.

Aware that both the girls were watching him, he cleared his throat noisily. 'Sorry, bit of a cold, must have picked it up in Scotland.'

'Don't you think my little sweetheart's done a good job on the room, Doc?'

'She certainly has, Kate.' Stephen looked about him. He'd never seen the room so clean and tidy.

'Well I've finished now. I'll see you in the morning, Kate.' Charity untied her apron, put on her coat and picked up the bucket. 'I'll empty this on the way out.'

'Here let me carry it for you.' Glad of an opportunity to be on his own with Charity, Stephen took the bucket from her. 'I'll be back in a second, Kate.'

At the bottom of the stairs, Charity stopped and turned

191

to face Stephen. Although it was a question to which she already knew the answer she still had to ask. 'Kate's real poorly isn't she?

'Yes, pretty poorly.'

'Is what she's got infectious?'

'In a way it is. But you're all right. Just be careful if she starts to bleed. If you've an open wound yourself don't on any account touch her. But I can't discuss Kate's illness here, I'll come and talk to you later.'

'All right.' Charity took the bucket of dirty water from him. 'I can see to this now. I'll empty it in the gutter outside. You go back to Kate. And Stephen,' Charity's dark eyes were pleading, 'try and make her better.'

Stephen raked his fingers through his hair in a helpless gesture. Why did everyone seem to imagine he was omnipotent.

'I'll do my best,' he answered. But there was something in his voice that told her not to hold out too much hope.

Charity stopped and clicked her tongue in irritation. What was the blind doing down on the door, and in the middle of the morning too? Of course she knew the answer. Eliza had heard of a cat in distress somewhere and never mind about *their* livelihood. She really was the limit sometimes. Exasperated by her aunt's unbusinesslike attitude, she was about to move round to the back of the house when she saw Leonard Willis picking his way with careful steps towards her. It's like watching doom approaching, she thought with a little shudder and hurried to get out of his way. But he caught up with her before she had a chance to slip down the side entrance.

He lifted his hat. 'G . . . ood morning, Mi . . . Miss Brown.'

'Good morning, Mr Willis.' As always he smelt musty and, hiding her distaste, Charity edged past him into the passageway. Preoccupied with thoughts of Kate, she was unaware he'd followed her until she'd retrieved the key from under a flower pot, fitted it in the door and tried to persuade the swollen wood to move under the weight of her shoulders.

'Here let me.' She stood back. Leonard Willis applied his strength to the door and it fell open immediately. Then, Charity wasn't sure how, he was in the parlour with her.

Ignoring him, she discarded her coat, hat, scarf and gloves, then with a frown of concentration, looked around her, searching for a note that might explain Eliza's absence. But she found nothing. Two places were set though and there was a joint of cold beef and a carving knife and fork ready on the table, which told Charity that with a bit of luck she'd be back by dinner time.

It was when she went to smooth her hair in the mirror that she saw Leonard Willis was staring at her. She'd come to hate that look, hot and intense, and she shivered as if someone was walking over her grave. What was he doing here anyway, uninvited and in their parlour. If he'd come with another of his so-called religious tracts, she'd throw it back in his weasly face. She swung round and, trying to keep her tone civil asked, 'Was there something in particular you wanted, Mr Willis? I really have to get the shop open.'

He moved round the table in a strange, jerky movement, until he was standing very close. His neck above his clerical collar was a dull red, he was panting as if under extreme duress and she could feel his sour breath on her face. Suddenly he lifted both hands as if offering benediction. 'Yes, my angel, you.'

Charity took a startled step backwards and found herself hemmed in by the horsehair sofa, the wooden frame of it cutting into her legs.

'Thy lips O my spouse, drop as the honeycomb; honey and milk are under thy tongue,' he babbled, moving nearer.

'Stop it you disgusting creature,' Charity screamed, blocking her ears.

193

He closed his eyes, pressed his hands together and, swaying backwards and forwards began reciting the Lord's prayer. 'Our Father, which art in heaven . . .'

Charity began to shake violently. There was no doubt about it, this man was deranged, and she was also alone in the house with him. 'Wi . . . will . . . you please leave, this . . . this minute,' she ordered, battling against a rising fear.

Her words roused him from his trance, he blinked and stared at her with mad eyes. 'I must have you, do you hear me, I must have you.' Then before she had time to dodge clear, he leapt forward, caught her in a pincer-like embrace and forced her down on the sofa. Smothered under his weight she found his wet lips on hers, then he was forcing open her mouth and filling it with his tongue.

Charity thought she would faint with disgust. She tried to wrestle free but he was too strong, and he'd now imprisoned both her wrists in a vicious grip. Drawing away, he grabbed the collar of her dress, there was a sound of tearing and buttons went flying all over the room. 'Stop it! Stop it!' she screamed and tried to defend herself as he took her nipples in his mouth, sucking on them like a child, then nipping at the soft flesh of her breasts with his teeth until she was sobbing with pain.

Her muscles seemed to have liquified but when she felt his hand up her skirt trying to force her legs apart and pulling at her drawers, she found a small residue of strength. He would not touch her there, she'd rather die. Frantic now, she remembered words of advice from Kate a long time ago. 'Always go for the balls love, where it bloody 'urts.' Managing to dislodge her knee from his smothering weight, she gave it to him, right on the spot too, judging by his satisfying yell of pain and rage.

Leonard Willis leapt away, staring down at her with wild eyes. 'Oh my God what have I done,' he blubbered. 'What will Mummy say. I'm done for, finished.' He pointed a finger at Charity. 'You brought me to this,' he accused. Reaching out he grabbed the carving knife and held it above her. 'It's all your fault, temptress, whore of Babylon. Nothing now can absolve you from your sins. You must die before you pollute the world further with your wickedness.'

Frozen with terror, unable to save herself, Charity stared up at the steel blade, knowing at any second it would be plunged into her heart. 'Kill me and you'll be hanged, then burn in hell,' she managed to say at last through numb lips.

He started back making the sign of the cross. 'No, no, that's impossible, I'm a priest. I won't let them,' he screamed and wielding the knife in the air he ran from the room.

Silent tears of relief at her deliverance spurted from her eyes and ran down her cheeks. Wiping them away with her fingers, she looked down and saw that he'd bitten so deeply into her breasts he'd drawn blood. Ashamed and flinching with pain, she made a futile attempt at covering herself up.

Through the window, terrified cats were diving for cover as Leonard Willis wove an erratic course down the path towards the privy. He was still waving the knife aloft as if seeing off an invisible enemy as he entered the WC and slammed the door closed.

Charity stood up. She must bolt the back door, quickly, before the madman returned. Shaking and distraught, she moved into the scullery, found the door swinging on its hinges and heard strange noises coming from the privy. A burst of hymn singing, 'As pants the hart for cooling streams, when heated in the chase . . .' which broke off into garbled prayer, followed by bitter weeping. Cautiously Charity approached the privy and heard the sound of vomiting. A long low groan followed, then complete silence. Charity moved still closer. Something dark and viscous was oozing under the door and she watched hypnotized as it dripped on to the snow, staining it bright red.

'Oh no.' She clapped her hand to her mouth and backed away, but the blood seemed to be pursuing her. Turning from her nightmare she ran, slithering in the snow. Almost beyond reason and without any sense of where she was going she swayed from side to side down the passageway and out into the street. Watched by astonished passers-by she reeled around on unsteady feet, only half clothed and screaming like one possessed.

Then she felt firm hands on her shoulders. 'Charity, what an earth . . . tell me what's happened.' She recognized Stephen's voice, paused, fell into his arms and the screams modified to heart breaking sobs.

'What's happened?' Stephen repeated, then seeing it was going to be difficult getting any sense out of her, he gave her a little shake. 'You must tell me.' Her teeth started to rattle violently and he took off his coat and draped it around her shoulders, hiding her nakedness from prying eyes.

'It's . . . it's Leonard Willis.' She stopped, tried to compose herself, failed and stumbled on. 'There's b . . . b . . . been a terrible accident. I . . . I think he's killed himself.'

Stephen found it hard to take in what Charity was saying. 'Killed himself? Where for God's sake?'

'In . . . in there, in the privy.'

Stephen turned to one of the men in the small, curious crowd now gathered round them. 'Go to the police station. Tell them Dr Trevelyan says it's extremely urgent and I want a constable here immediately.'

With Charity almost swooning against him he helped her back down the passage. 'You go inside,' he ordered and, leaving her at the back door approached the privy. There was blood there all right, a huge spreading lake of it.

'Mr Willis,' Stephen called, he didn't know why, then banged on the door. He tried the latch but it was bolted from the inside. Grabbing the door at the bottom and top he tried to wrench it from its hinges. But it was made of stout oak and wouldn't budge. By now blood was dripping on to the tops of his boots and soaking into his trouser bottoms. In desperation he looked around, saw an axe by a pile of wood, grabbed it and brought it down with all his force on the door, splitting it in two so that it swung open like shutters.

The sound of splintering wood brought Charity running. 'Go back,' Stephen shouted, waving her away with his hand.

But it was already too late, Charity had seen him. Leonard Willis was in a kneeling position, the head was all lopsided, the jugular vein had been severed and there was a great gaping red hole in his neck. Blood dripped from the sleeve of his coat on to the carving knife lying at his side.

Charity just couldn't take any more. She'd been tested to the limits of her endurance. Her body surrendered and she slid to the ground in a dead faint.

Chapter 15

For several days after the Reverend Leonard Willis's suicide, Stephen feared that Charity's sanity might be in jeopardy. He and Eliza could glean little from her incoherent ramblings, although the torn clothes and bite marks on her breasts told them enough not to waste time mourning the vicar's death.

It was a scandal of gigantic proportions. What people didn't know they invented and embellished, and with only rumours to feed on, it spread through the community unchecked. Mrs Green, whose tears of grief were spilt mainly for her daughter Alice and her dashed hopes, started a whisper around the congregation of St Bidolph's: what decent girl would be in a house alone with a man, her poisoned tongue suggested. It was obvious to anyone she'd enticed the dear vicar there to compromise him then blackmail him into marriage.

Like the rumours, the tragedy gathered momentum. At the news of her son's death poor old Mrs Willis suffered a massive stroke. She survived, speechless, for several weeks but was mercifully spared the true story and the terrible knowledge that her son would be buried in unconsecrated ground.

Temporarily laid off by his lighterage firm because of the severe weather, Danny heard this mish-mash of half truths and downright lies from his mother when he returned from Tilbury where he'd been with Boscoe looking for casual work.

'You an' me, we know Charity's not a girl like that. I should go round there and find out what really has happened, love, so that we can put paid to these vicious rumours.'

'Well, she better not 'ave bin up to anything wiv him,' Danny threatened and filled with an urge to thump someone good and proper, he marched round to Filbert Street and banged on the door with his clenched fist.

His temper didn't improve when Stephen answered and said with a touch of asperity, 'I thought from the noise, someone was trying to break in.'

Danny pushed past him into the scullery. 'Never mind about that. Where's Charity? I want to see her. Find out what the hell's been going on.' His stance and tone were aggressive, which did nothing to help his cause.

'You can't see her at the moment.'

'Oh, who says so.' Danny gave him a challenging look. Stephen's superior attitude really needled him and he was so worked up that for two pins this time he really would have given him one on that nose he seemed to look down all the time.

'Me.'

'She's my girl, I'm entitled to.'

Behind Danny's bluff exterior, Stephen could detect a

real fear. All that was needed was for him to provide some reassuring words then the boy would calm down. But for the life of him he couldn't. Instead he found himself rather unprofessionally snapping, 'It seems to me Charity's your girl when it suits you. But that's beside the point. She's under sedation so it would be a waste of time. She suffered the most dreadful trauma. But until she's ready to give a statement to the police we won't get the full story.'

'There's been a lot of talk. Some folk are goin' around saying she invited the vicar in.'

'They are vicious rumours put round by people with sick minds. You know yourself Charity couldn't stand the man. And her instincts proved to be right. He made a violent sexual attack on her.'

Danny paled. 'He didn't . . . ?'

'No.'

'It's just as well that bugger slit his own throat or I'd 'ave done it for 'im.'

Stephen knew it wouldn't do to say so but Danny was rather expressing his own sentiments, and that the man was dead by his own hand caused him no regrets whatsoever. Leonard Willis's dreadful legacy was the emotional damage he'd bequeathed to Charity, although it was still too early to know whether it would be permanent.

'If you come back tomorrow, she'll be awake then and you might be able to see her,' Stephen said in an attempt to be more conciliatory.

Danny shuffled his feet. 'I dunno about tomorrow. I'm helping out a mate you see, and I've got to go down to Tilbury again.'

'Well when you return then.' Stephen opened the back door. 'And Danny, I'll tell her you called, I know she'll be pleased.'

Extremely pleased, in fact, Stephen thought as he climbed back up the stairs. For it had been Danny's name she'd repeatedly called in her most fevered state.

* * *

By the end of the week Charity was back downstairs and showing every appearance of being on the mend. But in making her statement to the police, she had to re-live her ordeal and even with Stephen there to cushion her against the constable's more pressing and intimate questions, she broke down several times in tears.

But because of everyone's concern, the anxious looks that told her they were wondering whether her grip on reality had loosened, Charity felt almost obliged to recover as quickly as possible. So, she answered their solicitous questions with a reassuring smile and buried her agony away deep down inside her. There was nothing she could do about the nightmares though, they came of their own volition. Always he was walking towards her, arms outstretched, mouthing a prayer, the great gaping hole spurting blood and his head hanging loose like a flower broken from its stem. She would try to scream but she could force no sound from her paralysed throat, and when she turned to flee she found her feet were weighted with lead. Charity would wake sweating with terror. Longing for daylight and the normality of everyday life she would force her eyes to stay open. But, awake, she still felt threatened. The moving curtains became a ghostly presence, the dim outline of the washstand was transformed into the decomposing features of Leonard Willis.

It gradually emerged that Leonard Willis had been removed from previous parishes because of his obsessive pursuit of young women, but the knowledge that the gossips could no longer blame her for the tragedy didn't console Charity, who came to dread going to bed. With Lolly curled up on her lap she would sit by the dying fire until the clock struck one and she could no longer keep her eyes open. 'Lolly m'love, you're coming upstairs to keep me company,' she would murmur into the cat's soft fur as she gathered her up in her arms. Stroking her and tranquillized by the cat's contented purring, Charity would gradually drift off to sleep, praying tonight she would be spared the bad dreams.

But she never was, because although Lolly was the arch enemy of mice, she couldn't scare away the nightmares, which nightly grew more vivid and terrifying. Other recognizable faces joined Leonard Willis: Grimbold, Bill Slawson and the aristocratic Lord Prendergast. With greedy, lustful eyes, they would form a circle round her and like vultures, tear at her clothes until she was stood naked and ashamed. Then, although she fought desperately to protect herself, they would squeeze her breasts spitefully. But the true terror began when rough hands were thrust between her legs, forcing them apart.

Charity's sobs would bring Eliza running. 'It's all right my dear, I'm here.' Setting the candlestick down, Eliza would gather up the distraught girl in her arms and silently curse all men.

And it went on like this for some time. Eliza spent her nights comforting Charity as best she could and her days bustling around after her. For Charity had sunk into a dazed lethargy and nothing could persuade her to move from her chair by the fire. In the end, in desperation, Eliza dropped Danny a note, asking him to visit. But Danny was in still in Tilbury and it wasn't until the week-end that he was able to call round.

When he did call that Saturday, he moved into the small room filling it with his health, vigour and news of the outside world and was just the tonic Charity needed.

In a whispered aside Danny was warned by Eliza that on no account must he mention anything connected with Charity's ordeal. 'It would set her recovery back weeks. Just try and cheer her up,' were her instructions.

But when Danny sat down beside Charity and solici-tously took her cold hand in his, he was shaken to the core of his being by the suffering on her face. That sod, what's he done to my little girl. And such an anger welled up in him, Danny knew he was capable of murder. If Leonard Willis hadn't done himself in, he would have throttled him with his bare hands. But although all these

201

emotions surged within him his behaviour was exemplary. He didn't say one word out of place.

'I'm sorry I ain't been ter see you, Charity,' he said, trying to massage warmth into her fingers. 'But I'm working down at Tilbury just now.'

'Why's that, Danny?'

'Well, there ain't much work around at the moment. I don't s'pose you've seen the river, but the local vestries 'ave bin dumping snow from roads and bridges into the river and there are great masses of floating ice. The river's unnavigable, and boats are gettin' stuck all the time'.

'Tilbury seems a long way to go just the same.'

'With the new docks it's an up and coming place and Boscoe's got contacts down there.'

'What sort of contacts?'

'Oh you know, this and that,' Danny said vaguely. 'Anyway, don't worry yerself, it won't be much longer before I'm back at me regular job. This freezing weather's bound to end soon.'

But it didn't. In fact by February the thermometer had dropped even further and ten degrees of frost was nothing. Bored with being a invalid, Charity slowly pulled herself out of her apathy. Eliza noticed it in small things: the return of her appetite, an interest again in what she wore, undisturbed nights. So, when Charity suggested returning to work, she had Eliza's wholehearted approval.

But the severe weather provided her with an excuse not to move from the security of the shop. When the curious came to peer and probe, she just smiled and smiled and only the truly observant could see that her eyes were dead.

Stephen was one of them. Something needed to be done, he decided and took her aside one afternoon.

'You've been cooped up indoors long enough, young lady. What you need is some fresh air to get the sparkle back in your eyes and the roses on your cheeks.'

'I don't want to go out.'

'Yes you do,' Stephen insisted. 'And I won't take no for an answer.'

'But where can anyone go in this sort of weather?'

'What about St James's Park? We could go skating on Saturday afternoon.'

'But I've never been skating in my life.'

'With me as a teacher, you'll soon learn.'

'What about skates?'

'I'll buy you a pair. Make them a belated Christmas present.'

Charity shook her head. 'I couldn't allow that.'

'You're quite right you couldn't, so *I'll* buy you some,' said Eliza, sweeping into the room so suddenly Charity was sure she'd been listening at the door. 'Then there's nothing to stop you accepting Stephen's invitation, is there?'

Charity gave a shrug. If other people wanted to take control of her life they were welcome, it saved her thinking. 'No, Auntie,' she answered in a passive voice, 'there isn't.'

By determined effort, on the Saturday not only had Eliza bought Charity skates, she'd also made her a hip length jacket in holly green wool fastened with braided frogging and trimmed all the way round with fur. A matching fur hat and muff completed her ensemble and the new outfit did more than any medicine could to restore her self esteem. She positively luxuriated in Stephen's open admiration when he came to pick her up.

He stepped back and studied her. There was still a look of fraility about her. It was there in the alabaster colour of her skin and a faint bruising under her eyes. Somehow, though, this emphasized rather than detracted from her beauty. Feeling a conflict of emotions building up in him, Stephen said rather tamely, 'My word, Eliza's done you proud.' Then, taking her skates he slung them over his shoulder.

By the time they climbed aboard the tram to the

Elephant and Castle, Charity had decided to enjoy her day, to put the past behind her. Leonard Willis's mind had been unsound for a long time, that day it had tipped over into madness. It wasn't her fault and he wouldn't destroy her life.

Crossing Westminster Bridge, Stephen pointed out to her the huge ice floes Danny had spoken of which had helped bring river traffic to a virtual standstill. Another hazard to shipping was ice adhering to the bottom of barges. This caused them to break adrift and Charity and Stephen could see them now, floating rather dangerously up and downriver.

When they reached the park laughter, music, the cheerful sounds of people enjoying themselves, carried over the still, frozen air and propelled them forward. The sun was an orange globe in the smoky sky and when, through the leafless trees, Charity caught sight of the lake it immediately reminded her of a Dutch painting. Men, women and children glided across the ice, creating ever-moving skeins of colour against the stark winter landscape. Couples were waltzing to tunes played on a barrel organ and even the tiniest tot seemed to skate with utter self-assurance.

At the sight of such expertise Charity's own confidence faltered and she stopped dead. 'I can't go on there, I'll just make a fool of myself.'

'Now you mustn't be faint-hearted. I promise I'll hold on to you the whole time.' Refusing to listen to any more protestations, Stephen sat her down and helped her on with her skates. Then, with his arm firmly around her waist, she wobbled on to the ice.

'Just take it carefully,' he advised. 'Push one foot forward, then the other.'

Conscious of Stephen's hand resting on her hipbone Charity advanced gingerly, knees bent and expecting to suffer the indignity of falling flat on her bottom at any moment. To her surprise after a few yards she was still standing.

Stephen looked down at her with an approving smile. 'You're doing fine.'

'Am I?' She beamed back at him and felt her nervousness evaporate. Straightening her legs, she threw back her head and moved away from the support of Stephen's arm. Unfortunately at that precise moment a young man speeding past caught her a glancing blow on the shoulder and sent her spinning like a top.

'Ow! Help!' she yelled, flailing her arms and struggling to stay upright.

In the nick of time, Stephen reached out and grabbed her. 'Don't worry, I've got you.'

Breathless, she found herself pulled tight against his chest. Even through their thick winter clothes she could feel his rapid heartbeats and he was looking down at her with a strange expression in his eyes.

She gazed back at him, aware of a constriction in her throat and her own pounding heart, then the world went silent. Skaters whizzed past, children circled them laughing, but they were oblivious to anything but each other. For the first time Charity saw that Stephen's hazel eyes were flecked with green and that he had a small scar over his left eyebrow. Wanting to absorb every tiny detail of him, she searched his face, longing to trace her fingers over the generous curve of his lips and the smooth plane of his cheekbones.

Lifting his hand, Stephen tenderly stroked her cheek, and the rough wool of his glove against her skin was like an electric charge, sparking her body into desire. It was strange, discomforting, exhilarating, all at once.

'You are the most beautiful girl in the world and quite irresistible, do you know that?' Stephen's voice was husky with emotion. He lowered his head, bringing his mouth close to hers. Charity knew he was going to kiss her in full view of everyone but she didn't care. In a dreamy sort of stupor, her eyes half closed, the lids fluttering, her lips moist and slightly parted, she waited.

'Stephen!' The voice was female and peremptory and it cut through them, prising them guiltily apart.

Startled, Stephen lifted his head. 'Blanche! What are you doing here. I thought you were staying on in Scotland.' Feeling he'd been caught out, he looked uncomfortable.

'I couldn't stand all that haggis and tartan and Highland fling nonsense any longer. The Scots do carry on about how nasty we English are too, and they insist on living in unheated piles of granite, which is very trying in winter. So I got brother Simon to rescue me with a telegram and an interesting but not fatal illness. He's over there with Emma.'

Pretending to notice Charity for the first time, Blanche turned to her with an expression that was as cold as the day. Feeling like a schoolgirl, Charity shifted awkwardly under Blanche's scrutiny which took in every detail of her dress. And when she was finished, Blanche signalled the message to Charity that she knew the fur was fake, the material of poor quality, the skates second hand. Finally she spoke. 'Aren't you going to introduce us, Stephen?' Her smile flickered on and off before it had time to reach her eyes.

'Oh . . . oh yes,' Stephen stumbled, and Charity could see he was discomfited by Blanche's presence. 'Miss Charity Brown, may I introduce you to Miss Blanche de Vere.'

By this time another couple had appeared on the scene and the young girl skated up to Stephen, flung her arms round his neck and gave him an exuberant kiss.

Over her head Stephen was watching Charity, and he knew by her unhappy expression that if it had been physically possible, she would have turned and fled, and he silently cursed Blanche for making such an ill-timed appearance.

'This very familiar young woman,' he explained with a laugh and trying to put Charity at her ease, 'is my cousin, Miss Emma Moore.'

'Don't forget me, old man,' said the young gentleman, who was obviously Blanche's brother, for they were alike as two peas in a pod.

'Oh yes, Mr Simon de Vere.' When he made this introduction, Charity noticed that Stephen's voice was several degrees cooler.

'You'll both come back to Harley Street with us for tea, won't you?' Emma pleaded.

Stephen glanced at Charity. 'Oh, I don't know.'

Emma turned to Charity with a display of even white teeth. 'You will let him come, won't you Miss Brown? It's absolutely ages since we saw him.'

'Two weeks to be precise,' interrupted Stephen.

'Daddy will be terribly disappointed if you don't come.'

Young Emma, it seemed, had a very persuasive tongue. And although the last thing Charity wanted was to spend any time in the company of people who made her feel gauche and ill dressed, she was in a state of such total confusion she found herself insisting it was Stephen's bounden duty to return with them to Harley Street.

Simon made his excuses and left but a short while later Charity was sitting in a cab next to Blanche, casting desperate glances at Stephen. Her one consolation was that she was apparently far too humble a creature for either young woman to have any recollection of meeting before and she could only hope that went for the uncle too.

The door was opened to them by a butler. His look was one of haughty disdain and Charity could tell by the way he flicked his eyes over her that she'd been weighed up and found wanting.

But Stephen greeted him in a cordial tone. 'How are you, Evans?'

'I am very well, thank you, Mr Stephen. May I take your coat, Miss.'

'Oh . . . yes.' Charity struggled to remove it.

'Allow me, Miss.' The haughty voice was reprimanding

her. Mortified, Charity felt a blush rise from her neck to her scalp.

As soon as they were indoors the two girls tore upstairs, and Charity was certain she heard smothered laughter from the landing. She just wasn't going to get through this. Without her new coat she felt spectacularly shabby and she also had a desperate need to go to the lavatory but was to shy to ask.

'Tea will be served in the drawing room, Mr Stephen. Doctor Moore and Mrs Moore are already in there.'

'Thank you, Evans. We'll see ourselves in.' Stephen took Charity's hand and gave it a squeeze. 'Chin up, you're doing fine. We won't wait for Blanche and Emma, they'll take ages titivating. Let's go in.'

Deciding the best course was to sit tight, say nothing and that way she couldn't put her foot in it, Charity took a deep breath and with a hammering heart, followed Stephen.

It was a light, elegantly-furnished room and, as they entered, Stephen's uncle rose to greet them.

'Stephen my boy, how delightful to see you.' The man moved forward, putting his arm round Stephen's shoulder and patting him affectionately.

'Hello Uncle Richard.' Charity had shrunk back as the older man approached, but Stephen turned and pulled her forward. 'This is Miss Charity Brown, a friend of mine. We met Emma and Blanche in St James's Park and they talked us into coming back for tea. Didn't they Charity?'

'Yes.' Totally overawed by the doctor's rather grand manner and the opulence of the room, the word came out as no more than a squeak.

Stephen then led her to a large woman who was sitting on a *chaise-longue* knitting. 'This is my aunt, Mrs Moore. How are you, Auntie Margaret?' He bent to kiss her and the woman looked up and smiled.

'I'm fine, Stephen.' Mrs Moore replied, and Charity noticed that her left eye was a grey gelatinous mass with no pupil or iris. She flinched slightly at the disfigurement.

'You come and sit here, next to me, my dear,' Mrs Moore said to Charity in a kindly voice, and patted a space on the *chaise-longue* beside her. 'Then, once the girls are down, I'll ring for tea.'

Totally miserable and ill at ease, Charity did as she was bid, her fingernails digging into her palms as she tried to control the tremor in her hands. She half expected Dr Moore to start probing her, as he would a patient under the scalpel, to try to establish whether she was a suitable companion for his nephew, but instead he and Stephen started discussing medical matters. Realizing no one was paying any attention to her, the tension in Charity's neck eased a fraction. She thought it might look rude if she started studying the furnishings so for something to do her eyes followed the movement of Mrs Moore's large knitting needles. She was trying to fathom out what anyone could possibly want to make with a large ball of string, when Mrs Moore, noting Charity's interest, held up the piece for her inspection. It was a mystifying, indeterminate cat's-cradle of a shape but she still couldn't pluck up the courage to ask what it was.

'It's a dishcloth, my dear,' Mrs Moore explained, noticing Charity's puzzled expression. 'I make them all the time for the kitchen. Cook says they're very useful.'

'I'm sure they are,' replied Charity in a polite tone.

Mrs Moore turned her sightless eye to her. 'My eye, does it notice, dear?'

Charity shifted uncomfortably and fought not to avert her glance. 'Oh no, not at all,' she lied.

Mrs Moore beamed. 'Oh that is good. I fell, you know, down the stairs, from top to bottom, two years ago.' Guarding the side of her mouth with her hand, she cast her husband a sly glance then said in a stage whisper, 'I'd had a little bit more than was good for me.'

'What was that you said, Margaret?' Dr Moore swung round in his chair and his tone was sharp.

'I was asking Miss Brown about my eye, that was all.' Mrs Moore replied serenely. 'She says it looks quite normal, dear.'

Dr Moore said nothing but he smiled at Charity as if apologizing for his wife, and she gained the impression he found her an intolerable burden socially. She was almost certain that if he'd had any notion a stranger was calling on them, Aunt Margaret would have been quickly tidied away. Well, at least she wasn't the only person in the room for whom things could spin out of control. It was a comforting thought and it helped her to feel more at ease.

'Your eye is fine, Auntie.' Stephen's voice broke in. This was probably a familiar domestic situation for him and one, Charity assumed, he had his own way of dealing with. Tactfully changing the subject, he went on, 'Look, here come the girls, so shall I ring for tea?' Then without bothering to wait for a reply, he went over and tugged on the bell pull by the fireplace.

Although she pretended not to, Charity was watching Blanche and Emma as they came prancing into the room, confident, pretty, well-dressed and whispering and giggling behind their hands. If they imagined they were about to reduce her to a quivering wreck, they could think again. It was apparent that Mrs Moore was ever so slightly batty and, Charity decided, she would have no scruples about using it.

Blanche sat down and looped a slim arm along the arm of her chair in a graceful movement Charity could only admire. Emma was delegated the task of serving tea. The sandwiches she handed round, minute, crustless triangles, were the daintiest Charity had ever seen in her life. Her instinct was to reach out and grab one and she gazed at them with a hungry longing. But she wasn't sure how one juggled a plate, a cup and a saucer so she had to refuse for fear of making a fool of herself.

Blanche helped herself to an eclair, bit into it, took a sip of tea, and studied Charity carefully. Stephen must be amusing himself with this lowly little creature. Probably out of male pride and to pay her back for her own dalliance in Scotland. And parading her in St James's Park, that was a bit obvious, when he knew it was likely they would be there too. She'd had trouble in the past with Stephen and his weakness for pretty girls, particularly blonde ones, but she tolerated it because although it was accepted in their circle that she and Stephen were a pair, nothing was official between them – yet. They were from the same social background, understood its mores and, although in all honesty it couldn't be said that this girl was common, there was no style there. Those dreadful clothes! Upstairs she and Emma had laughed themselves sick over them. They were so pathetically cheap, one would have imagined Stephen would feel ashamed to be seen in the girl's company. Blanche's eyes narrowed. He wasn't becoming smitten, was he? Getting into deep sexual waters. But he was a prize worth having and supposing the girl used her wiles on him, and heaven forbid, got herself pregnant . . . it didn't bear thinking about. For what would then become of her, Miss Blanche de Vere, of impeccable lineage but unencumbered by wealth and with a wastrel for a brother. With a chilly sense of unease, Blanche patted her mouth with a lace napkin and sat up straight. This needed nipping in the bud, right now. It was working down there in the docks amongst the criminal classes, that was the trouble. Stephen was losing all sense of perspective. He needed to be back in civilized society where he belonged, with people of his own kind.

'Have you known Stephen long, Miss Brown?' Blanche asked with a smile that dripped venom.

Charity glanced at Stephen and he answered on her behalf.

'We've known each other a few months.'

'You live in Rotherhithe then?'

'Yes,' put in Charity.

'I can't for the life of me understand why Stephen

211

seems so intent on doing good works down there. Bit of a lost cause, Rotherhithe, I would have thought.'

Anger loosened Charity's tongue. Stoutly she defended her territory. 'It certainly is not! Being poor doesn't mean people have given up, you know.'

'I could get Stephen into a very prosperous practice but this do-gooding, his concern for the underdog is in his blood, I'm afraid,' intercepted Dr Moore in his well-bred voice. 'He's just like his parents were. Although some people might consider trying to rid the Indian sub continent of disease and at the same time convert it to Christianity something of a hopeless task.'

'My mother and father were medical missionaries,' Stephen explained to Charity. 'They died in a smallpox epidemic in India. And uncle Richard and Aunt Margaret kindly took me in, brought me up and educated me.'

'It was the least I could do for darling Catherine, and I've never regretted it. Although I did warn her not to marry your father, Stephen. No sense of reality at all, Edward. A complete dreamer he was.'

Stephen had obviously heard the speech many times before for his features took on an obstinate, faraway look.

Aunt Margaret's needles ceased their clicking and she rested her knitting on her lap. 'It was the only sensible thing she did in her life. At least it got her away from your beastly father. At his beck and call day and night and little more than a slave.' Mrs Moore leaned towards Charity in a confidential manner. 'I helped them elope. They might not have had long together but at least Catherine knew Edward loved her deeply. I would have settled for that.'

A nerve-stretching silence ensued and flustered by this rattling of family skeletons, Charity stared with a deep interest at the pattern on the carpet. This was a most unexpected turn of events. Interesting too, in a way, because it was obvious Mrs Moore was deliberately stirring up mischief as a way of getting at her husband.

Certainly if looks could kill she would have been stone dead. But none of this appeared to trouble her. Smiling innocently, she picked up her knitting again. 'And Stephen was such a lovely little boy too. Dear Edward to a T.'

Stephen smiled at his aunt in warm complicity.

'But what a heathen!' Emma exclaimed, taking over the conversation to an audible sigh of relief from everyone else. 'Do you remember, Papa? All he needed was a turban and he'd have looked like an elephant boy with his brown skin. And he spoke a very strange tongue. However, we quickly civilized you didn't we, Stephen?'

Stephen's brow creased with irritation. 'My dear cousin, India had an ancient civilization when the people of these shores were still running around wearing nothing more than woad.'

Not in the least put out, Emma laughed. 'Well you know what I mean.'

Stephen finished his tea and stood up. 'Anyway, I think we'd better be on our way.'

'Must you?' Blanche rose, too, and moved close to him.

'I've got a surgery this evening and calls to make.'

'Forget about those people for once.'

'A lot of "those people," as you call them, are very sick. Some are even dying.' Stephen moved over to the bell pull, tugged it and the butler appeared. 'Our coats please, Evans, Miss Brown and I are leaving.'

Before they left, Charity found the courage to ask Mrs Moore if she could use the WC, then Evans went out on to the step and blew a small whistle to summon a cab.

'You are a very pretty young woman and you must get Stephen to bring you again, my dear,' said Mrs Moore warmly. 'Do you hear me Stephen?' she gave him a playful tap as he kissed her on the cheek.

'I hear you, Auntie, and I'll certainly do that,' he replied affectionately and went to kiss her and his cousin farewell and shake hands with his uncle.

'What about me,' said Blanche, lifting her face.

Looking ill at ease, Stephen brushed her cheek with his lips.

Blanche gave Charity a knowing look then said, 'Don't forget the Coulson's Ball next month, Stephen. You will be coming won't you?'

'I suppose so,' he mumbled.

'And there's the theatre on Friday,' Emma reminded him.

'Oh, yes of course.'

'And please try not to be late,' said Emma, hanging on to his arm and walking with him to the door.

'I'll do my level best, but I do work for a living, young lady.' Stephen smiled down indulgently at his cousin then kissed the end of her pert nose. Charity, watching him closely, saw just how different their lives were. Harley Street and Rotherhithe, it was a gap of unbridgeable proportions.

In the cab they were both quiet. The afternoon had been so unreal that if Charity hadn't been so conscious of Stephen's thigh touching hers she might have thought she had dreamt the whole thing, particularly that incident on the ice. And Stephen, what did he think of it all. Street lamps occasionally illuminated his face and Charity stole him a glance. He had almost turned away from her and there was something unapproachable about the set of his jaw. Did he regret bringing her? Had she made a complete and utter fool of herself at his uncle's house? Still, afternoon tea had been an eye-opener. She'd been led to believe it was a sociable event, not the backbiting, knives out sort of occasion she'd just witnessed. She'd felt sorry for Mrs Moore though.

'Poor Aunt Margaret,' Stephen sighed, almost as if he could read her mind. 'It's difficult to believe now, but she was once a talented painter. I'm fond of my Uncle but in his attitude he's not unlike his own father. He thought my aunt would be better occupied dancing attendance on him and organizing their social life. So he made her give her painting up. With nothing else to fill her days, she started drinking heavily and as you probably gathered, it's become something of a problem.'

Charity was outraged on poor Mrs Moore's behalf. 'That's a terrible thing to do, deny a person their talent so entirely they end up knitting dishcloths.'

'The world's an unfair place. Take your friend Kate for instance, whom I have the sad job of visiting this evening.'

Kate. With a jolt, Charity realized she hadn't given a thought to her sick friend in weeks. Even allowing for her own problems how could she have done that? 'May I come with you?'

'It would probably be better if you didn't.'

'Why?'

Stephen spoke quietly. 'I'm sorry, I thought Danny would have told you. She's sinking rapidly.'

'What are you saying?' Charity's voice was sharp, edged with fear.

'I'm saying she's dying.' Stephen knew the words sounded brutal, but it would have gone against his nature to deal in anything other than the truth.

Charity turned on him accusingly. 'But you said you'd make her better.' In the dim interior of the cab, Stephen could just see her face, angry and crumpled like a bewildered child's.

'There was nothing I could do that would cure Kate. It was already too late when you brought her to see me.' He took her hand. 'Charity, what I'm telling you must not be repeated. Kate has something called syphilis. It is a disease that goes with her calling, unfortunately.'

'What do you mean?'

'It is sexually transmitted. Do you understand what I'm saying?'

Charity nodded, then burst out, 'It's the Grimbolds who are to blame and if there's any justice in this world, one day there'll be a reckoning and I hope I'm there to

215

see it. Anyway, whether you like it or not, I'm going to see her.'

'All right, you can come with me, but you'll find it upsetting, and I doubt whether she'll recognize you.' By now the the cab had reached his house and stopped. Stephen opened the door and jumped down. 'Wait here while I get my bag.'

He was hardly gone a minute and, in the short distance to Davis Street, Stephen tried to prepare her for the worst. But no words could have aptly conveyed Kate's condition, emaciated, her hair gone, she was way beyond recognizing anyone.

'Oh no.' Fist pressed to her mouth to stop herself from breaking down, Charity leaned against the door and watched Stephen roll back Kate's sleeve and inject something into her arm.

'That's all I can do for her now.' Stephen stepped back from the bed and there was a finality about the way he snapped shut his bag. 'At least she's not in any pain.'

'May I kiss her?'

'It would probably be better if you didn't.'

'Goodbye, Kate my love,' Charity murmured, her voice husky with tears.

And it seemed almost as if Kate heard, for one wasted arm lifted slightly and her hand moved in a gesture of farewell. There was such a terrible ache in her throat, Charity was unable to contain her anguish any longer, and she sank to the floor, weeping hot, bitter tears.

Gently, Stephen drew her to her feet. 'Come, my dear, I'm taking you home.'

Chapter 16

It honestly hadn't been in his mind, Stephen told himself afterwards, to take Charity back to his rooms. But she was so distressed he felt she needed a strong drink to help her calm down. Nevertheless as he supported her up the stairs, he admitted it was a relief to know Miss Fry was out and he was therefore spared her gimlet-eyed disapproval.

She was efficient though, the housekeeper and before she'd gone out she'd drawn the curtains, built up the fire and left tea things on a tray. But tea wasn't the refreshment Stephen had in mind for Charity, so as soon as he'd helped her out of her coat and sat her down on the sofa by the fire, he went over to the sideboard and unlocked it.

As he poured an extremely generous measure of brandy into a glass, Stephen watched her, moved by her pain and trying to assess her state of mind. Would she hold up under this further tragedy? In spite of her fragile exterior, Charity was tough, but there was only so much a person could cope with, before breaking.

Whisky was rubbing himself against her legs in a persistent, wanting-to-be-noticed manner, but Charity had withdrawn so far into her misery, she was totally unaware of the small cat.

Bending, Stephen held the glass against her lips. 'Here, drink this,' he said in a quiet, professional way.

The fumes assaulted her nostrils but Charity obediently took a sip of the fiery drink. 'Ugh, it's horrible.' Screwing up her face in distaste, she pushed his hand away.

'Just try a drop,' Stephen persisted, 'it will make you feel heaps better.'

Charity gave him a strange look. 'Will it?'

'Yes, I promise.'

'Give it here then.' Grabbing the glass from him, she threw back her head and let the golden liquid trickle down her throat.

'Hey, what are you doing?'

Too late Stephen wrested the empty glass from her and Charity had the not-unpleasant sensation of heat exploding in her throat and stomach. 'Making myself better like you said,' she answered, as her head begin to spin. 'And, do you know, it works.' With a cherubic smile Charity lay back on the sofa. The room was pitching slightly but otherwise she felt deliciously woozy and marvellously free.

But Stephen was not amused and he stood over her looking stern. 'I think I ought to make you some tea young lady, or I shall be accused of making you drunk.'

'And just think of your good name.'

Charity, evidently rather tipsy, was mocking him, but Stephen ignored it. 'And yours. I can hardly take you home to Eliza smelling of strong drink. Perhaps a better idea would be for you to sleep a while.'

'I don't want to sleep.'

Exasperated Stephen answered, 'Well at least try closing your eyes.'

Fetching a cushion Stephen bent and tucked it under Charity's head. Her lids drooped immediately and Stephen indulged himself in admiring the silky lashes and the creamy perfection of her skin. Stirred by her beauty and vulnerability, he was smoothing back loose strands of hair from her forehead when she opened her eyes again and regarded him with an expression that made his breath catch in his throat. Then in a languid movement, slim arms reached up, fingers were linked behind his neck and raising herself up slightly on the sofa, Charity murmured, 'Unfinished business,' and kissed him.

Only momentarily astounded, Stephen hungrily returned her kisses. Then, all notion of honour deserting him, he scooped her up in his arms and carried her to the bedroom. 'Oh my lovely girl,' he murmured, kissing her eyes, her ears, and the hollow of her throat.

Everything swam slightly out of focus, but Charity was totally relaxed. Today there was no grotesque image of a small girl being taken forcibly. No tensing, no pushing away when Stephen slowly undid the buttons on her dress. No shame, no fear. She shivered with pleasure as his hands cupped her breasts, then, teasing her with his tongue he took a nipple in his mouth and a primitive, throbbing lust spiralled down through her body into her groin. Her surrender was so complete that she gave no thought to the possible consequences when his hands moved under her skirt, pulling off first garters, then stockings and drawers. Her body now was a hostage to sensations exquisite and unfamiliar and over which she had no control.

Still somewhat dazed that this virginal creature had taken the initiative, Stephen watched her, gauging her reactions. Although he'd fought against it, this was something he'd been longing to do for months. For what man with blood pumping through his veins could fail to be moved sexually by her astonishing looks, he asked himself. And in some of his lonelier hours, without a hope in hell of them happening, he'd had his share of erotic fantasies about Charity, imagined situations similar to this. He was experienced enough as well to read the signs, knew by the flush on her neck and the rapid rise and fall of her small breasts that he would find no trouble taking her as far as he wanted. Unbelievably, he could act out those fantasies. The universe had shrunk to a mere pinpoint of desire. Him and her. Love didn't enter into it, just the entirely selfish need to be released from the pumping hardness between his legs. Mustn't hurry though, must hold on. This was her first time and he had to make it good. Gently but skilfully he stroked the firm mound of her stomach, moving down without haste to the soft skin of her inner thigh, his fingers slowly gaining ground until he was touching her in the most intimate of places.

For a moment commonsense almost submerged her desire and Charity stiffened slightly. This almost imperceptible stepping back brought Stephen abruptly to his senses and as he saw clearly the folly of his actions, his ardour ebbed rapidly away. Good God in heaven, what was he doing? This girl's inhibitions had been loosened by drink and he was taking advantage of it. It was the sort of situation that could lead only to regret once his passion was spent and she was sober. And supposing she got pregnant? Stephen's blood chilled at the thought. Well there'd be no turning back then. Duty would demand he do the honourable thing and he'd find he was tied to a girl, who for all her beauty, was still working class. And to be cut off from his own kind, Blanche, Emma and all his other friends, would he really want that? He should never have allowed things to go this far.

Ashamed and disgusted with himself, Stephen rolled away and stared up at the ceiling. It was dark in the bedroom but light filtered through from the sitting room and he could see Charity's bewildered expression as she leaned over him.

She touched his face lightly, tenderly, and he had to smother the urge to pull her down beside him again.

'Stephen, what's the matter?'

'Quite a lot. I think we were both in danger getting rather carried away. It was my fault and I'm very sorry, my dear.'

'Why should you feel sorry?' Charity asked in a puzzled voice. Wasn't that all men ever wanted from women.

'Because I respect you so much. Besides, something else could have happened.'

'You mean a baby, don't you?' Charity was now stone-cold sober, she had a slight headache and her mouth was dry. A baby. A hammer banged out the words in her head. She wasn't a freak, Stephen had liberated her from that fear, and she'd always be grateful to him for that. But a baby, perish the thought. Unaware of Stephen's own inward tussle, she sat up and busied herself pinning up her hair and buttoning her dress. 'Will you make me that cup of tea, Stephen, then I want to go home.'

Leaving Charity to finish tidying herself up, Stephen went through to the sitting room. It was working out better than he could have hoped. He didn't want to cause her pain but he would have to nip the relationship in the bud. Let things cool between them, but gradually so as to not hurt her feelings. She was romantically disposed towards him at the moment, but he'd encouraged it so it was his own fault. But she belonged to Danny, you only had to see them together to realize that and he'd be home as soon as the weather improved.

Relieved to have got off so lightly, Stephen bent to pick up the poker. Whisky, who was busy giving himself a pedicure, stopped and, paw in mid air, stared at him with an air of thorough disapproval. Or was it a reflection of his own guilt he saw mirrored in those yellow orbs? Hell, what a ridiculous notion. Trying to dismiss such strange ideas from his head, Stephen pushed the poker into the fire and furiously rattled the coals.

It arrived by the last post a couple of days later. Puzzled, Charity turned the envelope over in her hand. Only Mollie wrote to her, but she could never have afforded such expensive stationery – she held it to her nose – particularly not the sort that smelt of violets. Besides, the handwriting was small and cramped with none of her friend's generous loops.

Something made her push the letter into her pocket and later, finding an excuse, Charity rushed upstairs to her bedroom. She sat down on the bed to read it, fumbling to tear open the envelope with awkward fingers. Her eyes skimmed over the page, only half taking in the words, then she re-read the letter with more attention, her heart racing uncomfortably.

Dear Miss Brown
I really think it is in your own best interest to know that Stephen and myself have been acquainted for several years and have been on *intimate* terms for much of that time. Stephen is in no position to enter into matrimony at present but just as soon as his financial situation is stable, he and I will marry. That has always been the understanding. A girl of your class could so easily be misled by the attentions of

someone like Stephen, reading more than was intended into the friendship he has offered you. So this letter is meant with the best of intentions and to spare you future hurt.

Yours sincerely
Blanche de Vere

'You toffy-nosed bitch!' Cold waves of anger rolled over Charity at the condescending tone and she stared at the letter for so long the words danced before her eyes. Finally, in pure fury, she screwed it into a tight ball and flung it across the room. The letter hit the wall and landed on the washstand where it lay, mocking her from a distance.

It took some time but when she'd finally cooled down and given some thought to the matter, she went to the washstand, picked the letter up and smoothed it out. Stephen had rather given the impression that there was no longer anything between him and Blanche, so one of them was lying. And which one, she was about to find out.

Mumbling an excuse to Eliza that she was popping round to see Mrs Weston, Charity put on a warm coat, thick woollen gloves and, because it was snowing heavily, she covered her head with a shawl.

To keep traffic flowing, the roads were more or less kept clear of snow. But no one bothered much about the pavements and under this fresh fall, Charity could feel it packed hard as iron, which meant that as well as deciding what she would say to Stephen, she also had to concentrate on not falling over. Going like this she would catch him unawares. Show him the letter, and wait for his reaction. Unless he was clever at hiding his feelings, she was bound to discover the truth.

Turning into Princes Street, a bitter wind blew snow with shards of ice in it straight into her face. To protect herself, Charity pulled the shawl up like a veil until only her eyes were visible and plodded on. Traffic was light but a cab overtook her, the horse going at a slow pace. Envying the occupant who was warm and dry, Charity saw it come to a halt near the end of the street. A woman stepped out on to the pavement and peered up through the snow at the houses as if looking for a number. After a moment Charity heard her call to the driver, 'It's all right, I've found it, you may go now.'

She delivered the order in a tone of one who was used to being obeyed and as the cab moved off again, Charity stopped dead in her tracks. That arrogant tone was unmistakable. Waiting, with a sense of inevitability, for events to unfold, she saw Blanche bang the knocker as she had done so often herself, heard Miss Fry's voice, then after a brief pause, Stephen appeared on the step.

'My dear, I didn't think you'd make it. Come and get warm.' And taking both Blanche's hands in his, Stephen drew her inside and closed the door.

Charity hadn't moved and the snow was gradually covering her like a white cloak. Mercifully, she had been spared a humiliation. She had all the evidence she needed, in the letter and there, before her eyes. 'Well, you were almost taken in, weren't you, my girl, by fine manners and a posh accent,' she chided herself. 'But in the end he's no different from the rest of them.'

It hurt but squaring her shoulders bravely, Charity turned back home.

During the course of the evening, while sitting pretending to read, she made her decision and waited.

The air grew warmer, the days longer, the ice on the river began to melt and Danny and Boscoe returned from Tilbury.

March moved to its end and, deciding the time had come, Charity prepared herself with care. First she washed with the rose-scented soap she kept for special occasions then changed into clean underwear. Next, she coiled her hair into the nape of her neck knowing that was how Danny particularly liked it and put on a berry-red, wool dress. When she'd completed her toilet, Charity studied herself with a certain interest in the small mirror nailed to the wall. Would she look different, act different tomorrow, she wondered, then with a purposeful step she made her way round to Danny's. Stephen might not want her but Danny did.

Although she continued to insist there was nothing wrong with her, as they sat in the front parlour that evening, Charity could see that the energy was seeping away from Mrs Weston's spare frame.

Trying to discuss his mother's health with Danny was almost as difficult. 'There's no good you goin' on about it Charity. I've argued wiv her 'till I'm blue in the face but she won't go near a quack. Refuses point blank. Won't even 'ave 'im here.' This had been his argument until a few weeks ago. If she broached the subject, he clamped up, not because he didn't care for his mother but out of pure fear, she knew that. He was as well aware as she was of the lines of pain etched round his mother's mouth, the swelling stomach. Her tired body still swept and polished, but a scrubbed floor or whitened step usually meant she spent the following evening in bed.

Not tonight though. With the fire lit in the front parlour, and rejuvenated by the return of her beloved youngest son, Danny, (flush with money too, judging by the presents he'd brought them) Agnes Weston gazed at the two young ones benignly. It was nice they were still together, in spite of a few ups and downs. And Charity could count it as a personal achievement, because usually a month of courting was a lifetime for Danny. Much as she loved her son she wasn't blind to his faults, and unfortunately he couldn't resist a bit of skirt. But there, he was a chip of the old block in that way, although she'd heard that woman of Jim's was about at death's door. No doubt he'd grieve for a week or two but he'd soon

224

find someone else daft enough to take him on. Welcome to the old sod they were too. He'd be all charm at first but it wouldn't take long for the bad temper to show through.

Agnes had been hoping she'd be able to stay up for a game of cards, but after they'd been chatting for a while, the pain came on and making an excuse, she lit a candle and, still smiling, dragged herself upstairs to bed.

Danny went up with her to check that she was comfortable and give her her medicine. When he came back down, he stood in front of Charity smiling and with his hands behind his back.

'Which one?' he asked.

Charity looked puzzled.

'Which hand is it in?'

Grasping his meaning, Charity pointed to his left arm and he brought his hand round. Lying in the palm was a small, square, red velvet box.

Charity's uncertain gaze went from the box to Danny and back again.

'Go on, take it, it's for you,' he urged, looking pleased with himself.

Half expecting him to snatch it away again, Charity reached out, took the box and lifted the lid. Lying on a pillow of white satin was a gold locket inscribed with the initial 'C'. 'You bought this for me?' She gazed at the locket in wonderment. 'Gosh, Danny it's really beautiful. I don't know what to say.'

'It's none of your rubbish either. Real gold, that's what I buy for my girl.'

'But how could you ever afford it?' Charity held it up by the chain and the gold glowed in the firelight.

'I did quite well for meself down at Tilbury. Sometimes I wonder why I'm wasting time slaving away working all hours for a pittance when I could be earning real money. I could buy you dozens of presents then.'

'I don't want anything else.' An intense feeling of love

for Danny welled up in her. She ran her index finger over the curve of her initial, then prised the locket open. 'Look there's a place for a photograph. Perhaps we can have one taken together to put in it.' She smiled up at him, took his hand and pressed it to her cheek.

Danny bent and kissed her lightly. 'Why not. We'll get all dolled up shall we? Have one taken for Mum and one for your aunt, 'cos I sometimes think she'd rather see you going out wiv that snobby doctor chap than me.'

'Dr Trevelyan's already spoken for.'

'I'm glad to hear it. He was a bit too interested in you for my liking.'

Changing the subject quickly, Charity said, 'Put the locket on for me, Danny.'

She lifted the knot of hair from the nape of her neck in a graceful movement and Danny bent and fastened the chain. 'It's the same colour as your hair,' he said softly, removing the pins as he spoke. And indeed when the heavy weight of it was free, it flowed down her back like liquid gold.

A woman with loosened hair has loosened inhibitions, thought Danny, going over to the door and locking it. Coming back he coiled the thick swathe round his fingers, pulled her to him and kissed her neck, then her mouth. He was aware of a slight tremor of doubt when he unbuttoned her dress and pulled it over her head, but she sat passively until she was naked except for the locket resting on the curve of her breasts.

Breathing harshly, and hardly able to credit his good luck given her past behaviour, Danny rapidly divested himself of his clothes then stood in front of her, proud of his erect manliness.

Charity had crossed her arms over her breasts in a sub-consciously protective gesture but Danny pulled them away and pressed her down on the carpet, gripping her wrists so that her arms were spreadeagled.

He'd never had a woman of such beauty or class as

Charity before and the sight of her naked, the translucence of her skin in the firelight, made him so excited he became clumsy. He didn't dare wait in case she changed her mind.

She tried not to hold herself tense, but his callused hands were rough on the tender skin of her breasts and, knowing from Stephen how sensual just touching could be, when Danny rammed himself into her, Charity cried out in protest. But he didn't hear. He was grinding himself into her, sweat poured on to her upturned face and the only sensation she felt was pain. Remembering the state of sweet pleasure Stephen had brought her to, she wept. This wasn't how it should be at all, she knew that.

There was some final frenzied pumping then Danny collapsed, lying on her heavily. He got his breath back, gave her a brief kiss and rolled away on to his back.

'Doing . . . you know, that, it'll get better so there's no need to cry, Charity. And I loves yer, yer know that.'

Charity clung to him. 'Oh Danny, do you? That makes me feel so happy.'

He turned his face to hers. 'Let me see you smile then,' he ordered.

She gave him a brief tremulous smile, failed to hold on to it and instead broke down and cried into his shoulder with a deep sense of loss.

Danny let her cry. She'd get over it. After all she'd just been deflowered and sometimes girls regretted it, for a little while anyway. He, though, was filled with a sense of achievement. By God, buying her that locket had certainly paid off and the way things were stirring he was going to want her again very shortly.

Chapter 17

Kate's funeral was a splendid affair, the best the other girls in the house could afford. Plumed horses, mutes – hired mourners accompanying the cortege – and a mountain of greenery and white hothouse lilies. All of them were dressed to the nines, defiantly cheerful and aware of how short their own lives could be if they were cut down by the same dread disease.

At the burial ground where brown earth was piled on top of melting snow, Jim Weston stood staring down into the grave as the coffin was lowered, hands clasped in front of him, head bent and sobbing with the abandon of a child. Stephen was there too and he smiled and nodded in Charity's direction. But she deliberately ignored him and instead stared stony-faced over his shoulder. Discomfited by this slight, Stephen shifted uneasily.

Then, with a blink of disbelief, Charity saw standing behind him looking suitably pious, the Grimbolds. All the old corrosive hate welled up in her and her fingers curled into tight balls of anger. How dare they come here. She managed to contain herself until the priest had intoned the final amen of the burial service, then, pushing her way through the dispersing mourners, she stormed after them.

What a ludicrous pair, Charity thought mockingly, coming up behind them. Her with her acres of undulating flesh, him with his skinny legs. Evil personified. They were easy to catch up with and, once she'd overtaken them, she swung round in their path, spreading her arms wide and forcing them to stop. Then, her eyes glittering with hate and indifferent to the solemnity of the occasion, she hissed at them, 'How dare you come here, you bloody hypocrites, when it's through you two Kate's lying in her grave at twenty-one.'

'Oh my God,' exclaimed Pearl. Then, seeing it was Charity, she screamed, 'Grimbold, get that bitch away from 'ere,' and started to wheeze alarmingly. Then pressing both hands against her chest, she sank down on to the path. She lay there in the slush like a dying elephant, surrounded by the last straggle of mourners.

Grimbold turned on Charity with a raised fist. 'Now look what you've bin an' done.'

'Good, I hope she dies. The world would be a better place without her.'

Grimbold took a step forward as if to strike Charity. But just in time, a voice, Stephen's, intervened, probably saving her from a cracked skull. 'What's happening?' he asked, cutting his way through the circle of spectators.

'My wife's just 'ad an 'eart attack 'cos of that wench there. If she dies, I'll bloody well see she swings for it.' Grimbold's eyes bulged with hatred.

Stephen bent down seeking Pearl's pulse through the bracelets of fat. However he judged there to be little wrong for her eyes were open and she was swearing lustily at Charity. 'That shitty little miss wi' her uppity ways. And to think we rescued 'er from the gutter. Pity she didn't go the same place as her ma did. She deserved no better.'

With the help of several men, Stephen had heaved Pearl to her feet and Charity leapt towards her, ferocious as an alley cat. Grabbing Pearl's massive neck she shook her so hard her fat cheeks wobbled like jelly. 'And where was that? Go on tell me before I bleedin' throttle you . . . you great bag of tripe!' The years were peeled away and Charity was a small, defiant guttersnipe again.

'Charity, for heaven's sake!' This was a girl Stephen didn't recognize and he tried to pull her away. But she delivered several vicious, winding blows to his stomach with her elbow and he gave an exclamation of pain and let go.

'Leave me alone. They've got to tell me what happened to me ma. I've a right to know.'

229

Pearl nursed her neck and stared at Charity with a murderous expression. 'Arright, you asked for it so I'll tell you and serve you bloody well right. She ended up on a slab at the anatomy 'orspital like you should 'ave done.'

A shudder of revulsion ran through the small crowd. The greatest dread of the impoverished was to die an unclaimed pauper in the workhouse. It hung over them like the sword of Damocles. For if such a misfortune befell them, they knew they, too, would end up on the surgeon's dissecting table. And rumour had it that when the hospital was done with you, any parts left were cut up and sold for dogs' meat.

Hearing these chilling words, Charity's brain froze with shock. She wanted to reject what she'd heard, but images she'd blanked from her child's mind resurfaced. Dark wet streets, harsh voices, a pale, thin arm and the rattle of wheels on cobbles. So that was it. With a proud expression and looking neither to left nor right, she turned and walked away, through the respectful space the small crowd had made for her, out through the burial ground gates into the street. She heard Stephen calling, but she couldn't cope with his, or anyone else's sympathy today and she hurried away from him, dodging down an alleyway then cutting through the back streets home.

A few words had forced her to confront her past, to know the worst about herself. There could be no more fantasizing about noble forebears now. The brutal truth was that her mother had most probably been a whore like Kate, although Kate, at least, had had the benefit of a Christian burial. Charity gave a wry smile. Not much of a heritage really. But she comforted herself with one thought. Death had parted them but she knew with an absolute conviction that her mother had loved her. It was enough.

Chapter 18

'Bloody 'ell, you can't be!' Danny hurled the words at her with such savagery, Charity flinched and took a step backwards.

'Well I am,' she retaliated with a bravery she didn't feel.

The pupils of Danny's eyes had dilated and were hard and black. He stood, hands on hips, feet planted wide apart and looking for all the world like his dad. 'This is a fine kettle of fish, ain't it?' He began to circle the table, round and round, compulsively, his pacing making the small room seem like a cage. In his agitation his shoulder caught the edge of the glass cabinet and the fragile cups clattered in alarm. Suddenly he stopped. 'It's no good, you'll just have to do something about it.'

'What, for instance?'

Danny waved his hand vaguely. 'There are plenty of ways of gettin' rid of a kid, girls are doin' it all the time. Take something. Go and see a woman.'

'But you always promised we'd get married if anything happened.' Charity's voice grew tearful as she echoed the cry of all wronged girls down the ages. 'This is our baby, Danny, if you love me like you say you do you should be glad.'

Because she had experienced no sickness, it wasn't until she missed her second monthly in November that Charity knew all was not well and was beset by a deep panic.

Danny was a vigorous, demanding lover, but if she ever suggested she might fall for a baby his reply was always the same. 'It's quite simple, if you do find yourself in the family way we'll get hitched. You'd like that wouldn't you? Every girl wants to get wed, to have that gold band on her finger and a husband and babby to look after. So don't worry your little head about it, I'll take care of everything. Now come and give Danny a kiss.'

But he was singing a different tune now.

'Think about it,' she heard him say. 'How can I marry? I've my apprenticeship to finish.'

'You've talked often enough about leaving the river. Said you didn't like the long hours, complained about the poor pay. Said there was better money to be earned elsewhere. Anyway, if you'd like to know, I don't want to get married any more than you do, but this baby's not going to be a bastard.'

Danny's eyes narrowed and he studied Charity intently, his gaze lingering on her belly. 'How do I know it's mine anyway?'

'What are you suggesting?' Her face was ashen.

'Well you're mighty friendly with that doctor chap, that's all I'm saying.' It was a crude accusation, Danny knew that, and, although he regretted it immediately, he couldn't bring himself to say so, to take her in his arms, in the way she needed, and comfort her, not for the life of him.

Lacerated by the cruel jibe, Charity closed her eyes. Rational thought had deserted her. The blood swirled round in her head, her breathing became tight and her hand groped for the nearest weapon, a half empty cup of tea on the table. Her aim was accurate but seeing it coming, Danny ducked. The cup whizzed over his head, hit the wall, and fragmented into a dozen pieces while lukewarm tea spattered all over the wallpaper then dribbled to the floor.

Mrs Weston, who retired to bed earlier and earlier each evening, had been dozing on her pillows, and the commotion made her sit up with a start. The voices in the room beneath her were raised, angry. A common enough sound in their household, and at first she imagined it to be Danny and his pa at each other's throats. Except that one of the voices belonged to Charity. A lover's tiff she thought and might have left the two of them to make it up in their own way, but the anguish of Charity's sobs betokened more than a mere argument.

Agnes sighed, swung her legs out of bed with care and stood up gingerly. Bleeding was a problem these days and she had to be careful or it could gush from her with the force of water from a fountain.

Wrapping a shawl round her shoulders and thinking to herself, there was a time when I could take these stairs two at a time, she eased her way down, holding on to the banister for support.

'Lord, luv a duck, whatever is going on?' Agnes asked, opening the door and glancing first at the fragments of cup, one of her good ones too, then at Charity's heaving breasts and stricken white face. But the girl's eyes, glazed with hurt and tears, Danny's expression of sulky indignation, together with a touch of feminine instinct, told her nearly all she wanted to know.

'Danny, put the kettle on while I go and get dressed. I think there's some talking to be done here.'

Agnes dressed slowly to conserve her energy, swallowed two tablets to kill the pain and deliberated on what course of action she should take. Time was running out for her. She was tired and life hadn't exactly been a bundle of laughs so she could accept this. But she fretted all the time about Danny, wondering what would become of him when she was no longer around. If he stayed under the same roof as the old man there'd be a murder done eventually. It would be better if he was settled and Charity was a good girl who would look after him. 'It's an ill wind . . . she thought, and went back downstairs again in quite a cheerful frame of mind, knowing what had to be done. A marriage would take place, she'd see to that. Danny might not realize it but it was for his own good.

'Pour the tea, love,' she ordered, sitting down by the fire and noticing with a feeling of deep compassion how the girl's hands trembled so much, tea slopped into the saucers.

But she didn't beat about the bush. 'You're in the family way, aren't you, my dear?'

Charity blushed and fiddled with a tassle on the chenille tablecloth. 'How did you know?'

Agnes smiled. 'I've been around a while y'know and it didn't take a lot of working out. It happens often enough,' she added philosophically, then thought to herself, thank heavens it wasn't that May Potter. With some of the games that lad of mine gets up to it could so easily have been.

'Well, what are you going to do about it, son?' From Charity's tears, Agnes sensed Danny was trying to wriggle out of his obligations, so it was with an unusually cold eye that she regarded him.

Danny picked at a lump of callused skin on the palm of his hand with intense concentration. 'You know I can't get hitched just yet, Ma. Not wiv me apprenticeship to finish, and it's not long now.'

'Perhaps you should 'ave thought about the consequences a bit earlier.' Her sympathy entirely with Charity, she went and put an arm round her shoulder. 'Does your aunt know about this?'

Charity shook her head, biting her lips to hold back the tears. She felt betrayed, unutterably desolate. How could Danny have even thought, let alone said what he did.

'How far are you gone?'

'About t . . . two months.'

'Right, we're going round there to see her now. This matter has got to be settled tonight.' Looking determined, Agnes fetched her best hat, pinned it in place and wrapped herself up well in a bulky jacket. She led the way, speaking to neither of them, banged on the door in a forceful manner and even in her misery, Charity had time to be surprised by Mrs Weston's authoritative air. In fact she seemed to be quite enjoying herself.

Eliza looked taken aback to see Charity standing on the step with Danny and his mother and she studied each face in turn. 'Is something wrong?' she asked at last.

'Yes there is. But if you don't mind me sayin' so Miss Pumfrey, I don't think the doorstep is the proper place to discuss matters of a personal nature.'

'Oh . . . no . . . of course not.' Eliza stepped aside and the three of them entered. Charity shuffled in, eyes downcast, Danny had the look of a surly child.

Shooing several cats from chairs, Eliza wiped them with her apron and invited her guests to sit down.

Although each was fully conversant with the other's life, Eliza and Mrs Weston were on hardly more than nodding terms. However, Agnes Weston's grave demeanour, and Charity's refusal to meet her eye was already preparing Eliza for the worst.

How could you have, child, she wanted to cry out. How could you have thrown your intelligence and beauty away on that young man. But it would do no good. What was done was done. She gave a deep sigh of regret and with a sinking heart waited for Mrs Weston to say the words that would chain Charity, in whom she'd invested so many hopes and dreams, to Danny for the rest of her days.

Eliza hadn't shed tears in a long time. But she did that night. After the arrangements had been sorted out and Danny and his mother had departed, she sat down and let them pour out of her.

Totally ill at ease with the situation, Charity stood, not knowing what to do. Her debt to Eliza was incalculable and this made her guilt double-edged. She understood her disappointment and could have accepted harsh words as a just punishment, but the indomitable Eliza in tears was something she found difficult to handle.

Moving over to her aunt, Charity reached out and touched her on the shoulder. 'I'm sorry, Aunt Eliza.' Her voice wobbled on the edge of tears. 'I know I've hurt you and I know you're disappointed in me, but I'm going to be a good wife to Danny, I promise you that.'

Eliza reached up and patted her hand. 'I know you will.

235

I just think you're too good for him. But it's too late for recriminations. Love makes fools of us all and I'm crying for myself as much as you. Anyway, I'm not in a position to condemn what you did. I've got many faults but hypocrisy isn't one of them.' She wiped her eyes and blew her nose. 'Sit down, dear, I want to tell you something. I've never spoken to you much about my past life, have I?'

Charity shook her head. 'No. Although I know your Pa was a sea captain.'

'That's right. And I was an only child. Mother didn't have me until she was forty. I think she was a bit surprised to find herself a parent at that age. But she was lovely; pretty and gentle. Not a bit like me. I favoured my father in looks and build, although I hope not in character. But what makes a man handsome, doesn't necessarily suit a woman. To put it bluntly I was plain. Father was away for much of the year and life with Mama was comfortable and secure. But then father retired from the sea. I can tell you, Charity, he was a stern, unyielding man and he treated Mama and me much as he would his crew. He demanded complete obedience. Mama was terrified of him, but as I grew older I started to question his authority, then oppose it. He tried to thrash me into submission but it didn't work.

'I hadn't got the looks to please men, so they didn't pay me much attention. Then I met Carlton.' Eliza paused and stared into the fire. She'd never understood why, even when she was dizzy with love, what anyone as handsome as Carlton could have seen in her. 'We started meeting,' she went on, 'in secret.' She looked Charity straight in the eye. 'We had an . . . er . . . relationship.' How cold that sounded, she thought to herself, for something that had been so wild and passionate. 'Then he disappeared from my life just as mysteriously as he'd appeared, leaving me pregnant. I was so ignorant it was several months before I understood why I was getting fat. Then I managed to disguise my condition until I was nearly eight months gone.' Eliza paused again. Even as a middle-aged woman she still felt a frisson of fear remembering her father's apoplectic, brutal rage. 'My father was a huge man and when he found out he ripped the clothes from me then took his leather belt and whipped my naked body until I was raw and bleeding.' Her voice cracking with emotion she went on, 'I . . . I went into labour almost immediately, but he . . . he refused me a doctor and Mama delivered the baby.'

'Was it all right?'

'Yes. A little boy. Beautiful too,' she tried to talk but couldn't go on. She could still feel that small, warm body against her breasts, remember that rush of love, her delight when her mother placed him in her arms. 'I told Mama I was going to call him Paul, then he started to exercise his lungs and my father came into the room and wrenched my little darling from my arms. I shall never forget what he said. "This bastard's not staying here to bring shame on my family name."

'I was very weak but somehow I managed to drag myself from my bed. I clung to my father pleading with him to let me keep my child. "I'll teach you to defy me," he said, and pushed Mama aside, kicked me and strode from the house. I tried to follow but collapsed on the pavement and developed a fever. I never saw my baby again.'

'What happened to him?' Charity asked in a very small voice. This tragedy was too enormous for her to comprehend. She took Eliza's hand and it felt like ice.

'I don't know. He would never tell me even when he lay dying a year later. But I used to walk the streets, peering in baby carriages, then later I would stand outside school gates. But do you know what I think?' Eliza looked up at Charity and there was utter desolation in her eyes. 'I think my father deliberately drowned his own grandson in the river.'

Chapter 19

The wedding wasn't the most joyous of affairs. After the ceremony, Danny's father expressed the opinion that his son was a bloody idiot getting himself hooked like that and had then taken himself off to the pub in disgust.

As women will, Eliza and Agnes did their best. Eliza by making Charity a dress in powder blue wool, Mrs Weston in providing a tea of sandwiches and cake afterwards.

Charity found it hard to concentrate on the marriage ceremony. Very little registered until the vicar declared them man and wife. Her husband. It didn't seem possible. Danny's my husband. The words somersaulted around in her brain. I'm his wife. Until death us do part. How long would that be? Forty years? Fifty? Maybe even more. They were both young and healthy after all. Charity gave Danny a sideways glance. He wore a new suit, a stiff white collar he kept trying to ease with his finger, and boots that squeaked when he walked. He looked awkward and hot, imprisoned by his clothes and circumstances. In fact, thoroughly miserable.

I'll be a good wife. Look after him, love him, make him so happy he'll stop regretting his loss of freedom, Charity swore to herself, then took her new husband's hand and squeezed it tight to reassure him.

She'd needed Mollie there that day and like the good friend she was she came. As soon as they all got back to the house, Charity dragged her away into a corner. There was a lot that had happened in both their lives that needed catching up on.

'No nursing career for you now then,' Mollie observed, in that blunt way of hers.

Charity gave a shrug, trying to dismiss such ambitions as no more than the dreams of an idealistic young girl.

'Doesn't seem like it. But then they'd probably never have taken an ignoramus like me anyway.'

'Don't put yourself down. You know that's not true. But my mind's made up. That's what I shall do when I finish at Bedford, study to become a doctor. It's one of the careers open to women now.'

'Oh Mollie, you are lucky.' But she didn't feel envious, just glad for her friend. Mollie was doing brilliantly at college and her social horizons were expanding, too. More and more of her free time was spent with her friend, Isabel, and Caspar's name was dropped frequently into the conversation. Still, no time for regrets, Charity thought. She had made her bed and she must lie on it.

She toyed with a sandwich. 'If only I'd had your brains.' She sighed, then deciding she must put a brave face on it, squared her shoulders and went on in a bright voice, 'Still, we've got a nice little room. Aunt Eliza gave us the money to furnish it and Danny's got himself a job in one of the flour mills. At least this winter he'll be warm and dry. Won't be put out of work if the weather turns bad. When we're settled you can come and see us. We're going to need every penny we can get so I shall keep working in the shop and Aunt Eliza will pay me a wage.' She looked towards where Eliza and her new mother-in-law sat talking. 'Actually, I think they're both really looking forward to the baby. Although it's months off yet, they've both started knitting.'

Mollie just hoped her friend wasn't going to turn into one of those women with no interests beyond domesticity and babies. It would be such a tragedy to see that bright mind dulled by too many pregnancies and too little money. 'You'll keep up your evening classes, won't you?' she asked, to change the subject.

Charity shook her head. 'Danny doesn't really like me doing things like . . .'

She didn't finish. 'What doesn't Danny like you doing? Go on, tell me.' He stood in front of her holding a glass of beer.

239

'I was going to say you don't like me reading and studying or such things.'

'Too right I don't. And mind you don't go giving 'er ideas.' He waggled his index finger at Mollie.

Mollie bridled. 'I see no harm in reading and little point in ignorance,' she snapped back at him.

'I'm her husband, I tell her what to do.' He turned to his best man. 'Have you ever read a book, Boscoe?'

Boscoe ruminated for a moment, then he shook his head. 'Perish the thought.'

'No, nor 'ave I, and it's done me no harm.'

The mutual antagonism that had always existed between her friend and her husband seemed about to erupt. Aware that Mollie was sharpening her tongue for the cutting retort that would humiliate Danny and turn him into her enemy for life, Charity quickly interjected. 'Danny, I think your ma wants you.'

'Does she?' Immediately his concern was for his mother and he turned away and walked over to her. Crouching beside her, he took her hand with a tenderness he showed no one else. Charity heard him say, 'What can I get you Ma?' then she turned back to Mollie.

'Phew, that was a close one. I thought you two were going to fall out. Try and be friends with him, Mollie,' Charity pleaded, 'or it's going to make life difficult.'

'Of course I'll be friends with him. Nothing will come between you and me. Boyfriends, husbands, children, no one, you must know that.' She lowered her voice a shade. 'Now tell me, what's happened about Stephen? Your letters were full of him at one time, then suddenly it all stopped.'

It could still make Charity blush with shame to remember what a fool she'd made of herself with Stephen. 'Oh I see him around. And he wrote me a nice letter when he heard I was getting married. But he's got a lady friend. That Blanche, do you remember her, the snotty-nosed one on the boat. It's all very serious, so there'll probably be wedding bells pretty soon. And he'll move away after that. Can you imagine Blanche living round here? Women like her don't come cheap and he'll need a practice that will pay for her expensive tastes.'

'I quite liked him myself at one time, but it passed,' said Mollie.

So did I, thought Charity. But rich and poor were like oil and water – they didn't mix.

Mollie stood up. 'Anyway, I'd better go. I want to go and see Mum and Dad, then I've got to get back to finish off an essay.' She bent and kissed Charity. 'Good luck, love and keep the letters coming.'

She said goodbye to everyone and Charity walked with her to the door and they waved and threw kisses to each other right until Mollie was out of sight.

When she'd gone, Charity closed the door with a sigh and leaned against it. She couldn't blame her friend but she had the feeling that if Mollie hadn't gone away, she wouldn't be standing here only a few hours married but with a sense of emptiness and devoid of joy. She was still standing there when Danny popped his head round the door.

'Hey, what's wrong?' He came towards her with open arms and that smile of his that could always melt her heart and she went to him with a feeling of love and gratitude, wanting to be absorbed into him. It was going to be all right. It was. He kissed her gently and nuzzled her neck, then said in her ear, 'Come on let's leave this lot and go to our own little place, there's something I urgently want to do to my wife.'

So they crept out of the house like a couple of truanting kids and ran, holding hands and shrieking with laughter down the road. The house where they had rented one room was at the bottom end of Kenning Street and, as they crept up the stairs, they could hear the subterranean rumble of trains vibrating up through the house.

'Hold on,' said Danny when they reached the door of their room. Picking her up he carried her over the threshold. 'And now Mrs Weston,' he said, letting her fall on the bed and giving her a kiss, 'you can get all that finery off.'

'Let me light the fire first or we'll freeze to death.' Charity went and drew the cretonne curtains Eliza had made for them, lit the lamp then put a match under the fire she'd already laid with paper, wood and coal. It blazed quickly and she looked round her with a feeling of satisfaction. There was new lino on the floor, they had a chair each, a table to eat at and a large brass bed was pushed against the wall. She remembered the first time she'd been shown the room. It had been filthy and what little view there was from the window, obscured by several years' soot. But it was cheap, so she'd taken it. First of all she'd had the chimney swept, ripped off the layers of wallpaper under which she knew bugs could breed and limewashed the walls. Then she'd set to work with carbolic and scrubbed away the smell of dirt.

She went and sat by Danny on the bed and rested her head on his shoulder. 'It looks cosy, doesn't it? And it might not be much but everything in this room belongs to us. If we save hard, when the baby comes we'll be able to move into something bigger.'

Danny didn't answer. Instead he started to undo the buttons on her dress. When they were both naked they slipped in between the cold sheets, shivering and clutching each other for warmth.

He was about to push himself into her without more than a perfunctory kiss, when she stopped him.

'Danny, there isn't any hurry, no one's going to suddenly barge in on us, so can't we take our time, enjoy each other.'

He held her away from him and shook his head in puzzlement. 'I don't know where you get these notions. From those daft novels you read I suppose.' But, as a concession, he fingered her nipples, kissed them, rubbed his hands between her legs. Then stopped. 'Is that what you mean?'

'Yes, but you don't have to stop just yet.'

He repeated his none-too-skilful techniques. 'Bloody 'ell Charity, I can't 'old out no longer.' He levered himself into position between her legs, and as usual there was no pleasure in the sexual act for Charity. She lay staring at the shadows on the ceiling, aware only of the rhythmic squeaking of the springs and the bed rocking against the wall.

Then a man's voice in the next room shouted, ''Urry up and be done, for Christ sake or you'll 'ave the bleedin' 'ouse down.' And Charity felt so mortified she blushed in the darkness.

While Danny slept, Charity slipped out of bed, wrapped herself in her coat and made herself a pot of tea. The day had been a strain but now it was warm, quiet and blessedly peaceful. She was staring into the fire when Danny woke.

He stretched, blinked and sat up. 'How about a cuppa for yer old man then.'

She refilled the pot, took him over a cup but when she handed it to him she could see his face wore that sullen look again. His good humour had lasted for all of two hours. She reached out a hand and pushed back his hair in a gentle, placatory gesture. Why was it Danny could always make her feel that their situation was entirely her fault. 'Are you happy, Danny?'

'Happy as a bloody chicken in a stewpot.' He flung back the bedclothes. 'I'm going out for a drink.'

'But we've only just got married. This is our wedding night. You can't, Danny!' she protested, near to tears and unable to credit his heartlessness.

'Oh, who's to stop me.'

'Me.' She ran to the door and stood guarding it. But he glared at her with such a threatening expression she felt nervous enough to step aside. Charity was sobbing bitterly now. 'Go on, go and don't bother to come back!' she screamed after him over the banisters.

'Perhaps I won't,' he yelled back, his last words before he slammed shut the front door.

Charity cried herself to sleep, huddled up in a ball, and wishing she was back with Eliza, sleeping in her own bed with Lolly curled in the crook of her arm, soft, warm and comforting. Everything was a terrible mistake and her life was in ruins.

It was late when Danny crawled in beside her, waking her with the cold night air he brought with him and the smell of drink on his breath. He made no apology but climbed on top of her, pushing up her nightdress without any preliminaries. But thankfully he was flaccid from the ale he had consumed. With a curse he rolled away from her and in a moment was fast asleep.

But over the months there were lighter, happier moments in their marriage. He had tremendous mood swings but when Danny tried, he could be a marvellous, entertaining and loving husband. And there seemed to be plenty of overtime at the flour mill so he was flush with money and spent lavishly.

Sometimes she'd protest over some unnecessary extravagance. 'Shouldn't we be saving, Danny?'

'Certainly not. You're only young once, so let's enjoy ourselves I say. Anyway, you're gonna be stuck indoors once the little 'un comes. Besides, there's plenty more where this came from.' And for her benefit, Danny would jingle the gold and silver coins in his pocket.

However, Charity had a rather more cautious attitude to money. So each week, without mentioning it to Danny, some of the wages she received from Eliza were placed in a large vase on the mantelpiece.

On Saturday nights they went to the market and stocked up for the week with a plentiful supply of food. They took regular trips to the Music Hall, stopping off afterwards for supper at the pie and eel shop. Although she often found they were accompanied by Boscoe and May, Charity didn't object or say anything. Over certain matters she was learning the wisdom of keeping her mouth shut. Rows she wanted to avoid, so she was

244

prepared to put up with a certain amount as long as it kept her husband in a happy frame of mind.

Given the chance, Charity often thought afterwards, their marriage might have continued to improve, their love grow, but for a train of events tragic and inexorable.

It had been one of Danny's bad days. He'd come home from work, looking like a clown with his clothes, face and hair coated with flour. Stripping off, he had silently washed himself in the hot water she poured into the bowl for him, then without a please or thank you, his hand stretched out for the towel she always kept warm by the fire. In spite of the limited utensils at her disposal, Charity had become quite a good cook, and Danny was usually fulsome in his praise. But today he pushed the plate of oxtail, dumplings and carrots away before he'd even half finished.

Insulted, she could no longer hold her tongue. 'Is there something wrong with your dinner?'

Danny levered himself up from the table and went to the window. Pulling back the curtain he stared morosely at the wet roofs. 'I'm just bloody sick of working in that flour mill, it's enough to put anyone off their food, filling sacks of flour all day.'

She went over and put her arm round his waist. 'Go back to your old job then. I know you don't like the river in the winter but it'll be getting warmer soon.'

Danny pushed her arm away. 'But I broke me apprenticeship didn't I?'

'But you could still get work. They know how good you are so a lighterage firm would soon snap you up.'

'Yeah but I'll never be able to enter Doggett's will I? Not this year, not ever. Never know what it's like to win.' He turned on her. 'And d'you know whose fault that is. Yours.'

'It is not,' Charity snapped back. 'It takes two to make a baby, or have you forgotten your part in it. And for heaven's sake stop feeling sorry for yourself all the time.'

245

'Oh damn and blast you, woman.' He strode to the door, picking up his overcoat and white muffler on the way. Charity didn't try and detain him, it was a waste of time. He'd go out, get drunk, come back, sleep it off and tomorrow ask her to forgive him. And of course she would, and wait up for him, too. But what worried her more than anything when he was unsettled like this was what he might get up to. She'd sooner trust a sewer rat than Boscoe.

She got up to make some cocoa, felt the baby kick out and sat down again. How much longer now. She counted on her fingers. Just over two months. Another dragging two months. Frankly she'd be glad to be done with it. The discomfort of pregnancy, the backaches, the fatigue, made her marvel that so many women endured it year after year. But that wasn't her intention and whether Danny liked it or not she'd be making use of some of the contraceptive advice that Doctor Forbes had offered.

In the early months the only emotion she'd felt towards the intruder forming in her womb was one of resentment. But once it began to move, it became an individual, someone with a mind of its own. Someone with its character already forming, along with its fingers and toes, and she began to feel a curiosity about it. Not strong maternal feelings, that only came after the birth she'd been told, but an interest. What colour its eyes might be, who would it take after in character, would it be a boy or a girl. She'd already decided on names, Kathleen if it was a girl, Andrew if it was a boy, although, of course, Danny would have to be consulted first.

Her preoccupations were interrupted by an impatient and unexpected knocking on the door. Startled, she jumped to her feet. Relieved it was locked, and trying to hide her unease with a brusque tone, she called out, 'Who is it?'

'Danny's Pa. I want to speak to him, it's urgent.'

Danny's Pa? He'd never been here in his life before.

246

She lumbered to the door, unlocked it, eased it open a fraction but didn't invite him in.

'He's not here, Mr Weston.'

'Can you come then?' He looked distracted and repeatedly combed his fingers through his hair. 'It's Agnes. I got home to find her lying on the floor out cold. She . . . she's bleeding like the devil . . . I . . . I dunno what to do.' His voice held a mixture of self-pity, fear and helplessness.

Charity's heart gave a lurch, and with a vision of Agnes lying there in her own blood she asked sharply, 'And you've left her all on her own?'

He was pretty thick-skinned but he heard the criticism in her tone and bristled slightly. 'Well I 'ad to fetch someone, didn't I?'

'Yes all right, I'm coming.' Trying to keep a hold of herself and not to lapse into panic, she thought, what should I do first? Keep calm for a start or you're no good to anyone, then get Stephen. She picked up her coat, remembered Danny in time and scribbled him a note.

Charity always thought of Jim Weston as being a big man. But as he stood waiting while she locked the door, he seemed diminished by the gloomy light of the landing, shrivelled, the bombast gone from him.

But she had neither the inclination nor the time to waste feeling sorry for him. Even hating him would require more emotion than she could spare just then. Her concern was centred entirely on Agnes and the alleviation of her pain. She loved her mother-in-law, admired her stoicism and courage. And, although he would have denied responsibility, it was Jim Weston's treatment of her, his violence, which had caused much of his wife's ill health, probably shortened her life. He'd never lifted a finger to lighten her load, shown her any sympathy as she grew more frail, and even his love for Kate couldn't redeem him in her eyes. But it was too late to berate him, and if he went to pieces now he'd be even less of a help.

Outside on the pavement she turned and said to him,

'You get straight back to your wife, make her as comfortable as possible and I'll go and fetch the doctor. There's nothing we can do on our own.'

'Don't be long, will you?' he pleaded. 'I ain't too good at managing things like this.'

'I'll be as quick as I can. I'm as worried about her as you are Mr Weston.'

During the past year, she'd made every effort to avoid Stephen and, by and large, she'd succeeded. But he was the only competent doctor in the area. So now, as Charity made her way round to the surgery with as much speed as her bulk would allow, she repeated to herself over and over again until the words became a chant, let Stephen be there, let Stephen be there. Otherwise it would have to be Dr Campbell. And if he was still standing on two feet at this time of night it would be a miracle, she thought as she rattled the knocker with a desperate impatience.

'Come on, come on,' Charity muttered, was just raising the knocker again when the door was flung open.

With an expression on her face that would turn milk sour, Miss Fry snapped 'I'm not deaf you know. I heard you the first time and it's a long way from the kitchen with my legs.'

Sorry Miss Fry,' answered Charity, forced to be humble, 'but my mother-in-law is seriously ill. Is Dr Trevelyan in?'

'As far as I know, he is.'

'Can I see him?'

'You'd better come up.'

'Charity! How nice to see you.' As Stephen rose to greet her, Charity hardened her heart against his welcoming smile and remembered instead the last occasion she'd been in this room and the deep humiliation he'd inflicted on her. But now wasn't the time to dredge up past hurts, dwell on wounds that hadn't quite healed. She was here because Agnes was desperately sick and needed his help and her own feelings didn't come into it.

Stephen had stopped halfway across the room and his hazel eyes were regarding her with concern. Charity was glad she had her marriage and pregnancy to protect her from any lingering attraction she might feel for him.

'Are you all right, my dear?

'I'm fine. But Danny's mum's not. Could you come, now, this minute? I wouldn't have bothered you, but it's very serious.' Charity's voice, stance and manner conveyed to him her anxiety and he went immediately to collect his coat and bag. 'What exactly are her symptoms?' he asked, as he checked instruments and bottles.

'I only know what Mr Weston told me. He said he'd found her unconscious and bleeding badly.'

'Where was she haemorrhaging from, the mouth?'

They were out in the street now and Charity was having a problem matching his pace. 'The . . . the other end I think,' she panted, slightly embarrassed.

'However did she reach this state? Obviously she hasn't seen a doctor recently.' The length of Stephen's strides were increasing in direct proportion to his anger.

'No. I kept trying to get her to come and see you, honestly I did. But she always refused point blank and just kept taking all these pills she got from the chemist. And Danny would never listen to me either. I think they both kept hoping the illness would go away.'

'Why in heaven's name people can't come to see me before they get really sick, I don't know. After all, I can't perform miracles,' he snapped.

'Perhaps they can't always afford it,' Charity suggested.

'I know money comes into it, but still . . .'

'Here's the house,' interrupted Charity, relieved to see that Mr Weston had had the good sense to leave the door ajar. She led the way down the hall into the small back room, found it was empty and went to the bottom of the stairs and called out, 'Mr Weston, I've got Dr Trevelyan here.'

'Bring 'im up.'

Agnes was lying on the bed. Her eyes were closed, blood was seeping through her skirt and, Charity thought ridiculously, her nice white counterpane, she won't like that being spoiled. Controlling herself, she moved over to the bed and took her hand. 'Mrs Weston, it's me, Charity,' she called quietly, then bent and kissed her cold cheek, wanting to pour some of her own robust health and love into her. But there was no response, not even a flicker of an eyelid.

'If you wouldn't mind I'd like to see the patient alone.' Stephen was preoccupied now, taking off his coat, opening his bag and putting his stethoscope in his ears.

'Righto, Doc,' Mr Weston mumbled, and they went downstairs and waited. For an age they sat, neither of them saying a word. The minutes, quarter hours, half hours and hours ticked by, hot coals moved in the grate and Stephen's measured tread could be heard above them. Then the footsteps quickened, became urgent then all at once stopped. And so, it seemed to Charity, did her heart. In the silence she held herself tense and stared at the ceiling. No sound came from the bedroom, and she wanted to yell out. After an age the footsteps started up again, very slow, reluctant almost, across the floor and down the stairs. Already knowing what he was going to say, they were both standing by the time he reached the bottom step and came into the room.

Stephen came face to face with death, and consequently an awareness of his own mortality, on an almost daily basis. However his features were grave but composed like the good doctor he was. 'I'm sorry, I tried my best, but there was just nothing I could do for your wife, Mr Weston. She had cancer and it had reached a very advanced stage. 'If only . . .'

Stephen was interrupted by Danny hurling himself into the room, eyes glassy and smelling like a distillery.

'Where's Ma. How is she?'

No one said a word. He stared from face to face, then

250

his own features seemed to collapse. 'What's wrong? Why don't you answer?'

There was no pretence from Stephen. 'I'm sorry, Danny, but your mother is dead.'

'No!' He threw back his head with a great roar like an injured beast then turned, and, pushing Stephen aside rushed up the stairs with Charity following close behind. 'Ma, it's me, Danny, you're gonna be all right, really you are. And I promise I'll stay wiv you until you're better.' He sank to his knees on the floor and took her hand, rubbing it frantically, then holding it against his chest. 'Ma, don't die, don't leave me please,' he sobbed.

Pitying him, feeling his pain, the tears rolled down Charity's face. Stephen had now come into the bedroom, followed by Mr Weston, who stood staring at his dead wife with an embarrassed expression. As her spouse he knew something was expected of him, but what it was, he wasn't quite sure.

Stephen went over and touched Danny on the head. 'Danny, it's no good,' he said gently.

'Go away.' Danny snarled, 'You didn't do nuffink' to save her.'

''e did what 'e could, Danny.' Mr Weston's tone was unexpectedly conciliatory.

Danny stood up and advanced towards his father, fists bunched. 'And that's more 'an can be said for you, ain't it? That's why she's dead, 'cos of you. You bastard!' He moved closer and pushed his fist almost against his father's nose.

'Danny, stop it!' Charity screamed, rushing to separate father and son. 'Your ma's just passed on, can't you two allow her a little peace?'

'Get away woman.' Confused, grief-stricken and not sure who to blame, Danny pushed Charity roughly away. Her shoe caught on the edge of some torn lino. Fighting to save herself, she reached out to grab the bedrail, but her heavy body lost its balance and she went flying, face first, arms out, like a swimmer diving into the water. She fell heavily on to her stomach, there was a sickening crack as her forehead hit the fender then she let out a scream of pain and doubled up like a jackknife.

Chapter 20

For several frozen seconds all three men stood staring down at her, mesmerized into immobility by shock. Then making a circling motion with his head, Danny wailed pitifully, 'Oh God, what have I done? What have I done?'

'Plenty by the look of it,' Stephen spat out and dropped to his knees beside her. He felt Charity's forehead and pulse, said gently, 'It's all right my dear, I'm here, I'll take care of you. How do you feel?'

Charity grimaced and waited for the vice-like pain low in her back to pass. 'It's my back . . . it hurts.' Another wave of pain made her hold her breath and close her eyes.

Danny covered his face with his hands and began to sob. 'I didn't mean to hurt her, I swear I didn't. I love her, truly I do.'

'Pull yourself together man, for Christ's sake. Come on, help me lift her. Is there another bed here?'

Danny rubbed his nose along his shirt sleeve and attempted control his sobs. 'My old one next door.'

Between them they got Charity into the next room where they carefully lowered her on to the bed. Her skin had a greenish tinge to it and was oily with sweat, and as Stephen took a cloth and wiped it away, she began to moan in distress.

'Is . . . is she going to be all right?'

'I wouldn't like to be in your shoes if she's not,' Stephen threatened. 'Now if you wouldn't mind leaving.'

'She's my wife, why can't I stay?' To cover his fear, Danny spoke in a belligerent manner.

'Because I think she's gone into premature labour that's

why and you'd be nothing but a hindrance. But if you do want to make yourself useful find me clean sheeting, a nightgown and put a kettle on to boil. Mr Weston, you go round and get Miss Pumfrey, she ought to be here. Then as soon as you can you must go and arrange for your wife to be laid out.'

'Right you are guv.' He touched his forelock then, relieved to be away from it all, Jim Weston quickly disappeared downstairs.

At eight the following morning Charity was delivered of a small, perfectly formed, but stillborn baby boy. The labour had been long and exhausting and although Stephen had fought for both their lives, the baby hadn't the strength to survive the gruelling journey.

Weak herself from loss of blood and the ordeal her slight body had been subjected to, Charity nevertheless accepted it quietly when he broke the tragic news.

'May I hold him for a little while,' was all she said, 'just to know what it feels like.'

'Of course, my dear,' Stephen answered and, wrapping the tiny body in a blanket he handed it to her.

Crooning, Charity rocked him back and forth, kissing each tiny finger, stroking the small head still covered in mucus and blood and almost choking on the rush of love she felt for her dead son. He was so beautiful, so perfect.

Stephen himself felt emotionally and physically drained but watching Charity, it seemed to him that she was bearing up remarkably well. And yet there had been several times during the long hours of the night when he'd thought it was about to become a house touched by the hand of death, not once or twice but three times. But calling upon all his medical knowledge, he'd fought like the devil to save her, for the alternative, a world without Charity, would have been unthinkable, unbearable.

'Would you like me to send Danny up?'

She looked up with a smile. 'Yes please, I want him to see the baby.'

253

His eyes were gritty with fatigue, his tongue, as he ran it round his dry mouth, felt thick and furred. With a sense of deep longing, Stephen thought to himself, oh for a fragrant cup of Earl Grey, then a hot bath and bed. But he wasn't done yet. The news still had to be broken to Danny.

He found him sprawled in a chair and fast asleep, his smooth young features as yet unmarked by the tragedy he'd set in motion.

Eliza sat bolt upright and wide awake. But her legs were stiff and cramped and when she saw Stephen she eased herself to her feet gingerly, preparing herself for the worst. 'Well, how is she?' Anxiety made her tone sharp.

'Worn out. I'll be honest with you, there were times during the night when I didn't think she'd make it but she must have a stronger constitution than I supposed. What she needs now is plenty of rest.'

And the baby . . . ?

There was no point in beating about the bush. 'Still-born, I'm afraid.'

'Oh.' Eliza closed her eyes and swayed. She'd so wanted this baby. Her arms ached to hold another small life in her arms, it would have made up for so much.

Stephen moved to her side, gripping her elbow. 'Are you all right, Miss Pumfrey? Try not to blame Danny. He was so distraught at his mother's death, he didn't know what he was doing.' God why am I making excuses for the young fool, Stephen thought. 'I know it's sad, but Charity's safe and that's the main thing. And she and Danny are young so I shouldn't be surprised if there's another baby along pretty soon, perhaps even next year.'

Eliza straightened her shoulders and cleared her throat. 'I expect you're right. I'll wake Danny now, he should go up and see Charity first.'

The firm grip of her hand on his shoulder woke Danny at once. He stared at her with a befuddled expression, blinked then jumped to his feet. 'What is it? It's Charity,

254

go on tell me, she's dead, ain't she?' He stared at Stephen then at Eliza, a blind terror in his blue eyes.

'No she's not and she wants to see you.'

Pure joy lit up his face. Without waiting to hear any more, he tore from the room, knocking a chair flying in his eagerness to see his wife.

Charity was still crooning over the tiny form when he entered the room. Weak with relief he leaned against the door. So everything is all right, I've been given a second chance, he thought. I swear to God from now on I'm going to be the best husband and father in the world. We're going to be as happy as pigs in clover, me, Charity and the kid. Eagerly he marched across to his wife. 'Is it a boy or a girl?'

'A boy.'

'Let me see.'

'You can hold him if you like.'

She held out the bundle and Danny received it with a feeling of reverence. His flesh, his son.

'Isn't he lovely?' Charity smiled up at her husband. 'Such perfect little hands.'

'Bu . . . but . . .' Danny stared down at the feathery eyelashes, the closed lids then his face crumpled. 'He's dead.'

'No, just gone to sleep.'

'Dead! Dead I tell you, dead like Ma!' Danny screamed. Then shoving the tiny corpse back at her he collapsed on to his knees and started pounding on the floor with his fists.

Almost deranged with grief, Danny wore his pain and guilt like stigmata, and only after Stephen had given him a sedative did he calm down and eventually fall asleep. He moved through the funeral of his mother and son like a sleepwalker. When they returned to their room, he paced it restlessly for over an hour then suddenly announced, 'I'm going out,' and disappeared for several days.

255

They should have been mourning the loss of their baby together, as a husband and wife, offering each other solace and comfort. But just when she needed Danny most, Charity sat desolate, either with her hands pressed against her empty womb or sorting compulsively through the tiny garments Eliza had knitted. But interwoven with her despair was a growing bitterness. She could so easily have blamed him for the tragedy but she hadn't. And yet as always, Danny's answer to it all was to slam out of the house and into the nearest pub. This time though, she decided, he would be made to see that he'd done it once too often.

It was obvious to Charity when Danny staggered back filthy and with a harsh cough that he'd been sleeping rough. But his indifference to her needs diluted her concern and although she cleaned him up and put him to bed, his self-pity just angered her.

Stephen dropped in regularly to check on Charity's health and this evening, when he saw Danny asleep he went over to the bed. 'So the prodigal has returned.'

'Yes, but I'm not killing the fatted calf.' Charity's tone surprised Stephen, it sounded hard for her. 'He's got a bad cough though. If he wakes up maybe you could take a look at him.'

Charity looked at Stephen and realized that the support and care he had given her through the recent dark days had, to some extent, counteracted her past bitterness and the old ease and friendliness had crept back into their relationship. They moved away from the bed, keeping their voices low, but Danny was already awake. He didn't let on but instead watched them through half closed lids, noticed how close together their heads were, all matey like, heard their voices low and intimate. A violent, dizzying jealousy surged up in him. What were they saying? Was it lovey-dovey talk? He strained his ears, heard his own name but that was all. Supposing she was planning to leave? His stomach gave a sickening jolt. But she wouldn't do that, not Charity, she loved him, didn't she?

She might, though, if he didn't pull his socks up and she'd always been a bit taken with the stuck-up bastard, heaven alone knew why. Well he wasn't having any of that. Charity was his. If only they could put all these bad things behind them. Make a new start, move to the country, Kent perhaps or Essex, and open up a little grocery store. But like everything it needed money, and not a piddling amount either.

They paid such a measly wage at the flour mill, he'd been pushed into helping Boscoe lift a few pieces here and there recently, just to stay out of the poor house. But now Boscoe had a new idea up his sleeve, the final big job he called it, the one that would leave them rolling in it. But Danny wasn't sure. A bit of pilfering was one thing but real thievery where you could be sent down for the rest of your natural, well that really needed a lot of thinking about. And Boscoe's idea was so wild could it even be pulled off? Danny felt a shiver of excitement. Maybe if it was planned well. And it would solve all the problems he had just now . . .

Hearing a snuffling noise, Danny opened his eyes a fraction wider. Charity was crying into her handkerchief and Stephen had somehow managed to get an arm round her shoulder. Bloody 'ell, he wasn't going to get away with that. He shot up in bed. 'Hey, what's going on?'

He expected both of them to jump guiltily apart, but all Charity did was wipe her eyes and blow her nose while Stephen said calmly, 'So you're awake Danny.'

'Too right I am. And not before time either, by the look of it.'

Charity's head shot up. 'What are you talking about?'

'You and is nibs 'ere . . .' Danny's accusations were interrupted by a bout of coughing.

'You'd better let me look at that chest of yours Danny.' Stephen opened his bag and went to take out his stethoscope.

But Danny drew back. 'You ain't looking at my chest, just sling your 'ook.'

'For God's sake Danny . . .' in her exasperation Charity couldn't finish.

'I want 'im to go.'

'Take no notice, Stephen, I think he's got some fever of the brain.'

But Stephen got ready to leave anyway. 'I'll call back tomorrow. That cough needs keeping an eye on, it could develop into something more serious. In the meantime see that he stays in bed.'

Charity contained herself until she heard the front door close, then, eyes blazing, she went for Danny.

'Is that all you can do when people are trying to help, make nasty little insinuations? And after leaving me here on my own for three days, not knowing if you were dead or alive.'

'Would you even care if I was dead?' Danny taunted.

'Stop being so childish and stupid. Do it again, and I promise you I won't be here next time. And that's no idle threat. I've taken about as much from you as I'm going to. You're not the only one suffering. He was my baby too, and I carried him, felt him move inside me. But have you ever given a thought to me, stopped to consider my pain? No, of course not. You're too wrapped up in yourself. But I don't know why I waste my breath.'

Charity turned away, her back rigid with anger.

She'd never lashed out at Danny like this before and it floored him briefly. So, changing tack in the face of her anger, he took her hand and pulled her down on the bed beside him. 'Every word you say my love, is true, I am a selfish bugger. But I'll make it up to you, I swear it. From now on things are gonna be different.'

But Danny's charm was losing its potency and Charity looked sceptical. 'Oh, in what way?' she asked, wriggling from his embrace. 'You make promises easily and break them as quickly.'

'Oh do I? Well I'll show you, just wait an' see.' Danny's eyes had grown dark, the lids hooded, secretive. Determined to act immediately he swung out of bed. He tried

258

to stand but his legs felt as if they were stuffed with cotton wool. Exhausted with the effort, he fell back on the bed and started to cough.

'You're not going anywhere, not in that state.' Tucking him in, Charity smoothed the blankets and felt his forehead. Her tone had changed from anger to concern and it made him feel safe, cherished, which was how he liked it. Nothing would come between them, not that doctor bloke, not anybody. And just as soon as he was better, he would have a word with Boscoe. He was going to get Charity as far away as possible from this bloody place.

Chapter 21

It had all seemed so simple at first but in the end it had taken a couple of weeks to set up and organize. The tide had to be right, the night moonless, contacts made. Most important, Mad Brady who, for a cut was coming in with a small steam tug, had given the nod that a load of copper ingots would be tied up at Deacons Wharf on the Monday night, which was exactly the sort of big haul Boscoe had set his sights on.

'But what about the river police?' asked Danny, and heard with shame, a tremor in his voice. Because, as the day grew nearer, the thought that he was going to get his hands on some money at last, filled him with terror and excitement in about equal measure.

'No trouble at all. Even if they do get wind of anyfink, which I doubt, what can three policemen do at night? Besides, them boats they use are just a joke. Do you really think they'll be able to keep up wiv us? Not a chance mate. Depend on it, Boscoe's your man. Wiv me running things everything will go without a hitch. You see it'll be dead easy. And I ain't never let you down before, 'ave I?'

'No Boscoe, I'll give you that, you ain't. But then we've never had anything big like this before either.'

Boscoe peered at him suspiciously. 'Hey, you ain't losing yer nerve, gettin' scared, are you?'

''Course not,' Danny blustered. And he couldn't, could he? Because this was his last chance to make a go of it with Charity. And if he bungled things, it would be curtains for him in more ways than one. It was all right for Boscoe, he'd always lived on his wits, never done a real day's work in his life and if he'd ever had nerves he'd obviously forgotten what they were.

It had all gone swimmingly at first. It was a wet, blustery, ink-black night. The night watchman, by previous arrangement, had been got blind drunk. Danny found he'd lost his fear, and was clear-headed and precise in his movements. In no time they had made Mad Brady's tug's tow rope fast to the barge. It was flood tide and with plenty of other river traffic on the move they were unlikely to arouse suspicion. Nevertheless, there was no point in making themselves too obvious, so Mad Brady made sure he kept them close to the north shore, in the shadow of warehouses, until eventually he turned into Barking Creek. Here, well up into the creek, they tied up and Mad Brady left them.

Once they were in the cabin, Boscoe stretched himself out on the narrow bunk. 'Our contacts and waggons won't be 'ere until first light. By then it'll be low water and wiv all the mudbanks, no one else will be able to get up this far. In the meantime we'll take it in turns having a kip. Keep your ears open just in case and wake me at one.' Then, looking as if he hadn't a care in the world, he wrapped himself in a blanket and was soon snoring loudly.

At that precise moment Danny couldn't have slept anyway, he was far too keyed up. So he sat in a cramped position beside Boscoe planning the rest of his life. Something, either a bird or animal, screeched in the darkness, startling him but reminding him, too, that they were in the back of beyond and out there lay the countryside and further on the bleak, secretive Essex marshes, home to nothing but waterfowl. He still couldn't believe how easy it had all been to pull off, a bit of a doddle really, like Boscoe had promised. And by this time tomorrow, he'd have the money in his hands.

With a feeling of anticipation he moved Boscoe's foot from the small of his back, settled himself more comfortably, and started to plan what he would do with it. He'd have to lie low for a bit of course, and not start spending too freely or that would arouse suspicion. Charity was always saying one of her dreams was to live in the country, so after a while, casual like, he'd suggest he look for a job and a house down there. After that he just knew everything would be all right again between them. They'd buy a pub, have a couple of kids or maybe three . . .

His head fell on to his chest and he was drifting off, when he was alerted by a faint sound, the swish of oars in water. Immediately he was wide awake and tense. A moment later there was the sound of footsteps on the deck above them. Danny leapt to his feet. 'Christ, the law!' he yelped, and terror curdled his stomach and made his bowels feel loose.

Shaking Boscoe violently, he hissed, 'Boscoe, wake up, someone's coming.' The words were hardly out of his mouth before the scuttle was opened and they had to shield their eyes to prevent the light from the lamp shining down on their faces blinding them.

Then a disembodied voice shouted, 'What's going on 'ere, then? Come on you villains, on deck.'

Danny heard his heartbeats, like galloping horses, in his ears and was certain he would disgrace himself and vomit. But he had no choice but to obey the policeman's orders. He was half way up the ladder when he heard Boscoe behind him hiss, 'Jump, when we get outside and make a run for it, we've nuffink to lose.'

On deck and fighting his terror, Danny tried to assess

his chances of escape, noted that only one policeman had come on board which meant there were two more in the boat. If I'm going, now's the time, he told himself, but found he'd lost the ability to move.

'Thought you could outsmart us, didn't you Boscoe, m'lad. But we've had our peepers on you for quite a while, bin watchin' yer every move and we've caught you this time, red'anded. And for this haul, you and yer mate here can expect to be sent down for a nice long stretch, an' about time too.' The policeman, who was a large bulky man, conveyed this information in an almost jocular tone, feeling at the same time for the handcuffs with which to convey the miscreants more easily back to the police station.

In that brief moment of distraction, Boscoe's hand slipped in and out of his coat pocket. A shot cracked the silence and Danny watched with the same sense of unreality as he would a melodrama at Gattis, observing how the policeman clutched his chest, staggered then fell, blood oozing through his fingers.

Danny stared down at the man then at Boscoe. 'Christ, what did you do that for? It'll be a murder rap now.'

'Not for me it won't,' answered Boscoe, flung the pistol down at Danny's feet then, with one leap and a loud splash, he was gone.

Danny could hear himself panting like a dog and although he wanted to step back from the firearm and its implications, he was riveted to the deck by blind panic. His instinct was to bend and see if he could help the policeman but then another shot rang out. The wild scream of pain that followed brought his legs back to life and he ran aft and jumped into the dark waters of the creek.

He surfaced, his mouth and lungs full of evil-tasting water. Danny expected to feel the agony of a bullet in his neck at any moment, and he was in the grip of such total fear, it sucked the strength from his limbs. He floundered and almost went under again but a small measure of self preservation still remained, enough for him to strike out for the river bank. Stumbling and slipping in the mud he finally managed to grasp some reeds. But they were as sharp as a razor and, as he pulled himself ashore, they cut spitefully into his hands and made them bleed. He wanted to lie there and just give himself up to a deep, gut-wrenching misery. But he had to keep going. For one sound and they'd have 'im, then he'd be hung for murder.

Soaking wet, cold and choking on his sobs, Danny kept his mouth clamped tight shut and crawled along on his belly, through the stinking slime he guessed was the fall-out from sewers then finally harder, stonier ground that ripped his trousers and turned his knees to raw meat. Every cracking twig made him hold his breath, but he didn't dare stop. He carried on in this manner until the rational part of his brain slowly began to function again and he realized it was unlikely he was being followed anyway. The other policemen's first priority would be their injured mate and after that the capture of Boscoe, if he was still alive.

Cautiously Danny stood up. Stiff and bruised, his clothes still clung to him damply and his teeth chattered with the cold. He banged his arms to get some warmth back into his body and looked warily about him. The darkness was complete, stretching into infinity with not even the dim light visible of a lamp from a farmhouse. But he was facing east and the light would come from there soon so he must keep moving until he found some-where safe, a barn perhaps. Then after a day or two when the hue and cry had died down he'd make his way down to the coast, change his name and get on a ship. And never see Charity again. He had a sudden vision of her in a straw boater with gaily fluttering ribbons and a great wave of desolation swept over him. He loved his little wife so much and now it was too late to tell her. If only he could wind the clock back, if only Mum was alive . . . He let out a long wild, wail and shook his fists at the heavens. 'It's your fault, Boscoe, you got me into this God-almighty mess, ruined my life, and if you're dead I hope you burn in hell.'

A shuffling noise made him stiffen, until he realized he was being observed by a herd of inquisitive cows. Danny had the town boy's distrust of the country and it didn't help his nerves being watched. 'Go on, clear off.' He waved his arms at the animals who scattered in panic. Then he thought, control yourself m'lad, after all it's only a few cows. If he was to get through the next week he had to watch his every step and keep a guard on his tongue. Some of his natural optimism returning, Danny flexed the stiff muscles in his shoulders with a circular movement. What was it Ma, bless 'er heart, always said. 'Remember son, it's not over till it's over.' Well, you could never question the truth of that and when you thought about it, no one's future was certain, not even the Queen's.

There was something so cheering about this idea, Danny straightened up in a soldierly fashion. Peering into the dark to get his bearings, he struck off across the field with determined strides. For no good reason he was suddenly possessed of an amazing confidence. Famished and without a farthing to his name, he did have his wits and he'd get by, just see if he wouldn't. And somehow or other he'd get a message to Charity just to let her know he was all right.

What happened to the rest of the year Charity could never remember afterwards. However, that night, or rather the early morning, would forever be etched on her memory. The hammering on the door, the voices demanding to be let in, the policeman standing there. His words, 'I have a warrant for your husband's arrest,' began an ordeal she would relive and torture herself with for months afterwards.

Barely awake, shivering, pushing her hair out of her eyes, Charity stared at him in bewilderment.

'But my husband's on night work.'

'Now where would that be?'

'At Foster's flour mill.'

'Your husband, Mrs Weston, was apprehended tonight along with Boscoe Hobbs, up Barking Creek in the unlawful possession of a load of copper. Unfortunately, in the affray he escaped.'

Charity sat down heavily. 'No.'

'And, in the course of his lawful duty, a police officer was shot.'

She began to shake uncontrollably. 'Shot? I . . . is he dead?'

'No, seriously injured.'

'It wouldn't be . . . not Danny, he'd never . . . anyone . . . shoot . . . never had a gun in his life . . . use one, wouldn't know how to . . .' Her voice had grown hysterical, her words jumbled.

'It is believed the gun was fired by Boscoe Hobbs. The police sergeant had no choice but to return fire and Hobbs is now dead. However, your husband is an accessory. It is a very grave charge he faces, Mrs Weston.'

'An . . . and you say Danny got away?'

'We have reason to think so. Although there's a possibility he could have drowned. However, there's a big search on for him and he might try to come back here. I don't need to tell you, Mrs Weston, that if he does, it will be your duty to hand him over to the law. Just to make sure, a constable will remain on permanent duty outside. We might want to question you further later today, but for the moment I suggest you go back to bed and try and get some sleep.'

Of course she didn't go back to bed and, hurrying round to her room an hour or so later, Eliza found her sitting there in a nightgown and thin shawl, mind and body frozen. In her practical way and without any further to-do, Eliza started stuffing clothes into a bag. 'Get dressed young lady, you're coming home with me.'

Charity, who was compulsively twisting her long hair

into a rope, stared at her with blank eyes. 'But Danny might come back, he'd expect me to be here.'

'Exactly, and that's what worries me. Husband or no, Danny has caused you enough heartache to last a lifetime. But he's not implicating you in this dirty business. If he turns up on my step I shall feel no compunction about turning him in.'

Charity began to rock backwards and forwards like a distressed child. 'Oh, what will become of him?' she wailed.

But Eliza, having no answer to that, let her cry, waited until she'd finished, then mopped her eyes and took her back to Filbert Street.

Chapter 22

For the rest of the year Charity saw Danny constantly. She'd catch a glimpse of him on the top of a bus, or he would just be turning a corner and she'd rush after him calling his name to the surprise of a complete stranger.

Her grief was public, raw, and realizing matters couldn't go on as they were after nearly a year with no sign of improvement, Eliza spoke to Stephen. 'I thought she would be over the worst by now, but she still seems obsessed with the idea of Danny returning. Anyway, I've come to the conclusion that she needs to get away, this place has too many unhappy associations.'

'What would you suggest?'

'Nursing. She was very taken with the idea at one time, went to all those classes, do you remember? She's a clever girl too, my Charity, and she'd make a first-rate nurse.'

'It's definitely worth considering, although of course she's still quite young. Certainly she'd find the work so absorbing and exhausting she wouldn't have time to think of Danny, or anyone else for that matter. How old is she now?'

'Probably nearing twenty-one, although we don't know exactly.'

Stephen looked thoughtful. 'Generally they like nurses to be a bit older but rules can always be stretched. My uncle's a consultant, so he could probably pull a few strings. But there is the question of her marital status, whether she's a widow or not, that could make things a bit sticky.'

'You'll think me hard, but I wish she were. It would solve a lot of problems. This not knowing if he is dead or alive, of not being allowed to mourn, is bad for her. But that's typical of Danny, no thought for anyone,' Eliza added.

'After a year and not a word, I think you can safely assume he's dead.'

'Don't assume anything with that young man. It's easy enough to disappear, people do it all the time. I've a feeling he'll turn up one day like the proverbial bad penny and put her life into a spin again. That's one more reason I want her to get away from here. She's got such a strong sense of loyalty I'm sure she'd feel it was her duty to help him and never mind the consequences.'

'Danny was always a bit rash, but I doubt if even he would come here and risk a long jail sentence.'

'I hope you're right. But will you talk to her? Get her round to the idea again. Charity's always had a high regard for you so I'd know she'd listen.'

'I'll have to sound my uncle out first, we'll need his good will if she's to have any chance of being accepted at a hospital. The competition is pretty fierce. Although of course you realize Charity still might reject the idea out of hand.'

Which is exactly what she did. And she would have gone on stubbornly refusing to consider the idea if it hadn't been for Mollie, who had already started her training as a doctor at the Royal Free Hospital.

'I can remember a time when you used to talk of nothing else but becoming a nurse. And now you've been given this chance and you refuse to go. I can't believe it.'

'I want to stay here. Danny might return any day.'

'You don't even know if he's alive.' Mollie found no difficulty in talking frankly to her friend.

'He is, I'm certain of it.'

'Well if he is, the last thing he'd do would be to come back here, to be sent down. You really ought to try and accept that and get on with your life.' It wasn't as if he even made you happy, Mollie wanted to add, but thought better of it. Because something she'd come to realize as she matured, was the unpredictability of human emotions. Frequently even the most unsatisfactory marriage became bathed in an idealized glow once the other partner was no longer there to prove otherwise.

Seeing, by the look on Charity's face, that she was getting nowhere, Mollie tried appealing to her strong idealistic streak. 'Think of all the people you could help, women like Kate and Danny's ma. Perhaps save their lives. That's what I've decided to do when I've finished my training, to come back here. And we could achieve a lot together, you and me. Set up a clinic for women, give them advice on family limitation. We've both said for a long time, haven't we, that the reason so many women suffer from bad health is because they have too many pregnancies. And whereas a lot of them are embarrassed about discussing ailments of a personal nature with men, I'm sure they'd come to us.'

Charity still hadn't said anything but Mollie could detect a heightened interest as she formulated her ideas.

'You're right, Danny won't come back, he never loved me enough to do that. In fact if he'd thought of me at all he wouldn't have become involved in such stupidness with that awful Boscoe.'

'Of course Danny loved you,' Mollie felt obliged to say. And perhaps in his way he had, although he'd often had a funny way of showing it.

'And, as you say, nursing is something I've always liked the idea of, and I've got to do something with the rest of my life. Stephen's uncle can get me an interview too, so what is there to lose. And if I don't like it, well I can always pack it in.'

'Oh Charity, that's marvellous. I means we'll see a bit more of each other, too. When we're both off duty we'll be able to go out together, to the theatre, art galleries and things.'

It was a beautiful warm September day when Charity took the tram for her interview at St Cuthbert's Hospital, but as she sat and waited to be summoned by Matron, she noticed only the mingled smell of ether, carbolic and cabbage. And the dampness of her palms. Removing her gloves she rubbed her hands furtively against her skirt and saw the mark on her finger where her wedding ring had been. On Stephen's advice she was *Miss* Weston now, so she hoped no one would notice it. Everyone moved around with a hushed, brisk efficiency and the only sound seemed to be the squeak of shoes on highly-polished floors. Already intimidated by the atmosphere, Charity thought to herself, what am I doing here? They won't want me, not in a million years.

Eventually, she was ushered into the presence of Miss Frobisher, the Matron, a formidable woman who regarded her severely, then said without preamble, 'I hear it is your ambition to eventually become a district nurse. It is an area of nursing I am greatly in sympathy with. May I ask why, Miss Weston?'

Quite overawed by the great lady, Charity could think of no earthly reason why she should want to be a district nurse. Then she remembered Kate and Mrs Weston and their terrible deaths and all the other worn out women with their sickly children she'd lived her life with. Aware that she was being assessed, she gulped and finally managed to blurt out, 'Be . . . because they care for the poor. And in Rotherhithe, where I come from, there are plenty of those. Some people won't even see a doctor until it's too late.' Charity had stopped floundering now and was well into her stride. 'As a district nurse going into their homes, I could teach them about hygiene, sanitation and diet and perhaps help prevent some of those awful diseases like scarlet fever and diphtheria. And see that nursing mothers look after themselves . . .' Suddenly wondering if she'd gone on too long, Charity's voice trailed away.

But Matron appeared quite satisfied. 'Well, those strike me as being admirable reasons, Miss Weston. Sometimes, I fear, girls take up nursing for entirely the wrong reasons. They come in here with their heads full of romantic notions, imagining they will be required to do nothing more arduous than hold the hand of a few handsome young men. To put it bluntly, they think a becoming uniform will win them a husband. This type of girl I might add, rarely lasts long. Nursing is a life of sacrifice. To be good at it, a young woman must make up her mind to give up the worship of such gods as pleasure and self.' She leaned forward, her large bosoms resting on the desk, her spectacles glinting with fervour. 'It requires stamina, too, Miss Weston, to be a nurse. Stamina.' Matron's gaze ran doubtfully over Charity's small frame. 'Have you got stamina, Miss Weston, to cope with the drudgery and long hours?'

'Oh yes, I'm very strong really.' Charity assured her, pulling back her shoulders and sitting up straight in an effort to appear wider and taller.

Matron glanced down at a file. 'I see you've already taken some courses in sick nursing.'

'Yes Matron, and biology.'

'Very commendable. Although of course you do realize that there is a great deal of competition to get into our hospital and we can take our pick of girls.'

Charity nodded and held her breath. This was it, she was going to be turned down flat. She wasn't educated enough or from a suitable background.

Miss Frobisher picked up a letter. 'I must say, you come highly recommended. Dr Moore writes about you in

glowing terms. I only hope you live up to his testimonial.'
She stood up. 'You will come initially on a month's trial
and, like all the other probationers, you will get two hours
off daily, and a free day once a fortnight. Material will be
provided for three print dresses and three caps. Your
salary will be £12 per annum, presuming you last the
course, and half a crown a week is allowed for laundry.
May I suggest before you commence your training that
you purchase of copy of a textbook for probationers
entitled *General Nursing*. I think you will find it
invaluable.'

'Yes, Matron, thank you Matron.' Realizing the interview was at an end, Charity backed out of the room,
managing to contain herself until she was in the street
where she leapt off the bottom step with a wild hooray.

'You arright, love?' asked a woman, pausing to regard
Charity with some concern.

'Oh yes, I'm fine.' She had to tell someone. 'It's just
that you see, I'm going to be a nurse.'

The woman grasped her arm. 'Well good luck ter yer.
Angels of mercy nurses is.'

When the time came a fortnight later for them to say their
farewells, Charity and Eliza were both awkward with
their emotions. Charity swallowed the lump in her throat
and bent to stroke the cats, Eliza blew her nose rather
violently then pressed a sovereign into her hand.

'Here, you might need this, and see you write regularly,
my girl.'

Charity kissed her. 'I'll be home every chance I get,
don't worry, and I will miss you . . .' the wretched lump
had risen in her throat again, '. . . and I'm sure I'm going
to hate it.'

'Nonsense, you'll love every moment of it.' Seeing that
tears were not far away, Eliza gave Charity a pat on the
behind and said briskly, 'Now off you go. Young girls of
today have opportunities we never did. This is your big
chance, make the most of it.'

So with the uniform Eliza had made packed carefully between layers of tissue paper in her suitcase, and feeling both apprehensive and excited, Charity took the tram for a second time to St Cuthbert's. And for the next year hardly knew what had hit her.

When she arrived she was shown to her room by a silent maid and left there. Not sure what to do, Charity changed into her uniform. Pleased with herself she studied her reflection from all angles in the mirror. Her blue-striped dress and starched apron transformed her and gave her an air of brisk efficiency, although her churning stomach told her otherwise. Feeling the stiff collar already chafing her neck, Charity tied her cap, with its pork-pie frills, in a large bow under her chin, then sat down and waited with a nervous expectancy.

The knock at the door when it came was a welcome diversion. 'Come in,' she called and jumped to her feet.

A head appeared round the door. 'You the new pro?' a girl of about her own age enquired, her eyes making a quick assessment.

'Yes.'

'Well, I've been told to look after you. To take you to tea. My name's Fraser, what's yours?'

'Charity Weston.'

'Right Weston, bring your sleeves and follow me.'

Charity was conscious of a silence and what seemed like a hundred pairs of unfriendly eyes staring at her when she walked into the dining room. She sat down where she was instructed to by Fraser then the chatter started up again, but throughout the meal not one word was addressed to her. Staring at her plate, feeling wretched and homesick, she chewed at the unappetizing bread and butter. But it stuck in her gullet like her misery and even the strong tea couldn't wash it away. Why, she thought miserably, had she ever wanted to be a nurse. It was all a great mistake.

Immediately after tea finished, Nurse Fraser said, 'Keep

close to me, we're in women's medical this evening. And two words of advice, unless the hospital is on fire, never run, and never address a Sister unless she speaks to you first.'

Charity exchanged her cuffs for the long sleeves that went half way up her arm and was then told to help take supper round. When they had finished, the women were settled down for the night and, those who needed them, provided with bed pans. After this, she watered the plants. Then just when Charity thought she might rest her weary feet for a minute, the Staff Nurse told her to tidy out the linen cupboard. 'Because,' she warned Charity with a fierce look, 'if Matron opens it on her rounds and finds it less than up to the mark, she'll be extremely displeased. That woman's got eyes like a hawk. I swear she can see a speck of dust at ten yards.'

Nervously, Charity set to trying to tidy a cupboard that, in her eyes, already looked immaculate. At ten o'clock she fell into bed with relief. But it seemed she'd no sooner laid her head on the pillow than someone was banging on the door and calling, 'Six o'clock, nurse.'

That first morning she leapt out of bed, was washed and dressed and had her bed made by half past six. But exhaustion quickly put paid to this early enthusiasm. Soon, like most of the other girls, she would lie in bed until the last possible moment, then go down to breakfast with her cap crooked, her bed barely smoothed over and yawning her head off. Breakfast, unappetizing porridge, was at seven sharp and woe betide the nurse who walked in after Sister had said Grace.

She wasn't afraid of hard work, but for the first month Charity walked around in a haze of fatigue. Free time proved to be rather illusory with lectures to attend in physiology and anatomy as well as medical and surgical nursing. There were also classes in bandaging and sick-room cookery. On top of all this, she had to try to fit in periods of study, but not much sank into her tired mind at the end of a twelve-hour day. Finally, there was spiritual guidance in the form of Bible classes and these they were expected to attend every week.

Her month's trial came and went without comment and she was promoted from the menial tasks of cleaning out lockers and dusting to handing round medicines, applying poultices, taking temperatures and dealing more directly with patients. Her first case was a woman admitted early one afternoon, who, she was instructed by the ward sister, to bathe. 'And see you give her a good scrubbing with carbolic,' had in fact been her order.

The woman, a scraggy, dirty little thing, whose clothes had to be taken away and fumigated, took one look at the bath full of water and stepped back with an expression of terror. 'I don't need a bath, I 'ad one this mornin',' she whined. 'Anyway, if I goes in there I'll be drownded.'

Charity was at a loss. She couldn't physically drag the woman to the bath. 'You won't be drowned, Mrs Fitch, I'll hold you as you get in, and the water's not deep anyway.' It's hardly deep enough to drown those lice in your hair, she was tempted to add, then decided it was time to show who was boss. 'Besides, it's hospital regulations. On admittance, everyone is bathed and has their hair washed and we make no exceptions.' She spoke in the same brisk tone she'd noticed most nurses adopted when dealing with recalcitrant patients.

But her authoritative manner obviously didn't persuade Mrs Fitch, who remained resolutely clamped against the tiled wall. 'Right, if you don't get in, I shall have to fetch Sister.' Charity had ceased to cajole, her voice was threatening and she made for the door.

'Arright, arright, keep yer 'air on, Nurse, I'll get in.' And as Mrs Fitch, with her help, dipped dirt-ingrained toes gingerly in the water, it occurred to Charity that the woman had probably never sat in a bath in her life before.

It was a punishing regime and she hardly found the time to scribble Mollie a note, let alone spend a day out with her. But her exhaustion at least meant she didn't lie awake, her mind churning away and sifting through

274

memories as she tried to understand what had driven Danny to such a fruitless and stupid act of crime that night.

Charity got over her loneliness, too, and friendships were forged. The hospital had a rigid hierarchical system and this drew the junior probationers together and made them dependent on each other. In the afternoons, in their precious free time, they would make tea and toast in the sitting room and relax and gossip and Charity became adept at reading tea leaves in cups. She made it up as she went along but her popularity increased by leaps and bounds. Often, too, when they came off duty at night, instead of going straight to bed, they'd make cocoa and, in their winceyette nightgowns, sit with their feet in the hearth of the dying fire. Sleepy and warm, they'd plan their futures, teach each other the words of popular songs or one of them would relate the plot of a novel she'd just read. Sooner or later though, the conversation would turn to men.

'Have you got a young man, Weston?' Fraser asked her one night.

Glad the only light there was came from the fire, Charity occupied herself by scooping up the disc of froth from the top of her cocoa. 'Not at the moment,' she answered and wondered what would happen if her secret got out. To cover her unease at her deception, she went on, 'Where would I find the time anyway. I don't know about you, but on my day off I do nothing but sleep.'

'Yeah, we might as well be nuns,' another girl remarked, 'I reckon we'll all die old maids.'

'Well there are worse things than that. Not all marriages are made in heaven.' Then, feeling she'd said enough, Charity yawned and stretched her arms above her head. 'I don't know about anyone else, but I'm going to bed before I fall asleep on my feet.'

And so the days went on. She wept when her first patient died, an old man who'd never had one visitor all

275

the time he was in hospital, and Fraser rebuked her. 'You can't weep over every patient who dies, you know,' she said as they put the screens around his bed. Fraser sometimes had such a brusque manner, Charity felt certain she was destined to become a matron. 'Emotional involvement is an indulgence a trained nurse can't afford, it gets in the way of her work.'

'Well no one else is going to shed a tear for the poor old chap so allow him my few,' Charity said, wiping her eyes.

'Have it your way,' answered Fraser with a grudging lift of her shoulders.

Which is exactly what Charity did, and she continued to shed a silent tear and offer up a small prayer for every patient she nursed through their dying hours. But it was the death of a baby that affected her most deeply, because, each time that happened, she was forced to endure again the pain of her own loss.

Flirting with patients was strictly forbidden and dismissal was the penalty for being caught. But human nature being what it is the rules were flouted outrageously. In the cloistered atmosphere, young men with nothing better to do than observe pretty nurses going about their task of caring and healing, easily became infatuated. And sometimes these feelings were reciprocated. Certainly Charity allowed her emotions to run a little out of control as far as Patrick Neill was concerned. But that was perhaps because, with his blue eyes, he had a look about him that reminded her of Danny. There was also an empty space in her heart and, for a short while, he filled a corner of it.

He was nineteen with a serious heart condition and she'd been sent to give him a blanket bath. After a few months at it she could perform this task quite detachedly but now as she sponged Patrick's belly and legs, his member hardened. Most boys were agonizingly embarrassed when this happened so, not wanting to discomfit him further, she went on washing him and pretended she hadn't noticed.

But, instead of flushing scarlet, Patrick gave her a cheeky grin and said, 'Sorry, nurse, but he's got a mind of his own,' and this time it was Charity's neck that reddened. She didn't answer, but keeping her head bent, hastily finished washing his feet then covered him up.

'Do you know, nurse, just looking at you does this poor old ticker of mine no end of good. You're a real tonic,' Patrick said, next time she went to give him his medicine.

But Charity was ready for him and she pretended to cuff him round the ear. 'Less of the blarney Patrick, you say that to all the nurses, I've heard you.' But it was impossible not to respond to the charm of the dark-haired boy. She instantly developed a soft spot for him and she found herself at his bed so often, smoothing his pillow and straightening his sheets, the other patients began to joke about it.

His mother came every day without fail to visit him. A tiny, exhausted looking woman with a thick Irish brogue and the pink-and-white downcast expression of a plaster saint, her religion and Patrick were her whole life. She would sit fingering the crucifix round her neck and drone on about the church and 'dear Father Brendan,' until her son's eyes glazed over with boredom. Charity, seeing this look, would rush to his rescue with an imaginary pill and glass of water and suggest he was feeling tired.

A huge sign with the grim warning that, 'No food must be brought into this hospital,' hung in a conspicuous place on the wall of every ward. But it was another of those rules made to be broken and Mrs Neill, like most other visitors, smuggled various dainties in to break the monotony of institutional food. Some nurses were sticklers for the letter of the law but Charity turned a blind eye to the bags of acid drops and pork pies she knew were regularly shoved away at the back of Patrick's locker.

Christmas was the time of the great unbending. Wards were bedecked with paper chains and holly, Doctors became almost human, ward sisters twinkled like the decorations on the Christmas tree and a spirit of good will prevailed.

Along with the rest of the junior probationers, Charity had been practising carols for weeks, and on Christmas Eve, wearing their red-lined cloaks and with paper lanterns hanging on broomhandles, they sang their way round the wards.

Some of the nurses and doctors were going on to midnight mass, a considerable amount of sweet sherry had been consumed, rules were relaxed and the atmosphere was festive and happy.

When the choir reached Essex ward, they gave them, 'The Holly and the Ivy,' then, 'We Three Kings,' after which everyone was invited to join in, 'Once in Royal David's City.' When the last notes faded away, the men clapped loudly in appreciation, then Patrick beckoned her over.

'Come here, there's something I want to say to you.'

'What?' Charity's tone was wary. Patrick was a bit of a prankster.

'Go and find out,' said one of the other girls with a giggle and shoved her in the direction of Patrick's bed.

'Nearer, I want to whisper something,' he ordered and suddenly he whipped a sprig of mistletoe from under the bedclothes and held it above her head. Leaning forward, he kissed her full on the lips.

From the explosive laughter behind her, Charity knew the others had all been in on the plot. 'Hush,' she reprimanded them, and leapt back from the bed expecting Matron or Sister to come bearing down on her at any minute. Then seeing no one in authority was around, she giggled as well. 'You shouldn't have done that, Patrick, you'll get me slung out.'

'That doesn't matter, because just as soon as I'm better and out of here, I'm going to marry you.'

'You can't marry me, I'm old enough to be your

mother,' she answered flippantly and went back to join the others.

As soon as the patients had been served their Christmas dinner, Charity could go home, but before leaving, she went and said goodbye to Patrick and slipped him the second hand book of adventure stories she'd bought him as a present.

He was lying back on his pillows and looked tired. 'How long are you away for?'

'Three days.'

'Will you be going out?'

'Yes. I'm going to a pantomime on Boxing Day.'

'I bet a fella's taking you. What's his name?'

'Stephen.'

'And do you like this Stephen?'

'You are an inquisitive young man. Yes I do like him, but I like you too. Very much.' Charity put out a hand to rumple his black curls and he grabbed it.

'But I love you.'

Charity wanted to say, 'No you don't, Patrick,' but that wouldn't have been true. Love was written all over his earnest young face.

'Thank you, that's a great honour. Now I must go, my aunt's expecting me.'

'Promise you'll come and tell me all about the pantomime when you get back,' he called after her as she walked away.

'I promise,' she answered, and paused at the door to give him a final wave.

Charity returned to St Cuthbert's three days later, refreshed and light-hearted and looking forward to seeing everyone again. Eliza had fussed over her, cooked special dishes, made sure she had enough sleep. Having had Christmas Eve off, Mollie was leaving just as she arrived, so their paths crossed for barely an hour, but oh, how their tongues wagged in those sixty minutes.

However, Stephen more than made up for her not

seeing much of Mollie because as well as treating her to *Jack in the Beanstalk* at the Camberwell Palace, he'd also bought her the best present she'd had in her life: a bicycle.

'Close your eyes,' he'd said and then had guided her outside to the back garden. 'Now open them.'

'Whose is this?' she'd said when she saw the bicycle, shiny and black, leaning against the wall.

'It's yours, from me. Happy Christmas, Charity.'

'Mine?' She'd gazed at it first in disbelief, then delight, then doubt. 'But I can't accept a gift like this, it's far too expensive.'

'It's not a frivolous gift, I do have an ulterior motive. What I'm hoping is that it will persuade you to come back here and work when you're a Queen's nurse. It'll speed you up no end, if you can do your rounds on a bicycle.'

'I don't need a present to persuade me. I always planned to come back, it's my home. It was you I thought who'd be moving on.'

'Oh, where to?'

Although it wasn't mentioned, Blanche's name hung heavy between them. 'Oh, Harley Street or some such place, I suppose.'

'Well I must admit there are times when I've been tempted. But with only Dr Campbell left, who would look after the patients?' Blanche was, in fact, forever trying to get him to leave, and he was beginning to suspect she saw him more as a meal ticket than anything else. Of course he understood her parlous financial situation and the worry it must cause, and on more than once occasion he'd been poised to surrender. But he was damned if he was going to support that idle brother of hers. And this was perhaps why he'd dug his heels in. In fact he and Blanche had reached stalemate and sometimes he almost hoped she would meet someone else.

Then there was the question of Charity. As he'd watched her plucky struggle to survive the multiple tragedies life had thrown at her, he'd come to realize she was worth ten of Blanche or any of the crowd he mixed with. He wanted to tell her this and a thousand other things, but he was kept very much at arm's length now. Serve him right, after the the way he'd mucked things up before. It was also pretty obvious that the absent Danny was still a powerful rival and the best he could do was hope and wait.

'Happy Christmas,' he heard Charity say, then she was pushing a small parcel into his hand. I'm sorry, it's not much of a present,' she added, as she watched him undo the paper and try on the gloves she'd laboured over for several weeks. 'But it's all I could afford and I did knit them myself.'

'Hey, there's no need to apologize, they're just what I need this cold weather.' Bending, Stephen kissed her chastely on both cheeks and savoured the lightness of her in the circle of his arms. 'Come on now, let's give you a lesson on this bike.'

The bicycle was her ticket to freedom and now that she'd learned to ride it, she could see herself cycling out into the country, in the summer. And that was something else to tell Patrick, Charity thought as she changed into her uniform and hurried along to the ward. Describing her early attempts at trying to stay upright on two wheels would certainly bring a smile to his lips. The wobbles, the spills, the jeers of small boys, then the sudden mastery of the machine.

But Patrick's bed was empty, the pillows smooth. Charity turned to Fraser, puzzled. 'Where's Patrick, has he gone home?'

Fraser came and put an arm around her waist and said gently, 'No. He died on Boxing Day, it was a very peaceful end.'

'He shouldn't have, not without me here,' Charity protested in a tearful voice. But she knew she mustn't cry in public, Fraser would tell her it was unprofessional.

'Everyone misses him, the patients, nurses, even the scrubbers. But I know you were particularly fond of him.'

'It was just that he reminded me of someone I once knew.'

'If it's any comfort, his mother was with him, and Father Brendan to give him the Last Rites.'

Charity adjusted her cap and blew her nose. 'Poor Mrs Neill, I'll have to go and visit her. Patrick was all she had.'

'Perhaps her religion will sustain her,' Fraser said but without much conviction.

It was almost like losing Danny again and she felt a terrible sadness. Why wasn't I there? Charity kept asking herself. She could have kept Patrick alive and, instead of the empty bed, he'd be sitting up, charming everyone including Sister.

Charity tortured herself like this for many weeks. It was having the look about him of Danny that had made it easy for Patrick to steal a little bit of her heart. While Patrick was alive, she could believe Danny was too. Now there was nothing left.

Then one morning Charity woke and thought, this has got to stop. People came into hospital because they were sick and she was a nurse, not some deity; she had no power over life and death. If she continued to place such an intolerable emotional burden upon herself, she would cease to be an efficient nurse. Fraser was right, she needed to build a defensive shell around herself. It was the only way to survive.

Chapter 23

At the end of the year they sat their exams, received their certificates, vowed eternal friendship and went their separate ways. At least some, like Charity, did. Her eyes were now set on the future and her district nursing training, and she took her leave of the hospital a little less tearfully than some, unaware that as time passed she would look back on the year at St Cuthbert's with affection. All the hardships would be forgotten and only the companionship remembered.

A further six months of intensive study and lectures on health and diet, sanitary reform, infectious diseases, care of nursing mothers and the newborn child followed, interrupted at regular intervals by forays into houses of the sick poor. Charity was always supervised and accompanied by a trained district nurse. And this is where her real education began. Because not even Mrs Craven's manual, *A Guide to District Nurses and Home Nursing*, could have prepared her for the poverty and degradation she found in some homes.

She got on with her supervisor immediately. Her name was Nurse Spencer, she was auburn haired and lively and Charity guessed her to be about thirty. There was little she hadn't seen in her years as a district nurse and not much shocked her. Today as they wove in an out of narrow streets avoiding uncollected night soil and dodging round coster barrows, she explained the situation of the next house visit.

'This child, Mabel, we're going to see, is twelve and she's just had a baby, a little boy.'

'Heavens that's a bit young,' exclaimed Charity.

'But that's not the worst of it. We think the baby is the result of an incestuous relationship between Mabel and her father.'

Although she knew she couldn't let personal feelings enter into it, Charity felt her head reel as if from a sharp blow and she had to stop. 'What about the mother? Doesn't she know? Couldn't she stop it?'

'Yes, Mrs Tubbs probably does know, but as for stopping it that's unlikely. In fact with ten other children younger than Mabel she might even actively encourage it, so she can have a break from him. But the whole family's a bit simple, and what you must remember is that these people live by different standards, so she probably sees nothing wrong in it anyway. And I'd better warn you, they occupy one room in a cellar and its pretty disgusting.

'The father, what about him?'

'A violent drunk. He probably won't be there, he isn't usually, but if he is, he'll be charm itself. He likes to ingratiate himself. Sees himself as a bit of a ladykiller, but don't be taken in.'

'Don't worry, I won't. I know his kind. Does he work?'

'Not at anything legal as far as I can make out. Probably a bit of thieving and picking of pockets and he's training the children to do the same, I should imagine.'

They moved deeper and deeper into squalid streets, so narrow that in places they had to walk in tandem. Charity kept her thoughts to herself but peering into the stygian gloom of a court or yard, where houses looked about ready to collapse, Charity knew that, in places like this, the human soul could only shrivel and die. For there was nothing to nourish it, not a flower, a tree, nor even a blade of grass. At some houses linnets, imprisoned in cages, hung outside doors. But they were poor, miserable little specimens with drooping feathers and had long since lost the will to sing.

At an upstairs window in a cramped alley, a woman with wild eyes and hair springing snakelike from her head, harangued the world in colourful language.

'Watch out!' warned Nurse Spencer as a gobful of spit missed them by an inch.

It was obvious the woman's mind had tipped over the edge into madness, which hardly surprised Charity. For here lived the forgotten of society and she realized that, in comparison, Rotherhithe suggested affluence and calm.

Nurse Spencer's curls poking out from under her bonnet glowed bright and positive, but following her, Charity still hoped she had a good sense of direction. Because she herself felt bewilderingly lost and the irrational feeling was beginning to grow in her that they might be condemned to tramp this maze of streets and alleys for ever more.

'Don't feel nervous,' Nurse Spencer reassured her as some barefoot children, their legs bowed by rickets, began to trail after them. 'They might look an evil bunch of cutthroats but our uniforms protect us. They know we're here to help. What we must try not do is condemn or pass moral judgement on these people. They've never had a chance. They live and die in total ignorance.'

Well, that was a fact no one would argue with, decided Charity. But she wished her own attitude to her personal safety was as positive and that she didn't feel such a tension between her shoulderblades or the need to cast nervous backward glances every few minutes.

There was no reason why she should, but when they at last turned into a dank, evil-smelling yard, Charity felt safer. There was no knocker on the door so Nurse Spencer had to bang it with her fists and this brought an aged, toothless bundle of rags shuffling to the door.

'Whatdyawant?'

'May we come in please, I have a patient to see. Mabel Tubbs.' Nurse Spencer put her small foot firmly in the door and gave a slight push.

'Them lot owe me rent and they better pay up pretty bleedin' quick, or they'll be out on their ears.'

'Yes, well I'll have to leave you to deal with that,' answered Nurse Spencer firmly. 'Now if you'd just let us past.'

'Y'know where they are.' The rags shuffled off again to the back of the house, leaving Charity and Nurse Spencer to descend the steps to the cellar on their own.

How can human beings live like this? Charity asked herself in appalled disbelief as she stood on the bottom step and gazed about her. Pigs in their sties would fare better. The only light and air came from a grating in the pavement; for furniture there were a few orange boxes and the sleeping arrangements consisted of several shake-downs scattered around the earth floor. This isn't just a place that breeds bugs but where vice flourishes unchecked as well, a place from which all human decencies must have fled, Charity decided, and her skin began to crawl. There was a smoky fire of sorts and some grimy washing slung over a line but the overwhelming smell was of unwashed flesh and faeces. A gaggle of sickly, squint-eyed, half naked children appeared as if from the woodwork and formed a half circle round them. Then a woman sporting a black eye and cut lip and with two more small children clinging to her legs stepped forward. Troglodytes, that's what they all look like decided Charity and wondered how nurses from more genteel backgrounds coped with a situation like this, for she was finding it difficult enough. There appeared to be no sign of the husband for which she was grateful. She would have found dealing with him hard to cope with and her professionalism might have slipped a fraction.

Somehow, Nurse Spencer managed to greet the woman in a bright cheerful voice. 'Hello, Mrs Tubbs. How are you, and how's Mabel?'

'She's arright but the babby's bin took bad.'

'Well let's have a look, shall we.' She moved over to where a girl lay on one of the shakedowns and Charity followed.

'Hello Mabel.'

A lank-haired, heavy-bodied girl rolled on her back and pointed a finger at Charity. 'Ooz zat?'

'Nurse Weston, a colleague of mine. You'll probably be seeing a good deal more of her from now on.'

Charity gave the dim-witted looking girl an encouraging smile, but Mabel just stared back slackjawed and with pale uncomprehending eyes.

'Can I have a look at little Billy?' Nurse Spencer held out her arms and the girl handed her a small bundle in a tattered shawl.

'Oh!' she exclaimed and looked at Charity.

Charity stepped forward and saw that the infant's cranium was grotesquely deformed and bulged at the brow, completely obscuring its eyes. She also understood Nurse Spencer's exclamation for it was obvious the baby was dead.

They looked at each other, then Nurse Spencer turned

to Mrs Tubbs. 'I'm awfully sorry, Mrs Tubbs, but little Billy has passed on.'

'Has 'e now, poor little bugger. I wondered why he'd stopped crying.'

Nurse Spencer went and knelt by Mabel, and taking her hand spoke gently to the girl. 'Mabel, I've got something to tell you. Try not to be upset, but little Billy's gone to the angels in heaven.'

The girl gazed back at her blankly. 'Heaven? Where's zat?

Miss Spencer looked slighty put out at having such a heathen on her hands. It was also a written rule that discussion of a religious nature with patients was strictly forbidden. But she'd started so she had to go on. 'A better place where he'll feel no more pain and be very happy. And because he hasn't sinned, God will make Billy an angel I'm certain.' Her tone was designed to comfort and reassure.

'Will 'e come back?'

'I'm afraid not.'

'Good. I 'ated 'im. He was ugly and the little sod screamed all the time. Never let up 'e didn't.' Turning over on her side, Mabel put her thumb in her mouth and closed her eyes.

The two girls exchanged glances, then Nurse Spencer gave a faint shrug of defeat. After this she spent some time advising Mrs Tubbs about the burial of the baby, then they left.

'Phew, what a relief to get out of that place,' said the older girl when they were standing on the pavement again. 'That baby had been dead for some time. And I know I shouldn't be saying this, but it's a blessing he died. The poor little mite, as you no doubt realized, was a cretin. What can we do about people like that? It makes me feel so helpless.' Nurse Spencer had lost some of her bounce and her shoulders were slumped, her expression dejected.

'You did what you could,' Charity answered quietly

and paused to wonder if ever she found herself in a similar situation, whether she would cope even half as well. Certainly in this work miracles were going to be few and far between.

She did learn to cope though, under Nurse Spencer's continuing tutelage, extremely well. At the end of six months it was considered that she had reached the standard of efficiency deemed necessary for her to be placed on the roll of the Queen's Nursing Institute and to work unsupervised. She returned to Rotherhithe proudly wearing on her left arm a brassard embroidered with the Queen's cipher and, suspended round her neck on a cord, a bronze badge bearing the initials VRI. She also carried home with her a diary crammed full of her experiences.

Her training had changed her. Charity knew that without a doubt and was thankful for it. She'd moved out of the narrow confines of Rotherhithe, met a variety of people from all backgrounds, enjoyed female companionship, learnt to cope with horrific and tragic situations and it had given her a confidence she'd never possessed before.

With her black bag strapped to the handlebars she sailed forth from the nurses' home on her bicycle that April morning, knowing that her uniform and qualifications gave her authority. And she couldn't deny it, it was a comforting feeling for a girl with no background to speak of, being treated with a new respect by people she'd known since childhood.

It went without saying that Dr Campbell disapproved of district nurses, seeing them as women trespassing on his territory and denying him his fees. But since Stephen had more or less taken over the running of the practice, she had little contact with the older man, for which she was profoundly thankful.

Although her grief at Danny's disappearance had, to some extent subsided, he was still a powerful presence in her life. Stephen and Eliza wanted her to believe he

288

was dead, but he was alive all right, Charity knew that because an invisible thread stretched between them and she frequently felt its pull. And whatever he'd done, she was still bound to him by the sacred vows of marriage, which meant she owed him her fidelity and loyalty.

But there was the question of Stephen. Again he was unsettling her with his attention. But she was wiser this time round. And warier. So far love had brought her precious little happiness and she'd been misled both by men and the books she'd read. Or was it that men and women just wanted different things, Charity wondered, as she pushed her bicycle across the school playground and leaned it against the wall. Anyway, from now on she would be perpetually on guard and would steer clear of emotional involvement. Liberated by her decision, Charity unstrapped her bag from the bicycle and pulled open the school door.

Inside there was the same bilious mustard-coloured paint on the walls and that familiar smell of chalk. As she walked along the corridor where she and her schoolmates had been forbidden to talk or run, Charity could hear the sing-song voices of children chanting their tables and alphabet and was immediately back in her childhood. It didn't seem so long ago that she and Mollie had sat behind those desks, and yet so much water had flown under the bridge since then.

Although there had been a change of headmistress since their time, Charity still found herself tapping on the door of her sanctum with the same diffidence as she had when a child. Old habits die hard she thought, straightened her spine and smiled a confident smile as the door was flung open.

'Ah Nurse Weston, you're here,' said Miss Bunn heartily. 'We've got quite a few absentees, as usual, I'm afraid. Some of them are away because it's wash day, and have only the clothes they stand up in, others are sick, while quite a few, I suspect, are just playing truant. What hope is there of them ever acquiring an education, I ask you.

Well never mind, we'll get those who are here lined up for you, one class at a time. If you'll just follow me. At least they are all clean this morning in anticipation of your visit. I hardly recognized some of them, their hands and faces fairly glowed with all that scrubbing. The girls are wearing clean aprons and some of the boys even managed a bit of spit and polish on their boots. You should consider yourself honoured.'

Charity donned a long all-enveloping apron, filled a bowl with water and disinfectant then set out, on the table, scissors, a nit-comb for the hair and a spatula to examine tonsils. When she'd finished, she beckoned to the bobbing, curious faces she could see peering through the glass-panelled door and her first customers marched through in single file. What immediately struck Charity was how undernourished most of them looked.

'Will you all hold out your hands please. Good, nice and clean,' she said encouragingly as she walked along the line. 'Now who here cleans their teeth?'

One small girl, better dressed than the rest, put up her hand.

'I does, Nuss, on Sundays afore I goes to church.'

'You should all try to you know. Get your mum or dad to buy you a brush and use salt to clean them with, it will stop your teeth going bad.'

The children gazed at her blankly as well they might, because they knew like she did, that no parent struggling to keep body and soul together was going to spend hard-earned money on such unnecessary luxuries as tooth-brushes.

'Now, as I call your name, will you please step forward. Ida Pym.'

A small, snuffle-nosed girl stepped forward.

'How old are you, Ida?'

'I'm eight and one month, Nuss,' she answered in adenoidal tones.

'Right, I want you to stand against the wall so that I

can measure you to see how tall you are, then I'll test your eyesight, take a look at your tonsils, and lastly go through your hair. Is that all right?'

The girl, whose chin was burrowed in her chest, managed a nod.

Ida was undersized for her age, as were most of the others. A few had defective eyesight, another had very bad catarrh and enlarged tonsils, all of them had several decaying teeth and offensive breath. Lastly, she lined up the girls and went through their hair thoroughly with the disinfected nit-comb in search of head lice, and they weren't hard to find. Those infected she had to direct to the cleansing station and they went off weeping and knowing that their long hair would be cut off and in the playground they would be jeered at by the more fortunate children.

By the time Charity had finished at the school, written up her case notes and made her recommendations, it was dinner time. She stopped briefly for a coffee and sandwich then went on to her second call, an elderly woman with crippling leg ulcers that wouldn't heal. Charity dressed them, washed the woman, combed and plaited her hair, tidied up the room then promised her grateful patient she would call back again in a few days' time.

Her next visit was to a young mother with newly-born twins. The house was clean, the young woman, Mrs Lee, of some intelligence, but obviously anaemic. Charity examined the twins, two lusty lunged boys, and pronounced them fit and strong.

'I wish I could say the same for meself, I feel worn out. I'm twenty-five, and I've got four kids already. What am I to do, Nurse? By the time I'm thirty, I could 'ave another five. And all this about how when God sends a baby he also sends a pair of breeches is a load of rot. We're poor enough already, kids just push you that bit further nearer the workhouse.'

'Have you talked to your husband about this?' Charity asked, hoping she sounded worldly and knowledgeable.

'Till I'm blue in the face, but you know what men are, even the best o' them. I can tell you nurse, if I knew then what I do now, I would never have wed. Marriage is a trap for women.' She shook her head in disbelief at her own folly. Charity saw there was already a permanent frown between the young woman's eyebrows and the once rosebud lips were tightening into a thin line of bitterness. If she went on having children at the rate she was by thirty she would be old, at forty worn out and maybe even dead.

'I'll make no bones about it,' Mrs Lee went on, obviously wanting to get things off her chest, 'the next one I'm gonna get rid of, it's easy enough, I've heard.'

'Not always safe though, Mrs Lee. Some of the stuff women swallow is poisonous and if you use an instrument on yourself you could easily bleed to death. And it is against the law to do things like that,' Charity felt bound to mention.

'What does it matter, I often feel like giving up the ghost anyway. Nature ain't kind to women, is it Nurse?'

'No, it isn't,' Charity agreed. 'But you do have your little ones to think of.' Then, seeing the woman was about at the end of her tether and badly in need of practical advice, she added, 'Have you considered using something to stop babies coming?'

'Yeah, but it all costs too much. Our pockets ain't up to it.'

'I have a book which I'll bring so that you can read it. It gives you lots of advice and some cheap methods you might be able to use. I can't say any of them work one hundred per cent, but it's better than doing nothing. I'll drop it in tomorrow.'

'Will you? I'd be everso grateful, nurse.'

As she left Charity wondered if she was could get into trouble passing on family limitation information. Then she gave a shrug. What the hell did it matter if she did. At least she might ease one woman's misery, perhaps even save her life.

Chapter 24

The four of them collapsed on to the seats gasping and grinning and fanning their faces, but pleased with themselves at having caught the train, even if it was by the skin of their teeth.

It was Mollie and her young man Caspar who were the culprits. Charity had watched anxiously as the hand of the clock moved round to a minute before the hour. Almost choking on her disappointment, she'd turned to Stephen. 'After all that careful planning, now they aren't going to turn up.'

'Never say die, look here they are,' he answered and over her shoulder she saw Mollie and Caspar come tearing into the station.

'Save the explanations until later, let's run,' Stephen yelled as Mollie opened her mouth to speak. For already the porter had a whistle in his mouth and the green flag poised. Taking his advice, they tore down the platform, jumping into a compartment almost as the train moved off.

'Coo, heck, that was a close one,' said Mollie. 'Crisis at the hospital, wouldn't you guess. My day off and even then I'm called in.'

'Well, the offer is still open, my love. You could put all that behind you, marry me and live in penury in an attic instead.' As he spoke Caspar put an arm round Mollie's shoulder and pulled her to him.

'Thank you Caspar, but I've had enough of poverty and training to be doctor has been hard work. But having got this far I'm determined to finish if only to prove women can be just as competent in their chosen careers as you men. Anyway, you haven't even decided whether you want to be a painter or writer yet.'

'Yes I have. I decided yesterday. I want to paint.'

'I'll marry you when you're famous then.'

'That might take a long time, my love.'

'Never mind, I've got plenty of plans in the meantime.'

'Don't you think your friend is a trifle hard hearted, Charity,' Caspar beseeched.

'No. She sounds like the practical, level-headed Mollie I've always known,' Charity answered, and for some reason her remark seemed to amuse Caspar, who threw back his head and laughed uproariously.

Caspar had a head of thick black hair, inherited from his Spanish mother and, by all accounts, a quixotic nature. Although Charity had never met his family, she'd heard so many stories of their goings-on she felt knew the Rogets intimately. She also suspected, from the way Mollie regaled her with these tales, that she was almost as much in love with Caspar's family as she was with him. Her noncomformist soul might often be shocked by their free-flowing lifestyle but it was obvious she was utterly fascinated, too. From what she said, debt didn't trouble them in the least and money flowed in and out of the artistic, liberal household with the regularity of the tide. So did the scantily-dressed nubile young women who acted as models for Mr Roget, a successful painter. Inez, his mother, equally successful, smoked Turkish cigarettes, wore her gipsy curls loose down her back, scorned corsets and wrote slightly risqué novels about young men falling in love with mysterious older women. Once Mollie had related to Charity with a slightly embarrassed giggle how Max, Caspar's father had grabbed her on the stairs and given her a whiskery kiss and had even suggested she sit for him, 'Naked, mind you,' he'd said. Rows, when they occurred between these two exotic birds of paradise, usually over extramarital affairs, were apparently monumental, with furniture frequently having to be replaced once the household had returned to normal.

But weighing it all up, witty and charming as Caspar was, Charity still thought Mollie's basic good sense, plus her ambition to prove herself in an overwhelmingly male profession, would protect her from making any starry-eyed decisions about marrying herself into the family, love them as she might.

'Not very interesting at the moment, I'm afraid,' said Stephen, breaking into her thoughts. 'London seems to have stretched its nasty tentacles farther and farther into the country every time I come.'

'Yes, just look at those perfectly horrible villas. The architect who designed them needs shooting.' Caspar's high-bridged, aristocratic nose wrinkled in distaste.

They seemed rather nice houses to Charity, spacious with neat back gardens where children could play and, no doubt, to most of the people she knew, they would seem like palaces. Certainly, she could see herself living quite contentedly in one. However, since it was obvious they didn't meet Caspar's stringent aesthetic requirements, she said nothing.

She had vast areas of ignorance, architecture being one of them, and the middle classes, with one well-chosen word, could squash the likes of her totally. And another thing she had no intention of letting on about, imagining Caspar's look of disbelief, was that today Stephen was fulfilling a promise he'd made to her a long time ago and this was her first proper visit to the country.

Only she did wonder if Stephen might be having second thoughts about the excursion. He looked tired, burdened with worries and added little to the conversation during the journey, although the razor-sharp repartee that went backwards and forwards between Caspar and Mollie did bring an occasional brief flicker of a smile to his face.

Charity was still new enough to her job to feel optimistic about what she could achieve. However, Stephen frequently expressed doubts about his ability to improve the quality of the lives of the people he treated. 'What they need is decent housing and a living wage, Charity, and anything else is a waste of time.' This was usually said at the end of a particularly exhausting day and it often took her some time to persuade him that what he was doing was actually worthwhile. Yet she understood his feelings of hopelessness. She'd lived all her life close to poverty, was more accepting of it, but for someone of Stephen's background, driven by a strong moral sense, it must be so much harder.

But as the train plunged deeper and deeper into the lush green countryside and they caught tantalizing glimpses of small villages, white weatherboard houses and the spires of old churches, she saw his features lighten, his hazel eyes lose their dullness.

'Look, Charity, oasthouses and hop gardens, we're really in Kent now.' He was pointing through the window at some buildings with oddly-angled chimneys, then field upon field of strung poles around which green bines were already winding.

A short while later they crossed a viaduct and down below them Charity saw a river and gardens with apple trees in blossom. 'That's the Darent, it means we're nearly in Eynsford, get your things together.' More his old self again, the train hardly had time to stop before Stephen had the door open and was jumping down on to the platform. Then, reaching out, he clasped Charity round the waist and swung her to the ground. 'Well, I've finally got you here,' he said, smiling down at her. Leaving the other two to catch up with them, he pulled her towards the exit.

When they'd left London it had been one of those days, neither one thing nor the other, but gradually the cloud had broken and now the sun was out on this early summer's day, and as they walked down into the village Charity lifted her face, enjoying its warmth and inhaling pleasurably. 'It smells so different from London.'

'Yes, clean for a start. With all this fresh air, I bet everyone here lives to a ripe old age,' said Mollie.

Stephen gave a rueful smile. 'Some do, some don't.

It's not so obvious but you can find rural slums to equal anything in London. But let's not talk about depressing things.'

'No, let's not,' interrupted Caspar. 'And may I suggest that for today you three try and imagine you've left your social consciences behind you in London. Just for once be self-indulgent sybarites. As a way of life it has a lot to recommend it, and I speak from personal experience.'

Slightly shocked by Caspar's attitude, the other three stood silent for a moment, then Stephen grabbed both the girls' hands. 'Caspar's quite right, we are here to enjoy ourselves, so first of all I'll show you the village.'

As he had promised, Eynsford was a delight. A fifteenth-century bridge straddled the Darent, with a cornmill on one side and on the other a ford where local children paddled.

Pausing to watch them, Charity said to Stephen, 'Perhaps, like you said, there are poor people here but even so, any child that grows up in a place like this is lucky. Look how healthy they are. Not pale and stunted like some of the children we treat and they haven't got rickets or running sores.'.

'True,' answered Stephen as they walked on.

But Charity had an observant eye and she began to to notice that for all its quaintness and flower-filled gardens, there was indeed considerable poverty. She could see it in slipping tiles on roofs and broken window frames and fences. After Caspar's remarks, she wisely kept her thoughts to herself, but she could also see the disturbing consequences of in-breeding: vacant-eyed children; shuffling, grinning adults, making it obvious the village idiot wasn't just a myth.

They'd just done a quick dash round the church and were about to move on when Caspar said, 'I've never believed in neglecting the inner man so shall we repair to a hostelry for a little something before we embark on our hike?'

'Why not,' answered Stephen and he led them to an

inn with a bench outside. At ease with the world, they leaned against the warm brick, drank strong ale and ate great crispy hunks of homemade bread and cheddar cheese with the healthy gluttony of the young.

Sitting along from them was an elderly man who was wearing a smock-frock and gaiters and puffing on a clay pipe that was almost buried amongst his thick grey whiskers. 'Well that's the genuine article, a real son of the soil,' observed Caspar, and drawing a pencil and sketch pad from his haversack, in several quick strokes immortalized the old man on paper.

'Why that's brilliant, Caspar,' said Charity, who up until now had figured him out to be a bit of a dilettante. 'Isn't it good, Moll?'

Mollie rested her chin on Caspar's shoulder. 'It certainly is. But the wretch writes just as well. The trouble is because he's so talented he can't decide which career to pursue and so ends up doing nothing.'

'Tomorrow, my love, I will get down to the serious business of making my way in the world, I promise you. But in the meantime since you admire my simple drawing so much, Charity, would you like it as a memento of today, of fleeting youth and transient happiness?' Caspar gave her a melancholic smile.

'I'd love it.'

He signed the sketch with a flourish. 'Keep it safe. Who knows, one of these days, m'dear, when I'm an honoured member of the Royal Academy, and married to your friend, it might be of great value.'

Charity was in no hurry to move from such a pleasant spot but Stephen pulled her to her feet. 'There's much better to come. Just wait until you see the orchards and the view.'

Crossing the bridge they followed a lane out under the viaduct. Here the Kent countryside opened out before them, a fertile valley of hop gardens and orchards. And just as Stephen had hoped, they'd caught the blossom, massed like pale pink clouds, at its moment of perfection.

Tomorrow, nudged by a gentle breeze, he knew it would start scattering its petals on the ground like confetti.

To the right was gently rolling wooded downland and pastures where sheep and cattle grazed, in front of them a meadow of wild flowers through which Caspar and Mollie were already tramping.

Charity watched them with an indulgent smile. They both had books in their hands and earnest expressions on their faces, and she knew they were trying to identify each flower before deciding whether to pick it to press.

'Well, what do you think?' asked Stephen.

'Idyllic. Everything you promised and more. I can see what draws you down here. Rotherhithe can't really compete.'

'I envy Caspar, if I could paint like him then I'd be able to take it back to London with me. Now I just have to rely on my memory. But I've promised myself this is where I'll live one day.'

'So you won't stay in London.'

'Not if I marry. It's no place to bring up children.' He reached for her hand. 'Would you like to live here?'

Charity pulled her hand away. 'I could never leave Rotherhithe. You see I've got to be there when Danny comes back.'

Stephen decided it was time to be firm. 'Charity, it's been three years now, you really ought to try and accept that he won't return.'

'In other words he's dead. That's what you're saying isn't it?'

Stephen nodded.

She stared at him, a stubborn look on her small face. 'Well, you're wrong, see,' she snapped, then turning, strode on, presenting to Stephen a back that was ramrod straight, and a thick coil of hair that fairly bounced with indignation. There was no reason why she should go on believing Danny was alive, she had to admit that, no letter, no small personal token to fuel her hope. But she

299

just knew, with a sort of obstinate certainty, that he was alive, somewhere, although it was a waste of time trying to explain this to anyone else, even Mollie.

But it was rather too hot to remain irritated and feeling she'd made her point, Charity flopped down in the shade of a willow and watched as Stephen walked toward her. She'd expected some sign of remorse but he had his jacket slung over his shoulder and was whistling happily, which put her back up slightly.

He joined her under the tree, made a pillow of his jacket, then settled himself as if for sleep, his long legs stretched out full length on the ground. 'Mmm this is nice, isn't it?'

Charity made no comment but when he opened one eye, he detected a small frown marring her smooth features. So that was it, she was expecting him to apologize for being such a doubting Thomas. Well he could do that, although it wouldn't alter his opinion.

'I'm sorry, Charity, I didn't mean to upset you, particularly not today. I want today to be perfect, something you'll remember for the rest of your life.'

'I haven't had so many good ones that I'm likely to forget this.' Charity plucked sulkily at some young leaves and her tone was cool, unforgiving. 'Anyway, hadn't we better tell the other two we're here.'

Looking perfectly relaxed, Stephen closed his eyes. 'It's all right, they're just a bit further along. Caspar's stopped to sketch the gatehouse of Lullingstone Castle.'

Aware of the dangers that lurked for girls in the shade of overhanging branches, Charity stood up. 'Well I shall go for a paddle then. Keep your eyes shut while I take my stockings off.'

As any red-blooded young man would do, Stephen ignored her order. Through half-closed lids he caught a glimpse of neat ankles and the gentle curve of white thigh and knew keeping a tight rein on his emotions was going to be a problem today.

As she ran to the river's edge, Stephen eased himself

up on his elbow. Through the umbrella of leaves he saw her hitch up her dress and gingerly dip her toes into the water. She looked so young and vulnerable, the urge to protect her overwhelmed him. Why, he wondered with a gut-aching surge of jealousy, did she cling so doggedly to the idea of Danny returning? Why was she wearing her wedding ring today? And that locket round her neck? What was in it? Danny's photograph, he'd bet his life on it. Was this her way of telling him she still loved her husband, or was it an excuse to remain in an emotional limbo? Of course if it was, he couldn't blame her, for she'd hardly been well served by men. He was quick to condemn Danny, but there was his own dubious behaviour to be considered. He hadn't exactly covered himself in glory, and he held himself more than half responsible for her disastrous marriage. A marriage to which she was still legally bound until it could be proved conclusively Danny was dead. And that was the great problem, would they ever find out?

Charity was now standing in the river, holding her skirt bunched up in front of her and staring down into the water with the self-absorption of a child. Her honey-toned skin had darkened slightly in the sun and her hair was bleached white like late summer corn. Alone and apparently content. But he wanted to rouse her from that emotional half-world she inhabited, to make his presence felt again in her life, to gather her up in his arms and show her tenderness and passion, to protect her from life's ills, but most of all to tell her he loved her. Ardent, impatient now to declare his feelings, Stephen tore off his shoes and socks, rolled up his trousers and leapt to his feet.

Perfect happiness is possible, thought Charity, this moment, now. And in simple things. Golden floating motes of sunlight, scented air assaulting the senses, the sound of running water over pebbles, darting, long-winged insects. On the bank, bees and butterflies

301

supped drunkenly from cowslips and golden kingcups and then, unbelievably, a heron dropped into the water just a few yards from where she stood. Not daring to move a muscle she watched as it waded about on spindly legs with slow, sedate movements. Then suddenly the bird froze, giving Charity a chance to study him more carefully. With his grey, black and white plumage, long neck sunk into his shoulders and small plume of feathers sticking out from the back of his head, like a pigtail, she thought him magnificent. And being so close to nature added to the perfection of the moment. He seemed to be regarding her with one sharp yellow eye and although she was sure he already knew, she felt she wanted to speak to him, to tell him how beautiful he was. Then out of the corner of her eye she was aware of Stephen approaching, noisily displacing the water and startling the heron, which gave a loud *kaark* of annoyance and took off slowly and clumsily, its large wings bowed, its thin legs dangling.

But the bird's annoyance at being disturbed was nothing compared to Charity's. 'Now look what you've done, frightened him away.'

'Sorry.'

'Being sorry's not enough,' Charity answered and, to show her irritation she bent and bringing her arm back, scooped up a great handful of water, feeling the tension of it against her fingers as it arced through the air, dousing Stephen in a most satisfying way.

'Why you . . .' Rendered speechless, Stephen stood there, water dripping from his hair on to his clothes. He'd come to offer her his love and he'd got this. And her laughter too, full-throated and mocking, echoing around the countryside.

Noticing a dangerous glint in Stephen's eye, but still unable to curb her laughter, Charity struggled to the water's edge. But the hem of her dress dragging in the water impeded her progress and she was just scrambling up the bank, clawing at the damp earth with her nails when behind her she heard Stephen say, 'I'll get you for that, young lady,' and she felt her ankle being grabbed. When she tried to kick free, she was caught in a tight lock around the waist and lifted bodily.

'Put me down,' she yelled, flailing her legs.

'All right, if that's what you want,' said Stephen and, without further ado, he let go and she landed on her backside in the river, her dress ballooning out around her.

'You beast, now look what you've done, ruined my dress.' Charity had changed her tune and was no longer laughing, in fact she looked dangerously close to tears.

'No I haven't, the water's quite clean,' answered Stephen unsympathetically. 'Anyway, it will soon dry in the sun. Come on stand up.' He held out his hand.

'I can manage quite well on my own thank you.' She tried to struggle to her feet but she was dragged down again by the weight of her saturated dress and petticoats.

Forced to take the extended hand she said petulantly, 'Stephen Trevelyan, I shall never forgive you for this.'

'Never?' As he drew her up, he slipped an arm round her waist.

'No never.' But Charity's voice had lost some of its petulance. Closer and closer, Stephen drew her, and his hand was now on the back of her neck, their lips almost touching.

'Charity, where are you?' At the sound of Mollie's voice Charity leapt guiltily away and Stephen cursed under his breath. Of all the ill-chosen moments, he thought as Mollie's cheerful face appeared round a tree.

'Good Lord, what ever has happened to you?' Mollie stared in astonishment at Charity and Stephen standing ankle deep in the river. 'Are you all right.?'

'A little mishap, that's all,' replied Stephen, as they emerged dripping from the river.

'What sort of mishap?' Mollie had never seen her friend looking so unkempt.

'I slipped,' Charity lied, 'and Stephen came and helped

me. I'm sorry, Moll, but we'll have to stay here until I've dried off.'

'That will suit me just fine,' said Caspar who had now joined them again. 'My sketch book is already half full but there's still so much I want to draw. I can see why Samuel Palmer called this his valley of vision, it's beautiful. I feel inspired by the fact that he did some of his best landscapes when he lived at Shoreham. Just think, he and his friends must have come into these same meadows to sketch and paint.'

Charity had taken off her petticoat and spread it on a bush to dry. Usually so neat and tidy, sitting there on the grass beside Mollie, hatless and sunburnt, her wet, mud-spattered dress and bare feet gave her a gypsyish air. And the two of them together, weaving necklaces and crowns of wild flowers, made a perfect composition. Caspar studied them both a moment longer then took up his pencil and pad again. With a look of intense concentration, he started to sketch. And perhaps he *was* inspired because in the drawing he seemed somehow to capture the fleeting perfection of the afternoon, the languid heat, the girls' simple happiness and affection for each other, the tangle of daisies and buttercups in loosely falling hair. It had an unaffected pastoral charm, and when the painting was finished, Caspar would call it, 'Friendship'. He couldn't have known it but it was destined to become one of his most enduring and popular paintings. It would be reproduced by the thousand and copies of it would adorn the walls of cottage and mansion alike, from one end of the country to the other.

Charity's clothes had already been dry for some time when they eventually moved on to Shoreham in the late afternoon. Although they complained they were ravenous, Caspar insisted that first they must take a look at Water House, where Palmer had once lived. Only after this were they allowed to find a cottage serving tea. Here they sat in an overgrown, sweetly-scented garden of lilac, primroses and violets and gorged themselves on scones with cream and strawberry jam.

Originally they'd had no intention of going any further than Shoreham. But without saying anything, all of them knew there was something so special about the day, so touched with magic, they would probably never recapture it. Because none of them could bear the thought of letting it go, they decided they could just as easily walk on to Otford and catch a train home from there.

So in a long, luminous twilight, and with hands linked, they walked across wide green meadows where a spectral mist lay suspended over the river and a pale sliver of moon hung in the pink-flushed sky.

'I wonder if I'll ever again feel as happy as I do at this moment,' said Mollie a trifle pensively. From a copse a bird started to sing, and his song was taken up by another, then another.

Stephen stopped. 'Listen, nightingales.'

'Exquisite. My friends, I think my heart is going to burst with joy and love for you all.' Caspar flung his arms wide in an expansive gesture and Mollie went to him and he enfolded her in an embrace and kissed her.

Stephen moved closer to Charity. She watched him, her lowered lids hiding a wicked gleam. She waited until their lips were almost touching, then she turned and ran, so swiftly and lightly, it wasn't until she'd reached the other side of the meadow, that Stephen finally managed to catch up with her.

Chapter 25

They didn't need much of an excuse but during that last summer of the century the intolerable heat of London often drove them into the country. They went in June when sweet-faced dog roses tumbled from hedgerows and the curd-white heads of elderflowers bowed heavily over the wayside. Teams of mowers would be out in the fields until it was too dark to see, swishing away rhythmically with their scythes and filling the air with the vanilla sweetness of new mown hay.

Charity came to see how ploughing, sowing and harvesting marked out the cycle of the year for the country dweller. Because in late August when they went, the corn had been cut and women and children were gleaning in the fields. By September the smell of hops drying in oasts told them the hop pickers had arrived.

They came from London by the trainload with their pots and pans and children, whole families to live in small corrugated huts without any amenities and to cook on open fires. In some ways they were welcomed for the money they spent in the local shops and inns, but in other ways resented. Drunken fights frequently broke out, many of the children were allowed to run wild, and in the way of the town-bred they would carelessly leave gates open so that cattle could wander and many a time farmers caught them red-handed, scrumping from orchards or stealing eggs from hen coops.

Wanting to preserve their happiness, the four of them made it a rule that they would not discuss the disturbing news from South Africa. However, by mid-September this was almost impossible because Britain had decided that Mr Kruger, President of the Transvaal, must be made to see reason over the *Uitlanders* wish for their rights and their hunger for gold. By dint of "the mailed fist," if all else failed, the *Observer* reported as the 1st Battalion Northumberland Fusiliers, 'Who may be depended upon to give a very good account of themselves and to prove a very hard nut for the Boers to crack,' embarked at Southhampton.

That day, before they could silence him, Stephen had burst out furiously, 'What I can't stand is this sickening wave of patriotic fervour and jingoism which is sending young men so needlessly to their deaths.'

'Perhaps everyone will see reason and it'll all fizzle out,' suggested Caspar in an attempt to calm him.

'Whoever heard of human beings behaving reasonably,' answered Stephen.

'You're forgetting the rules. Can we change the subject please,' interjected Mollie. 'Did Caspar tell you he sold his first painting, a landscape? He's paying for dinner today.'

Later, coming home on the train, they decided between them they could manage one last trip to Kent to catch the autumn colours before winter set in.

'You won't believe this, but I've got a whole weekend off at the end of October,' said Mollie.

'Well, why don't we do that then? Go from the Saturday to the Sunday.' Stephen suggested. 'I sometimes rent a cottage down there from a farmer I know. It's got two bedrooms, Caspar and I could share one, you and Charity the other.'

Caspar took Mollie's hand. 'I think that's a splendiferous idea, don't you, my love?'

Mollie wasn't so sure. She could see that Charity, like the others, had no doubts. The difference was, she lodged in the nurses' home where no questions would be asked and she'd also been married so her virtue wasn't at stake. But how would her own parents greet such an idea? They didn't altogether approve of Caspar or the artistic circles she increasingly moved in.

'You would like to go, wouldn't you Moll? It would be such fun.' said Caspar, made anxious by her silence.

'What shall I tell my parents? They're hardly likely to think it's a good idea, are they?'

'Who says you have to tell them. What they don't know isn't going to hurt them, is it?'

'I suppose not.' Mollie answered, then got to thinking; what was she bothered about? Her good name? Her virginity? None of those models she met at Caspar's house seemed to mourn the loss of theirs so perhaps she'd held on to hers long enough anyway.

* * *

On that October morning, there was the usual nail-biting wait for Caspar and Mollie but this time it was hard not to notice how many khaki uniforms there were amongst the crowds of travellers. Young men posturing a bit, cracking jokes, having their shoulders slapped by fathers, being wished good luck or kissing sweethearts and mothers goodbye.

'Can you understand why anyone should volunteer to be killed,' asked Stephen, shaking his head at men's folly.

'They're young, they see it as an adventure. They don't expect to die,' answered Charity, her attention diverted by the porter, who was now walking along the platform slamming doors. She looked around expecting to see, as always, Mollie and Caspar flushed and apologetic pushing their way through the crowds. But this morning there was no sign of them.

Recognizing them, the porter held open the last door. 'It looks as if them friends of yours 'as been and gorn and let you down terday. If I was you I'd 'op in, guv.'

'What do you think, Charity.'

'Yes, let's go. I'd rather be walking in the country than standing on a sooty platform. They know where we're staying and they'll just have to catch the next train.'

The porter looked pleased with their decision and handing their bags in after them, said with a wink, 'Enjoy yerselves.'

They reached the other end to find it a still day and the sky a cold, pale blue with little wisps of cloud like bridal veils. And the smell was of autumn, of woodsmoke and burning leaves.

Getting to the farm where they were to pick up the key to the cottage meant a walk along a winding, deeply-rutted farm track. This, Charity soon discovered, was a torture to feet, particularly in unsuitable city shoes. Wishing Stephen had warned her about the condition of the lane and trying not to think how much her shoes had cost, she gritted her teeth and soldiered on. Until she wrenched an ankle. Letting out a yell of pain she stopped.

'I'm not walking an inch further.' Even to her own ears her voice sounded fretful and childish.

Stephen, who was a little way in front with the bags, stopped and turned round. 'Come on,' he said with an encouraging smile, 'not far now.'

'It hadn't better be,' Charity muttered darkly, hobbling after him and wondering if this weekend was such a good idea after all.

'Look, there it is,' Stephen shouted back to her and sure enough, round the next bend, she saw with a sense of relief a farmhouse and out-buildings.

'Thank the Lord for that.'

'You wait here and look after the bags,' Stephen ordered when she caught up with him, then went off to collect the keys from the farmer. In no time he was back, cradling a large basket in his arms.

'Can you manage to carry this to the cottage? It's provisions. I bought them from the farmer's wife. Milk, eggs, bread, butter and bacon. I don't know about you but I could eat a horse.'

Talk of food made her forget her sore feet but then she remembered the other two. 'But what about Caspar and Mollie? Shouldn't we wait for them?'

'Right, the next train is in an hour, if they haven't arrived by then we eat.'

The white weatherboard cottage was only a few hundred yards from the farm, and Charity was glad to reach it. Putting the basket down on the scrubbed table, Charity eased her feet out of her shoes, flexed her toes gratefully and looked about her with an approving eye. The parlour floor was stone flagged, but brightly coloured homemade rag rugs stopped it from seeming spartan, so did the fire which someone had thoughtfully lit. As well as the two wheel-backed Windsor chairs on either side of the fireplace there was an oak settle and a Welsh dresser with blue and white cups dangling from its hooks.

'Well . . .'

Charity nodded her approval. 'It's very nice.'

309

Stephen breathed easily again. He'd noticed her cross expression on the way here. Eager to show her more, he took Charity's hand, led her up the narrow staircase and pushed open a heavy oak door. 'This is where you and Mollie will sleep.'

The floorboards shone, the room smelt of beeswax, lavender and crisp white sheets, the brass bed was so large it nearly filled the room. 'Oh, I must try it,' said Charity and, leaping on to the bed, she was almost submerged in the deep feather mattress. Then she saw that Stephen was watching her, with an expression that made her scramble hastily off the bed and go to the window. He came to stand behind her and she was very conscious of his hand resting lightly on her shoulder.

'What do you think of it?'

The view across the valley was of heavily-wooded downs in a wash of colours: russet, brown and gold. 'Absolutely perfect.' She turned to face him. 'Did you ever bring Blanche here?' Somehow the question slipped out unbidden but Charity found she was holding herself tense as she waited for his answer. It would all be spoilt if Blanche had stayed here. She and Stephen, arms and legs entangled, making love in that bed.

She watched his slow smile of amusement. 'This is all too rustic and primitive for Blanche. Can you imagine her going outside to get water from a pump? She likes hers brought hot to her room each morning by a subservient, bobbing maid. And not a minute before ten either. No, in the past, I either came with a friend from my student days or on my own. Actually I quite enjoy the solitary existence as long as I know it's not going to last longer than a weekend.'

'So I should consider myself privileged, being invited here?'

'Definitely privileged. The main thing is that you like it.'

'Oh I do, I do,' Charity breathed, forgetting her earlier doubts.

'Good. Let's go and make ourselves something to eat, then we'll go for a walk.'

Charity upacked first, laying out her nightgown on the bed, then changing into stout leather shoes and a tweed skirt suitable for walking in. Finding water in the wash-stand jug, she rinsed the grime of London from her face then went downstairs.

Stephen, who knew where everything was, had already produced a large cast-iron frying pan, and soon Charity had rashers sizzling away in it. When they were crisp, she lifted the bacon out with a fork and, keeping it warm by the fire, fried four golden-yoked eggs until the whites were nicely frilled round the edges. While she was doing this, Stephen, humming to himself, set the table, cut bread and made the tea and Charity was struck by how very cosy and domestic it seemed.

'Gosh, that was good,' said Stephen, when he'd wiped his plate clean with a piece of bread and drunk his second cup of tea. 'I don't know if it's unrequited love or not makes her such an awful cook, but Miss Fry's eggs arrive at the table swimming in congealed fat, with the yolk overcooked and the white leathery. No chance of getting overweight with her cooking. Now yours, Charity is another matter.' He patted his stomach. 'I think what we need now is a ten-mile walk.'

'But we can't, not before Mollie and Caspar come.'

Stephen looked at his watch. 'I think we've given them a fair chance.'

Charity gave a perplexed frown. 'I can't understand it. It couldn't even be an emergency at the hospital. Mollie was staying at Caspar's last night.'

'You know those two, they'll turn up sooner or later. But if we hang around any longer it won't be worth going. The days are too short. As long as we leave the door unlocked it'll be all right.'

With a slight sense of guilt at not being there to welcome her friends, Charity scribbled a note.

Gone for a walk, back in an hour or so, help yourself
to food.

She signed it, then drew a little clock with the large hand
on twelve and the small one on three to show they had
waited. Slipping it under the oil lamp, she told herself
that by the time they returned, Mollie and Caspar were
bound to be here.

Stepping out at a brisk pace, they set off for the woods.
They didn't meet a soul and it all seemed very quiet and
secretive there under the high vaulted branches, with the
only sound the crunch of dry leaves and the snap of twigs
under their feet. The peaty earth gave off a smell of decaying vegetation and fungi and roots spread themselves out
over the surface of the ground like large veins, to trip up
the unwary. In a grove of chestnut trees, however, there
was movement, a sound of busyness: rustling leaves and
nuts falling at their feet as if the branches were being
shaken.

Stephen stopped and pointed upwards. 'Look,
squirrels.'

'So there are.' Bushy-tailed, the russet colour of
autumn, Charity watched them with a sense of absorbed
delight. One sat on its hind legs, a nut held between its
claws and nibbled rapidly. Another performed amazing
acrobatic feats for their benefit, leaping from swinging
branch to swinging branch in his search for food.

'I don't want to deprive them of a meal, but I love roast
chestnuts, let's take some home,' said Charity and began
scuffing her feet in the leaves. They gathered them up as
if they'd discovered lost gold, stuffing them into their
pockets until they bulged. Into the swing of it now,
Stephen filled his arms with wood for kindling.

They were walking home across the fields when
Stephen stopped. 'Look,' he said and pointed with his
toe at mushrooms big as plates.

'We must have those.' Bending, Charity plucked them
from the ground and they bore nature's bounty home,

feeling as pleased as primitive man must have done returning from the hunt.

Night was closing in over the countryside as they walked down the lane. 'There's a wind blowing up, perhaps we're in for a storm,' said Stephen, and as if to confirm it, Charity felt a spattering of rain on her cheeks.

She'd taken it for granted they'd be welcomed by the golden glow of lamplight spilling out into the lane, but when they reached the cottage it was in darkness.

'Oh, they haven't come.' Her voice carried in it her deep disappointment. She'd seen the four of them sitting round the fire roasting chestnuts, catching up on each other's news and perhaps even playing charades. Then in the morning after a large breakfast of fried bacon and mushrooms, going for a long walk in crisp, bright sunshine. She turned to Stephen. 'What are we going to do?' But as she spoke a spiteful gust of wind blew them indoors.

She waited until Stephen had lit the lamp, watched him throw some of the wood they'd collected on to the fire, emptied her own pockets, then coming to a conclusion, said firmly, 'Well, one thing is certain, we can't stay here alone. I'm going to pack. There is a train, I assume, to London this evening.'

'Yes. But take a look out of the window. It's raining cats and dogs out there. The lane is the only way out and it quickly becomes an impassable quagmire. I'm afraid, Charity, you are stuck here with me. But what are you worried about, that I'll compromise you?'

The question was put jestingly, but Charity didn't answer. However her eyes rebuked him and Stephen, remembering, like she did, that other night, felt a sense of shame.

'There is the question of my reputation. I know working class girls aren't supposed to, but I do value mine, you know.' Her tone was chilly. 'What do you imagine the farmer's going to think, me here alone with you.'

'If he bothers to come near us, which I doubt, he'll

assume we're married. After all, you are wearing a wedding ring.'

Charity stared down at her hand, twisting the gold band round on her finger. 'Oh yes.'

'Even if Mollie and Caspar made it to Eynsford they won't be able to get through now. They'll have to put up in an inn for the night. But they could still turn up here in the morning. After all, they were looking forward to the weekend as much as we were.'

Stephen went over and took a final look out into the darkness. 'It's a positive deluge out there. I bet it's set in for the night.' He drew the curtains across the window and the room seemed to wrap itself around them. Everything suddenly seemed cosier, more intimate.

Aware by her silence that he still hadn't convinced Charity of the rightness of the situation, Stephen took her arm and drew her to the fire. 'Come on, since we're virtually marooned and you've no choice but to spend the evening in my company I'll do my best to entertain you. While we roast the chestnuts I'll tell you about when I was a little boy in India. Would you like that?'

Charity nodded, watching while Stephen, with a surgical precision, made a neat cut in the tough chestnut skins then placed them on a large shovel. The fire, drawn by the wind whistling round the chimney pot, glowed red hot and the sweet nutty smell of cooked chestnuts and charred skins soon filled the room. And as he'd promised, he told her stories of his childhood, of the ayah who had looked after him, the intense heat of India, then the monsoon, which when it came, would put any rain England had to shame.

'Did you miss it when you came back here?'

'Yes. I was a very unhappy little boy. I'd lost two loving parents within a week of each other, I arrived here in winter and I'd never experienced such cold in my life. And after the intense colours of India it all seemed so drab. Emma said I was a little savage, in fact I was rather withdrawn, and if it hadn't been for Aunt Margaret's kindness I think I might have died too, of sheer misery. I used to dream about India a lot when I was a child. In fact I still do.'

'Would you ever consider going back?'

Stephen threw a shovelful of cooked chestnuts into the hearth. 'Perhaps if things didn't work out here, I might consider it.'

'Not work out? In what way?' As she spoke Charity absentmindedly reached out and helped herself to a chestnut then shot back with an 'ouch!' as the charred skin seared her flesh.

Startled, Stephen looked up and saw she was cradling her hand against her breast. 'Let me see,' he said, and taking her hand examined the burn. The end of the finger was red and about to blister so without a second thought he put it in his mouth, and sucked on it gently.

For so long Charity had made her body deny the attraction she felt for Stephen, but now she forgot her pain as a tidal wave of desire surged through her.

Stephen felt the tremors, faint as the beat of a butterfly's wings, and he watched her closely as he drew his lips slowly down each finger in turn until, with a wild protest, she tried to pull her hand away. But he held on to it hard and pressed it against his heart. 'Feel how it beats for you, Charity. With real love.'

She shook her head in denial. 'No it doesn't, you're lying.'

'I swear to God I'm not. I want us to share everything, a life together, children. I want us to have that love for each other that my parents knew, so intense it made them almost one.' He watched her face in the firelight, saw her struggling to believe him, wanting to trust but not daring to. But he wasn't going to lose her this time.

Finally she turned slowly to look at him. 'What are you saying?'

'I want you to be my wife.'

'That's easy enough to say, isn't it?' she challenged, 'when I'm already someone else's.'

'I mean every word of it. You must know I do, you must feel it.' His voice rose, wanting her and angry she should doubt his passion, angry that she could still resist him when he was almost dying with love.

Her cheeks were rosy, whether from the fire or his avowals of love he wasn't sure. She didn't say anything, though. Instead, keeping her head bent, she twisted her wedding ring compulsively round on her finger. God, was she thinking of Danny, Stephen wondered, and as he reached out to stop her, he felt her tears wet on his hands. 'Please don't cry, my dear,' he pleaded and as she broke down with loud sobs, he gathered her into his arms and kissed her tears away. When she was quiescent in his arms, he took her hand and drew her to the stairs.

In the bedroom he lit the candle, undressed her, then unpinned her golden hair. In a sort of dream state, Charity allowed herself to be pressed down into the deep feather mattress. Gently, skilfully, Stephen began to stroke her, setting her skin on fire. Feeling him inside her, their moving bodies making shadows on the wall, she knew she'd never experienced such sweetness and joy in her life before, and when they shuddered to a climax together she clung on to him, almost weeping with the power of her emotions.

'I love you, never forget that, my dearest,' Stephen murmured. Then he gathered her to him and in the security of his arms and with her head upon his chest, she fell asleep to the regular rhythm of his heartbeats.

When Charity awoke a crack of light was showing through the curtains and she could no longer hear rain gurgling in the gutters. She turned her head and saw Stephen still asleep beside her, his hair rumpled and a slight shadow on his jawline. Last night I had sex with a man who is not my husband. Last night I committed adultery. Last night Stephen had awoken her body to sensual pleasures that had engulfed her and left her wanting more. Why had she never felt like that with Danny?

She stared at her left hand and the solid gold ring he had put there and it was then that the guilt and shame at her own pleasure came.

I shouldn't be here, I'm a married woman. In a confusion of misery and remorse, Charity slipped out of bed. In her own bedroom she dressed hurriedly, hardly stopping to do up the buttons on her dress. Then, shoving the rest of her clothes into a bag, and aware of every creaking floorboard, she crept downstairs and eased open the door.

There was a fresh wind, but although the rain had ceased, the track to the main road was a sea of mud. She'd had the good sense to wear her stout shoes but as she struggled to stay upright, the oozing mud sucked at them, almost pulling them from her feet. She made a valiant effort to keep a hold of the hem of her skirt, but, with her bag it was impossible and she soon let go and left it to drag behind her like a recalcitrant puppy.

There were few people around when she reached the main road, which was just as well since her self-control was beginning to slip and with her filthy clothes and hair hanging loose, she was sure she'd be mistaken for a gipsy.

She didn't have to wait long for a train and when it pulled into the station, she found an empty carriage, sank into a seat and truly wretched and still assailed by a deep guilt, she allowed the tears to gush unchecked from her eyes. For herself, for Stephen, but mostly for Danny. A great unstoppable deluge which rolled down her cheeks, then splashed like raindrops on to the backs of her hands.

Chapter 26

Mollie often pondered on it afterwards, that curious chain of events. The explosive marital row, then Caspar's father, roaring drunk, rushing outside to get himself knocked down by a cab, so forestalling their trip to Kent and inadvertently altering the course of Charity's life.

Because Charity, finding it impossible to cope with the emotional mess her life was in, had, in the end, taken the coward's way out and had simply run. It hadn't been easy. She had had to give notice to the superintendent of the nurses' home of her intention to leave, say goodbye to her many patients, then try and explain to Eliza.

'South Africa!' she exploded, whatever for?'

'To nurse. Many of our soldiers are dying out there and they're desperately in need of trained nurses. I've volunteered to go, been accepted and the ship sails from Southampton at the beginning of December.'

'You must be off your head, my girl. You realize you could get yourself killed.'

'Of course I won't, I'm not going to be in the firing line. I'll be working in a hospital in Cape Town.'

'I often wonder if I'll ever understand you, Charity. You seem sometimes deliberately to commit the most awful follies.'

Coming on top of her bewildering and wounding flight, for Stephen the news was like a bombshell. 'I can't believe you're doing this to me, Charity, and just when I thought that at last everything was right between us. First you run away as if I were some seducer. Now you tell me you're going to embark on this damn silly exercise. Why?'

'What happened the other night was a terrible mistake. I'm still married and that means we can have no future together.'

'I know we can't marry, but that doesn't mean . . .'

'. . . we can't have an affair,' Charity finished for him. 'Sorry, but I couldn't cope with that hole-in-the-corner stuff, snatched weekends, meetings in hotels. It would be no life for either of us. This way is the best and it severs your obligation to me. And, if it came to it, would you really marry me, a girl from the slums?'

She could see he was bruised by her coldness, saw the muscles in his jaw working, then all the emotions of rejection cross his face: disbelief, then pain and finally anger.

'Why are you shutting me out? Why?' he raged.

'I have no choice,' Charity answered wretchedly and turned and walked away.

The situation wasn't made easier by an outbreak of pneumonia in Rotherhithe, which threw her and Stephen together during her last two weeks in England. Trying to behave professionally and deal with the sick while passions simmered just below the surface, had put a great strain on them both. But Charity stuck grimly to her decision, even though another great dread hanging over her was that she might be pregnant. However, by the time she embarked on the SS *Princess Maud* bound for Cape Town, to her great relief, this particular worry had resolved itself.

But homesickness was another thing, and she was getting her first taste of it while the ship was still steaming down the English Channel. She stood on deck feeling the cutting edge of an icy wind on her cheeks and watched with a sense of loss isolated villages and neat fields slip by. Suddenly, her country seemed very dear to her. What on earth am I doing here, she asked herself and knew with the most awful certainty she would never see England again.

Gulping back her tears, she tried to hold the scene in her mind like a photograph. Here and there the countryside was already whitened by a smattering of snow, and although it was hard to imagine, in South Africa, that strange, hostile land where she was heading, it would be getting on for summer. She wasn't even sure why the English were fighting the Boers. People explained about the rights of *Uitlanders* being denied in the Transvaal but that hardly seemed worth going to war over. The more likely reason seemed to be the gold that had been found there.

The actual day of her departure had been harrowing for everyone. Tears from Eliza, who was convinced she would never see Charity again, bitter words from Stephen.

'I will write to you,' she'd promised, reaching out for his hand.

But he'd shaken her off. 'Don't bother,' he'd answered and rejecting her he'd turned and left without a wave or backward glance.

Watching him go, seeing his shoulders hunched in anger, caused such a tightness across her chest it hurt her physically. She longed to call him back, to tell him she'd changed her mind and wanted only one thing and that was that they should be together, but she knew she couldn't.

Only Mollie understood and approved of her decision. 'Life's a game of chance really, isn't it? But I think you're doing the right thing. It's a very difficult situation for you and Stephen and this will give you breathing space, time to sort yourself out. You can always come back and live in sin in Hampstead, nobody bothers up there.'

'I couldn't do that.'

'I know. Anyway, at least you're going to see something of the big wide world. I envy you for that alone. If I'd been qualified I might have joined you.'

Well she wished Mollie had, because at this moment she felt utterly alone and friendless. The miles between her and those she loved were lengthening by the minute and, apart from diving overboard and swimming for shore, there was nothing she could do about it. Her fate was irrevocably sealed. She was watching seagulls dipping and rising on air thermals, and wondering how long they would stay with the ship, when behind her she thought she heard her name. 'Weston?' there was a touch of uncertainty in the voice.

Wondering if it was her overwrought nerves playing games, Charity turned slowly. Then, staring in astonishment she exclaimed, 'Good heavens, Fraser! Fancy finding you here. I can't believe it!' and in an excess of

320

emotion at seeing a familiar face, flung her arms round the other girl.

After a moment they stood back and studied each other to see what damage time had wrought, neither having set eyes on the other since St Cuthbert's. Seeing none, they both started talking at once.

'How did you . . . ?

'What brought you . . . ?

'Go on, you first,' said Fraser finally.

'Well, how did you know it was me?' Charity finished.

'I'd been told there were two more nurses besides me on board and when I looked down the passenger list and saw your name I could hardly believe my eyes.' Fraser shivered and massaged her arms. 'Do we have to stand up here? It's freezing. And once they let the pilot off we'll be out in the Atlantic and it might be rough then.' She linked her arm through Charity's. 'Come on, lets go below, see if we can find the other girl and have some tea.'

Nurse Stansfield, soon to be nicknamed Stanny, was a bit older than they were, perhaps nearing thirty-five, Charity decided, with a coiled plait at her neck and a slightly spinterish air. She was also, the two younger girls were to discover, a bit of a mother hen and elected herself guardian of their morals. 'There are some predatory men on board, so watch out for them, particularly married ones without their wives,' she warned. 'They are by far the worst. What they are looking to do is pass the time pleasantly, and this means a romantic liaison with the first pretty young thing who shows an interest and who they'll forget the minute they set foot on shore.'

Stanny was right and Charity watched with detached amusement as they went into action. It was also apparent Miss Moira Fraser didn't intend to take a blind bit of notice of the older girl's advice and her somewhat homely features began to glow from the unaccustomed attention she was enjoying. Well, she's welcome, thought Charity. I've had enough of emotional entanglements to last me a lifetime. An amorous adventure, even of a transitory nature, was the last thing on her mind.

However, there was dancing most evenings to a small ensemble to which almost everyone went and Charity found herself being partnered rather too often by a handsome young deck officer, called Lawrence. But polite conversation was the most she would allow and she declined all offers to go and see the moonlight on the water, although she noticed Moira often disappeared after only a few dances, frequently with different escorts.

Watching her, Stanny would shake her head and tut-tut with displeasure. 'That girl will get herself the most awful reputation if she continues to flirt with every Tom, Dick and Harry.'

'Let her be, Stanny, she's never had such a good time in her life and anyway, where we're going, there aren't going to be too many laughs. Lawrence says that from the news trickling through, men in the war zones are not only dying of wounds but of dysentery and typhoid as well. There's also a shortage of medical staff, so it looks as if we'll have our hands full once we arrive, which won't leave us much time for a social life.'

After all the dire warnings, everyone was pleasantly surprised to sail through the Bay of Biscay on calm seas. The three friends went ashore at Madeira where the ship anchored briefly to let off passengers and to take on coal and fresh supplies. It was a beautiful and mountainous island with lush vegetation, but a thick cloud obscured the peaks and it soon started to rain too heavily for them to do any sightseeing. Instead, they went shopping, and, deciding one would be useful in the heat, each of them bought a pretty lace fan. In another shop Charity purchased a beautifully-embroidered tablecloth and arranged for it to be sent back to Eliza as a sort of peace offering.

As soon as she got back to her cabin she wrote rather dramatically in her diary: *Today I set foot on foreign soil for the first time.* She'd quite forgotten how homesick she'd felt at the beginning of the voyage. Now she was like a sponge, absorbing every new experience then writing it down and hours, even days could pass without her giving either Danny or Stephen a thought. Charity found it amazingly liberating, like unlacing over-tight corsets. Ship life, a world in miniature floating on the high seas and complete in itself, fascinated her. An elderly man died, he was sewn into a canvas shroud and, after a short burial service, committed to the deep. A thin, desperate-looking woman with seven awful children and a bullying husband went quietly mad one evening and stripped naked in the middle of the dancefloor. The astounded violinist dropped his bow, the other musicians lost their places and went off key. A hush descended and everyone stared in numbed embarrassment, first at her breasts, sucked dry by greedy infants and now just empty flaps of skin, then at the jutting hip bones and finally at her thin legs, over which ran a network of engorged varicose veins. Coming to his senses at last, her husband stood up, barked 'Ethel!' and made to grab her. But she fled and was only just prevented from throwing herself overboard by a nimble-footed steward.

But as well as these tragedies Charity watched people fall in and out of love, be intimate friends one day, implacable enemies the next.

However, a few days after leaving Madeira, normal human exchanges came to a halt when the weather took a turn for the worse. Waves crashed over the deck, with spray reaching as high as the bridge. The ship creaked and groaned, and its bow dipped into the ocean as if about to disappear forever into the depths. Hatches were battened down, portholes covered with great metal disks and screwed tightly shut. But cutlery and crockery and anything not pinned down, crashed to the floor. Although at first, there was some false bonhomie, slowly the public rooms emptied of passengers.

As they crossed the equator, Charity moaned on a bed of sickness. Never had she felt so wretched in her life. Even beef tea and dry toast, brought by the steward, wouldn't stay down and it wasn't until they were less than three days from Cape Town that she felt capable of dressing.

She was sitting on her bunk wondering if she could find the energy to move, when there was a knock on the door, then Moira's face appeared round it looking surprisingly chirpy. 'It's me. How about coming up on deck for a breath of fresh air, you look as if you could do with some.'

'I still feel like death but I suppose a walk would do me good.' Charity answered and stood up on slightly unsteady legs. On deck, the transformation was truly amazing. The air was balmy, the sky blue, the sea a sparkling millpond. Then Moira pointed and said in an excited voice, 'Look,' and the two girls watched joyously as a school of dolphins with smiling faces, swam along beside the ship, leaping out of the water, purely, it seemed, for their benefit.

There was a carnival spirit on the last night, paper hats, streamers. But when the orchestra struck up Auld Lang Syne and everyone joined hands there was a deep sense of sadness, a knowledge that the party was over. Tomorrow meant reality and a country at war.

Charity was startled out of sleep the following morning by the most unholy din and, looking out of her porthole, she saw that the ship was already berthed and the gangways down. Excitedly, she scrambled into her clothes and hurried up on deck.

Dominating the town was Table Mountain. Wide and flat, it looked as if someone had taken a knife and sliced off its peak. Africans, their skins glossy with sweat, were unloading the ship's hold and luggage and mail were being swung by cranes down on to the quay. Passengers appeared to be disembarking and soldiers were standing in line for kit inspection before being marched off, perhaps to their deaths.

Charity looked around for Moira, saw her gazing

324

soulfully into the eyes of one of her admirers, so decided to seek out Stanny instead. She was sitting on her bunk surrounded by luggage and, in spite of the heat, wearing a heavy woollen dress. 'What are we supposed to do?' Charity asked.

'Our instructions are to wait. Eventually someone will come and collect us.' Stanny had hardly finished her sentence when there was a tap at the door.

'I've a message from the Purser, Miss,' said the young bellboy standing there. 'His compliments and he asks that you young ladies go to his office, as soon as possible.'

'You go on up Stanny, while I try and drag Moira away from her beau.'

After some indecision, Moira's heart had finally been given to a young army officer called Alan, who was leaving immediately for the front line. Charity tried to comfort her but all she would say was, 'I know he'll be killed, I just know it,' and wept into her handkerchief all the way to the Purser's Office.

Here an RAMC corporal was waiting for them. 'Sister Weston, Sister Fraser and Sister Stansfield?' he asked, reading from a list in a broad Cockney accent that reminded Charity of home.

'That's us,' Stanny answered.

'I'm Corporal Morris and I'm to take you to the hospital. A servant will bring your luggage. So if you'd follow me please, ladies.'

On the quay they were helped into a carriage and soon the horse was trotting away from the confusion and babel of the docks and driving through Cape Town, overtaking columns of soldiers, cheerful young men, who waved as they passed.

The three girls were so excited at being in South Africa they hardly knew where to look first and they leapt around in their seats, pointing and exclaiming at everything. In her ignorance, Charity had imagined Cape Town would be a rather primitive place, but it was a splendid town, with buildings to equal anything in London. And equally astonishing was the rugged beauty of the country-side. In England colours were muted, rain-washed, here they were brash, vibrant and dazzled the eye. There was an extravagance about the flora and fauna. Everything was on a grander scale, blooms on flowers larger, trees taller and the plumage on birds gaudier. And it was warm, with just enough breeze to stop it becoming unpleasantly hot.

'It's all so lovely, I can hardly believe it' said Charity, who felt her senses being assaulted from every direction.

'I agree wiv you there miss. I've visited a few countries in me time in the army, but there ain't one to match this,' answered Corporal Morris. 'Mind you, it can get pretty windy at times. When there's a south-easterly blowing you can hardly stand straight.'

'How far now to the hospital, Corporal Morris?' asked Stanny.

'A mile or two.'

'And what can we expect when we get there?'

'Well I'll be blunt wiv you Sister, don't expect too much of a welcome from the the doctor in charge, Captain Hubbert. He don't approve of wimmin, says he don't want them in 'is 'orspital. He's been driven mad by volunteers, you know, Lady Bountiful types wanting to nurse the sick but wivout the faintest notion of what to do. The patients are fed up with them as well so he's banned them from the hospital, saying they're more trouble than they're worth. So seein' as you three young ladies are the first nurses we've had from England, expect the sparks to fly.'

'I'm quite used to dealing with trouble, Corporal Morris,' said Stanny, with a determined pat at her plait. Noting the gleam of battle in her eyes, Charity had a strong feeling Captain Hubbert was about to meet his match.

'Are there many wounded?' Charity asked.

Corporal Morris shook his head sorrowfully. 'A good

326

deal, I'm afraid. We've had some bad do's at Colenso, Stormberg and Magersfontein. The Black Watch and Seaforth had terrible losses and injuries. Awful week that was. Got ourselves into a devil of a mess. Incompetent officers underestimated the Boers, if you ask me. I'll tell you straight, all this talk about good old Tommy Atkins is a load of rot. The top brass couldn't give a tinker's cuss for other ranks, gun fodder that's all they are. You'll see that when they bring the wounded down on the hospital train. If this war continues to go badly for us, we're gonna need all the nursing help we can get.'

The corporal continued to give his opinion of the way the war was being conducted until they turned into a short drive, then pulled up at a low building with a wide, shady veranda. Here, Charity could see wounded soldiers were convalescing, some sitting in bath chairs, others propped up in bed. All of them were surveying the girls with intense interest.

Servants appeared to carry in the luggage and several barefoot African children ceased their games and stood in a half-circle regarding them with dark, solemn eyes. As she stepped from the carriage, Charity smiled and said hello. But this was too much for them and, with smothered giggles, the children turned and scampered off. And, for a moment, the scene was transposed as she saw a small flaxen-haired boy, his eyes blue like Danny's, running, not away, but towards her.

'Sister?'

Charity shook herself. 'Yes?'

'If you follow me I'll show you to your room,' said Corporal Morris. 'And I've got a treat in store for you young ladies. I'll be back in half an hour to take you to meet Captain Hubbert.'

Charity's room was simple but adequate. The walls were lime-washed; the furniture consisted of an iron bed with a mosquito net, a chest of drawers, chair and washstand.

She unpacked, and while she changed into her

uniform, an ankle-length grey dress, starched apron and shoulder cape, she thought about Corporal Morris's comments. His description of the doctor from whom they would be taking their instructions hadn't exactly reassured her. They had enough to grapple with, a strange country, extreme heat and entirely different nursing conditions, without added aggravation. And if he did decide to make their lives difficult there was no question of them just walking away. Slightly apprehensive at what might be in store for them, Charity went to seek out her two companions.

Unfortunately, when they were shown into Captain Hubbert's presence, it immediately became apparent that Corporal Morris hadn't exaggerated the Captain's hostility to women. Corporal Morris introduced each of them in turn, but rudely the doctor went on scratching away with his pen and the only view they had of him was of his pink, bald scalp. They stood in silence for several minutes like recalcitrant children in front of a head teacher, until finally Stanny lost her patience. Giving Charity a warning nudge, she spoke.

'I know of your dislike of incompetent females, which I understand, Doctor Hubbert, but we are three professional, highly-trained nursing sisters, sent here to do an important job, and as such, deserve a modicum of courtesy from you.'

This at least brought his head up from his writing. His complexion, which bore the stamp of a heavy drinker, went purple, his eyes, glassy green like bottles, bulged, and his moustache almost stood on end in fury. However he disdained to reply and instead turned to the orderly. 'Corporal Morris, show the sisters round the wards.'

He went back to his paperwork, the girls exchanged glances, then turned and strode out. Stanny bringing up the rear, slammed the door pointedly. 'Of all the . . .' she was speechless.

'I did warn you, didn't I?' said the Corporal

'Ignorant swine!' Stanny's rather stern features were animated by anger.

'You mustn't let it get to you, Sister Stansfield, or, excuse my French, the bugger's won. We've got one war goin' on, we don't want another 'ere. Come on, let me show you the wards, like 'e said. Then we'll have a nice cuppa.'

The wards were clean, well-organized and the injured men appeared to be well on their way to recovery. And at the sight of three young women, English ones at that, they bucked up even more.

'Some of this lot are going to be shipped 'ome shortly, lucky devils. On the battlefield it's best to be injured just enough to get attention but not enough to die. Hopeless cases are often left lying for hours in burning sun, screaming in agony. But lads never learn until it's too late. It's not their fault, I suppose, they've been taught to glorify war, to romanticise it. You should see the way these young fellas come out here looking for a scrap and straining at the bit, to be where the fun is, as they call it. But once they've had a real taste of war, have seen the blood and guts of it, they soon change their tune.'

Corporal Morris spoke with the weary cynicism of the soldier who'd seen it all and Charity asked him how long he'd been in the army.

'Twenty years, Sister.'

'Why do you stay?'

'Because I was brought up in the poorhouse, and this is the only family I know. When they kick me out it will be the old soldiers' home for me.'

What with the orderlies and now three extra nurses, it struck Charity that the hospital was going to be over-staffed and she said so to Corporal Morris. 'Wait until tomorrow when the hospital train arrives, our feet won't touch then.'

*   *   *

329

Charity had thought she was enough of a professional now not to let her emotions get the better of her. But when the wounded, most of them hardly more than boys, were carried in on stretchers, she wanted to weep. War injuries were like nothing she'd ever encountered. Faces half sliced away by shrapnel, crushed and severed limbs, sightless eyes. But perhaps worst of all were those brought in raving, sometimes even screaming, their minds completely gone. So this was what two so-called civilized countries were inflicting on their young men, Charity thought, and for what? There'd be no medals or glory for them, just blighted young lives, and for the dead, a formal army letter to a grieving mother or wife. Surely no cause was worth all the human agony and waste.

Doctor Hubbert loved red tape, the filling in of forms in triplicate, as much as he loathed female nurses. He took a sadistic delight in making their working lives as difficult as possible. Sometimes it was in paltry ways, like haggling over their time off. But his spitefulness often spilled over to the patients, as on the occasion when Charity was dressing the stump of a young soldier whose leg had been amputated at the knee. She was almost through, when an uneasy prickling in her spine told her the doctor was standing over her. He watched without a word until she'd finished, then barked out, 'Do that again, please, Sister Weston.'

Charity leapt to her feet and gazed at him with utter disdain. How dare he question her skills, her bandaging was immaculate. But unlike Stanny she strove at all times not to let him get to her, so her tone was icily polite. 'Would you explain to me why, Doctor Hubbert?'

The bottle eyes took on a vindictive gleam. 'Because it's a mess and because I say so.'

The stoicism of these men, the acceptance of their lot astonished Charity and they rarely complained. But even taking the greatest care it was difficult to dress bad wounds without causing the patient pain. The young private had endured it silently, apart from an occasional indrawing of breath. Now, wiping sweat from his upper lip, he cast a bewildered look at the doctor and a pleading one at Charity. 'Please Sister, not again,' she read in his eyes.

And she owed him that at least. With a mutinous expression, Charity sat down and made a great pretence of drawing scissors from her pocket and snipping away the bandage. As she'd expected, the doctor was soon called away by an orderly. She waited until he'd gone, gave the soldier a reassuring pat on the arm and slipped the scissors back in her pocket. It was a small victory but she'd had enough of the man's petty tyranny. This incident, one of many, started her thinking.

Stanny would come away from an encounter with him white and shaking; Moira, he often reduced to tears. However, there was a growing determination not to let him win, for they knew that nothing would have pleased the doctor more than to see the three of them on the next ship home. So, one evening, sitting on the *stoep*, where they came each evening to watch the spectacular sunsets, they made a pact.

'So come what may we'll stick it out here,' said Stanny, 'Is that agreed?'

'Agreed,' Charity and Moira repeated in unison.

But watching his behaviour become daily more impossible, his drinking more out of control, Charity began to wonder. She hadn't the least desire to go back to England but was there perhaps another way out?

Although expediency and a growing casualty list might eventually alter attitudes, Charity knew that at present, women were made about as welcome in field hospitals as they were here. However, there were the hospital trains and they always carried at least two nurses. The problem would be getting the transfer. Out of sheer spite, the Captain would probably try and block her application.

*   *   *

On the first day of the New Year, and to honour a momentous occasion, Charity printed in her diary in large bold letters: JANUARY 1 1900. Then underneath, she continued: *How peculiar that seems to write. I still can't believe it's the beginning of a new century. I wonder what it will hold for us all. Let's hope it's peace at any rate. Because, surely after this carnage, men will have learned their lesson and see the pointlessness of going to war for their so called principles.* She left a space then wrote: *Captain Hubbert has been drunk since Christmas Eve.*

Charity imagined the situation had deteriorated about as much as it could, until half way through January something occurred that, for her, was the last straw.

Woken from a deep sleep by a tremendous hammering on her door, she shot up in bed quaking with terror and certain the Boers had come. But she was hardly reassured when instead from the outside she heard Doctor Hubbert's voice, slurred with drink. 'Unlock ss . . . is door at once, Shister Weston, tha's an order. I've got somethin' very 'mportant t' discuss with you.' There was a loud hiccup. 'It's bout your bandaging, most unsatisfactory. D'you hear me?' He hammered on the door again then, working himself up into a fury at her lack of response, he put his shoulder against the door and, using it as a battering ram, tried to break it down.

Charity sat petrified, the sheet clutched to her breast, staring at the heaving door and waiting for it to splinter under the weight of his bulk. The noise erupted through the quiet hospital, doors opened and voices, rough with sleep, moved nearer. First Stanny's and Moira's, then Corporal Morris's.

'Now come on, Captain Hubbert, we can't have this sort of carry on, or you'll be getting yourself into deep trouble. Let's get you to bed.'

But the doctor had no intention of going quietly. There were grunts, the sound of scuffling, until at last, swearing profusely, he was led away by Corporal Morris.

'Charity, are you all right?' Stanny's worried voice called. But Charity could neither move nor speak. It was as if she'd had a seizure.

Stanny called again and this time Charity managed an uncertain, 'I think so,' and, on shaky legs, she moved to the door and turned the key.

Two pairs of anxious eyes studied her, then with a, 'Oh you poor girl,' Stanny enfolded her in an embrace. Taking charge, she sent Moira off the make cocoa and, by the time Corporal Morris returned, the three of them were sitting drinking it on the bed.

'I've locked 'im in 'is room; he won't trouble you no more tonight, Sister Weston.'

'Or any other,' Charity replied, cradling the comforting beverage in her hands. 'The man's a lunatic and I'm getting out of here.'

'But we made a promise to each other that we wouldn't go home. If you do that, it'll mean he's won.' Moira protested.

'Who said anything about going home? No, I've got other plans up my sleeve.'

Interested, the other two sat up. 'What are they'?

Charity smiled enigmatically. 'You'll find out in time, just be patient.' And even though they continued to badger her, she'd say no more and her two friends went back to their rooms consumed with curiosity.

Chapter 27

The train was travelling north across a limitless arid veld with nothing to relieve the monotony except a distant ridge of hills and the occasional stumpy tree. This was the Karoo, a roasting, semi-desert area, stretching across almost the whole of the Cape Colony and was as strange and fascinating as anything Charity had ever encountered in her life before.

Grass was baked dry as tobacco and a burning wind blew up small swirls of dust. Except for a few wheeling birds of prey, the desolate landscape seemed uninhabited by either man or beast. But there were creatures existing out there, so Charity had been told: springbok, hardy sheep and goats. There were also things to beware of, snakes with a lethal venom, scorpions and funnel spiders, swarms of locusts that could bring a train to a standstill, and, of course, the ever present flies.

Blackmail was a strong word to use, even to herself, but it hadn't been hard to arrange their transfer to the hospital train. At least not after that night, with all the witnesses and everything and Captain Hubbert knowing the serious charges he could face if she kicked up a stink. She'd been quite clear about what she wanted, made no attempt to veil her threats. A place on the hospital train that was about to be put into service or else . . . In two shakes of a lamb's tail their positions were confirmed and now she and Moira were clanking along on a single rail track, en route to De Aar and the main railway junction there, to pick up more casualties.

Fanning herself, Charity leaned back in her seat. Now at last she would get the chance to put her nursing skills to real use. Gratifying, too, to have landed such a plum nursing job, even though she guessed it had earned her Doctor Hubbert's undying hatred. Not that she cared. That was one of the advantages of a tough upbringing, it gave you an armour-plated skin. Looking across at Moira, she gave her a pleased smile. 'Are you glad you came?'

'Not half. Anything to get away from that petty-minded drunk.'

'Do you think Stanny's disappointed she didn't have the chance?'

'No, not for a minute. She wouldn't want to be parted from Corporal Morris.'

'Oh, why not?'

'Didn't you know, they're going great guns. I wouldn't be surprised if an engagement isn't announced soon.'

All ears, Charity stopped fanning herself and sat up straight. 'Stanny and Corporal Morris? Well I never.' She shook her head in disbelief. 'When did this start?'

'Stanny's quite secretive, but I think soon after we arrived.'

'It seems a bit of an odd match. He's a nice man of course, but a bit of a rough diamond and she's so prim. I wonder what brought them together?'

'I don't know, but I envy her.'

Surprised by her honesty, Charity said, 'Did you ever hear from the young man you met on the ship?'

Moira bit her lip. 'If you mean Alan, no.'

'Oh you probably will.'

'If he's still alive,' answered Moira and bent her head to her book.

Poor old Moira, thought Charity, staring at her reflection in the train window. So much killing and to what end? The sooner this lot was over the better.

She hadn't stopped to consider her own future, but it would have to be faced eventually. Worried letters reached her regularly from Eliza, and it was obvious she was following the course of the war closely, because they were full of how dreadful it all sounded and how desperately worried she was for her safety. Then, being Eliza, she would berate her for her thoughtlessness, saying she hadn't taken her in, brought her up and fed her, only to see her perish in some distant land.

Charity would reply by return post, reassuring her that they were hundreds of miles from the war zone and under absolutely no threat. And, to spare her more worry, in her last letter she'd omitted mentioning this new job on the hospital train.

Mollie's letters, as was to be expected, had a more positive tone.

I'm nearing the end of my medical training, thank goodness, [she wrote.]

335

Caspar is doing rather well with his painting and someone suggested producing prints of the water colour he did of us that day by the Darent, (do you remember it?) to see how it sells. He also wants us to get engaged, but you know me, although I love him I just can't decide. I just fear that all I've worked for and the years of study will disappear in a welter of babies, breast-feeding and colic.

Suddenly Charity saw the film of grit and dust that lay over everything, felt the enervating heat that made even her scalp wet and thought with a sick longing of Kent and those unending summer days, which, like youth, they thought would last forever. Oh for lush green meadows, stippled sunshine through willows, and Stephen. He hadn't written, but then she could hardly expect him to, not after the bitterness of their parting. And this way he was released from any obligation to her. She might have a profession now, but in Stephen's eyes she'd always be that girl from the slums, living with an eccentric woman in a house full of cats. Blanche had a clear field and she'd make a far more suitable wife. Perhaps by the time she returned to England they would already be married.

Charity could see she was proceeding down a familiar but unproductive line of thought that would get her nowhere. And that was the trouble with spare time, it was the enemy of a tranquil mind. However, until tomorrow there was absolutely nothing for them to do. The train was extremely well equipped and as well as themselves there were four orderlies and a medical officer on board. Everything had already been made ready to receive the wounded. Charity would like to have chatted but Moira was deep in her book so instead she answered letters and wrote up her diary. When the heat became intolerable they slept. Once it got dark the air cooled quickly and they ate.

*   *   *

A brilliant flame sunrise woke her and Charity saw that the countryside was beginning to show signs of habitation: isolated farmsteads, a kraal here and there, African children waving to them from the wayside, oxen outspanned on the horizon and mule carts being whipped along by their native drivers. An hour later the train steamed into De Aar.

Here they found the usual chaos; milling, curious crowds, wounded men left lying unattended on stretchers in the hot sun. Officers with lots of shiny buttons and loud arrogant voices rushed around issuing orders while quite a few other people, it seemed to Charity, appeared to be chasing their own tails.

'The stress is always on red tape and filling in forms in the army. I don't really think they give a fig for these poor chaps,' Moira muttered to Charity, when they'd eventually got some of the casualties on to the train and made them comfortable. However, eventually the Medical Officer, Dr Jones, had signed the last document and they were awaiting instructions to leave, when an exhausted-looking doctor who'd been supervising the transfer of his patients on to the train, pushed his way over to them.

'I'm Doctor Asquith and you might think this a bit out of order, old chap,' he said, addressing the MO, 'but I'm in desperate need of nursing staff, have you got someone you can spare? Everyone, patients, my orderlies, is going down like flies with typhoid and the injured continue to pour in.'

'Where are you stationed?' asked Doctor Jones.

'At Graspan, between Belmont and Modder River Station. I've just brought down casualties. But when I get back, there'll be more poor devils there, all with horrific injuries. Field Marshal Lord Roberts is coming north to take charge of things and that can only mean one thing, action, and frankly I'm just about at the end of my tether.' He ran his fingers through his pale, thinning hair in a distracted manner and looked about him. 'You're pretty well equipped, aren't you? Orderlies, nurses. The only people still standing in my small hospital are two African servants and me.'

'I understand your predicament, and it sounds bally awful, but I couldn't let my staff go. How would I explain it back at the base hospital?'

'If you can persuade at least one of the orderlies to come, I'll accept responsibility.'

'I'll go.' At her rash offer, Moira and the MO turned to stare at Charity. Both looked stupified.

'Have you any idea what you are saying, or even what it's like up there? There's been heavy fighting and with more to come it's a very nasty place for anyone to be, let alone a woman,' said the MO.

'I'm a nurse, I've been trained to tend the sick and Dr Asquith needs help, urgently by the sound of it. And, as he says, this train is very well equipped, you're not going to miss me and you can soon find another nurse to fill my place. I'll just go and pack.'

'I can't be held responsible for your safety then, Sister Weston,' the MO called after her.

'I'll write a short note and sign it absolving you completely. In triplicate if that would help.'

Moira grabbed her arm. 'Charity you mustn't.' Her eyes looked frightened, her face pale.

But Charity pulled her arm away her expression, in contrast, fiercely determined. 'Oh yes I must. And it's what I want to do. Why I came out here in the first place. Nothing we've done so far has been what I would call real nursing.'

Moira grew tearful. 'But you could so easily get killed.'

'Hospitals flying the Red Cross flag don't tend to get attacked. You know, Geneva Convention and all that,' Dr Asquith interjected, terrified this plucky girl was going to be lost to him.

But Charity shot him a reassuring smile. 'I know. Anyway, I won't be a tick, I haven't much to pack.'

Back in the carriage she shared with Moira, she quickly

338

scribbled a note, shoved everything she'd brought with her into a large leather bag and picked up her red lined parasol.

Moira embraced her and wished her good luck; the MO pushed some medicines and dressings at them. 'Here, take these, there's plenty more in the dispensary. Where you're going I think you'll be more in need of them than we are.' He shook Charity's hand. 'We'll be thinking of you, Sister – and praying for you.' His solemn demeanour made it clear that he did not expect to see Charity again in this world.

'Don't worry, I'll return her safely, just as soon as everything is under control again,' Dr Asquith assured him. Then, clamping his fingers round Charity's arm and without making it too obvious, he started to draw her away. Because his great fear now was that she might waver in her decision or lose her nerve. 'Well, we'd better be going, our train leaves in about five minutes. And thanks, old chap.'

They had another fairly long journey in front of them and weren't due to arrive at their destination until later in the afternoon, which gave Charity and the doctor an opportunity to get to know each other.

'I feel like some kind of kidnapper, dragging you away from your companions like that.' Now that the train was moving at some speed, making it impossible for Charity to leap off, Dr Asquith allowed himself the luxury of a little guilt. 'However, I don't need to say how deeply grateful I am to you.'

'You need help, Doctor, I've come to give it.'

'Yes, but I wonder if you really understand what you've let yourself in for.'

The doctor wore a permanently anxious expression, and, worried that it might be catching, Charity tried to reassure him with a smile and words of comfort. 'Don't worry about me. I've got quite a strong stomach and a good sense of survival.' Of course she wasn't prepared for the full horror of war at first hand, but then who could be.

At Graspan a mule cart with an African driver was waiting for them and while he helped her up into it, Dr Asquith introduced them.

'Pieter, this is Sister Weston, she's come to help us.'

Pieter awarded her a big smile. 'That's good, Missi. We need plenty help.'

'Not far now.' Dr Asquith smiled his anxious smile and, bumping along in the cart, Charity hoped he was speaking the truth. The wheels and the mule's hooves threw up clouds of hot, red dust, her parasol offered only minimal shade and she could feel a prickly sweat breaking out all over her body. All she could concentrate on was a cold bath.

Her first glimpse of the hospital was through the shimmering, dancing sort of heat that could play tricks with reality, and her immediate reaction was to distrust what her eyes told her. But it remained fixed in its place and as they drove into the compound, Charity saw it consisted of two small, crude buildings with corrugated roofs, surrounded by several bell tents. A Red Cross flag fluttered from a pole.

'Bit cramped, I'm afraid,' said Dr Asquith when he showed her to her room, and it wasn't a point she would disagree on. It was in one of the tin-roofed buildings used as an operating theatre, stifling hot, and hardly big enough to swing a cat in let alone accommodate a camp bed, the only furniture it possessed. Charity could see she wasn't likely to want for companionship though, not by the number of cockroaches scuttling away under the floorboards.

Desperate for air, Charity ill-advisedly flung open the door and was immediately invaded by large flies which clamped themselves on her and started to suck at her blood. 'Ugh!' she exclaimed in horror, and tried to swat them away with her hands. Slamming the door against any further unwanted guests, she went to enquire about the washing facilities.

It was then that she learned about the water. 'In these parts it's more precious than gold,' Dr Asquith informed her, but as a concession allowed her a bowlful, just enough to rinse off the red dust from her hands and face.

The heat here was far more severe than in the Cape and after the long journey she felt so drained of energy even the hard camp bed looked inviting. But this was no time for self-indulgence she told herself severely. All along she'd claimed this was what she wanted to do and there were desperately sick men needing her attention.

She found Dr Asquith in one of the tents where half a dozen beds were cramped into a very small space. He was bending over a patient.

He looked up as she entered and beckoned to her. The man's face was covered with a thick viscous sweat and it was obvious he was near death. 'Typhoid,' he murmured. 'Can you stay with him? It will all be over in less than an an hour.'

Charity nodded, and he moved on to the next bed. There was no room to sit so she had to crouch down beside the dying man. She knew the splitting head pains he would have suffered, the delirium, but he was past all that now and sinking gently. She carefully sponged his face and neck with a damp cloth, then so that he would know he wasn't dying alone she took hold of his hand and was terribly moved to feel his fingers flutter feebly in response. Then he half opened his eyes, cried out, 'Daisy,' and died.

Fighting back a tear, Charity thought, who is Daisy? His sweetheart or his wife, and would she mourn his death?

Covering his face with the blanket she called the doctor back over.

'At least there seems some point if a soldier dies fighting, but that young man died needlessly, because he drank contaminated water straight from the Modder. Whatever you do, Sister, never drink unboiled water here.'

The young soldier had to be laid out, ready for burial and after this there were the other typhoid patients to attend to then wounds to dress. When Charity next looked at her fob watch it was midnight, and she remembered she'd had nothing to eat since breakfast. But she was too exhausted to care about food. She unpinned her hair, took a quick look at herself in a small hand mirror and saw that her face was grey with fatigue. Just about managing to find the energy to undress, she collapsed on to her bed. But her aching bones chafed against the lumpy mattress and although the small room was airless, she didn't dare open the door. Trying to get comfortable she tossed this way and that, while her mind, refusing to wind down, dwelt on the strange twists and turns of fate that had taken her from a riverside pub to a shack here in the middle of Africa, close to the enemy line.

She'd almost dropped off when a deafening drumming on the zinc roof made her leap up in alarm. With a dry mouth, she listened. She had nothing with which to protect herself and it could be anything; wild beasts, the dreaded Boer. She'd decided that if it were the enemy she would make no pretence at bravery but surrender immediately, when she realized it was nothing more dangerous than rain, marvellous, life-giving rain. Jumping out of bed, she ran outside and, with her head flung back, stood there, letting it pour down her face. Not until her nightdress clung to her like a second skin did she go back inside. Discarding the nightdress she towelled herself dry, rubbing her skin until it tingled. Then thoroughly refreshed, Charity climbed naked underneath the rough blanket and slept like a babe in its mother's arms.

Chapter 28

9 February 1900
We think Field Marshal Lord Robert's rumoured great offensive
against the Boers is soon to take place. This morning a whole
division of cavalry came riding through in great clouds of suffo-
cating dust. After them came the foot soldiers, then the artillery.
A lot of them are now so sunburnt they're nearly as dark as
Africans, but the fair-skinned ones suffer agonies and I've had
to treat some men whose faces are so blistered they are blown
up like balloons. To keep their spirits up they sing a lot. 'Soldiers
of the Queen', or 'Goodbye Dolly' are popular, and so are the
music hall songs. Of course they remind me of Danny and home
and Friday nights at Gattis and that makes me feel a bit sad.

Perhaps I shouldn't but I can't help feeling sorry for the ani-
mals. The men know why they are here, they are soldiers by
choice, but not the poor horses and it's awful to see the pitiful
state some of them are in. And the oxen drawing the stores.
There's hardly any pasture, and most of them are so thin their
rib cages show through and today I saw a driver cursing and
whipping his team so unmercifully it made me really angry and
I shouted at him to stop. Of course he looked at me as if I were
quite mad. And perhaps with all this sun I am.

For a few days after Charity noted this great trek in her
diary, there was an eerie nervous silence as if the whole
countryside was holding its breath. But finally it came,
the sound of artillery fire, the rap, rap, rap of Maxims, the
dull thud of exploding shells, followed by smoke drifting
innocently up into the azure sky. Soon after the tragic
victims of these weapons of destruction poured in and
the following days blurred for Charity into a confusion of
blood and death. The more fortunate casualties had their
wounds bound on the battlefield and then were brought
down to the small hospital in mobile field ambulances.
Others, in the chaos and indifference of war, were just

slung into bullock carts and came in piled on top of each other like bloody carcasses of meat. Others walked or rather staggered in, some supporting sick companions, their crudely-bandaged wounds oozing blood, the agony on their young faces saying everything about the obscenity of war.

Charity and Dr Asquith, assisted by Pieter and John, did what they could in the the primitive conditions. Waging their own war against flies, ants, mice, poor food and lack of sleep they operated, amputated and stitched, then as soon as the men were well enough to travel, they were sent on down to Cape Town or to face death again on the battlefield.

Storms were violent and frequent. Charity would watch them with awe, wondering if God, perhaps angry at man's folly, was unleashing his wrath upon the world with this terrifying spectacle. For certainly it was nature who was in charge here. The sky would suddenly pile up with swollen grey cloud, there would be a great crash, like cymbals, followed by a zigzag of lightning so power-ful it seemed as if it might fracture the earth's crust. But even worse was the whine of the simoom, a hot, suffocat-ing desert wind that could last for days, blowing dust into the nostrils, eyes and mouth and testing everyone's self-control to its limits.

Nerves were soon in tatters anyway: the constant sound of battle, the lack of sleep, not knowing what to expect next or who the victors would be in this particular engagement. But whatever the outcome, they were depending on their red and white flag to protect them, for apart from one rifle, they were unarmed.

One morning Charity and Dr Asquith were setting out instruments, dressings and chloroform in preparation for the next operation when a violent and continuing ra-ta-ta-tat on the tin roof, like spitting bullets, made them both start in fright.

'Get down!' the doctor yelled, certain they were both about to get a bullet from a Mauser through their heads.

But as they ducked under the operating table, the door, fastened by a latch, was blown off its hinges by a violent gust of wind and, to their astonishment, hailstones the size of pigeons' eggs rattled on to the floor. Outside was a wall of crystal.

Charity thought that in time she might become inured to the suffering but she never did. In fact the more she saw of it the angrier she grew, and, one evening, in a rare spare moment, she sat down and wrote in her diary, five words: *War is an absolute evil.*

Her diary was a very private possession and she was shoving it away at the bottom of her bag when there was a knock. 'Come in,' Charity called, the door swung back on its rusty hinges and Dr Asquith stood there.

By nature the doctor was an anxious man and it showed in his face, which was prematurely lined. However, today his expression was unusually animated. And it was obvious he was bursting with news. 'General French has relieved Kimberley,' he declared in dramatic tones.

'Well I'm pleased, of course, for the poor souls who've been in the siege but how many more Boer, English and African lives has that cost?'

'A few, no doubt, but it's a turn in the right direction. Anyway I feel it's a victory that deserves to be celebrated. I've been saving this.' He sat down beside her, drew out a hip flask and silver cups hardly bigger than thimbles and poured them both a whisky.

'To General French, and a turning point.'

'To General French,' Charity repeated in a dutiful voice, went to take a sip of the drink, and felt a pain like a knife turn in her gut. With a surprised yelp she let the small beaker bounce to the floor and, gripping her stomach, she rocked back and forth in pain.

'Sister Weston, whatever is the matter?' Dr Asquith reached out and touched her tentatively.

'It's my stomach . . .' She screwed up her face as another violent spasm shot through her.

'Let's lie you down.' Quickly the doctor lifted her feet on to the bed and covered her with a blanket. 'I'll go and get a thermometer.'

The creases in his brow now deep furrows of concern, he tore back to his room. Panting from the heat and the effort, he gathered up a thermometer and precious medicines. He just could not afford to lose this nurse. Charity was being wretchedly sick when he returned, but he took comfort from that. If she had any poison in her system at least she was getting rid of it. He cleaned her up, took her temperature, saw it was a hundred and two.

The fever lasted forty-eight hours but Dr Asquith knew Charity's value and he lavished all the care and attention he could on her. On the fourth day she sat up in bed. 'I'm coming back to work today.' she announced.

'I really don't think you should,' the doctor protested.

'Well, tomorrow then.' Charity bartered, telling herself she would soon work off the shakiness in her legs.

'Oh all right,' he answered, caving in, too easily he realized. But with a hospital full to overflowing, what was he to do.

Cheers and smiling faces greeted her return, which was a tonic in itself. And when a young soldier gripped her hand and said, 'Glad you're better, Sister, we really missed you,' Charity's throat grew tight with emotion. In the nick of time, before it got out of hand, she saw Dr Asquith beckoning to her.

'There are a couple of new typhoid cases I'd like you to see,' he said, filling her in on the details as they crossed the compound. 'One looks as if he'll recover but I don't hold out much hope for the other poor fellow.'

He pulled back the tent flap and allowed Charity to enter first. After the brilliant African light it was dim in the tent, but as her eyes adjusted, Charity noticed one patient, obviously on the mend, sleeping peacefully. But the harsh, irregular breathing of the other indicated an extremely sick man. To confirm her diagnosis, she moved closer. The eyes were sunk deep in their sockets, the lips

346

cracked and blistered, the leathery skin covered in a film of sweat. But in spite of being ravished by sickness it was a face as familiar to her as the back of her hand. Not sure if was her recent illness, the unremitting heat or her mind slipping out of kilter, she took a step backwards. 'His name? What's his name, Doctor?' The words came out in a strange croaking sound.

'Private Daniel Smith, an irregular from Cape Town.'

Danny! The shock almost knocked Charity off her feet. For a second her heart stopped beating, then it started up again, pounding against the wall of her chest like a sledgehammer. Feeling the world receding, she reached out for some support and Dr Asquith grasped her arm. 'Are you all right, Sister?' His voice sounded troubled. She was falling sick again, he knew it.

She stared at him with a blank expression. 'It's the heat, I . . . I think I need some fresh air.'

'Come on, let's get you outside.' Solicitously he guided her from the tent.

Charity grabbed a guy rope and stood inhaling deeply, still too shaken to think straight. Even always knowing, to the inner core of her being, that Danny was alive hadn't prepared her for this.

'Stay there, I'll get you a drink.'

'No, don't bother, I'm all right really.' Smoothing her apron, Charity adopted her normal, brisk professional manner. 'See, I'm better already.'

'Are you sure?'

'Absolutely.' Her tone was emphatic. Inside the tent her husband was near death and while she stood there precious time was being wasted. 'Have we got any phenacetin left?'

'A little.'

'Right, I'm coming with you to get some. If I have any say in the matter that's one patient who isn't going to die.'

He nearly said it, it was on the tip of his tongue: 'I'm sorry, I can't give you any. We're in very short supply and there's no point in wasting it on that young fellow who isn't going to last the day.' But Dr Asquith was a compassionate man and somehow he couldn't bring himself to articulate what he thought. And miracles did happen. The very fact that anyone at all survived in this godforsaken hole was evidence enough of that. Often men would come in with such appalling injuries it seemed impossible they would last the hour but who clung on to life with an amazing tenacity.

So a short while later, unaware of the doctor's inward moral struggle, Charity carried back to Danny the precious phenacetin, freshly boiled water, and a clean towel and pyjamas. Inside the tent she stood quite still and listened. She could no longer hear his harsh breathing and fearing it was already too late, she dropped down beside him and felt his pulse. It vibrated faintly through her fingertips. Putting her mouth close to his ear, she whispered, 'Danny, it's me, Charity, can you hear me? I'm going to give you medicine which will make you better.'

Willing him to respond, she squeezed his hand and to her intense joy his eyelids gave the merest flutter. That was all, but it was enough to give her hope. But speed, now, was vital, and she had to get the medicine down him somehow. Praying he wouldn't fight against it, she pushed a spatula between his teeth. Forcing open his clenched jaws she managed to get a few grains of the drug and a several spoonfuls of water into his mouth. 'Fight, Danny fight,' she intoned in a desperate voice, and watched with a sense of frustration as most of water dribbled down his chin. All she could do now was wait and hope that enough of the drug had found its way down his throat to set him sweating and bring his temperature down.

But Danny was just one of many sick and dying men and Charity knew there wasn't the slightest chance she'd be allowed to sit with him through his crisis, when she looked up and saw Pieter hovering just outside the tent.

'What is it, Pieter?'

'Missi, Doctor want to see you. Urgent he said.'

'All right, Pieter, tell him I won't be a moment.' She waited until he'd gone, then bent and kissed Danny tenderly on the forehead. 'Get well my husband, soon.'

But her anxiety made it hard to concentrate on her tasks, so in her first free moment, Charity slipped back across the compound to the isolation tent. As she'd hoped, Danny's whole body was saturated in sweat, his bedclothes and pyjamas wringing wet. Removing the pyjamas, Charity gently sponged him down, wanting to weep at the sight of his emaciated body. He'd always been so proud of his hard, broad-muscled shoulders and to see him like this, bones protruding everywhere, was a heartrending sight. She patted him dry and was struggling to get him into clean nightwear, when his eyes opened. She held herself tense and waited for that first flicker of recognition. But she could see how much it had cost him in effort when the lids drooped and then closed. But she wasn't disheartened. She'd achieved what she'd set out to, got his temperature down. And his pulse was stronger now, his breathing regular. With a bit of luck and a lot of love, Danny might soon be on his way to recovery.

It was as well the other patient had been moved, Charity thought to herself, as she walked towards Danny's bed a few days later. Because it was pretty difficult to maintain a cool exterior when you were being observed with puzzled but intense interest by the husband you hadn't set eyes on for nearly four years.

'Good morning, Private Smith, I'm Sister Weston.' She bent and tweaked his sheets into place, revelling in his startled reaction.

Danny lifted his head, stared at her in disbelief, muttered a weak 'Blimey!' and sank back on the pillow.

'Is that all you've got to say to your wife after all this time?'

'I'm not imagining this am I?' A thin hand came up and touched her cheek. 'You are real?'

'Yes. I'm real enough.'

He stared at her with hungry eyes. 'It's not sinking in. This must be a dream. I've had enough of them wiv you in.'

She leaned over and kissed him lightly on the mouth. 'Now do you believe me.'

'By God, you're a marvellous sight, Charity. I never thought I'd set eyes on you again.'

'It just shows how wrong you can be, doesn't it?'

'As far as you're concerned, I've been wrong about a lot of things, haven't I?'

'Well yes, maybe. But we'll talk about that later. For the time being we've got to concentrate on getting you fit again. You've been extremely ill.'

She saw him quickly check his arms and legs.

'Not with injuries, typhoid. We didn't think you would pull through at first. I suppose you drank river water.'

'Yeah, me and several 'undred others. What else could we do? They'd made us march all day, there wasn't any fresh water and men were dying of sunstroke. Most of the time there wasn't much grub either. Christ, what a cock up. It's a butcher's shop out there.' As his memory returned, so did his anger.

'Hush, don't get yourself agitated. You're on the mend but you must keep quiet or you'll start the fever up again.'

'So I was nearly a goner, was I?'

Charity nodded.

'Do you remember Ma's favourite expression?'

Charity laughed. 'I do.'

'Well, that's bin my philosophy these past few years: It's not over until it's over, an' I promise you, I've a helluva long way to go yet.'

'You will have if you rest. But before I go, let me say something. Nobody here knows we're married and it would probably be simpler if it stayed that way, don't you agree?'

Having certain matters he would prefer to keep to himself, Danny nodded in compliance. When she reached the entrance, Charity turned. 'Go to sleep now.'

In reply he blew her a kiss. Like hell he was going to sleep, he had too much to think about.

Food shortages daily grew worse. All the cattle and fowl in the area had been slaughtered, so there were no eggs or milk, and for the most part everyone lived on a very restricted diet of tough goat's meat, bully beef and army biscuits. Charity found her dreams now centred almost exclusively on food. She dreamt she was at home and all the dishes Eliza cooked were spread out in front of her: roast beef, steaming hot pies with rich brown gravy, jelly and blancmange. With a greedy anticipation she would reach out to fork the food into her mouth and find it had dissolved into nothing. Her cries of frustration and the most desperate hunger always woke her.

Even so, she still gave Danny some of her own meagre rations and as much of her time as she could.

Danny would lie staring at her, dazed by his own good fortune. This was his wife, this beautiful young woman, who he'd found again, here in the middle of nowhere. Incredible to think that he'd sometimes resented their marriage, and like a bloody idiot had thrown it all away. But he'd paid for it, of course, during these last years. There'd been no shortage of women ready to take her place but they could only slake his desire and sometimes he'd longed for her so desperately it had made him ill. As well as this there'd been his guilt to contend with, and loneliness, and regret. Oh yes, there'd been bucketfuls of that, and the time to dwell on it. But at least something had come out of this blinkin' shambles. By some miracle, he'd been given a second chance and by God he was going to make the most of it. He would never let Charity out of his sight again, not for one second.

Danny reached out for Charity's hand and kissed it

fervently. 'I know I don't deserve it but you do still love me, don't you? I couldn't bear it if you didn't.'

Charity's expression softened and she pushed back the fringe of hair from his forehead with a tender gesture. 'I don't know why you even ask, you must know I do. But we have to do some serious talking. We can't get on with the future until we've sorted out the past. Why did you never let me know where you were? I suffered agonies. Just one word would have helped.'

'I wrote you 'undreds of letters trying to explain, honest I did but I was so ashamed of meself I chucked 'em all in the fire. Anyway, what with the shooting and everything, after a while I decided I'd messed up your life enough. I wanted to give you the chance to get on wiv it and that would be a lot easier if you thought I was dead. I never knew Boscoe had a gun, I swear it, or I wouldn't have done that job. Did 'e cop it, the policeman?'

'No, but Boscoe did.'

'I thought 'e might 'ave. Poor sod.'

'But however did you find your way here, to South Africa, Danny?'

'I managed to get on a tramp steamer going to Marseilles, jumped that and gradually worked my way down. It was a bit of a fluke really. But good fortune has to shine on everyone at least once in their lifetime, I suppose, 'cos I could have just as easily ended up in America or Australia. That's when I thought up the name Smith for meself. And it answers pretty well, don't you think? Not a name anyone's too likely to catch up with.'

Hearing his explanation and his voice, chirpy as a London sparrow's, Charity smiled indulgently. He doesn't change, she thought.

'Everyone else said you were dead, but I knew you weren't. I could feel it, ever so strongly.'

Danny looked impressed. 'Could you? That must have bin 'cos I was thinking of you all the time.'

'Truly?'

'Yeah, and cursing meself for the bloody fool I'd been.

352

They say you never appreciate what you've got until you lose it and truer words were never spoken.'

Charity was glad they had this time together to talk and feel the old intimacy return. In spite of the untold anguish Danny had caused her she found it easy to forgive him, perhaps because she'd had plenty of practice. And he did seem truly penitent. At first, after such a long separation, she'd been nervous of examining her feelings and instead she'd concentrated all her emotions on willing him to live. But watching his gallant fight, Charity came to understand and accept that as long as she had breath in her body she would love Danny. It was an immutable fact. But she was aware of a subtle shift in the balance of their relationship. Danny was dependent on her now in a way that he'd never been before, so it was a more balanced love that flowed between them.

He wooed her, cherished her, was tender with her and, in the midst of a war-torn country, Charity became a young girl again. Never had they been so close and it was a special time of sweet, intense happiness.

After a couple of weeks Danny took his first cautious steps. Watching Sister Weston support the young soldier round the compound, Dr Asquith was intrigued and curious. Forced into living in close proximity, he and Charity had always kept their relationship strictly professional and he knew as little about her life as she did his. But he could see that was a relationship which had gone past the professional stage, thick as two thieves they were and quite plainly they'd fallen for each other. His own tastes lay in a different direction, but he could see that Sister Weston was exceedingly beautiful, although a woman could look like a baboon in these parts and still turn a young fellow's head.

She obviously imagined she was being discreet, but, right from the beginning, he'd noticed the extra attention she gave to Smith, although he would have said she was a cut above the soldier, a mere private as well. Still, it happened and the most ill-suited people fell in love, he knew that from some of his own sad and furtive affairs. But they'd part soon, he to his regiment, she probably back to Cape Town, so let them enjoy what little happiness they could. As a celebration of their love he would offer, before they parted, to take a photograph of them. So far his Kodak camera had recorded nothing but images of war – a picture of two people in love would make a pleasant change.

When the news came through that the Boer General, Piet Cronje and four thousand of his men, had surrendered at Paardeberg, and that 'Bobs' was now on his way to Bloemfontein, Danny hugged and kissed Charity with delight. 'We've got Johnny Dutchman on the run now, I reckon this is the beginning of the end.'

In the rest of the camp there was a tremendous surge of optimism and the patients were jubilant, telling each other they'd soon be back home with their families, as if the war were already over.

As the fighting receded from their part of the country, the number of casualties dropped rapidly. Life became more settled and Danny was eager to discuss their future.

'You and me, we'll make a good life for ourselves out 'ere. It's not like England where everything depends on yer accent and the school you went to. They couldn't give a toss about that sort of nonsense 'ere. It's how hard a man's prepared to work that counts. Meself, I've managed to keep body and soul together quite nicely these past few years.' Getting carried away, Danny went on, 'And there's diamonds and gold, so a bloke could grow rich. Then we'd have a big house, servants, a carriage and you could be a real lady.'

They were standing watching the setting sun stain the sky and parched earth blood red, something they did every evening now that it was safe to stroll outside the confines of the compound. 'This is the best time of the day, when it gets cool,' said Charity massaging her tired neck, and trying to come to terms with the idea of life as a permanent exile. Because Danny had made one thing quite clear, he had no intention of going home to face the music, which probably meant she would never see Mollie, Eliza or Stephen again. It was cowardly, but she didn't want to face up to such difficult choices yet. 'You know there's not much point in us making plans until this lot is over,' she said, turning to Danny. 'As soon as you're declared fit you'll be called back to your regiment. You know that, don't you?'

'They can finish this war without me. I shall do a bunk when the time is ripe and you can come with me.'

Charity looked appalled. 'I'm a nurse, I couldn't just leave Dr Asquith and the patients in the lurch and if you deserted and were caught, you'd be shot.'

'It's such a shambles this war, nobody would know if we were dead or alive. Anyway they won't find us if we go up to Rhodesia. I'm not going back to any bloody regiment to get my head blown off. Before, it didn't matter, but now I've found you again, it does and I swear this time only death will part us.'

'Danny, please stop and think, we've got no money.' Charity could feel herself growing exasperated. He was still as impetuous, still unable to imagine the consequences of his actions. It was as if his past tragic experiences had taught him nothing. But they mustn't argue. Those days were over. They must learn to talk over their differences, resolve them like mature adults. She took his hand, 'It'll be dark very soon, let's walk on a bit.'

By a tree he pulled her to him. 'We never get any time to ourselves, do we? There always someone else around. What I want to do, is take all those clothes off you and make love naked out here in the open under the night sky. For the moment, though, I suppose I'll have to be satisfied with a kiss.'

Danny's body was filling out a bit more each day and now, as she moulded her body to his she was immediately made aware of his need for her. He smoothed back some loose strands of hair from her brow and explored her face, tracing his fingers over her eyebrows, nose and finally the long curve of her lips. 'My little wife, my one and only love, you are very beautiful, do you know that?'

Lapped by gentle waves of joy, Charity's arms slid round his neck. This was how she'd always dreamed of it being between her and Danny and now, at last, she had it, complete happiness. She closed her eyes and pulled him to her. Their lips were almost touching when she heard the clink of harness, followed by just one word, 'Britische!'

The hair rose on the back of her neck and, mouth agape with fear, Charity swung round. She saw him, middle-aged, bearded, wearing a floppy-brimmed bush hat and with a bandolier slung across his shoulder. The Boer had his rifle raised and for an eternity she stood there, hypnotized by the barrel which was pointed straight at her head. Then, from a great distance she heard Danny's voice, loud, imperative, 'Move, for Christ's sake!' and she was pushed violently. She went sprawling in the dust at exactly the same moment as the shot rang out.

Winded, lips bleeding and choking on a mouthful of grit and dirt, Charity lay there feeling the ground vibrate with the pounding of hooves, which moved in time with her own galloping heart. Her eyes remained screwed tight in terror and she didn't dare open them or raise her head until long after horse and rider had gone.

Danny was lying a short distance from her. 'Danny! Danny! Are you all right, please answer me,' she screamed in a frenzy of fear as she struggled to her feet. But she only managed to stagger a couple of paces then her legs buckled under her again. Desperate to reach him, on all fours and moaning pitifully, 'oh my love, my love,' Charity pushed her unwilling body forward over the rock-strewn ground.

Gently she lifted his head on her lap, her tears falling on to his upturned face. Danny opened his eyes and though they were glazed with approaching death, he struggled to speak. 'It . . . it's . . . over . . .' Then the blood bubbled up in his mouth and Charity's anguished screams brought Dr Asquith running out into the rapidly-falling darkness.

Chapter 29

She would allow no one else to touch him. As his wife that was her task, her final demonstration of love, to wash his young body, then lay him out. There was no coffin to lend dignity to his death and his shroud was an old army blanket, but she wrapped him in this as tenderly as a mother would her child. For Danny's final short journey Pieter and John acted as pallbearers and, followed by a straggle of mourners, they carried him to the cemetery marked out by boulders and shaded by a few camelthorn trees. Dr Asquith read the burial service then a small rough-hewn cross, with a name not even Danny's own burnt into the wood, was placed at his head, one more added to the sad row of crosses already there. Through it all Charity maintained a dry-eyed, straight-backed dignity. That is, until Pieter and John started to sing, a haunting chant in their own tongue. Overwhelmed by the melancholic sound, she wept, the tears falling silently and mingling with the freshly-turned earth of Danny's grave.

For Charity the hardest thing to bear was not being able to talk about Danny, to acknowledge their relationship, to mourn him in the proper way of a wife. She was also denied that part of the ritual of death which is a widow's due – and an important part in the healing process – the comfort and sympathy of friends. All her unhappiness was pushed away inside her. Dr Asquith seemed to understand something of her misery and once or twice she was on the verge of speaking out. But uncertain what her confession might set in motion, she thought better of it and held her tongue.

However, she felt no such constraints when writing in her diary and, in neat lettering, she marked Danny's passing: *On 14 March 1900, Danny my husband died saving my life, killed by a Boer bullet and laid to rest on foreign soil.*

Watching Charity closely, Dr Asquith marvelled at her strength of character and wondered time and again how her mind had survived the senseless, random killing of her lover. He knew she needed someone to whom she could pour out her sorrow, but he'd lived all his life in a masculine environment, apart from Nanny at home and Matron at school, where emotions were deliberately stifled. He could mend bodies but he had no capacity to deal with grief.

A few days later Charity succumbed to another attack of fever. This time it lasted a week and caused Dr Asquith even more heart-searching. He was torn, but he knew if he kept her here much longer in these conditions when she was in such poor physical shape, he might be putting her life at risk. He waited until she was well enough, then he spoke to her.

'I make no bones about it, Sister, in my selfish way the last thing I want is to lose you, you are far too valuable to me for that. But I also see what this place is doing to your health.'

But Charity dismissed his worries. 'Really, I'm as strong as a horse. I admit the heat and food have got me down at times, but that's the same for everyone, isn't it? But it'll soon be autumn and with some decent food starting to get through, there's no reason why I shouldn't stay as long as you need me.'

So, not being of a decisive nature, Dr Asquith let the matter ride until finally the problem was resolved for him by a higher authority.

Charity was sterilizing instruments when he told her. 'Ah . . . Sister Weston, orders have just come through that I'm to close down this hospital and move on to Bloemfontein within the week.'

'That's all right, I'm quite prepared to come with you.' She gave him a quick smile and went on with her work as if the matter were settled.

'I'm afraid it's not as simple as that. I appreciate your offer, of course, but to be honest with you, I don't think you are up to the journey. It will be across country in waggons and could take a week.'

Charity looked indignant. 'But if the army is as short of medical staff as it's supposed to be, how can you possibly go without me?'

'Actually for your own sake, I think it really would be better if you went back to Cape Town.' The doctor's tone was unusually firm. 'I don't know what I would have done without you these past weeks, but you really need a chance to recuperate. And try and see my point of view, Sister, you've already had two attacks of fever, you could easily succumb to another on the journey and what would I do then? Anyway, what's to stop you coming up country again, once you've got your health back?'

'Perhaps I'm not one hundred percent, but then who is? You're not, are you?'

'No, I'm not,' he agreed, 'but that's beside the point and I am a man.'

'What's being a man got to do with it?'

He shrugged. 'Men are stronger, I suppose.'

'Rubbish!' Charity heard her own voice and thought, how sharp I'm sounding these days.

But her arguments held no water this time and Dr Asquith remained adamant.

Charity had arrived with little luggage and was leaving with even less. As a small parting gift she gave Pieter her mirror and John a bead necklace and, since most of her clothes were in rags, she left them to be torn up for bandages.

In the hour she had before the train left, Charity went and said her final goodbye to Danny. Finding some shade under a tree she sat down, closed her eyes and, her throat aching with loss, allowed her mind to wander back over the years. She remembered her early childish love for Danny, their troubled marriage and the death of the baby, then their brief late flowering of happiness. Would they have gone on sharing that intense joy they'd found in each other? It was hard to know but she hoped so, and at least now she was carrying away with her memories untinged by bitterness.

She was disturbed in her meditation by the cawing of a large bird on a branch above her. Opening her eyes, Charity scooped up a handful of dry soil and let it trickle through her fingers. Dust to dust she thought. Perhaps like some people said, everything was predestined. But there was still a cruel irony in being allowed to nurse Danny back to health only to see him struck down by a sniper's bullet. Now she had to leave him here alone in this hostile landscape. And somehow go on herself. Charity crushed her hands together and cursing fate, threw back her head, let out a long, loud primeval wail of anguish, and rocked backwards and forwards in mesmeric grief.

'Missi.'

She stopped and looked up with wounded eyes. It was Pieter. Understanding and keeping a respectful distance, he said quietly, 'Train leave in short while.'

'All right, Pieter.'

Charity stood up, but she was beyond trying to compose herself. She waited until Pieter had gone, put her fingers to her lips then lightly pressed them against the wooden cross. 'Goodbye, my dearest. Rest in peace now,' she whispered, then through a blur of tears, she turned and stumbled back to the compound.

Parting from Pieter, John and the few remaining patients had been painful too. And obviously as much as an ordeal for the doctor, who as they waited for the train, stared at his feet and shuffled them awkwardly in the dust like a schoolboy.

'When I have a chance to get it developed, would you

360

like me to send on the photograph I took of you and Private Smith?'

'Yes please, and could you . . . would you take a photograph of his grave for me as well?'

'Of course.'

Charity held out her hand. 'Well, goodbye, Dr Asquith.'

'Goodbye Sister Weston, it's been a privilege working with you. And thank you, for everything.'

She stepped up on to the train then half turned and smiled at him. 'You haven't got rid of me, you know. I promise I'll be back.'

'I'm sure you will,' Doctor Asquith replied, although he knew with some sadness in his heart, that he would never see this brave young woman again.

Chapter 30

Charity had forgotten how green it was, how fertile, and how pretty the gabled, whitewashed homesteads were, set amid their vineyards. After the harsh landscape she had just left it was a balm to the eyes. The journey had been long and trying. The train had clanked and hissed, lurched to a stop then started up again so often, Charity had begun to doubt whether it would ever make it to Cape Town. But it had proceeded at its somewhat erratic pace, and with a bit of luck, pretty soon it would be steaming into the station and a short while after that she'd be back at the hospital.

No one was expecting her so she enjoyed herself for a while imagining Moira and Stanny's faces. Contemplating Captain Hubbert's reaction, she found, had less appeal. In fact she realized he had a good case for sending her home.

After their initial astonishment there was a rapturous welcome from Stanny and Moira. She was hugged, kissed and so many questions were fired at her her head began to spin. Then followed expressions of concern.

'Look at you, you're nothing but skin and bones,' declared Stanny, standing back and studying her with a critical eye. 'Still, we'll soon sort that out. Tell us what you'd like for tea.'

'Everything. Sandwiches, cakes, scones. Gallons of tea. You don't know how I'm longing for proper food after living on bully beef and dry biscuits you had to shake the weevils out of before you could eat them.'

For the first time in weeks she bathed, and as she sank down into the great steaming tub, Charity swore she would never take water for granted again. She soaped herself all over with sweet-smelling soap, then with a sigh of pure pleasure, lay back and closed her eyes. They were rarely out of her mind those poor fellows still fighting, and she prayed for them every night, but with a twinge of guilt she acknowledged it was good to be back.

The bathroom was large and contained heavy pieces of bedroom furniture, so, after washing her hair, Charity wrapped herself in an enormous towel, padded over to a dressing table and sat down. With a corner of the towel she rubbed the steam from the mirror then leaning forward, studied her reflection with the dispassionate eye of a stranger. She hadn't looked at herself properly in weeks and she hardly recognized the person staring back at her. Her hair was bleached white, her skin deeply tanned, her face all cheekbone. She'd lost her young girl's bloom and what she saw instead was the face of a woman moulded by pain and circumstance. No wonder Stanny and Moira were shocked, she thought, they had every right to be.

Charity rubbed her hair dry, plaited and coiled it round her head then dressed, savouring the pleasure of clean linen against her skin. She'd just finished when Moira knocked on the door.

'Tea is about to be served in the sitting room. And oh, here, these are yours.' Moira handed Charity a bundle of letters, then went on, 'By the way, I heard from Alan. He's up in Natal, slightly wounded but all right.'

Moira's face wore such a happy expression that although she was dying to read her own letters, Charity stuffed them in her pocket and took her friend's arm. 'Oh I am pleased. Come on let's go and get that tea and tell me what he said.'

Tea was brought in, then it was first things first, Stanny's engagement. 'You'll come to the wedding won't you?' she said, spreading her fingers wide so that Charity could admire the small circle of diamonds. 'Of course it won't be until after Leonard and I return home, whenever that might be. And he's promised to leave the army.'

Stanny's family were prosperous farmers in Norfolk and although it meant he would finally have a home, Charity did wonder how Leonard would fit into a rural community after his footloose army life.

'I'd love to come and I'm very happy for you, Stanny. And they say victory's in sight so perhaps Moira will see Alan again soon, and you and Leonard won't have long to wait before you can get married. But whatever happens I expect I'll be shipped off home anyway.'

'Why do you say that?'

'Well me going off like that gave old Hubbert plenty of ammunition. I suppose I played right into his hands, really.' Not looking too concerned about her fate, Charity heaped sugar into her tea then spooned a generous helping of jam on to a scone and with eyes closed, bit into it with a delicious sense of gluttony.

'You're right there. He kicked up a proper stink when I gave him the news, and I was taken off the hospital train immediately as a punishment.' Moira grumbled. 'But you don't have to worry, he's the one who blotted his copybook and was sent packing.'

'Why, what happened?' asked Charity, interested enough to pause in her eating.

'He was getting crazier by the day, operating when he

was drunk, hitting the servants. But you tell Charity the rest, Stanny.'

Looking faintly embarrassed, Stanny leaned forward and stirred her tea. 'Well the final straw was him trying to get into my room. Leonard nearly tore him limb from limb. Anyway, his behaviour eventually reached the ears of some bigwig and he was sent home in disgrace. The new MO is Dr White, who's a nice old codger. And as for you being disciplined, why it's quite the opposite. The reports coming down the line have been glowing. What you've had to put up with, the awful conditions you worked in, the way you looked after the patients. As far as the men are concerned, you're a real heroine and deserve a medal.'

Charity looked uncomfortable. 'Nonsense. It was my choice to go and once there I got on with the job as best I could. And I wasn't in the least bit brave. When the shelling started I was terrified out of my wits. But as soon as you see the appalling injuries you forget your own fear, there just isn't the time. The brave ones were the poor Tommies, not me. They were so uncomplaining.' But, in spite of her protestations, the two of them seemed determined to turn her into some sort of Florence Nightingale, a role that sat uneasily on Charity's shoulders.

Moira and Stanny only had an hour off, so when tea was finished, they went back on duty while Charity escaped to the solitude of her room. It was marvellous to see everyone again but she'd been through a gruelling time physically and emotionally these past weeks and sleep was a high priority.

Also, a pleasure lay in wait, the letters from home. More than a little homesick, she was hungry for news and with a sense of anticipation she sat down by the window and sorted through them. Five from Eliza, one from Mollie, none from Stephen. Her disappointment was acute, which was perverse of her, she knew, when she'd come out here to forget him. She read Eliza's letters first. Each one was more frantic than the other and with a growing sense of guilt, Charity realized that in all the time she'd spent up country, she hadn't once written to her aunt.

But some of Eliza's news made her sit up and take notice:

> I don't imagine you'll grieve when I tell you that the Grimbolds have been given a hefty prison sentence. They were caught red-handed with a haul of antique silver and jewels from a stately home. Everyone is glad to see the back of them, me included.

I second that, thought Charity, remembering the misery they'd brought to her life and Kate's, and all the other girls. They'd got their just desserts, and about time, too.

She turned to Mollie's letter with a sense of relief. If Mollie was worried about not hearing from her, she kept it to herself.

> Guess what? [were her opening words], Brilliant news, Stephen's invited me to join his practice. Dr Campbell passed on at the end of January and although I don't finish at the hospital until later this year, he says he'll keep the position open for me and either run it on his own or with a temporary assistant.

So Stephen hadn't moved away from the area, thought Charity as she put Mollie's letter back in its envelope. And there was her friend so excited about her new career she hadn't once mentioned Caspar. And no word of Blanche either.

Although Charity felt dog-tired, she was moved sufficiently by guilt to get out writing paper, ink and pen. She also needed to tell Eliza about Danny. She'd always had certain reservations about him, but Charity still knew Eliza would understand her desolation better than anyone. It was a long letter and the hardest bit was writing about the arbitrary manner of Danny's death. Fate had dealt her the cruellest of blows when it made her lose him twice, and sometimes her pen faltered and a tear dropped on to the page. But for the first time she could articulate her grief once she got into her stride, and it poured out of her. She kept on doggedly to the end and, when she'd finished, she felt the burden of sorrow lift. She signed off with love, then in a positive mood wrote to Mollie, telling her also about Danny, and congratulating her on her new career. The one question she couldn't bring herself to ask was about Blanche. When she'd addressed and sealed the envelopes, she shoved them in the letter box then went to bed and slept soundly for twelve hours.

'Mmm, I think we'd better keep an eye on you for a while, young lady.' Dr White had just finished examining Charity and his manner was serious as he removed the stethoscope from his ears.

Charity paused in buttoning her dress, alert to the tone of his voice. 'Why, what's wrong?'

'From my diagnosis I would say you are not up to the mark at all and certainly not fit enough to return to duty.'

'But I can't sit around doing nothing, I'm not used to it,' Charity protested.

'You have no choice, I'm afraid. I want you to have complete rest for at least a month then we'll see how you are after that.'

'Doctor White, if you make me do that I shall go mad with boredom.'

But the doctor prided himself on being a plain speaking man. No shilly-shallying, give it to patients straight on the chin was his motto. 'I doubt it. And it's either that or probably a permanent breakdown in your health with the rest of your life lived as a semi-invalid. You might not think so but these mysterious fevers you've twice been struck down with and the gruelling conditions you worked in have taken their toll. Your body needs a chance to heal itself. You're a nurse so you know what I'm talking about and if you behave sensibly and rest, as I say, it should do the trick. But if not . . .' he shrugged, '. . . well then I'm afraid I can't be held answerable.'

The doctor stood looking at her, daring her to dispute his professional judgement. But his words had such a doom-laden ring to them they frightened Charity into submissiveness. So, although she chafed at the inactivity, for the next month the most energetic pastime she indulged in was to complete a jig-saw puzzle. Never in her life had time passed so slowly.

'I don't know how much longer I can stand this,' Charity complained to Stanny on a permitted gentle walk round the grounds during her second week of convalescence. 'I'll end up as a mental case if he doesn't let me go back to work soon.'

'Old Whitey's a pretty good doctor you know, so you ought to listen to him. He's hardly likely to keep you out of circulation for the fun of it. And when he's examined you again, he might even suggest another month.'

Charity looked appalled. 'Another month? He couldn't do that.'

But Charity knew he could, so she ate and slept, wrote up her diary, read and tried not to look restless.

Mail was eagerly awaited by everyone and although Charity knew she couldn't expect a reply from England for several weeks, she looked every day for a letter. And then, unexpectedly, she received one from Dr Asquith. Enclosed with the letter was the photograph he'd taken of her and Danny. Studying it, Charity found it impossible not to cry. It was so unbearably poignant, the two of them standing there together in the middle of the compound, arms entwined, smiling a little self-consciously at each other as the doctor had instructed. We were so full of hope and plans that day, it's captured there forever

367

and yet it's gone, she thought. When she'd composed herself, she put the photograph back in the envelope and tucked it out of sight under a pile of clothes.

Dr Asquith's letter had little of any cheer in it. Apparently, a typoid epidemic was raging in Bloemfontein and men were dying daily and in large numbers.

How we could do with your nursing skills here Sister, [he wrote]. There just aren't enough medical staff to go round, we've no beds, no medicines and sick men are left lying on the hard ground – in fact in the normal army muddle. They miscalculate everything and care little for the common soldier, but there always appear to be luxuries for those officers who can afford them, even champagne I've heard.

Poor Dr Asquith, Charity thought. He was such a good caring doctor, she hoped he got through the war unscathed then perhaps they could meet up again in happier circumstances in England.

Sooner than expected, another letter arrived from Mollie, and Charity wondered how, until she saw from the postmark that their letters must have crossed. As she slit open the envelope, a newspaper cutting fluttered to the ground. Charity bent and picked it up. Under the heading, MARRIAGES, she read:

The wedding of Miss Blanche de Vere and Henry Read Esq of Holtby Hall, Leicestershire took place at St Swithin's Church, Westminster. Mr and Mrs Read will be spending their honeymoon in Venice, before returning to their London residence.

Bemused, Charity re-read the announcement. 'Well I never, Blanche married,' she exclaimed and turned to Mollie's letter for clarification.

Not a word from you for ages, but still thought you'd
be interested in the enclosed snippet. Interesting eh?
Stephen tells me Blanche has made the sort of marriage she wanted. Her husband is rather older than
she is but wealthy and intends soon to stand for
Parliament. Stephen might be putting on a brave face
for my benefit but he doesn't look particularly
broken-hearted. I think his decision to remain in
Rotherhithe probably killed any chance of their
marrying. Could you see Blanche dealing with nits
and scabies? Still, she's got brains and she'll make
an ideal political hostess.

Charity read on through the rest of the letter which was
mainly about Mollie and Stephen's ideas for the practice.

Stephen and I have done a lot of talking lately and
we've both got all sorts of plans for the future. One
in particular which you and me talked about, is to
open a clinic for women so that we can deal with
illnesses of a personal nature and perhaps help girls
like Kate too, who die through ignorance. Stephen
says it's also vital that we give women advice on how
to space or limit the size of their families. This will
have to be done discreetly of course, because you
know how opposed so many (male) churchmen and
politicians are to the idea. The last thing we'll want
is them breathing down our necks with threats of
perpetual damnation for interfering with nature . . .

Charity finished the letter and sat staring out of the
window at a group of children playing. She'd be deceiving
herself if she didn't admit to being delighted at Blanche's
marriage. But also for the first time in her life she felt
jealous of Mollie. There was no question about it, Stephen
and Mollie were two people who had a great deal in
common. She could see them, working together as
equals, sharing their daily life and its burdens, giving

each other mutual support, their interests binding them ever closer. And Mollie had always had a soft spot for Stephen and he admired her intelligence. In her imagination she saw them already married. I couldn't stand that, not Mollie and Stephen, not my best friend who'd once said that nothing would ever come between us. To smile, feign delight, no, no no, she'd rather make a new life for herself here in Africa.

Charity sat there for a good half hour, noises from outside gradually impinging on her thoughts. The children were now squabbling, from the kitchen came the clatter of pots and pans and back and forth along the corridor there were footsteps, always in a hurry. Each sound magnified her isolation, everyone except her had their allotted tasks. The enforced idleness was causing her imagination to run riot, and she couldn't stand it a minute longer. Going over to the mirror she smoothed her hair and pinched her cheeks. She was bursting with health, anyone must see that. With a resolute expression Charity went to seek out Dr White.

But before he'd make any decision the doctor insisted on examining her again. 'Well, your ticker sounds as if its working nicely, Sister and since it's only a few days before your month is up, I'll let you go back on the wards tomorrow.'

What surprised Charity was how little energy she had, and by the end of each shift, she was too exhausted to do much but go to bed. She kept very quiet about it, but after she and Moira had lifted a patient out of bed into a bath chair one morning, her legs were so trembly she had to sit down.

Moira peered at her worriedly. 'You all right?'

Charity stood up again. 'Fine, just a bit puff . . .' She didn't finish. Suddenly the earth became insubstantial under her feet in the frightening way she remembered and Moira's face went out of focus. She reached out to grab something, failed, and although she struggled with

370

all her power against surrender, she felt herself falling. The last thing she heard was her friend's voice, high and panicky, shouting at her from a long way off, then she descended into darkness.

This time the fever was even more vengeful and in spite of all the wonders of modern medicine and his own medical skills, it seemed to Dr White as if the beast still might win. They all watched with a sense of helplessness as Charity's temperature see-sawed; down to a hundred at one moment giving hope, soaring a short while later, to everyone's despair. For days it was touch and go but Charity fought back. After ten days it was apparent that although it was a close-run thing, she would pull through.

Too frail to even move from her bed, Charity was molly-coddled no end by her two friends, who tempted her with small, almost unobtainable, luxuries.

However, Dr White when he came to see her made no bones about it. 'You've had about all you can take of this country, England is the place for you now. The hospital ship, *Regis*, sails a week on Saturday, Sister Weston, and I'm going to make sure you are on it.'

'All right, Doctor, just as you say,' she answered passively. Lying flat on her back it would have been difficult to argue, but Charity was inclined to agree with him anyway, the time had come for her to go home.

'Have you parents, Sister?'

Charity shook her head. 'No.'

'Who do I get in touch with then? Someone will have to be sent the details and date of your expected arrival in England.'

'My aunt, I'll let you have her address.'

'I imagine she'll be glad to see you.'

'And very relieved. She brought me up, we only have each other and I think she'd come to the conclusion she was never going to set eyes on me again.'

'A few days ago I would have said it was unlikely she would myself. But fortunately, from some forebear, you inherited a pretty strong constitution.'

'My father, I expect,' Charity answered and enjoyed herself wondering how the doctor would react if she told him that it was highly unlikely that the man from whose loins she'd sprung even knew she existed.

Never had she spent so much time saying goodbye as over the past few months, Charity reflected as she took her final tearful departure from Stanny and Moira.

'We'll keep in touch, won't we? And I'm sure you'll both be home soon and when you are we'll have a grand reunion. Go to some posh hotel for dinner.'

'And you will write every week without fail, won't you, Charity?' Moira asked, and they kept on like this, exacting emotional promises from each other all the way to the ship.

Charity felt uneasy about being treated as an invalid when the ship was crammed full of casualties, young men returning to their families blind or minus a limb. Men no longer of use in the machinery of war. But although she tried, she was still too frail to walk, so after a final embrace and wave, she was carried on board by stretcher and put straight to bed.

She was made to stay there for a good part of the journey although once they'd crossed the equator and were in the northern hemisphere again, Charity could feel an energy flowing back into her. At first she was content to sit up on deck enjoying the sunshine and watching the albatross. These birds with their enormous wing span, twelve feet she'd been told by a member of the crew, fascinated her and she wondered how they managed to follow the ship for days without ever appearing to rest.

But the life of an invalid quickly palled and before long she was taking a turn round the deck. Each day she did one more. Gradually her leg muscles regained their elasticity and she no longer puffed from her exertions. By the time the ship reached Brixham and stopped to pick up the pilot she was telling anyone who asked that she'd never felt better in her life.

As the ship moved up the Channel soldiers, overjoyed to be back, crowded against the ship's railings, cheering exuberantly as they caught their first sight of England. Along from her, Charity heard one Tommy observe to another, 'By God, that's a bloody marvellous sight and one I never thought I'd see again neither. I'm minus a bit of arm, but I've got 'ome and that's the main thing and I swear I shall never leave England or me missis again.'

His friend nodded. 'You're right there, mate, it is good to be back,' and Charity silently agreed. After the untamed African landscape, she was struck by the orderliness of the countryside: downland sweeping to rocky coastline, small fields stitched neatly together by green hedgerows. Like the soldier, she'd often wondered if she'd ever see her country again. In danger of becoming emotional, Charity furtively searched for her handkerchief.

It was supposed to be a fast train from Southampton to Waterloo but to Charity the journey seemed interminable. She was sure every signal was against them and each time the train slowed down or stopped, she'd jump to her feet, pull down the window and lean out, muttering impatiently, 'Come on, come on.'

Finally, an elderly gentleman sitting next to her growing exasperated, said, 'The train will get there in its own good time, young lady, with or without any encouragement from you.'

Feeling like a child that has been reprimanded, Charity went pink and shut up. Here she was getting herself in all of a flurry and there might not even be anyone at the station to meet her. Eliza definitely wouldn't come, she never moved far from home, and Mollie was probably on duty, so that left Stephen.

During the long journey home with time on her hands, Charity had attempted a logical dissection of the romance she'd dreamed up between Stephen and Mollie. She told herself that Mollie loved Caspar, that Mollie was uninterested in marriage anyway, but if she did enter into matrimony it would be to Caspar. But even if this was the case, Stephen still might not care a jot for Charity now. He hadn't written to her and it was getting on for a year since their fairly bitter parting. His life would have moved on, just as hers had and they would meet again as different people, changed in indefinable ways by their experiences. But she still couldn't help nursing a small hope that either he or Mollie, or both of them would be waiting for her at the barrier.

To the gentleman's intense annoyance, as soon as the train steamed into the terminus she leapt over his feet and poked her head out of the window. The train juddered to a halt. Charity turned and gave the man a sweet smile. 'Goodbye, I hope you enjoyed your journey,' she said and picked up her hand luggage. Stepping down on to the platform, she peered through the smoke and rushing crowds, hungry for the sight of a familiar face.

Luggage was unloaded, sacks of mail were thrown on to the platform. She heard doors slam, felt people push past her, saw them greeted and embraced by friends and move off, but no smiling Mollie came running towards her and she stood there in a small island of loneliness. She could hear the ring of the wheel tappers' hammers against steel but, except for a refreshment trolley and a couple of porters, she was alone on the platform. Not one person had remembered or even cared enough to come and meet her. She blinked away a prickle of self-pity. It was only a minor setback and after the miles she'd just travelled surely she was capable of getting herself home.

'Want a hand Miss?' A porter had come up behind her with a trolley.

'Yes please.' Charity was moving towards the luggage van when she saw him. Out of breath, the straight brown hair dishevelled, he was looking up at the clock. 'Stephen,' she yelled, and waved frantically. She saw his face light up, and a great surge of joy lifted her up and carried her along the platform towards him. Then, remembering their parting she slowed down, watching

374

as he walked towards her, both of them now a bit awkward. He paused a couple of feet from her.

'Hello Charity. It's been a long time.'

She nodded.

'Well let me take a good look at you, then.' Moving closer, Stephen took both her hands and studied her intently. 'You've changed.'

'A lot's happened to me.'

'I know. I don't know what to say about Danny, just that I'm terribly sorry. And the way he died, that must have been the worst part.'

Seeing she was struggling to keep control of her emotions, Stephen put a comforting arm round her shoulder. 'Cry if you want to my dear, let the pain come out.'

Soothed by his compassion, Charity cleared her throat. 'I'll be all right. It's just sometimes, you know . . . when I talk about it. Danny and me meeting again like that at least gave us the chance to make our peace with each other. There aren't any bitter memories now, just good ones.'

'I'm so glad.'

A discreet cough made them both turn. It was the porter. He was leaning on the trolley waiting patiently. 'You'll be wanting me to do somethin' wiv this luggage Miss.'

Stephen searched in his pocket then tossed the man a half crown. 'Yes, find us a cab, will you, please.' He linked his arm through Charity's. 'Everyone is dying to see you, so let's get you back to where you belong, young lady. Caspar and Mollie allowed me to come on my own to meet you on the strict condition I wasted no time in getting you home. And I don't suppose you have any idea of the anxiety you've caused Eliza these past months. She's been cooking for days too, enough to feed an army, so you'd better be hungry.'

Without any prompting from her, Stephen brought up the subject of Blanche's marriage, while they were still

375

driving along Waterloo Road. 'I must hand it to her. She's done very well for herself,' he said, sounding, Charity thought, remarkably cheerful, considering the young lady in question might just as easily have become his wife.

'So you weren't upset by the marriage then?'

'Good heavens no. In fact I wish her only happiness, because, even when it seemed there was no hope for you and me, I still knew I couldn't marry her. It would never have worked between us, we have different priorities. I suspect Blanche still thought something might come of it, though. Until I started asking some of my uncle's rich associates to dip their hands in their pockets to help equip this new clinic Mollie and I are setting up, that was it. She realized finally I was a lost cause and being a practical girl, and a poor one, she wasted no time looking elsewhere. But enough of Blanche, wait until you see the clinic.' Stephen grabbed her hand and his eyes were alight with enthusiasm. 'It's very bright and modern and Caspar's painted a mural. We are definitely planning to give women advice on family limitation. But of course it's a delicate, personal subject which they will probably only discuss with another woman, so that's where you come in. You will come and work with us at the practice, won't you? We are in desperate need of a good nurse.'

'I haven't given much thought to my future, Stephen.'

'We'd be a team, and think what the three of us could achieve together? And I know it's something close to your heart.'

'Well, if you really want me.'

'Want you? Of course I do.' Gauging her mood, Stephen unfolded her fingers and lifting the palm of her hand to his mouth, kissed it gently. 'Nothing's changed for me, Charity, I want you in my life, permanently.'

Charity closed her eyes, saw a mound of earth, a small wooden cross and felt a burning desert wind on her cheeks.

'Charity?'

She opened her eyes. Stephen was studying her with

376

a concerned, loving expression and, knowing he would understand, she pleaded quietly, 'Give me a little time, Stephen.'

Stephen pulled her close. 'Of course, my dear. I'll wait just as long as you like, we've got all the time in the world now. Anyway, look, we're almost there.'

Charity leaned forward eagerly. Through the cab window she could see the familiar forest of masts and spars, smell resin and pitch, then they were turning into Filbert Street. Red, white and blue bunting was strung across the front of the shop; Eliza was standing with Lolly clasped in her arms; Caspar and Mollie were waving frantically. All of them were smiling. Hot tears of emotion scalded Charity's eyes, but she made no attempt to brush them away. She belonged and she was loved, it was a good feeling.

Stephen took her hand and squeezed it. 'Welcome home,' he said and Charity kissed him lightly on the mouth.

'Thank you, Stephen, for everything.' As she stepped from the cab and into Eliza's embrace, Charity felt a tremendous surge of optimism. From turbulent waters she'd reached safe harbour. For the first time in a long while she could see the future, and it didn't look bad at all.